Trumpets Sound No More

Jon Redfern

A Victorian Detective Story

RendezVous
Crime

Cover art: The Drama (1860)
by Honoré Daumier (1808-79)

Cover design: Vasiliki Lenis

Le Conseil des Arts | The Canada Council
du Canada | for the arts
depuis 1957 | since 1957

Napoleon & Company acknowledges the support of the Canada Council for our publishing program.

Published by RendezVous Crime
an imprint of Napoleon & Company
Toronto, Ontario, Canada
www.napoleonandcompany.com

11 10 09 08 07   5 4 3 2 1

Library and Archives Canada Cataloguing in Publication

Redfern, Jon, 1946-
        Trumpets sound no more / Jon Redfern.

ISBN 978-1-894917-40-7

        I. Title.
PS8585.E34218T78 2007   C813'.6   C2007-903847-6

For Lucy and Zazu

So quick bright things come to confusion.
-William Shakespeare

LONDON, 1840, a singular immensity, a Babylon of curiosities, none more splendid than the edifice on the corner of Brydges and Russell Streets, the queen of theatres, Old Drury. Granted, she is formidable, a pile of marble dressed with a portico. Her classical exterior suggests a court of law. But enter her front doors, draw in the perfume of oranges and human sweat. The huge auditorium contains benches, boxes, gaslight chandeliers. Listen as the orchestra fills with violins and trumpets. Beyond them arches a frame of gold opening into a realm of shadows. Here is the stage, the terrain of the painted actor, Hecate's Cave of illusions: farces, tragedies, burlettas, extravaganzas. Old Drury stands oblivious, a glittering domain of dreams beyond the grime, cruelty and injustice of the greater London world.

Chapter One

FRIDAY, DECEMBER 18, 1840

We begin on Brydges Street at seven o'clock, the hour the farce begins in Old Drury. There on the steps across from the theatre's entrance sits Betty Loxton, fourteen, a basket in her lap. December cold turns her little hands blue. On her head is a tattered nankeen bonnet, the one she has worn now for four years, the one she sewed herself, when her brother's eye was not upon her, from remnants of the yellow cotton, a tag of silk and ribbons once belonging to a younger sister gone six months to her grave. Thin shivering waif, Betty slowly looks up and sees through throngs of rushing ticket-buyers the still figure of a man in a black long-coat.

He stands tall, round in the chest, his dark hair tangled and straggling.

Betty wishes he were no more than a phantom come to haunt the city's moon-washed back streets. He seems so like a spirit, she thinks. He appears then disappears momentarily as pedestrians cross to and fro in front of him. Passing carriages along Brydges Street spray him with cobblestone mud, for he lingers too close to the kerb. "Serves him right," Betty whispers to herself. When the man starts to meander toward her, his broken-heeled boots slip on the slick paving stones. He stops to blow his nose, one finger to one side, then to the other, his head bent over. Betty shifts her basket. She tastes the icy December air deep in her throat.

"He won't do you no mischief," she prays.

Betty Loxton knows enough about mischief, especially

from the roughs of Hart Street who loll by her spot in the evenings where she does her hawking. The Willy Gangs she calls them, coster lads and message-runners, runts and fools no older than she by a year, caps pulled low, kerchiefs tied with double knots around their skinny necks. "Hey, Pretty," they tease. "Come for a dance and a kiss, too?" Foolish is as does, thinks Betty. She is just fourteen this past November, with no cough in her lungs. A pretty girl with ivory-coloured skin and blue eyes. There is a steadfast quality about her when she lifts her face to the frosty sky, her arm held out. She never clutches her little ones too hard, in case she bruises their delicate skins: "Apples, Winter Reds. London's finest."

Now Betty must look smart. Though her boots are too loose and her sleeves soiled from carrying her basket, she must practice her smile. Soon the "quality" will draw up in their phaetons and private carriages; the ladies in silk may deign to stop and admire her polite nod and perhaps toss a ha'penny to her for a spit-polished Winter Red. Betty finishes counting her pennies in her basket. She puts the plumper fruit on top, all the while avoiding looking at the tall man moving faster through the crowd. The pain in her ribs still presses against her. *Now don't be foolish on that,* she scolds herself. *Don't vex yourself with the memory, or the pain will only hurt more.* She dares to peer ahead through the brown drizzle. *I do wish he was a stranger,* she thinks of the man, like one of those brutes who stumble along Brydges at this hour, one with a hunger in him, needing a visit to the back stairs of Covent Garden theatre, where ladies of the town charge tuppence for a favour.

"I know Jacks like him what walk with that look to their eye," she murmurs.

Alas, no time for slacking, for the man is nearly upon her. Tall, yes, a country man with thick fists and knuckles. Just as Brother John said at breakfast this very day: "Look you sharp, sis," he warned. "Uncle comes to aid you. He shall find you at your spot by the stroke of seven, no doubt he shall."

Laughter erupts from the theatre. Watermen line up by the side entrances, hauling slopping buckets from the pump in the alley to cabs and gigs, the horses stamping, their mouths dipping into the buckets to suck in the water. *What a shoving place*, Betty complains. The tall man now looms beside her. She pulls back and studies his flat collar and his cuffs, old but of good weave. What a sorrow rests in his face. The man crouches on the pavement below Betty's step. His smell reminds her of a stall. His great hand delves into his coat pocket to retrieve a bit of brown paper.

"Hallo, young pippin."

His voice is rough. Betty stands immediately and curtsies.

"So, you are *she*. The one. Little Betty."

Betty looks down. "Welcome, Uncle."

"I am Thomas, brother to your mam."

"Yes, sir."

Thomas hands Betty the piece of brown paper. On it are a number and scrawled lines.

"I read very little, sir."

"I none at all, mite. But my wife, she wrote it for me, she can read and write pretty good, and she said, now Thomas, if you shall get lost, show this to any London policeman; they are a good lot and can point you the way."

"I can lead you, Uncle."

"Come then, gal. No time for shyness. Go on, you're a good hand, you've done famous for yourself. Your Uncle Thomas has come as good as gold. I can settle accounts for you, Little Betty."

Betty hears kindness in his words, and yet she does not want him to come with her. She is in a pickle. "A pickle indeed," she whispers. But her uncle waves his arm. She gets up and slings her basket onto the top of her head. She points to her right, and Uncle Thomas squints into the distance then shakes his head. "You are sure, mite?"

Betty wants to laugh at him and his country ignorance. She has worked these streets since she was four and is cousin to every shop window, every doorstep, every iron fence and painted sign. "Sure, Uncle," is her answer. She scrambles on ahead, her footsteps quick and deliberate. Straight to Russell Street, then a turn to her left and onward toward the arcades of Covent Garden market. Thomas follows close behind. He gawks at gables and dormers. When he stumbles on the kerb, he curses the toiling horses and carriages in the road before him.

"Careful, Uncle, stay awares," Betty cautions.

"I aren't used to city lanes, you know it, mite."

"All the more reason to take care. You came by coach to Surrey side?" Betty amazes herself for asking such a bold question.

"Aye. With a lot of chattering monkeys, I wager. Too loud for such as me."

Betty wants to fly away. It is not Uncle Thomas she fears, it is what he can do *for* her that made her toss in her sleep the night before and lay aside her meagre breakfast of bread and coffee. The memory of her sweetheart pricks her, and she starts to weep. Yes, he has done her harm, but he was so dear, so lovely in his voice and his way of talking. Sweetheart, he called her, sworn to love her. Promised to cherish her, so she imagined. Not so. And not deserving of what Uncle Thomas is to do to him. Oh, no. The machine was never meant to hurt her. Her sweetheart said so. He shouted at her afterwards when she tumbled down. Yes, he sent her then into the street with only a penny. But he was kindly in doing so, and such a sight of him in her mind's eye makes Betty wipe her tears and ignore her aching ribs.

Beside her now walks a man just arrived in London. He is here to right things, even if Betty herself does not want things righted. No good can come from hurting, for that is what this business is all about.

"Little Betty, hurry on." Thomas's voice startles her.

"Come then," Betty says, her voice again full of resolve. Gaslight shines all the way along Henrietta Street. Betty points at last to the tavern of the Two Spies. All around her are the sounds of laughter and drinking. She hesitates at the entrance to the raucous place then motions to a set of gloomy stairs just inside the tavern's swinging door.

"And so, mite, where are they?"

"Yonder, Uncle. Yonder."

*   *   *

The second floor chamber above the Two Spies spread narrow and long, with a brick hearth at one end. Two candles in sconces pooled light near a large table with chairs. Blackened beams stretched overhead. A woman occupied one of the chairs. Her drawn face, lit by a taper on the table, showed the toil she'd suffered since childhood. Pockmarks dappled her cheeks. Sandy-coloured hair shorn to ear-length framed two mean eyes. Thomas went up and embraced her. Pineapple Pol held her country brother then let him go. She leaned forward into the taper's flickering light and pointed at young Betty Loxton now standing beside her.

"Show him," she said.

Betty Loxton reluctantly lifted her cotton bodice. "See," Pineapple Pol said. Her finger pressed the blue bruise like a ring around Betty's puckered belly.

"See here. He hung her up from the contraption and nearly killed her."

Uncle Thomas sneered. Another man was in the room. A big man Betty feared more than she did her mother, Pineapple Pol.

"Right rounder, he is," Brother John said.

John the Pawn stepped forward into the taper's light. He shook the hand of Uncle Thomas. John the Pawn's thin face resembled his mother's, as did his short, sandy hair. A scar scored his chin. He wore his costerman's cap far back on his high forehead. Betty smelled on his clothes the familiar market stench of straw and wet fruit and dung. John the Pawn tapped his clay pipe on the edge of the table. From his upper pocket he took out a fresh plug of tobacco and stuffed it hard into the bowl of the pipe before leaning it into the taper's flame, pulling in breath so that the plug ignited in a red glow.

"You, you foolish girl," Pineapple Pol said. She held Betty's chin. "No more of that dreaming. No business of yours is the stage. A stager you wanted to be? No, my girl."

"Let it lie, mam," John the Pawn said.

"I cannot, son John. See, here, Thomas, how her whole self was almost killed by him."

Uncle Thomas raised his head toward the beamed ceiling. "We can do it, back in kind, for sure. I will do it."

Betty pulled down her bodice. Pineapple Pol waved her aside, and Betty sat in a corner by the hearth. Thomas took a pint offered him by John the Pawn and drank the entire contents in one swallow. John the Pawn pulled out a chair and suggested Thomas rest his legs. "No. I thank you, nephew. But there is no time for resting. We must to our commotion soon, for my wife wishes me back home in Surrey by noon tomorrow."

On hearing these words, Betty began to weep once more. Pineapple Pol came to her, her hands planted on her hips. She leaned close to her daughter's ear.

"You make nine pence a day. Don't you grumble and mew, do you hear? You keep dry and gets your bread and butter."

"Leave her, mam," said John the Pawn. "She's not about to go at it again. Though you can make a shilling in the theatres, you can, for the crowd actors. I seen it put on the bills near Covent Garden. What is the shame in that?"

"No shame at all," Pineapple Pol replied. "But my Betty ain't no dancer or singer. Not her. And the likes of stagers, they can turn a young fool's head. See here, what the villain caused us. We almost lost her. What good is a cripple-child in the market? On the streets? I'll no more of it. He needs a lesson, that villain. And you, stupid gal, you shall get a beating again if you go nears him ever at all."

The door to the room opened, and a thick-set man walked in. He wore a costerman's cap, and he tipped it to Pineapple Pol and the others.

"Thomas, this fellow's here to help you and John with the business." The thick-set man put out his hand to shake Thomas's.

"Well, then, all of you," said John the Pawn. "We have tonight to go. We know where to follow him. But it must be late. After the theatres are shut up for midnight."

"Betty, get off now," snapped Pineapple Pol. She yanked her daughter's arm and made her stand. Then she shoved her toward the door. "You get back to your spot, you hear. Get rid of the rest of your Reds tonight. Get along. No use staying here."

Betty wiped her eyes, tied her bonnet and lifted her basket.

"Do you have it, Thomas?" asked Pineapple Pol, turning and walking back to the table.

Betty hesitated at the door to the stairs and looked toward the three figures standing around the table. The taper threw a huge shadow on the wall as Thomas pulled open his black long-coat. Betty stepped forward to see better. A pocket inside the coat was heavily stitched. Along one seam, a strap of leather held what Betty thought at first was a snake. But then Thomas unbuttoned the strap and slid out a rough-hewn club.

"Oh, no," Betty whispered. "You cannot."

"This will do it," Thomas said. He cracked the club hard across the table top. Dust puffed up, and the taper tipped to the floor amidst harsh laughter from Pineapple Pol.

"See, girl," John the Pawn shouted at Betty, his voice full of mocking anger. "A bruise for a bruise. Mr. Arrogance will not be walking so tall tomorrow breakfast time."

Uncle Thomas grinned at Pineapple Pol. "Best he hide himself," he said, "if he wants to keep breathing."

Betty rushed out the door and pulled it shut behind her. She stopped two steps down the stairway. From below her came tavern laughter and chatter. Even through that noise she heard her own mother say: "Then tonight it shall be. And I thank you all for your pains."

Chapter Two

SATURDAY, DECEMBER 19, 1840

Dawn hovered over the inner city as a young police constable in a stiff collar hastened through streets near Chancery Lane. His bull's-eye lantern rocked to and fro, and by the time he stopped at Number 6 Cursitor Street, he was breathless. His right fist knocked hard on the door.

"Inspector Owen Endersby?" he shouted. "A pressing matter, sir."

Presently, the self-same man appeared, a broad, tall figure wearing a frown and a rumpled nightshirt. After a short conference with the nervous constable, Inspector Endersby went back inside. Within moments, a cab arrived and soon after, as light showed golden on the window panes of Cursitor Street, the constable and the inspector climbed into the cab and rattled up passageways north to Holborn, bypassing the Inns of Court, Gray's Inn and northward to Doughty Street where, the constable explained, a body had been found, a body most "foul and bloodied, sir. No doubt a murder, sir."

"No doubt," answered Owen Endersby, his eyes still heavy with sleep.

The cab pulled up to a wide, handsomely-kept three storey brick house. An iron railing guarded the area staircase leading down to the kitchen below street level. Over the polished front door was a half-moon window. Two stout chimneys capped the steep roof. Inspector Endersby noted immediately that they were oddly smokeless for such a brisk December morning.

"Are the servants not up and about?" the inspector asked of the constable keeping guard at the railing.

The young man stood at attention, wearing white leather gloves. "No evidence of such, sir. No below-stairs residents as far as we can determine."

Inspector Endersby told the young policeman to stand at ease. Endersby then reached into a pocket and took out a candied chestnut from the box his wife Harriet had given him. In spite of his hasty house-leaving this morning, he'd had time to put on his favorite plum-coloured waistcoat. His gouty foot was merely a dull ache for the moment. As always, elation and anxiety preceded the viewing of a mutilated body.

A man in a black Mackintosh approached. "Inspector, sir."

"Caldwell. Here on the dot? No doubt you have been efficient." Endersby tried hard to mask his snide tone. Detective Sergeant Caldwell, in his early forties, had restless peering eyes and a mouth too full of teeth. He reminded Endersby of a rat-catcher's terrier with his closely-shaven head. On its top sat a frayed, low-crowned hat.

"Sir. I have done a bit of rummaging already. It was the neighbour's servant who informed the police at the station on Gray's Inn Road in the early morning. Said his master heard crashing noises in the night and was afeared. Seems the night-watch sergeant had trouble locating the station inspector—he has an ill wife—so Gray's Inn notified you."

"Thank you, Caldwell."

"There is more, sir."

"Carry on," said Endersby.

"Schools are rampant in this quarter, sir," Caldwell continued. "The Boswell School has been caught hereabouts, nicking silver and such."

"No servants, but crashing noises. Where is the body, then?"

"In the front parlour on the first floor, a male in evening clothes." Sergeant Caldwell glanced sharply at the two constables standing near the inspector. "These young constables have kept out of harm's way. Nothing's been touched."

"Do we know the name of the victim as yet, Sergeant?"

"Not as yet, sir. I apologize, but I neglected in the rush of things to ask the name from the neighbour's servant. I can go now if you wish and enquire."

"I think we can wait for the moment. I'd like to poke around first and view the body."

"That would be best, sir. If I may be so bold to say."

"I am an inquisitive man, indeed, Sergeant Caldwell." The sergeant was about to respond again, but Endersby cut him off. "I see the street is curious soon enough."

Faces peered out from behind curtained windows. Two boys gazed from across the laneway. Doughty Street was clean and lined north to south with rows of brick houses. At either end of the street were iron gates, one of which was manned by a porter in mulberry-coloured livery. Damask curtains betrayed the comfortable wealth of many of the lease-holders. A maid in a canvas apron was washing down the steps of the house opposite, and she stood up, her brush dripping, to stare at Inspector Endersby and his retinue of police.

"Caldwell."

"Inspector?"

"Best send one of these constables to fetch a surgeon. And have him obtain the beadle while he's at it. The coroner, I assume, has been summoned?"

The constable in the white gloves answered. "The night-watch sergeant sent word from the station, sir, so we were told."

"Inspector Endersby is my name."

"Thank you, Inspector."

"Under the jurisdiction of Borne and the central Metropolitan."

"Thank you, sir."

"Where is your detective branch at Gray's Inn?" inquired Endersby.

The other constable, the one who had knocked on the inspector's door, explained. "One's off with a broken arm. He was in a tussle last week with a bounder. The other has a sickly wife, sir, as the sergeant explained. Such was the situation this morning that my superintendent suggested I run to you and to your sergeant, Mr. Caldwell."

The two constables stood at attention in the manner taught to all members of London's constabulary. Sergeant Caldwell sent the one in the white gloves to fetch the surgeon and the beadle.

"Shall we, gentlemen?" Endersby then said.

Caldwell stepped forward immediately. "Inspector."

Caldwell held open the gate to the stairs leading to the area below street level and the front entrance to the lower kitchen. Endersby made his way first down the curved staircase. Over his shoulder hung a leather satchel with a broad strap, a legacy from his days as a Bow Street Runner. Endersby had put on his suede gloves and long-coat of coarse canvas, his usual plainclothes costume, which his wife Harriet called his "hunting" outfit.

"You next, Constable," commanded Caldwell. He then clicked the gate shut and hurried down the steps behind the others, passed them and stood at attention before the kitchen door. It had the standard four panes of glass, two of which were broken. Caldwell snapped his fingers at the constable, as if to cue him for a line. The young policeman quickly responded. "The door was ajar when we arrived on the scene. There was bits of glass all over."

"I can see," said Endersby. "Notice, gentlemen, the door has neither latch nor lock. Only a simple turn knob. Why would someone shatter the glass?"

"Odd, sir," said Caldwell.

"Perhaps the owner of this house had no fear of thieves?" said Endersby.

"Curious, sir," replied Caldwell. He stood stiffly in a posture he had perfected over the past two years of working with Endersby. It had become his way, even though it was forced and bordered on belligerence. The men entered the house into a large, low-ceilinged kitchen with a deep hearth and a simple wooden table upon a slate floor. A single cup with tapers and candles sat on the wide mantel. There were no spoons, no pots nearby. No cabinets nor bins cluttered the corners. The floor in the kitchen and hallway was dirtied with muddy footprints.

"Such sparseness," said Endersby, popping one of his wife's candied chestnuts into his mouth.

"This table appears new and unused, sir," said Caldwell examining its surface by brushing his hand over the top.

The constable then said: "Makes one wonder if a ghost lives here."

"One does now for sure, Constable," quipped Endersby. "Ah," he then cried and leaned forward. Endersby studied the muddied slates along the hallway leading from the kitchen toward the back of the house. From his satchel he pulled out a brown paper envelope, the kind his brother-in-law sold to law clerks. "Caldwell, put a smudge of that stuff on this envelope. That's it. Now come to the light. Well, well, we have boot track here."

Sergeant Caldwell put on a pair of wire-rimmed spectacles. Inspector Endersby examined the lump of dried mud lying on the flap, picking out a piece of apple peel from the brown-coloured mass. Then a corner of green. "Cabbage."

Caldwell sniffed. "So it is, sir."

Endersby shoved the wad of mud into the envelope. "From the looks of all this mud, there was a host of visitors. Big feet."

"Men with large boots, surely," reiterated Caldwell.

With a huffing and puffing, there appeared at the front kitchen door a bent man in his sixties. He was wrapped in a madras house-coat, a tasselled Turkish cap perched on his head. His face carried a most perplexed expression. He paused to catch his breath. "What a terror," the bent man said.

Caldwell leapt toward him. "State your business, sir."

The old man recoiled in alarm.

"Sergeant Caldwell," said Endersby, "please, let me handle this gentleman."

Endersby calmly introduced himself and his men. The affronted gentleman straightened in response and regained his composure. About him was an air of one who spends too much time with books as sole companions. There was, as

Endersby noted, a parchment-like look to his skin.

"Ratcliff," replied the man testily. "What a ruckus. My servant tells me the fellow is deceased."

"I have yet to see the body, sir," answered Endersby. "You are, I presume, the neighbour from next door, the one who sent for the police?"

"Most certainly. I shall grant my neighbour one thing; he was quiet enough most times."

"Did you speak with him yesterday?"

The bent man shook his head and lifted his right hand in a wave of dismissal. "I knew little of his habits. Mr. Cake kept himself close. My servant tells me he was in the theatre. That is all. But then, I keep to home."

"Can you suggest if any of your servants might know more about this Mr. Cake?"

"Servant, sir. I have only one. He is partly deaf and hears little and sleeps most days. If this be murder, God save us. God save us all."

"And what of these crashing noises you heard?"

"Much banging indeed. And late in the night. I heard windows smashed. And yelling. I thought gypsy bands had invaded." The neighbour then queried in a shaking voice if the former Mr. Cake had been dead some time.

"I cannot predict as yet, Mr. Ratcliff. Not until a surgeon comes."

"But what shall come of this, sir?" the old man wondered.

"An investigation, Mr. Ratcliff. If we do our duty, and with your aid, we can discover a culprit."

"But are we safe? Have we become victims of a rowdy gang?"

"These questions are, as yet, to be answered, sir."

"God help us. What can we do but wait and see?"

"Would you surmise the hour in which you heard these various noises?"

"Oh, my. Late, sir. After midnight. I was up and about, reading and thinking. But what else? I am confused at present, what with lack of sleep."

"You will remain indoors for the day, will you, sir?"

"Indeed. Most likely. I must keep guard, do you not think?"

"I shall come presently to speak with you, if I may. I can offer some advice in securing your home, if you wish it."

"Indeed, and thank you. Then I shall depart from you gentlemen, if I may?" Ratcliff threw a disdainful glance toward Sergeant Caldwell. "I have been up half the night and need my rest."

"Mr. Ratcliff," replied Endersby, "please, sir, will you also make yourself available this day for the coroner's inquest. Be prepared to answer more questions about this matter—about times, people you may have seen."

"I have informed the constables already of what I have seen. And I shall do so at your request for the coroner."

With this word, the neighbour mounted the area stairs into the street.

Endersby allowed a moment for Mr. Ratcliff to walk out of earshot. Impatient, Caldwell scratched his head under his low-crowned hat. He sucked on his teeth. In reaction to this and to all the new information he had just encountered, Endersby decided to walk and ponder. "I shall take but an instant," he said, not looking Caldwell in the eye. With little hesitation, Endersby turned and walked about the ground floor of the house, from room to room. He took his time, glancing into corners, peering through shadows. Cupboards presented empty shelves; rooms echoed like deserted caverns. To his deft eye, the place seemed even more odd than before. He returned, pensive, and announced: "The other rooms here are empty. The back door leading to the yard and alley also has no latch or lock. The door is intact."

"Inspector?"

Endersby turned around to see the constable in the white gloves at the front kitchen door stepping aside for a blond man carrying a black leather satchel. Caldwell kept his distance, waiting for his superior to greet the man. A gentleman too, but years younger than the neighbour, his status confirmed as a professional in his top hat of brushed beaver, his knee-length coat fastened by brass buttons. The warmth of his quick smile did not extend to his bare right hand, chilly from morning cold as it took hold of the inspector's.

"I beg your pardon," said the man. "I am John Sloane, surgeon."

"Good morning, sir. You have come in good haste." Endersby smiled. Fond of surgeons, especially the young ones, Endersby particularly respected their new metal gadgets and medical language. "Edinburgh, Mr. Sloane? I detect a Scots accent."

"Yes, Mr. Endersby."

"You look young for a member of the Royal College."

The surgeon smiled. "The college has a wide open door, Mr. Endersby. I am proud to be of service."

Sergeant Caldwell then suggested each of the men take a candle upstairs to the first floor, as the shutters there had been nailed closed, and light from the grey sky was insufficient for viewing the body.

"Nailed shut?" asked Endersby.

Caldwell replied, "We could not open the two in the parlour, sir, without damaging the wood."

With a tilt to his chin, Inspector Endersby went ahead up the staircase leading to the first floor of 46 Doughty Street. On reaching the top step, he paused for a quick breath, the surgeon, Caldwell and the two constables directly behind him in a line. Endersby noticed a back room, its window smashed. He told Caldwell to investigate to see if there might be a weapon or some item left behind by the intruders. With a taper, the constable in the white gloves illumined each of the men's candles then waited with the others in the hall leading to the dark front parlour. "Light me again, please," Endersby asked.

"It seems the intruders came up here as well. Look at this mud. Caldwell?"

"Yes, sir," answered Caldwell from the back room. "Right away, sir."

Caldwell joined his superior, who was holding the others back from proceeding.

"One indulgence, gentlemen. Caldwell, hand me an envelope once again. Do you see it? This particular mud.

Here is a separate set of foot prints, the mud entirely different in colour."

Caldwell bent down and scooped up a piece of dried, reddish earth.

"What do you make of it?" Caldwell asked.

The surgeon stepped forward and glanced over Caldwell's shoulder. "I can enlighten you," said the surgeon. "That reddish muck is from Mecklenburgh Square close by. I have a house there. Workers are digging a foundation to replace a burned-out building." The surgeon lifted his boot, and in the candlelight Endersby could make out the same colour of mud stuck to the man's toe and heel.

"Extraordinary," Endersby said. "What a bunch came calling on Mr. Cake." Before proceeding, Endersby took a few moments to instruct and remind his present entourage to touch nothing and to be careful not to move any object without his permission. "All of you swear to make no hasty judgments," he then counselled. "After all, we are dealing in grave matters. *Sic Gloria transit mundi.*"

"Hollah. Hollah?" They heard a voice from downstairs.

"Who is there? Come up," Caldwell shouted.

A quick-stepping gentleman in a yellow frock coat and broad woollen hat appeared at the foot of the staircase. He brandished a brass-tipped staff. "Good morning," he blared and rushed up the stairs.

"You are the beadle, sir?" asked Endersby.

"No doubt of it," the man replied. "No doubt at all. I was told one of you was the esteemed Mr. Owen Endersby of the Bow Street Runners."

"I am he, sir. But we no longer claim that appellation."

"I beg your mercy, sir. No doubt you mistook my attempt at light humour at this early hour."

"Did I, perhaps, beadle? And your name?"

"Thaddeus Arne. I am pleased to meet you." The beadle quickly shook hands with all the men and adjusted his hat, which had been knocked to the side of his head by his rushing up the stairs. "No doubt, from what this young policeman has described, I reckon we have a corpse badly done in."

"So it seems," replied Endersby. "What do you know of the former Mr. Cake?"

"A fine, upstanding gentleman. Never once did he come to me with complaint. I understand he was associated with the theatre in some capacity. He was a successful gentleman, given the size of this fine house. Mr. Samuel Cake, Number 46, yes, this building belonged to him—a new lease-holder, as our record indicates." The beadle had brought with him a ledger from which he read out the information on Samuel Cake.

"Was he an actor, Beadle?" asked Endersby.

"I do not know, sir. I record only the lease-holder's name and his lot number. It is my little efficiency, peculiar to me in our parish. But I find such information helps me to remember names. I am notorious for my forgetfulness."

"Can you recall any complaints against Mr. Cake?"

"Against him?" The beadle flipped hurriedly through his pages to the end of the ledger. He asked the constable beside him to hold his candle closer. The beadle's fingers raced down the page of numbers, beside which were minutely written short entries. "None, sir. Not a one. A most respectable man. Although we never saw him at service on Sunday. But no, no complaint, no judgments, no inquiries as to his business or welfare."

"I thank you for your kindness, Beadle. Gentlemen, we must go to the parlour. Please step very carefully and keep your gaze down for any items we may locate which could be relevant to Mr. Cake's demise."

Six men now in single file hugged the wall, candles held up as in a procession. Shadows jumped onto cornices and ceiling mouldings. The men paused at the entrance to the parlour. Inspector Endersby ventured in first. Broken glass and overturned furniture filled the room. Jagged nails hemmed the shutters, refusing the thinnest crack of light to enter. The grate held a meagre handful of fresh coal. A sofa, legs pointed at the ceiling, lay beside two toppled chairs, their cane kicked out of them. The only object left standing was a desk with its drawers gaping open. It was as if,

Endersby thought, the desk had bravely held its ground against the marauders. He took two more steps in, signalling to Caldwell and the surgeon to accompany him. The beadle sighed, and one of the constables coughed; outside, the street was stirring with chatter and the passing of horses.

In the corner across from the cold hearth lay a colder and more frightening object: the body of Samuel Cake. Reddish mud led away from the redder stain surrounding the body. Cake sprawled, dressed in a red sash, a cloak and boots; his beaver hat sat right side up a few feet from his battered head.

"Mr. Sloane, if you please," Endersby said in a respectful voice. "Poor chap," he whispered as the surgeon knelt down and opened his medical bag. From a pocket, the surgeon lifted a mirror the size of a saucer and held it to the mouth of the corpse. Cake's hair was mussed and crusted with dried blood. Endersby walked to the opposite side of the body, across from the surgeon, and raised his candle. The wall closest to him was splattered with large drops of blood.

Caldwell was suddenly beside him. "Smashed good and hard, I'd say, sir."

Endersby reached down and picked up a walking stick. Its ivory head was shaped like a dog's. The muzzle was bloodied, and bits of dried hair and flesh stuck to the metal ring under the head. Endersby held his candle closer. Two initials in brass were inscribed on the handle: S.C. Caldwell took hold of the walking stick and placed it on the mantel.

"What physical force caused this?" Endersby said to the surgeon. "Gaze at the skull, pummelled and cracked. One of the eyes is slightly swollen, do you see?"

"I do, sir."

"A blow before death, if my experience of beaten bodies can give us guidance," said Endersby.

By now the surgeon had opened Cake's jacket and shirt and listened to the heart with a brass instrument that the beadle, Thaddeus Arne, exclaimed resembled an ear trumpet. "Indeed it does," was the surgeon's curt answer.

"Mr. Cake, he was kimbawed right hard," the constable in

the white gloves added. The room fell silent again as the surgeon passed his candle over the pale bluish face. Cake's hands lay stiff, fingers curled on the parquet. Inspector Endersby questioned the surgeon if Mr. Cake had been dead a long time.

The surgeon stood up. He wiped his hands on a flannel. "Probable but not certain, sir, this man died four to six hours ago."

The bystanders did not move or make a comment. The surgeon then asked the beadle if anyone on the street was related to Mr. Cake.

"I believe not. No doubt we can discover some kin," was Thaddeus Arne's hasty reply.

The surgeon turned to face Inspector Endersby and his sergeant. "Mr. Cake has died of severe blows to his head. The skull appears cracked in two places—on the crown and over the right ear. There is also some bruising by the shoulder, which suggests he was struck there by the same instrument, but that his clothing cushioned the blows, thus creating a bruise. The weapon most likely was that walking stick on the mantel, since the cuts in the flesh of the cheek and chin were caused by sharp edges, similar to those of the stick head's carved shape. I shall write these details on requisition and present them to the coroner."

"I thank you, Mr. Sloane."

"I assume the burial will be covered by Mr. Cake's income or savings," the surgeon then said. "He appears to have been—God grant him grace—a man of some means."

"Most likely, sir," replied Thaddeus Arne. "I shall, of course, send soon enough for the coffin maker. We in the parish can look into such a matter."

Inspector Endersby then spoke. "My sergeant and I will endeavour to find some clues to his connections—to kin, to friends, to hirelings, if there are any—to all that may concern the unfortunate."

Agreeing, the surgeon said, "He was a strong, youthful man. What revenge was this that must befall such a fellow?"

"If in fact it was revenge," replied Endersby. "We must

investigate further for the sake of aiding the coroner's inquest. We must see if there are any papers or documents in this house which may afford us a direction—a by-way, as I like to call it—toward a suspect."

The beadle stepped forward. He seemed restless and impatient, his shoulders shifting as he waited to speak. "There is a tavern of good repute two streets from here, The Oak and Crown, where the coroner will swear in his jury and hold proceedings," he said, his words separated by huge breaths. "Gentlemen, I beg your leave and rely on your presence at the tavern this afternoon. I must start my soliciting."

Thaddeus Arne hesitated at the doorway. As the beadle, he had to act quickly to petition for a jury of peers and go about knocking on the neighbours' doors to select reliable witnesses—a footman, upstairs maid, water carrier, any idle watcher at a window—who must have seen *something*. The beadle rushed down the hall, his ledger open to take notes, a flurry of loose-flying paper hampering his progress.

"We must all testify honestly to what we have seen, gentlemen," Endersby added. "So please be alert and look once again on this horrible place. The coroner is a busy man and must have straight answers."

With formalities finished, the surgeon shook hands with Endersby and left, requesting beforehand that one of the constables come and fetch him in Mecklenburg Square for the coroner's inquest. The two young police officers moved their eyes around the dank room one more time before walking toward the staircase. Endersby followed close behind. "Wait," he whispered, though Caldwell was already moving down the stairs. In the hall, Endersby took a step toward what resembled a black sooty ball lying on the floor. On picking it up, his broad fingers felt the coarse grains of a cheap cut of tobacco. Part ash, part raw leaves, the plug gave off a salty perfume. He pinched some of it into another small envelope then closed his shoulder satchel, his hand brushing against the brass ear trumpet he carried and used when inspecting bodies. Endersby had been pleased to see the young surgeon use a similar instrument, proud that his own method was like that of an Edinburgh-trained professional.

Downstairs, Endersby spoke quietly to Sergeant Caldwell. "Go round the theatres this morning, before the inquest."

"Whatever for, sir?" Caldwell spoke peevishly.

"Sometimes, Sergeant, you are too quick."

"Pardon, sir. I see no…"

"Play the rube," Endersby said, cutting Caldwell off. "Play the gull. I suggest you try the Surrey side theatres first. The Coburg, Aston's Palladium, you know them. I have not heard of this Cake fellow. Find out who he was, what he did, who he knew. Do not mention what has happened."

"Right away, sir."

Caldwell pulled down his frayed hat and reluctantly left by the front area stairs. Endersby next instructed the two constables. One walked outside to the front railing on Doughty Street. The constable in the white gloves offered to guard the backyard gate and also to go later to alert the surgeon of the inquest. Endersby then stood by himself in the muddied hall near the kitchen. He showed neither fatigue nor impatience, neither bewilderment nor anger. He reached into his pocket and to his astonishment discovered his candy tin empty. All the chestnuts, every one Harriet had given him, he had eaten. He burned with shame for the instant: he must have been chewing the wretched sweets without consideration as the surgeon examined the corpse. "None of these any more," he cautioned himself, snapping the tin shut.

Once again he climbed the staircase to the first floor, a candle held aloft. He moved to the front door entrance leading to Doughty Street. He stepped around the mud-prints and stopped. The door had a turn knob. "But no lock or latch," Endersby muttered. "Why did this man not lock up his house?" He moved back down the hallway and decided to look into the room next to the parlour. In passing, he glanced briefly again at Samuel Cake, lifeless as dust on the floor. The second room had a bare window. A large dining table of polished mahogany appeared in the flutter of candlelight, taking on form like a spirit-figure in a vampire play. The table had been marred by some kind of blunt instrument. A cabinet behind it leaned forward; broken glass from its upper shelf doors lay like shimmering snow on every nearby surface. The shelves were empty of crockery and silverware. "If, indeed, there were any for thieves to take." *This whole house seems uninhabited*, Endersby thought. His eyes continued to scan the floor and walls. The heavy bootprints of mud streaked the parquet, but in this room there was no colour of reddish earth.

Endersby did not move for a second, though now he had situated himself at the staircase leading to the ground floor kitchen. It was his habit to ponder a crime scene, to imagine it before the crime had taken place, piecing together what he surmised was its original state, then matching that image to what his eyes presented to him in the present moment. This was one of his by-ways, one of the paths he liked to wander to gather a first impression. After thinking for a time, he took the steps to the ground floor. He went slowly as he descended, the gout beginning to pang him already. He moved to the backyard door, opened it and went into the shallow sunken court. There was the constable in the white gloves pacing and beating his hands to keep warm. Endersby climbed the four stairs to the brick yard, a squalid space surrounded by a low wall. Looking at the backyard gate, he kept thinking that perhaps this might have been a way in or out for the villains. What forced him forward was an itch he always felt when he thought a clue would soon turn up. His eyes started searching the low brick wall.

He paused, then smiled to himself. "Ah, there you are," he whispered. Owen Endersby opened his satchel and slipped out an envelope.

A single glove lay on its side, its palm of canvas coarsely sewn to a yellow leather backing. The fingers were slightly shredded; blood spots, on closer inspection, speckled the thumb and two of the forefingers. "So, you rogues," Endersby said, his bulky frame all sweaty from his exertions. "Here is a part of one of you, blood and all."

Endersby raised the glove and folded it into the

envelope. He adjusted his hat and his canvas coat. He looked
up at the sky. "Well, this is the start of things. Now, Mr. Cake,
we shall endeavour to find out a thing or two about your sad
departure from this foggy world."

*   *   *

By the time Endersby walked back down the hall on the first
floor and opened the front door of Number 46 Doughty
Street, the news of Samuel Cake's body had reached the
neighbourhood. Milling children gawked at the windows.
Servants and masters were asking questions of the constable
standing guard. Inspector Endersby interrupted them.
"Good neighbours, please go about your business. This
young policeman is here to provide some security to Mr.
Cake's house. Do not be alarmed. My cohorts with the
detective force are now in pursuit of the villains." The crowd
stepped back. Endersby heard grumbling and the clearing
of throats, but soon the street returned to its placid state:
doors were closed, servants cleaned windows and washed
down steps, carriages pulled up with packages, a postman
began his duties distributing the first of London's five daily
mail deliveries—dinner invitations, calling cards, solicitors'
letters, love notes, relatives' requests for money—the whole
range of human communication slipping through the brass
mail slots of the doors on Doughty Street. Endersby beheld
the spectacle and pondered how the world was always ready
to return to harmony and order.
    "I shall go to the coroner," he told the young constable
on guard. "To The Oak and Crown, in Guildford Street."
He then reminded the young policeman he would return
later on for a final inspection of the crime site. "So, please
keep all in good stead," Endersby said, pulling on his gloves
and starting off down the street.
    Endersby began to stroll along Doughty southward to the
corner at Guildford. At exactly two o'clock in the afternoon,
the coroner would make his entrance into the smoky,
sawdust-smelling confines of The Oak and Crown.

*   *   *

When the clock struck the appointed hour, Mr. Thaddeus
Arne, his beadle's chain about his neck, preceded the
coroner and led him into the tavern. As a man of sixty, the
coroner impressed the tavern's guests with his lively step,
his head of white hair, and his hawk's beak nose. He and
the beadle passed into the narrow room at the back of The
Oak and Crown.

The coroner placed himself at a long, greasy table and
around him herded a group of serious-faced gentlemen
holding their summonses in their hands. The coroner
instructed Mr. Arne to name the jurymen he had found, one
after the other, and to call each to be sworn in. Penny-a-line
journalists from the crime rags, as well as the beadle's collected
witnesses, were then allowed to enter. Soon after, a crush of
spectators crowded the low-ceilinged room, all of them wearing
what Endersby called their "roast-beef Sunday clothes".

The coroner then stood. "Gentlemen."

Silence fell.

"Gentlemen, you are worthy men all, and have been
summoned under law to inquire into the death of Mr.
Samuel Cake. Your verdict shall be given, but only after you
have been afforded evidence, and testimony from witnesses
as honest and reliable in their cause as you are in yours."

The jury spread itself over a group of chairs, benches,
and perches by the hearth. Endersby and Caldwell stationed
themselves beside the penny-a-liners with their lead-tipped
pencils poised to scribble down details of the proceedings.

"Call Mr. Ratcliff."

The neighbour, Mr. Ratcliff, dressed now in proper
frock coat and trousers, approached the table.

"Sir, you live beside Mr. Cake and reported the noises in
the night. You also notified the constables and night-
sergeant at the Gray's Inn station?"

"Yes, sir. I did indeed." Mr. Ratcliff spoke in a shaking voice.
Endersby nodded to Caldwell when the bent man came to the
point in his story where he stood at his front window.

"I saw the front door of Mr. Cake's house open. The gaslight from the street was sufficient to show three men rush out and run up to the north end of the road. They wore caps was all I could tell."

"Three men? At what time do you reckon this occurred?"

"Late, sir. Quite past two o'clock in the morning."

"Thank you, Mr. Ratcliff."

"And then..."

"Then?" queried the coroner. Endersby nodded to Caldwell.

"I took a glass of wine in my study. At the back of my house. I was attempting to calm myself, you see, from being awakened by such violent noise-making."

"I see," nodded the coroner.

"While in my back study, I saw a fourth, a lone man."

"A fourth man? Where?"

"Leaving the back entrance of Mr. Cake's house. I am sure of it. He was tall and wore a cloak, and at first I thought it was Cake himself. I presumed such and made no further note of the matter until the constable arrived to announce there was found a body in the very house next to mine."

"And what of this walking stick, sir?" asked the coroner, pointing to the stick's ivory head which had been partly covered by a cloth.

"Good heavens, your honour. That is surely not blood?"

The spectators let out a muffled chorus of "ahs."

"Answer the question, Mr. Ratcliff."

"It belonged to Mr. Cake, sir. He carried it on every occasion that I saw him."

Sergeant Caldwell was then brought forward and sworn. "Now, Sergeant," instructed the coroner, "tell us about Mr. Samuel Cake."

Caldwell stood at attention. "In summary, sir," said Caldwell, to both coroner and jury, "Mr. Cake had means. His stage manager informed me Mr. Cake rented warehouses. He used the profit to hire his players and musicians for the Coburg Theatre, Waterloo Street. Seems Mr. Cake was the manager, and he also wrote many of the pieces presented to the public. I asked after the stage-door keeper about Mr. Cake's whereabouts last evening. He replied that his employer had taken his usual supper at the theatre, with his many assistants. He had then dressed for the evening in his dressing room where he kept clothes for all occasions. What his business was for the evening, the stage-door keeper did not divulge, mainly because he did not know. Mr. Cake, I learned, was a bachelor of twenty-nine years and had few acquaintances. One young mistress I encountered in the wardrobe department was fearful for him, as she wondered what had happened to him since he had, not returned for his usual breakfast. The matron in charge spoke highly of him but was much inclined to keep silent. On instruction from my superior, I did not reveal the true purpose to my questions."

"Oh, mercy, mercy," cried the next witness, a Doughty Street heiress, a nervous woman of about forty in a rich blue coat and velvet bonnet.

"Take care listening to her, Caldwell," instructed Endersby.

"That Mr. Cake, he was a suspicious gentleman. How did he live without servants? Never did I see a one. Never were any deliveries of any kind. Mind, he had a full purse. Never came *once* to Sunday service. I did not notice much else, really. To be truthful. Then, of course, there were the frequenters. My husband—he's gone to Manchester—my husband labelled them that. These frequenters came and went during the early afternoons. Always came in proper hansoms, always properly dressed. A veiled woman in a bonnet and two young men in top hats. Most respectable, as I could tell. The woman's face was hard to make out. There was also a tall man in a Mackintosh with a wool cap, dressed like he was a costerman from the Covent Garden market. I found that intriguing. Yet I could tell from his trousers and boots he had a purse. He once came, I swear, and was wearing a red beard. I am sure he was the same gentleman. His beard was most certainly red and bushy. Must have shaved it off perchance. Though I reckon from his height he was no Irishman, he being so tall."

The jury took a break. The clock struck four, and Inspector

Owen Endersby then approached the table.

"It was found, sir, by the back wall of Mr. Cake's house." Inspector Endersby held up the bloodied glove. "There are marks on it. Blood and soot." The jury and spectators peered at the object.

The coroner concurred. "Much violence to the establishment, much breakage." The penny-a-liners scribbled, the spectators once again leaned forward.

"Is there any other witness, Mr. Arne?" the coroner demanded.

The beadle shook his head in an official manner. "The porter of the street gate was indisposed, sir. His wife claimed he was out of town on Friday night at his mother's funeral. The street gate was locked at eight o'clock, as usual. The wife had gone to bed early and claimed to have seen nothing— hence I did not ask her to appear before you today."

"Call the surgeon, then, Beadle."

Mr. Sloan stood up. He described his findings on the state of the body. He surmised the number of times Mr. Cake's head had been struck—sufficient enough to cause death. Mr. Sloan sat down.

"Very good, sir," the coroner stated. The jury members rose from their places. All of them clustered around the table. The scribblers continued to write, and Endersby nodded to Caldwell. When the jury of men parted, the coroner stood alone at the centre of the room.

"Gentlemen," he began, "our verdict, accordingly, is murder. No doubt of it. Our witnesses spoke of men coming and going. Mr. Sloane described to you the state of the beaten body. No doubt of what the crime *is*. But we must now discover for what reasons and by whom it was committed. You are all discharged." The jury bowed.

"Mr. Endersby?" The inspector faced the coroner. "I grant you permission, Inspector, to guard all items connected to the murder and to hold them for the magistrate."

"Yes, sir."

"There is no doubt, Inspector, your discoveries may lead to something most important, and I therefore implore you to find out as much as you can, to find out, for instance, if the owner of this glove may have been guilty of killing Mr. Cake. Please be advised that all items, papers, objects which you deem important must be carried to the magistrate."

Endersby bowed his head to the coroner and watched the older man retreat into the street, surrounded by the men once commandeered to be his jury.

"What time are we, Caldwell?" Endersby asked.

"Half past four o'clock, sir."

"Come with me, will you, to Number 46. I want to explore the second and third floors while the light is still sufficient."

As the two men made their way back to Number 46 Doughty Street, Endersby thought out loud: "And so Mr. Ratcliff, the bookish neighbour, witnessed three men in caps rush out of Mr. Cake's front door and head up to the north end of Doughty Street. You must speak again to the gate porter or his wife, Caldwell."

"I took the liberty earlier today to do just that, sir."

"Well done, Caldwell," said Endersby. At times, his subordinate could impress with his initiative.

"Indeed, sir," answered Sergeant Caldwell, "the beadle's story was correct. The porter's wife was alone and told me she had seen nothing in the night. Only Mr.Ratcliff claims to have any idea of the time when the three culprits fled— two o'clock in the morning."

"Or thereabouts," said Endersby.

"And then, sir, there was the fourth lone man."

"Yes, Sergeant, the lone man coming out a while later. But leaving from the *back* entrance of Mr. Cake's house."

"Perhaps the assailant, sir."

"Likely, Caldwell. Or a witness to the brutality and the smashing."

Sergeant Caldwell rushed ahead to Number 46 Doughty Street and spoke to the constable with the white gloves who was now guarding the front door. Endersby arrived limping from his gouty foot and entered the area leading down to the kitchen. "Caldwell, make certain these two young policemen are relieved for the coming evening. Also, instruct one of them to have the superintendent from Gray's Inn send over a locksmith to secure these doors."

Inspector Endersby waited and thought about the other key fact learned from the woman in the blue dress: Mr. Cake received "frequenters". Visitors who came and went in the afternoons. A veiled woman with two young men being regulars. And a tall gentleman—coming at one time wearing a beard. Or perhaps it was two different tall gentlemen? "Indeed," mumbled Endersby.

He entered the house with Caldwell behind him and climbed the two flights of stairs from the basement to the second floor. By this time in the day, the doubt he felt was clearly embodied in the level of pain in his foot. In fact, Endersby measured the success of his fact-finding by how much the gout bothered him. He dipped into his pocket. He had secured at the tavern a bit of bread and pickle wrapped in brown paper. He quickly ate it, thinking that at this point facts were many, but the logic of their patterns was still obscured.

"Let me catch my breath, for the moment, Sergeant," Endersby said, wiping crumbs from his lips. "Do you recall that bit of business, Caldwell, the witness claiming the tall man once came dressed as a Covent Garden coster?"

"Certainly, sir. One of the frequenters, you mean?"

"Precisely."

"A tall man in a Mackintosh and coster's cap."

"A coat not unlike your own, sir."

"I beg your pardon, Inspector."

"A casual comparison only, Sergeant."

"Thank you, sir."

"And the red beard."

"Yes, sir. The witness was most insistent it was red."

"Most emphatic about it."

"Notice, sir," Caldwell then said. The floor was muddied. The red earth was more plentiful than below on the first floor.

"Whoever the person was wearing those boots did much tramping about, didn't he?" said Endersby.

Caldwell walked ahead and opened the door to the front bedroom.

"Only red mud in here," noticed Endersby. "Curious."

"And look here, sir."

"Another desk with its contents scattered. What are those, Caldwell?"

The sergeant picked up a wad of crumpled papers.

"Letters?" wondered Endersby. "No. Notes," he said on examination. "Promissory notes. Here is one for ten pounds. Was Cake a lender?"

"Here is another bunch, sir."

"Promissory notes again. Ten pounds. Twenty-five pounds. From what we've seen of this house, Mr. Cake must have hidden his money well. Perhaps the ruffians were looking for ready cash."

"This bed, sir, is still made. Unmussed."

Endersby opened his satchel. "Hand me the papers, Caldwell. There are three notes here signed by a P. Buckstone. The two others have the signature of…can you make it out?"

"Looks like a P, Inspector. Simmons…no, Summers. P. Summers."

"Fellow theatre folk, you imagine?" Endersby placed the notes into his satchel.

"It is odd, sir. Actors are always wanting money, I presume."

"Not so odd, then, Caldwell, given the hazards of their profession."

Inspector Endersby yanked open one of the curtains in the room. Shadows fled from the pillows and coverlets. "Cake has not slept here recently. He did not sleep here at all last night, if these bedclothes indicate anything. Might he have come home and discovered the burglars and his assassin? Make a note, Caldwell, to have Mr. Arne bring the cloak and hat and the other clothes found on the corpse to our station."

"Noted, sir."

"See how this blasted red mud is everywhere in here, but scant evidence of the other variety. And look at that curtain."

A long green damask on the other window drooped

from its rod, as if torn by a violent pull. Endersby drew it aside and found a porcelain chamber pot tipped over. Its yellow liquid had pooled under the window, and floating up from it was a faint, acrid odour. "Curious," commented Endersby. "No top to the potty. And why has it tipped?"

Caldwell's knees cracked when he knelt down to inspect the small corner covered by the drape. "Clusters of the same red mud here, sir, and a distinct foot print."

"Let me see. A large boot indeed. And the toe facing out to the room. Check the hem of the curtain."

"Telltale mud on the inner panel, sir."

Endersby straightened. *What to make of this,* he wondered. "Picture the room, Caldwell. A desk rifled. A curtain torn. But no bashing up here. Perhaps a man was hiding here, behind that curtain?"

Caldwell scratched his head. "Hiding?" he asked impatiently.

"Yes, perhaps. Not one of the bashers. Someone else. Someone who also needed to pay a visit to Mr. Cake. A lone figure. If a thief were desperate for money, why would he not search *this* room and wreak havoc? Unless, Caldwell, he knew what the desk contained *before* he broke in."

"All possible, sir. You do love your rambles."

"I do, indeed, Sergeant. The by-ways of crime lead us in many directions at once."

Caldwell went back to the desk and pulled open the drawer once again. "What do you make of this, sir?" He held up a folded parchment with its wax seal broken. Endersby read the first few lines.

"It's a letter of offer from Lord Harwood. He is the proprietor of Old Drury and the lease-holder of other properties near the Strand. It appears he wished to contract Mr. Cake to take over Old Drury's management duties." Endersby slipped the parchment into his satchel. "How odd that Mr. Cake kept such a document here."

Endersby sat down on the edge of the bed. He wiped his brow with a handkerchief. "I shall wait here, Caldwell. Go to the third floor and see what you can find."

Sitting alone, Endersby reflected on the objects and

papers and mud samples and the positioning of the corpse and the bashed chairs and scratched tables and...

"Nothing, sir," said Caldwell on his quick return. "No mud, empty rooms. No cupboards. No sign of thieves breaking any wall or floorboard. This place is as cold as a tomb."

"Appropriate, then, for Mr. Cake's present state, I reckon," quipped Endersby.

"Sir?"

"Sergeant, I think it best for you now to contact the beadle, find a locksmith and relieve our young constables. I am in need of tea and a hot soak of this wretched toe."

"Very well, Inspector."

"Tomorrow being the Lord's day, we shall rest. But Monday, we must meet early and plan our strategy. Superintendent Borne will need a brief meeting, and we shall also speak to the magistrate. I think we need to start our investigation, first, at Mr. Cake's Coburg. Kindly pass by the man's theatre this evening and inform his stage manager."

"I shall do so, sir."

"A good deed on your part, Sergeant. The gutter press will have the story out on the streets soon enough. I shall go to my table and my good Harriet. I bid you good evening."

"Good evening, sir."

*   *   *

With his mind in much turmoil, Inspector Endersby held his gaze on the passing parade of London. He had left Doughty Street and hired a hansom cab. On his way home, he asked the driver to stop in Mecklenburgh Square. One stone wall of the Foundling Hospital blocked the western entrance. To the north, toward Heathcote Street, a line of houses stood with an open space, like a gap in a row of teeth. "Drive past there, cabby," said the inspector. The mud pit was red, and the timbers lining the foundation hole showed smudges of the same colour. The cab then rumbled on, clacking its way toward Cursitor Street. "Curious" was the only word which planted itself in the inspector's thoughts. What to do, indeed, he wondered, as the cab pulled up to his front door.

After a bath in his copper tub, he joined Harriet at the table for a quick supper of capon and potatoes. Without further delay, the two of them then hired a hansom cab to Old Drury for the performance of the hit melodrama, *Rachel; or, the Hebrew Maid.*

As the hansom rattled forward down Chancery Lane across Carey Street and into the hurling gigs of Drury Lane, Inspector Endersby looked out mournfully at the misery beyond the cab window. Beggars huddled in corners, barefoot children with blackened hands cried out for ha'pennies to buy food. Thick mud and slush and smoky brown air had become the three elements of London's streets. A stench of sewer and a sharp smell of rotted timber and sulphur brought to Endersby's mind images of war and hell. "How dismaying," he whispered to Harriet.

She nodded to him. "Terrible," she said. "And to think, dear Owen, of all you do to help alleviate such misery."

The inspector shook his head. "One man is not enough. We need a miracle. Or a revolution."

Harriet frowned. "Now, now, dear, we know well enough what happened to the French."

The cab slowed and turned a corner, and when Endersby looked up, Harriet was fussing in her handbag.

"Owen, my dear," she said, an expression of dismay marking her face. She pointed to his hands held in his ample lap. "You cannot wear those day gloves, those stained suedes, into Old Drury. I shall not allow it."

"Harriet," replied Owen Endersby, "can we not…"

"Mr. Endersby," she interrupted. "You may command your sergeants to bring order to our city, but as the proud wife of a public official, I cannot let stained suede stand for black kid. Thank goodness we have time."

In her flowered bonnet, Harriet Endersby seemed younger than her forty years. Owen Endersby had few, if any, complaints about his two decades of married bliss, though at fifty he continued to suffer gout, an ailment he attributed to his wife's rich cooking. He watched his beloved draw a pair of black kid gloves from her small handbag. "You see, Owen," she said, handing him the gloves, "I imagine you will look the part much better now." Harriet helped Owen change his suedes to the black kid, and by the time she had folded his workaday "mittens", as she called them, into her handbag, the hansom had drawn up to the portico of Old Drury.

"No less than nine minutes," quipped Owen as his wife pushed open the door.

Before them rose the great theatre, its portico crowded with theatergoers. Shadows from the streetlamps played across the theatre's marble façade. The odour of horse dung, the glitter of the nearby shop windows, the very loudness of the street only increased the excitement Owen felt on going to the play. "Careful," Harriet said, taking his hand. They mounted the steps and pushed through the high open doors. The ticket-taker recognized him and Harriet at once.

"Good evening, sir. Mum."

"Isn't this wonderful, dear," Harriet said, as she always did when they first stepped onto the marble floor of the foyer. Above them, the ceiling was painted gold, with frescoes of gods floating in clouds. Indeed, the place was much like a temple, as Endersby had often observed. Portals, saloons, mezzanines, boxes and galleries, all aglow with candles and gaslight. Like a temple, it inspired awe, but instead of silence, there was always shouting and laughter and much stomping of feet. Owen nodded to the two statues of Shakespeare and David Garrick as he and Harriet moved beyond the foyer into the broad, bustling, echoing tiered auditorium, rows of benches, five levels of boxes and galleries, the stage framed by a golden arch, while amidst all, like a giant glass tulip, the great chandelier shimmered with yellow gaslight.

A man in a green coat approached them. "Good evening, sir. Mrs. Endersby."

He tipped his hat to Harriet and shook Owen Endersby's gloved hand. Then the man moved into the crowd toward a place on one of the long pit benches which faced the stage.

"Remind me, dear," Inspector Endersby whispered to his wife.

"A colleague of my cousin, if I recall. We have met him once before. How polite of him to remember us." Harriet helped him up the steps and into their first-tier box. "I believe he is a jobber in the stationery trade," she said.

"More likely a copy clerk, my dear."

"How do you know?"

"Look at his rigid back. From sitting all day at the tilt. Did you notice his thumb and forefinger when he shook my hand? Black with India, which never rubs off."

"Pleasant enough fellow, he seems." She removed her bonnet and opened a small tin of candied chestnuts.

"He could be a rabble-rouser just as easily."

Harriet raised her eyebrows. "No, surely not."

"Did you spot what was in his pockets, dear one?"

"What were those in there?"

"Political weeklies. I saw clearly the title of one in his left coat pocket. *The Eye.* A disgruntled man, I surmise."

"Owen, dear. We are at the play. Let the poor man be."

Endersby nodded consent to his wife's request. His natural tendency toward critical analysis of the human race led him to perceive the perverse in people. For most of his twenty years as a London policeman, he had dealt with the brutalized nature of Man. Now he recalled the nails in the shutters in the house of Mr. Samuel Cake, but halted himself saying, "You must leave this for the time." Endersby knew the details of his day would harass him with doubts, questions. *And the bloodied glove? Left in terror or haste? But come now, old gander.* Endersby stretched his arms forward. For further relief, he raised his sharp eyes and his heavy eyebrows to survey the laughing bonnets and caps. High above his head, the fussing members of the shilling and two-penny galleries began to clap and shout out their impatience. There were cutters and seamstresses and coffee runners and footmen and upstairs maids and hall porters' wives holding their sleeping infants. *A veritable sea of Man*, thought Endersby, as a hush fell over the auditorium.

The canvas front curtain slowly rolled up to reveal a second curtain of luxurious green.

"I hear she is wonderful."

"Who?" asked Endersby.

"Owen, I told you. Miss Root."

"We have seen her before?"

"Of course. In *The Tempest*. But tonight she plays a Hebrew maid in disguise."

"Don't tell me…"

"A pilgrim."

"Thank you, Harriet."

"Mr. Weston plays the prince. He can bring a tear. Pathos is his great talent."

Owen Endersby ate a candy and watched a young boy across the pit slip his hand into the coat pocket of a drunken gentleman to pull out a clutch of coins. The boy slipped back and disappeared into the crowd. "Is he the tall fellow who sword-plays so well?"

"Yes, dear. Mr. William Weston. A tenor voice, too. Oh, look." Harriet pulled at her husband's sleeve. A pregnant woman had fainted in one of the boxes, and two ushers in livery carried her out. "I hope she will not be ill," said Harriet. Owen patted her hand and watched her cheeks flush with excitement as the orchestra began tuning up. As drums rolled, shouting and whistling started up in earnest, but then quieted when there was a loud knocking from the right wing of the stage.

"Here," said Harriet, holding the candy tin. "Take another before we start." Owen lifted his broad hand and delicately secured a candied chestnut before settling back in his seat. A violent drum roll now pummelled the chattering in the pit. A trumpet blew, and the galleries at last fell to silent wondering. The luxurious green curtain tore apart in its centre and lifted like a cloud. To Owen Endersby's delighted eyes, a painted city appeared, towers, dormers, lanes and a phalanx of drummers whose rat-a-tat-tat brought clapping from the slips and boxes. A fountain floated up through a trap door as a crowd in multi-coloured robes rushed onto the stage holding chalices.

"Oh, Let the Trumpets Sound," sang the men, arms raised. A figure in pilgrim's dress scurried onto the scene.

"There she is."

"Yes, Harriet."

"What lovely hands Miss Root has."

Owen Endersby took hold of his wife's plump wrist and placed it in his lap. She leaned into him in rapt attention as the yearning words of the pilgrim recounted a tale of loss. When Miss Priscilla Root sang her first air accompanied by a flute, the audience hummed along, bursting into deafening applause on the final stanza.

"Once agin,' lovely. Come agin', Miss Root," shouted a bravo from the upper benches.

"Sssh," lifted a chorus from the pit. "Quiet, quiet."

A round of cymbals and brassy fanfares announced the retinue of a prince, and the entire scene filled with men mounted on jumpy horses; banners waved, shields and pikes lined up on either side of the stage. The prince rode in and dismounted. His cloak embroidered in gold braid bore the insignia of an eagle.

"Mr. William Weston," pointed Harriet, breathless.

Owen sat forward. "Yes, indeed," he winced and shifted his throbbing foot.

A host of dancing village maidens later inspired his eyes to tear as his foot cramped with pain.

"Are you unwell?" Harriet asked, her eyes held by the movement on the stage.

"To be truthful," Owen replied, "it is like sticking my foot into hot mercury. But it shall pass."

"Here." Harriet offered the tin of chestnuts.

Into the fourth act, Inspector Endersby discovered the pain in his foot had lessened somewhat. Now before him appeared a crowd of townsfolk and a row of sneering cardinals in blood red robes. Miss Priscilla Root struggled nobly toward the scowling churchmen. She rolled her eyes toward heaven. Praying, she clasped her delicate hands before her heart. Drums thundered; gasps exhaled from the audience's two thousand faces; one of the cardinals pointed toward a boiling cauldron raised at the back of the stage. Slowly shutting her eyes, Miss Root opened her pilgrim's cloak to reveal her delicate neck as the chorus hummed a slow dirge. This dark moment prompted the inspector to reflect on the sordid lives in the streets which lay just outside the theatre's doors. How irrational and brutal all life is, he thought. Owen Endersby straightened his heavy back and entertained a sudden wonderment: did Old Drury herself remain but a mute observer of the tragic trials played upon her boards? Was there in her brick and mortar a capacity to harbour ghosts of sensations, to register the exaggerated cries of her powdered and wigged victims? If so, what use was such sympathy when the misery in the streets remained? No amount of paint and powder could fool one's eyes *not* to see it.

A braying trumpet cleared the inspector's mind. Watching the audience around him, he approved of their dabbing handkerchiefs, which rose like white petals blooming in the amber glow of the gaslight.

Harriet suddenly clutched him. Tears glistened on her cheeks. A hooded man led Miss Root toward the cauldron. She, in turn, suddenly faced the audience, and in a grand spasm of defeat let out a death scream from her powerful throat. The sound shot into the auditorium; the actress collapsed to the stage boards; mute faces stared at the prone body; then tumultuous applause arose like summer thunder. The pit and boxes jumped up in unison, clapping. The galleries followed close behind with such whistling, the orchestra drums held their fanfare for two extra rounds while Miss Root lay still as a stone, the life beaten out of her by Cruel Fate.

"Most enjoyable," exclaimed Mrs. Endersby at the close of the play. Owen and Harriet stood waiting for a hansom cab under the portico, damp coal smoke greeting them in the late evening air.

"Fine indeed, my love," Owen Endersby agreed. "Let us to home."

*   *   *

Back at Number 6 Cursitor Street, Harriet prepared a tea table before the fire in the parlour.

"Not professional thieves," she said, handing a steaming cup to her husband.

"Unlikely. The thieving schools train their chappies well."

"What would possess a man not to lock his doors?"

"A pertinent question, Harriet. Why indeed?"

"Professional thieves would know what was in a house, know about the silver, have accomplices among the servants, would they not?"

"From my experience, yes, most likely they would. I surmise that Mr. Cake did not hold anything of value in his house."

"Yet, you have evidence that he lent money? I imagine he kept it in a bank."

"Or in the theatre. But the man had no servants, no dishes. He did not reside at Doughty Street so much as visit it."

"How eccentric."

"My first concern is noise."

"How do you mean, Mr. Endersby?" Harriet took up her embroidery screen, yet Owen knew she was fully listening.

"The intruders broke glass. Made much noise. It was as if they wanted to be noticed."

"What would possess them to do that?"

"Ruffians. It is hard to figure. Did they want a fight to ensue? The police to come and have fisticuffs?"

Harriet laughed. "I suppose younger men might find that amusing."

"Precisely," agreed Owen. "The doors were without locks. One could clearly see that. The house was as bare as a moor."

"What a mystery," Harriet sighed.

"And the motive. What was the motive for all? Money? Revenge? Playful sport? Were the men playing a cruel jest on Mr. Cake?"

"Do you think he knew who they were?"

"Heaven only knows that, Harriet. But one man certainly hated Mr. Cake. The beating…"

"Oh, please, Mr. Endersby. Please do not describe the cruelty."

Later in his study at the end of the hall, Owen Endersby sat down at a round table and peered at the pieces of a French puzzle he had unwrapped from the post the day before. The puzzle's wood sections were polished, varnished shapes which implied a body of some kind of animal—most likely an elephant—and a group of men, if the elbows, knees, shoulders and heads indicated such. The puzzle was his favorite kind, cut and hand-bevelled in Paris, available only from the import dealer of toys and games in the Burlington Arcade. Endersby shuffled the pieces, the click and glide on the table's surface affording him calm. He sorted body parts. He set aside the trunk and howdah of the elephant; a palm tree was the first full picture he was able to form, a lower corner. *Here we can begin, monsieur,* he thought to himself.

For an hour he placed pieces together, then apart. He rose slowly and walked to the window, where there stood a longer table. On it were his mud samples, the glove, the ball of tobacco, all taken from Mr. Cake's house on Doughty Street, each on its own section of rough paper. The promissory notes had been unfolded and flattened. Endersby examined the signatures—Buckstone, Summers —and decided he must first determine who these people were and why their notes had been left in the house along with the contract from Lord Harwood.

"Curious," he muttered aloud. "Much can be indicated by what was left behind. Were there other notes; was ready money taken—bills, coins? Evidently, the ruffians had no interest in the contract."

Endersby fingered one of the nails he had picked up from the broken shutters in the front parlour where Cake's body had lain. He had taken it during the coroner's visit and was surprised to find that it was an old nail, a seconder, usually bought from the vendors of used metal or the Jew pedlars near Covent Garden.

"Taken into the house, perhaps, by the ruffians. Did they bring their own hammer as well? A planned ruckus, for certain." Endersby replaced the nail by the ball of tobacco. He leaned forward and smelled the tobacco again. "Cheap, coarse cut. A man of small means. Surely not belonging to Cake himself, if his cloak and sash were signs of his spending." Endersby passed his eyes over the whole collection. "And who would benefit from this sad death? A greedy relative? A wastrel brother?"

And what of the lone man seen escaping from the back of Cake's house? And the veiled woman with the two male companions? Were they the same three figures seen leaving by the front door?

The loss of this young man's life was so wasteful. Endersby paced before stopping at the dying hearth. Wanton brutality must not run unchecked. To effect retribution...indeed, this was the stone wall he must scale. Endersby knew now he was caught. He knew his passions for truth and justice would twist him, pang him worse than his gouty foot, force him to lie in an uneasy bed. Like a light in darkness, he thought: as a man, a husband, a Londoner, a policeman—all my energy will be bent on vindication.

"Ah, Harriet," he whispered.

Owen Endersby carried the candle from the room and watched his shadow move toward the bedroom door. He peeked in. Harriet was asleep. "Good night," he whispered to the sound of her breathing. Closing the door, he returned to his study, pulled out a long wool blanket from a trunk near the hearth and stretched out on the divan, plumping the pillow to support his head. Would sleep come tonight? His mind relished questioning and searching, even though his tired, bulky body, in particular his aching foot, finally forced him to give in, his dreams rushing toward him as his slow intake of breath began to rumble and fill the study with the steady blast of his snoring.

Chapter Three

SUNDAY, DECEMBER 20, 1840

We continue our story on this, the Lord's Day, a solemn time, the London air still cold and forever grey with chimney smoke. A figure stood gazing at a window into the morning light. A well-known London fixture, as the press called him, a noted swordsman and lead player at the great theatre of Old Drury, Mr. William Weston. His face was as pale as soured milk. He pushed open the window pane of his bedroom in his set of rooms on Cromer Street and, holding onto the sill of painted wood, stared at the frost on the trees which ran in a line along the pavement below him. The actor, known for his tenor voice, had taken his breakfast of cold ham and toast long before. His mood was as sanguine as it could be, considering he had spent the very earliest hours of the dark morning tending his sick sister, Sarah.

Mr. Weston breathed in the sharp air. He would not attend church services this morning. His cheerless, devout aunt was always ready to drive him out of the house into a church pew. He would have none of it. Was there not enough misery in his life? He did not need scolding Christians to tell him he was an evildoer. It was December, shortly before Christmas, and even though he felt troubled, fearful and restless, Mr. Weston wished for the season of cheer to suffuse him with joy and warmth. Beneath this icy sky, he imagined citizens of London at their breakfast tables, their newspapers in hand, their secrets on Yuletide presents to be revealed in a few days.

Mr. Weston did not indulge his imagination to picture the poor or the destitute. As an itinerant player, he had lived in poverty too long ever to consider its cruelties as one of his daily reflections. With this set of rooms in Cromer Street, and his string of fine performances in *Rachel; or, the Hebrew Maid,* one of his greatest ambitions had come about: he was a famous actor in the greatest city in the world.

Weston stepped back from the window and closed it. He sat down next to his cheery fire. He rubbed his eyes and breathed in slowly. He wanted to weep from fatigue and from worry, but he forced himself to turn his thoughts elsewhere. On the table beside his chair rested a small portrait of his mother. She had died giving birth to his sister, Sarah, when William was three. Their father had then abandoned them to the care of William's dour, mournful aunt. She had been kindly if cold towards him. She loved the girl, Sarah, more than him, as she could teach her sewing and reading. His aunt had been impatient, believing boys should be whipped to control their rambunctious urges. William Weston had been an active youth, playing hard at games, often losing his temper with his playmates, frequently finding himself being caned at school for disobedience and raucous behavior. His harried aunt had tried her best, as he grew older, to find him employment with the help of her brother, who had suggested, when William turned sixteen, that he should enter the army. The day Weston told his aunt he had joined a travelling theatre troupe, her shocked face had turned ashen before she had fainted. Yet, William Weston soon realized he loved his profession, and that an artistic life could offer him many rewards.

Life also punishes with many cares, he thought. He looked again at his mother's portrait. Sister Sarah had inherited the same delicate features. William sat up. Was that Sarah calling now? The poor sickly angel had wept most of the night. Her restraints had cut into her arms, and the bed she lay in had been soiled. But thus was the way of her terrible illness. Over the past year, ever since Sarah and Samuel Cake had broken off their relationship as friends—

the aunt had never dared mention the word sweethearts—
Sarah had been suffering from strange mental lapses. For a
month or two she'd be happy, busy at her sewing, running out
to the theatre to see her brother perform. Then, abruptly, her
entire character would change. Overnight she would refuse to
bathe, to take food. With the loss of appetite came fits,
tantrums, followed by long days of staying in her bed curled
up into a ball under the covers, her face wan and thinning.

Weston believed it had been love between Sarah and Cake.
Love built on false promises and Sarah's hopeless dreaming.

"William?"

Weston leapt up, startled. His aunt stood in the doorway
behind him. A female caricature of her nephew, she had a
mannish figure, erect and tall as his, her bearing supported
by her corsets and stays; her long chin and broad forehead
were as pale as his, made all the more ghostly in contrast to
her black floor-length dress. A Bible sat smugly in her right
hand. William apologized for scaring her. She took a
moment, then asked him if he would accompany her to
church. He did not hesitate. He said no and sat down
again. Before she could open her mouth to say another
word, he fell into a sudden crying aloud: "Oh, Lord Jesus,
horror upon horrors!"

The dour aunt froze in the doorway, her eyes full of fear
at nephew's outburst.

When he stood up again, anger reddened Weston's face.
"I cannot abide this any longer," he shouted. The room
seemed shattered by the power of his full, sonorous voice, as
though a bolt of lightning had struck and run through the
house. Weston rubbed his face, pulled at his hair. "I am sorry,
Auntie," he said.

His dour, sallow aunt moved toward the fire, her dress
whisping and hissing as it dragged over the Turkish carpet.
She gazed into the flames, prompting Weston to ponder the
notion of Hell.

Then, in a suppressed tone, she addressed him. Her voice
sounded low at first before it took on strength and steel. "I
know you are tired, William. We both are. Sarah is more tired

than either of us. I know that you have worked hard this week, playing and sword fighting. There is one thing, however, I must express to you which I feel is very hard to say."

William Weston came over to his aunt. He did not touch her. He faced her as he had so many times in his life, waiting for her to berate or beat him. He placed his hands on his hips and bent his head toward her to show he was paying her absolute attention.

His aunt was about to speak. She reached down and lifted up his hand. "What have you done?"

"It is nothing, Auntie. A wound from a sword-play last Friday evening. Common enough."

"Shall I bathe it for you?"

"What did you want to say, Auntie?" William asked, pulling his hand away.

"Only this, nephew. You are working *too* hard. I can see it in your tired eyes. Leave the tending of Sarah to me. This is what we agreed to do, is it not?"

"Yes, Auntie," William said. His voice had a tinge of shame in it.

"Yes, indeed, Nephew. You have taken me in, you have provided for me in my old age. You know very well I am grateful for this kindness."

"It is only right to do so, Auntie."

"You are a man of too much passion, William. I know Sarah and I are burdens on you. Such is your life, however. You must let me play my part, too. I must be her nurse, for I am a woman and can better understand her turmoil. You cannot let your sadness—your passion to help her—cut away at your life. Save your emotions for the theatre where they belong. You give in to them too much at home. Yes, I see it in you. Angry like Macbeth, doubtful and fearful like Prince Hamlet. You are the man in this household. Sarah and I must depend on you to be strong and stalwart."

William's aunt put out her arms to embrace her nephew. He took them and let her hold him for a brief moment, then he broke free. "If you wish," he said, "I will relent and accompany you to morning service."

His aunt left the fire and walked to the door. She held up her Bible. "Come if you wish, Nephew. Come for your heart's sake. I will await you in the front hall."

After she left the room, William stood still, gazing blankly around. He had given in. He had placated her. After he dressed, he went from his bedroom down the hall to Sarah's room. Through the half-opened door he saw her, quietly asleep. In his pocket he had the necklace he knew he could sell to the broker to get money for medicine.

He found his aunt waiting in the hall. Taking her arm, he led her down two flights of stairs to Cromer Street. In the fresh air, he felt revived. He admitted to himself that it was his aunt who had given him his chances in life. It was she who had taught him to fight against despair, for the two of them together had learned to face the terrors of the world. And with what he had to face now in his life, he was thankful she remained with him.

*   *   *

Young Reggie Crabb dumped the ashes from his bucket into the bin at the rear of Old Drury and ran back into the long, darkened corridors of the great theatre. Early afternoon light did not pursue him beyond the slammed door. Reggie liked sun, but he had chores to do before his tea. He and Mrs. B., the costume mistress, would take theirs by the hearth in the costume room, as would the cutters and the hearth sweeper who worked, ate and slept within the grand building. Old Drury surrounded young Reggie Crabb like a city. Tall stairwells like towers, avenues of hallways, the open space of the stage as great to him as the park leading to the palace of the Queen.

Reggie Crabb was fourteen, sinewy and obedient. Mrs. B. called him her "lamb". The gruff stage manager addressed him as Master Crabb or just Crabb. He ran for his living, and he liked his title of call-boy. At fourteen, he was proud to be a part of Old Drury. He was happy to be working for his shilling a week rather than being down in a coal mine. Reggie raced along the corridor to Miss Root's dressing room. Sundays bored him with the quiet, the eerie emptiness. No actors backstage, no scene shifters upstairs, downstairs, only Reggie and Mrs. B. He tapped and waited, though he knew Miss Priscilla Root would not be in her dressing rooms at this hour. Or at least he guessed she was not in, as Sundays were Miss Root's time to ride in the park and take luncheons with her actor friends. He tapped again. To his surprise, the door knob turned. Crabb stood frozen with his hands at his sides. Then a sudden glow of light fell upon him.

"Enter, and make smart."

A mannish woman stood before him, her haughty nose held up. Reggie recognized her as one of Miss Root's constant companions. The woman held the door ajar and gestured to Crabb to step in. He bowed to her and to another woman dressed in similar clothes standing across the room by a tall dressing cabinet. Both of the women reminded him of ravens; they always wore men's black breeches, frock coats and top hats. The raven by the cabinet crossed the room and came up to Crabb. The cigar in her right hand left behind a thin trail of smoke. She peered at him, cocked her head as if her eye was like a bird's, paused then spoke in a snide voice: "Little Peter still in need of a fitting?"

Both the ravens laughed.

"What peephole could we find for him, dear one?"

The ravens bussed each other mockingly on the lips. The one with the cigar spat into the brass spittoon by the door. Like a police sergeant, she made a hasty inspection of Crabb's trousers and waistcoat, then jerked her head toward the inner room. "Go on, look lively."

A tan and white spaniel opened its eyes and blinked. Beside it on the sofa lay a pair of silk slippers with torn ribbons. Crabb's eyes took in the sweep of tasselled velvet that led into the inner room, its walls lined with playbills and portraits in faux metal frames. On one side of the room rested a bed. Across from it, a long narrow table stretched. Upon it leaned a mirror framed by rows of oil floats. With no order to them and with some spilling over, pots of colour, puffs, brushes, powder satchels, pins, rouge sticks, quills and boxes of lozenges crowded the table top beside stained wine glasses .

Miss Priscilla Root sat on a stool before the mirror. *Here she is*, thought Reggie, staring, finding Miss Root still dressed in her riding clothes, a rich top hat with a trailing veil, grey gloves, a long full dress with velvet buttons. Her high forehead was smooth with pearl powder. She was a statue to Crabb, a fairy from a tale. And she was gentle with him, even when she spoke to him with rum on her breath. "Come and sit by me."

Crabb obeyed. Miss Root lifted a glass of liquor to her lips and drank. Putting down the glass, she patted her mouth with a silk handkerchief.

"Were you surprised to see me today, dear little Crabb?"

"Yes, Miss Root. Mighty surprised I was."

Priscilla Root laughed. She was famous for her fluttering hands and her poignant playing of sad heroines in the melodrama. If any of the gossips were to be believed, she was as famous for her rich clothes as she was for her jealous rages.

"Can you keep a secret, my little Crabb?"

"You know I can, Miss Root. Surely I can."

"Yes, I believe you can, my lad. Now will you help me?"

"Yes, Miss Root."

"Sit as quiet as a mouse beside me. Can you do that?'

"Oh, surely, Miss, I can."

One of the ravens stood in the doorway, suppressing a laugh. "What's this little Peter hanging about for? Let him get on with his cinder bucket."

"Hush now, dear one. Our little Crabb is only a mouse. He will not understand, nor will he tell a soul of our visit here today."

Miss Priscilla Root leaned toward her reflection in the glass. "*He* has put me in my coffin," she said, her voice raised to the raven in the doorway.

"Stuff and nonsense," replied the raven. "He was a bluffing prick is all."

Miss Root lit a cheroot and drew in deeply. "Go on, Kean, go on," she said, shooing away the spaniel. "Oh, dear Crabb, what can I do?"

Miss Root spoke to her own image, but Crabb could hear tears in her voice. He watched the statue breathe in.

The raven spat into a handkerchief. "Priscilla, buck up, sister."

Miss Priscilla Root rose from her dressing table. Her voice shrill with impetuous command, she instructed Crabb. "Take," she said, handing him an envelope of brown paper. Crabb felt the hard shape of a sovereign inside. He tucked the envelope into his waistcoat pocket. "Deliver this to the gentleman outside the stage door," she said. "He is waiting in Vinegar Yard. You can tell him by his yellow cravat. Hurry on. But remember to tell no one. I shall give you a sixpence if you do my bidding."

Crabb nodded and ran with the envelope. He slammed the door behind him, descended two steps and turned past the scene docks into the shadowy world of the backstage. Then, with his stomach wrenched into a knot, he headed for the stage door. He unlatched its large handle, pulled the door open and gazed furtively around Vinegar Yard. By its arched entrance, a man stood; he was exactly as described: oiled hair, a yellow cravat at his neck. Crabb dashed up to him. He dared not look into the man's eyes; he handed the man the brown envelope. "Lad," the man said, his hand up to give a penny. Crabb refused, grabbing a breath, his feet pulling him back towards the theatre.

When he reached Miss Root's dressing rooms, the light was out and the place empty and still smelling faintly of Miss Root's cheroot. "Miss Root?" He waited then sighed.

Lighting a taper, Crabb began to sweep the hearth, his brush fast like a wind whipping a tree branch. He laid fresh coal in the grate for early evening, stacking the pieces neatly so Miss Root would be pleased. With his blackened hands held behind his back, with his breath held, he moved, finally, on tiptoe to peek one more time into Miss Root's dressing chamber. What a magical Temple! Crabb then left the dressing room and wandered back down the myriad halls to the rear door. At the outside bin, his stomach rumbled for his tea. He dumped the ashes, the dust forcing him to squint and look up at a chimney across the courtyard. A little sparrow had flitted onto its ledge, ruffling its sooty feathers.

Crabb thought suddenly of Mr. William Weston's lonely life. His old aunt, his sparrow of a sister, sick and lost, not at all free like that bird on the upper ledge. And what about Mr. Weston's strange behaviour on Friday night? London's finest actor had arrived late, his hat pulled on low. Mr. Weston had not been himself for some time. *Lor' bless him,* Reggie thought. He remembered how he'd tapped on Mr. Weston's door that Friday night to cue him for his stage entrance. Reggie heard noises, coarse mumbling. Was Mr. Weston fighting with someone? Reggie called out to him. "Enter," the actor cried. What a shock to see Mr. Weston all alone, his face made up, with but a broken goblet on the floor.

Perhaps the great actor was rehearsing lines for a new play, Reggie pondered. Perhaps that was it.

Young Reggie shivered as he scampered back inside the cavern of Old Drury, its echoes suddenly raising up another story, this one about Mr. Samuel Cake. Reggie stopped to recall: he was out of the theatre, on the streets, running an errand. There, before him, crossing Waterloo Bridge, walked Mr. Cake. Tapping his walking stick, Cake wore a red sash; he was whistling a tuneless ditty, a here-and-there jumble of notes. So confident, so sure of his dress—his cloak, his high beaver hat, his brass-tipped walking stick with a handle the shape of a dog's head. Reggie was proud to be near him. Mrs. B. once said he was a gentleman. "I hears," she said, "he made his money from American cotton, from ownin' half the warehouses on Surrey side." Reggie followed Cake a few blocks into the Strand, onto Catherine Street, where he saw the man stop abruptly by a clockmaker's shop. Reggie held back, but could see Cake's reflected face in the glass. A sudden melancholy, the great man's eyes showing a sadness that made Reggie's own heart start to beat. *Poor man,* Reggie thought. *What's he got to be sad about?*

Reggie now brushed away his thoughts—*move on,* he said to himself–whereupon he ventured across the empty stage, keeping his eyes down to make sure the trap doors were closed. Imagine falling through this floor down to the mezzanine, cracking apart on the stage boards below. A few minutes later, Reggie had clambered down the stairs to the basement costume room. There Mrs. B., the costume mistress, was pouring water from the kettle. He told her about the sparrow.

"Yes, boy," Mrs. B. said. "Old Drury has many birds—in her chimneys, inside her courtyard and the auditorium."

"Do they live here like we do, Mrs. B.?"

"Some do, boy. Some live and die here. I'm always finding little dead ones even down here, by the hearth."

"Do they fly down the chimney?"

"I suppose," Mrs. B. said. "They live and they die, just like we do, my lad. And there is not much you nor I can do about such things."

Reggie thought about her words. He wondered about birds—were they so free? as he blew the steam from his hot tea.

· *   *   *

Inspector Endersby returned from taking the evening air, pondering the case of Samuel Cake. He felt refreshed by his exercise—gentle though it had been—and fatigued at the same time. He made his way to his copper tub to bathe. Afterwards, in his small study near the kitchen, he searched in his bureau drawers for a cravat, the penultimate item of his dress needed for this Sunday evening's dinner with Harriet. Owen Endersby did not think of himself as a fashionable man: he liked colour, he demanded a good fit in both trouser and frock coat, but he was not what the London intelligence might call a "smart" dresser. Simple comfort for him, and care. After all, he was noted for being pointed in judgment, especially in matters pertaining to the "Criminal Mentality." This last observation was made by his wife, Harriet, a fair woman in all things. Whenever he thought of her, he thanked Fate. Life before Harriet had resembled a ramshackle building, crazy lumber all about, angles out of plumb. But Harriet had brought domestic order, encouraged him to find a respectable roof over their heads. And it was she who had given introduction to the man who provided Endersby the opportunity to become a London detective policeman.

"Come along, old gander." He stood before his bureau, reprimanding himself for dawdling. He lifted up several cravats, inspected them for grease spots, and decided on the violet with stripes. For an instant, the stripes reminded him of the cloak of the dead Mr. Cake. He paused to remember: *such a loss*. Searching for a cravat pin, he recalled putting it in a drawer of his writing desk. The drawer squeaked as he pulled it open. Beneath the pin box lay the citations from the Police Division, their words deeming him a highly respected working member of London's law and order establishment. These paper accolades, however, raised in him a cold reminder of the bloodied skull of Mr. Samuel Cake. *What a cruelty*, Endersby thought. *A forlorn house, a gentleman's body mangled in anger by whom? A mere intruder?* Endersby raised his head, whisking away his present thoughts. "Now hurry up," he mumbled.

The last maid had broken his looking glass, so he had to guess the effect of his dressing. He looked down. "Belly needs attention." To his wardrobe in haste, since time was pressing. Here before him was the collection of wear he favored most—the treats of his private closet. Owen Endersby's waistcoats complemented his ample stomach with pomp and sartorial authority. He chose green for the evening and placed his arms slowly into the waistcoat's form before brushing its front to smooth the wrinkles. "There, you are set," he mumbled.

"Mr. Endersby?" called his wife.

"I come within the second."

Passing by the parlour into the kitchen, Owen realized that despite the evening's promised merriment, he had not been able to hold back a vexing confusion of feelings. Not only pity for Mr. Cake but others. Guilt, regret, remorse— all were lurking like a gang of vicious street boys ready to attack his peace of mind. All were brought about by the cruel shade of memory, which this winter's day—December 20—cast upon the contented light of his marriage.

"Good evening, sir."

Owen Endersby's maid had a Scottish accent and a face round as a pot lid.

"It is the twentieth once again, I fear," Owen said, facing the maid and the cooking hearth.

"Yes, sir, it is." The maid lifted up a small parcel wrapped with fancy white paper. "I shall place it on her pillow, as usual, sir," she said in a soft voice, "once you have begun your soup."

"Thank you. And the ribbon, of course."

"Certainly, sir," From another small packet, the maid pulled out a blue silk ribbon. Owen touched it briefly as if to bless it then watched as his capable maid folded and tied it into a bow. "There, sir. Like always. His little cravat."

"Yes, indeed." Owen stared for a moment more at the ribbon.

"Come, sir, let me arrange this for you, since Mrs. Endersby is waiting." The maid's words stirred Endersby from his sudden melancholy. *Do not let this bully you,* he thought. Owen had trained his heart to counter this harsh souvenir of loss, realizing that later this evening he would have to gird himself and hold back his tears when the hour of reckoning came.

"You visited him not four days ago, sir, on your own?" asked the maid.

"Still as tiny as ever. But the whole place is in shambles. Stones tipping over, many graves heaved up. It is worse than last year, as it seems the city keeps burying one on top of another. The green of eleven years ago is hardly in sight."

"Terrible, sir. But your wee Robert lies at peace, safe and sound."

"I believe so. I thank you for your kind words." Owen left the kitchen and decided to clear his mind of this sorrow.

*   *   *

After dinner, Owen Endersby studied his wife's face. It held a smile; it presented a brave gaze to the warm room around them. "Never an easy day," he mumbled.

"What, dear?" asked Harriet.

He reached out and patted her arm. "Haddock superb," he complimented. "As was the tart."

Harriet blinked and let out a quick breath. "It is time," she said in a low voice.

Darkness greeted them on entry to the hallway. Harriet lit a candle and walked alone to the bedroom while Endersby retired to his study to get the blue ribbon. Afterwards, with his shoes safely off and his night dress and cap on, he strolled back to the bedroom door. The blue ribbon bow lay clasped in his left hand. "Mrs. Endersby?"

"Yes, my dear."

Owen heard the coverlet of the bed being pulled away. "May I come in?"

He entered the room without waiting for her reply. Banked coal twinkled in the hearth. Shadows danced on the walls from the light of six candles. Harriet was in bed, the canopy curtains drawn back to admit more candlelight. She sat with her hands folded, her nightcap placed high on her curls, her face cleaned of tint. She looked at him with that same look she had given him for eleven years. Could the little creature who was once their son feel the sorrow in this room? Would God himself listen to their tears and one day grant them peace?

"I thank you for the brooch, Owen, dear."

Harriet held up the small cameo she had unwrapped. The fancy white paper still lay on the pillow beside hers. It was close in the room, and Owen wished time could somehow speed up. He handed Harriet the blue ribbon bow. She placed it with eleven others in a small book kept in her side table.

"Please, Owen, sit here, on the edge."

Owen moved to the bed and sat facing the street window. Harriet leaned toward him. "Our Robert is fifteen as of this day. Fifteen and among the angels."

"He is indeed, Harriet."

Both had said it now. Both welcomed the silence, each of them staring into the space of the room.

"Are you comfortable, Owen?"

"Yes, thank you. My toe has ceased biting me."

"I feel most elated tonight," Harriet said.

Owen bent forward. Tears fell from his eyes. He sat back, and Harriet passed a handkerchief to him. He blew his nose. "I beg your pardon."

"More comfortable, now, Owen?"

"Thank you, yes."

"Do you wish something to eat? I can warm you some soup."

"What I need is sleep, most of all."

Harriet smoothed out the counterpane. "Come then, stay with me tonight. Come along."

"I am so sorry, I..."

"I have been stalwart this evening, Owen. I don't know why. Perhaps time is healing me, as the sage says."

"Sometimes, Harriet, I think it is all in vain."

"Come, Owen. You are tired. You are a strong, good man. Come and be beside me."

Owen moved himself farther onto the bed and carefully crawled under the covers. He lay close to his wife for a few moments. Harriet smiled at him, reached to her side table for the book and showed him the array of blue ribbons. "Cheers me up," she said softly. "I shall wear my new brooch the next time we go to Old Drury. Would you like that?"

"I would."

"I shall say good night then, Owen."

"Shall I put my arm around you?"

"With pleasure, Mr. Endersby."

Chapter Four

MONDAY, DECEMBER 21, 1840

Bludgeoned?" Superintendent Borne had a pinched face and a long neck. The early morning meeting in his Scotland Yard office found him standing before his inspector and sergeant. It appeared to Inspector Owen Endersby that his superintendent had been in a rush before the meeting: Borne had mussed hair, and a button was missing from his frock coat. Frost speckled the windows behind the superintendent's broad desk. Endersby knew Borne could be an impatient man who liked to find cause for conflict.

"Beaten with his own walking stick," explained Endersby. "A most savage scene."

"What the devil," complained Borne. He shot a cranky glance at Sergeant Caldwell. The sergeant held his head up, his back as stiff as the gallows post in Fleet Prison.

"Well, I don't like this at all," Borne went on. He sat down at his desk. He folded and unfolded his hands.

Endersby sensed the man's weariness and bewilderment. He, too, had awakened early, his entire body aching from tossing and turning. His brown waistcoat suited his sombre mood this morning. He regretted having refused a tin of candied orange from Harriet, recalling his shameful and thoughtless eating of chestnuts over the body of Samuel Cake. But now he was hungry. This nudge of appetite would grow insistent through the day. *Pity,* he thought, snapping to attention and speaking. "It is most urgent, sir, that we move on this case," Endersby said, looking directly at his superintendent's tense mouth.

"Move, sir? What a vulgar expression. Most certainly we must proceed in our investigation, as the coroner has pronounced."

"Indeed," said Endersby, sweetening his tone.

Borne sat restless in his chair, his hands now picking up papers and putting them down. He then jumped up. "We have little choice, Inspector Endersby. You, in fact, have no choice at this point. I am already vexed enough with the St. Giles fire. I still need from you a report due today, I believe."

"Yes, sir. We have but little to go on as yet."

"And now a prominent—or at least a notorious figure in the capital—ends up in a bloodied state. What with Christmas at hand—this bodes poorly, Inspector."

"What would you have me do, sir?"

"Do? Find a culprit, sir. Surely that is obvious."

"Certainly, Superintendent. And shall I then begin my search, as the magistrate…"

"Yes, yes. By all means. Hardly the best time, with the holiday season. Surely this Cake murder can be looked into within the next forty-eight hours. Surely you can find some angry, jealous fool who was drunk enough to beat the man to death?"

"That supposition, sir, had entered my own mind for consideration."

"Most happy to hear of it, sir," snapped Superintendent Borne. "But we have no time to *suppose*. We must search and capture."

"You give me permission to proceed?"

"I want an arrest, Inspector. This kind of violent display will rile the general public. Make them think we are not doing our duty to keep the capital safe from random acts of murder and mayhem. I cannot afford—nay, I will not abide—bad business such as this to harm the reputation of the Metropolitan Detective Police."

Borne paused for a second. He clasped his hands behind his back. He stood in a regal-like stance, then with a glow to his face, walked around his desk and stood in front of Endersby and Caldwell as if he were a general about to pin on a medal.

"You have my firm wish, Inspector, that this case be resolved by this Friday. I want evidence, I want arrests. I want to report to the press that such an act cannot go unpunished for long. And I want above all to show that my detective force can work diligently and quickly."

"Certainly, sir."

"No hesitations, Endersby. I want you to proceed immediately. Keep this Caldwell on his toes and running, and by Friday, I want Mr. Cake's villain presented to the courts. You will also continue to investigate the St. Giles fire, although it may turn out to be a more complicated affair."

Borne almost saluted his two colleagues. "Until Friday, with warrants in hand."

*   *   *

Having sent Caldwell to investigate the matters of the found glove and the plug of tobacco, Inspector Endersby found himself in a calmer state of mind by the time he walked through the stage door of the Coburg Theatre. A squat narrow building on Waterloo Road, in a neighbourhood of wharfs and warehouses, its front was decorated with large showy playbills announcing the "blood tub" melodramas for which it was renowned. Tonight the fare was *Jack Wilson, The Tar of the Mary Dee; or, Revenge for the Red Fox*. A fetching title at least, thought Endersby, as his nose took in the heady smell of oil and sawdust of the backstage wings.

Endersby had slept for only a few hours the night before. As the stage manager led him down a corridor into a dusty room, the intensity of his fatigue doubled. His gouty toe began to bite into his concentration, even as his natural inclination to be blunt took hold. Endersby pulled off his suede gloves, shook the stage manager's hand, eased his way into a chair and arranged his questions. The stage manager lit a pipe on sitting down.

"A most unfortunate death," Endersby began.

"Most brutal, Inspector. I am grieved and shocked, as are all of Mr. Cake's colleagues."

Endersby was impressed by the man's expression of sentiment.

"How long had you been acquainted with Mr. Cake, sir?"

"Two years, or just under, Inspector. He took on the lease-hold of the Coburg in January of '39."

"He was a successful manager?"

"Most astute, sir. Good with his staff. Clever with his purse. A fair man, too, when he needed to be."

"I understand he owned warehouses?"

"Your sergeant came by the other morning. I told him such. Mr. Cake rented them out to dry goods companies. Made a profit from them, which feeds us here and pays us all good wages."

"A man of means, then."

"A man of talent, sir."

"Where did he keep his money? I mean, did he bank it, invest it?"

"I only know he kept his accounts in his head. I do not know else. I figured that was Mr. Cake's business, sir."

"Did he have kin?"

"A half-brother. Mr. Barnwell. Gregorious Barnwell."

"Still living?"

"Most certainly, sir. He is our machinist, and a fine one at that. A genius, I would say, at levers and contraptions."

"May I have the chance to meet him this morning?"

"I have been sent word, sir, that he is off for the day to arrange matters with the gravedigger."

"Ah, certainly."

"But he will be in attendance this evening, for our *Jack Wilson*. Barnwell is always here to supervise his machines. Might you wish to meet him this evening, I can secure an order or two for you, but they would have to be in our gallery."

"I thank you. I would be delighted. On the night of Mr. Cake's demise, was his brother here in the theatre?"

"Yes, sir. He stays late as well, to re-set the machinery of the stage. Mr. Barnwell lives in a small room over his workshop."

"I am also curious about this particular item. And why it was found in Mr. Cake's house."

Inspector Endersby pulled from his satchel the contract from Lord Harwood. He handed it to the stage manager, who ran his eyes over the details.

"What a stroke," the stage manager exclaimed. "Mr. Cake gone across the river? A sea-change for the better. He was a clever man." These last words caught in the man's throat, and he paused for a moment before handing the document back to Endersby.

"You knew nothing of this then? That Cake was to manage the great house?"

"No, sir. Not a jot."

"And what of these? We found these on the floor of his house. It seems Cake lent money as well as made it. Are these names familiar to you, sir? I caution you that I require truthful answers, even at the expense of shaming someone's reputation. Mr. Cake's murder overrides any consideration of confidentiality. As I am sure you shall agree."

The stage manager sat forward and studied the promissory notes. He sniffed and wiped his mouth.

"Well, first, I do not know of a P. Summers. At least in our theatre circle. But I imagine these other three notes are all from one man, Mr. Percy Buckstone. He is one of our actors. I am surprised at his need for money, he being one of our better performers. But I reckon he likes his drink and his horses. Yes. No doubt it is he. Though I am surprised Mr. Cake would have been into usury."

"Mr. Buckstone may not want to speak to me about these matters. But I must insist."

"I shall have him fetched, sir. He comes to the theatre early, as there is rehearsal for the Christmas extravaganza. He is also our Jack Wilson and does a fine hornpipe."

The stage manager rose and left the room for a moment. His voice called out, and someone came running. There was subsequent murmuring by the doorway. Endersby went over the facts so far, repeating them twice to set them into his memory. He glanced at the pale morning light seeping in the high window. *Mr. Barnwell, Mr. Barnwell,* he repeated to himself. The stage manager returned followed by a young boy carrying two pints of porter.

"Will you join me, Inspector? Mr. Buckstone will be here presently."

Endersby took the pewter pint and raised it in a toast.

The stage manager's voice cracked again as he spoke. "To Mr. Cake."

"To Mr. Cake," Endersby said, wiping his lips.

*   *   *

Betty Loxton lay on the cold mattress, morning air brushing her tear-stained cheek. She wished she were a cloud like the ones high beyond the smudged sky light. Gone in an instant, gone he was, and sister Clare stirring the coffee only knew him as a name, a Mr. Cake, his murder an oft-told story in the market. A cousin of a friend had been in the public house with the other spectators and seen the bloodied walking stick and the old coroner with skin whiter than a turnip's. Smoke filled Betty's cramped room, curling blue over the hearth and the rickety shelves of white mugs and tin plates. She huddled under the thin quilt. *These walls are blacker than widow's crepe,* she thought.

"Get you up, sis, before mam finds you there. We are all so late this morning." Clare handed her a steaming cup and a slice of bread with drippings. Betty did not take even a sip of her coffee.

"I want to die, Clare. All I want is that."

"What are you up to?" crabbed Pineapple Pol, suddenly coming in from the other room. Her bonnet framed her scowling face as the doorway framed her threatening body, an arm held up like a club. Betty threw back the quilt. She struggled to the wash basin, pulled on her bonnet and skirt. "Hurry, lazybones," her mother's sharp voice shouted. Pineapple Pol left the doorway, her footsteps soon stamping down the stairs to the open street. Passing into the other room, with its table and other beds and its string across the far wall hung with dripping rags, Betty dared not look at the mound of covers where Uncle Thomas had spent the night. The shadow over his bed was like a shroud. Betty wiped her nose.

"Girl," her mother shouted up the stairwell.

"Coming," Betty hollered back.

"Slowpoke, you are," Pineapple Pol scolded when Betty came into the street. "It's Winter Reds again for you today, and I'll hawk bosky pears. Berries and mistletoe, too, if you want 'em, but they're dear. Keep up, girl, keep up. We are so late today. I don't want you lagging now, not never, you hear me?"

The cobbles wore a slick coating of mud. Frost and powdery snow whitened window sills. "Ice coming soon," Pineapple Pol announced. "Keep your feet dry. Get a bit of canvas to sit on, from your brother. Them lords and ladies at Old Drury like a clean-looking git, you mind. 'Tis Christmas, after all," she laughed. "Merry times for us all."

Betty halted. She dropped her basket. Her fists tightened into stones.

Pineapple Pol reddened and said, "Don't you gawk at me, you ingrate pox box. I got two of you useless daughters." She took hold of Betty and shook her.

Betty pulled away. She kicked her basket and sent it rolling. Pineapple Pol struck Betty hard on her right temple. She grabbed her neck and shoved her toward the basket. "Bend, you. Fetch it!" Betty reached out. Her hand clutched the handle as her temple throbbed and a hoarse whisper burnt her ear: "You'll starve if you don't strap, you hear?" said Pineapple Pol. "Scraggy fool, I won't have you on the scamp. Get along, get."

From Longacre they came, Betty holding her eyes down all the way. She refused to gaze at the vast square of the Covent Garden market. Under the archways, shop windows glittered with morning light. Lines of donkey carts reminded her of a funeral parade, and she told herself to "buck up" as she held back her tears. Paving stones slid with cabbage leaves; bags and sacks, like lumpy corpses, held leeks and potatoes and rhubarb. "Need a dozen, sweetie?" the apple-woman cried, her voice singing in an Irish lilt.

Pineapple Pol disappeared into the crowd past the hordes of greengrocers in their blue aprons, all of them like dogs of Hell, thought Betty.

She bought a basket of Winter Reds. She spat on them and rubbed them bright on her skirt. Between the pillars were the coffee-stalls where other coster girls sat talking, but Betty wanted none of that rattle today. A flower girl in bare feet dashed by carrying an armful of hardy violets, their trail of perfume streaking after her.

"How much a bunch?" asked Betty at the girl's stall.

"Ha'penny," was the sharp reply. Betty selected the plumpest violets and paid the girl. They curtsied to each other. Then Betty headed east toward her corner. Old Madge would already be on the opposite side of Russell, her brazier roaring with chestnuts on the grate. The murmur of the market faded as Betty walked under an arcade and hurried along a side alley, where she dodged barrows of piled vegetables. Eventually, she wound her way to the far corner of Brydges, to the very place where her sweetheart had first met her. He had come strolling along, his skin ruddy as a plum's, his coffee-coloured trousers so clean and pressed. He had tipped his hat and called her by her first name.

"It is Betty, is it?"

Betty stopped at the place where his words had been uttered. The gentle hand of memory touched her cheek. "Samuel," she said under her breath, "take these." She laid the bunch of violets on the kerb, their weak, lonely petals soaking in the muck.

"No more tears. Keep them close," Betty whispered. "Think of what you must do. You've a load of apples that'll crick your neck hard enough, you silly lamb. Think of what you *want* instead." Betty crossed the street, her little frame shadowed by the bulk of Old Drury. She did not look over to Madge the chestnut seller. She was breathless by the time she found herself under the tall columns of a portico. Hurry on, she cried to herself. Around the corner, down the side lane, past the water pumps, through the open air

of Vinegar Yard toward an arched doorway, a red wooden
door at the side of the great theatre where a kindly, frizzy-
haired gentleman sat in a small booth. His green waistcoat
and yellow leather boots proclaimed to the world that he
guarded the entrance to a magical world. There Betty
Loxton took pause. She gathered her courage.

"Stand to one side there—what's your business?"

"I beg you, kind sir…"

"Stand aside, girl. Out of the way. And take that basket
out, too."

"I beg you, sir."

"Ah, good morning, Mr. Dupré. Good morning. There
are twelve letters for you, and I have sent up the coffee boy
to the stage manager's fire."

"Thank you, Hartley, and a fine morning it is. I shall be
taking interviews after midday, as we have arranged. Then
I shall need to see the list and the names of the tryouts. The
same procedure as last holiday time."

"Very good, Mr. Dupré. Good morning to you. Stand
aside, young one, stand off. What is your business?"

"I come, sir, to the call, sir. I heard it told in the market."

"For the panto, you mean? We want dancers and singers,
youngster, not coster girls. Stand aside. Mr. Dupré shall be
receiving very soon."

"Sir?"

"What again, foolish child? Can you not see I am a busy
man? This stage door is not for sellers and hawkers."

"But sir, the call. Can I have my name put on? I beg you,
sir. I sing, I dance a hornpipe as well as any."

"Why really, you have come too early, and I have so
many this morning to oblige."

"But, kind sir, I can wait. I can see the manager when he
is free. And the dancing master."

"You are a saucy girl. You must not stop here, crowding
the foyer. Can you write your name?"

"I can initial, sir. Right quick."

"Then take this….ah, Miss Root, a good morning to you."

"Dear Hartley, what a chilly day it is. Any letters?"

"I have sent Crabb with them already, to your parlour."

"I thank you, dear Hartley. How is your leg?"

"Rheumatism is a burden, Miss Root. But I manage. I can sit most times here, by the door. Mr. Dupré has allowed it."

"You dear man. And what of my interview?"

"This afternoon, Miss Root. In the stage manager's chamber."

"And who are you, young miss, may I enquire?"

"Miss Betty Loxton, mum."

"What a sweet face. How much for the Winter Red?"

"Penny, mum. But I come not to sell. I want to sign for the call. For the panto."

"Can you sing and dance? Mr. Dupré will like your pretty face. But we shall need quick bodies for the fairy chorus."

"I can sing, mum. I dance at the Gaff near St. Paul's, Wednesday nights and Sunday afternoons."

"Hartley, take this sweet girl. Here, take Hartley's quill and sign. There. There you are. What time does Dupré see the supernumeraries, Mr. Hartley?"

"I believe at six this afternoon, Miss Root. Yes, at six on the dot."

"Good morning to you."

"Good morning. As for you, get along now, saucy girl. That'll do, you've got what you want. Come sharp at six. Be on the spot, you hear, with the others. Wash your face and hands before you come. Mr. Dupré is not in the habit of hiring mud hens for his stage chorus."

*   *   *

A tall man with red hair and a large red beard appeared in the doorway. "Sir, you have a request?" The man sounded winded. His face was sweaty, his freckles so thick he seemed like a countryman with a field tan.

Endersby stood and introduced himself, and the man's eyes looked down to the floor then toward the hearth, as if the simple invitation to meet a policeman had caused some pinprick of guilt to surface.

Percy Buckstone was thirty years old, tall and muscular. His orange hair and beard formed a striking frame to his high cheekbones. He had the face of an actor, thought Endersby. The lips a little too large for real life, but ample to show in the wavering of footlights—a telling face, as his Harriet would have said.

"Please be seated, Mr. Buckstone."

"I prefer to stand if I might." The voice was cooler now, resistant. Mr. Buckstone's right hand was sheathed in a thick rawhide glove, yellow in colour.

"May I see your glove, sir?" Endersby replied. The actor pulled off the glove. It was leather through and through. The found glove had been smaller, yet as flamboyant in design. "What do you use this for, sir?" the inspector continued, his pitch and tone full of genuine curiosity.

"Fencing. In rehearsal only. I fight off villains, sir, every night of the week but Sunday."

Inspector Endersby smiled. "Do you, Mr. Buckstone? Admirable." The actor pulled on the glove. "Does this glove have a mate, Mr. Buckstone?"

The actor looked bewildered, then answered: "I never use it, sir." Percy Buckstone pulled the mate from under his shirt, clean and new-looking.

Endersby examined it and handed it back to the actor.

"Will there be much else, sir?" Buckstone asked, relieved. "I am rehearsing the middle of a scene."

"Tell me about these, please."

Buckstone looked at the three promissory notes containing his signature. He fidgeted. "I am sorry to hear of Mr. Cake, sir," he stuttered.

"Are you indeed, Mr. Buckstone? What luck for you. I perceive a large debt of eighty-six pounds from these notes. Why was it necessary to visit Mr. Cake's house in Doughty Street to secure these funds, when you could have easily arranged such gentlemanly matters here in the theatre?"

Percy Buckstone drew back. His face paled noticeably. "I resent this intrusion, sir. And your insinuations."

"What insinuations, Mr. Buckstone? A man has been

bludgeoned to death. His skull cracked open. Surely such matters override a mere inquiry into your financial dealings with the deceased." Endersby's voice had taken on an insistent quality, his final words punched out like shots from a pistol.

"I shall not be bullied, Inspector. Not at all. I beg your leave."

The stage manager shuffled forward. He glanced at Endersby, then he replied. "I am afraid, Buckstone, our guest has a few more questions to ask."

"Were you a friend of Mr. Cake's?" Endersby put out his hand to induce Buckstone to sit down. The actor lowered himself into the chair across from the inspector.

"Friends? No. I knew him as an honest man. I knew he lent money. Actors like to spend, Inspector. We like our pleasures." Buckstone's confident air had returned.

"And so you took advantage of Mr. Cake's generosity?"

"I would hardly call it that. Not generous, sir. He was practical is all."

"How so?"

"He knew my kind. My love of the horses. The gaming table. He lent out at a fair price, better than old Eleazar across in Fleet Street."

"A Jew lender?"

"Popular amongst we actors and stagers, sir."

"And did you find Doughty Street a fine abode?"

"I did, sir. But I saw none of it. I was let into the kitchen only. Mr. Cake was always obliging. He had his cash ready and his quill to sign, and that was the end of it. 'Short and done with', as he liked to say."

"Your beard is a fine one, if I may compliment you, Mr. Buckstone."

The actor was taken aback at the sudden shift in Inspector Endersby's line of investigation. He smiled immediately, his actor's vanity bringing a sudden blush to his cheeks.

"Is it a kind of specialty of yours, sir?" the inspector went on.

"How do you mean?" the actor puzzled.

"Not unlike Mr. Young's famous moustache? Or, indeed,

the venerable Kean's eyebrows. Which I understand were combed each night with wax so that they would shine in the stage light."

"I never thought of my beard in that way," the actor mused, clearly delighted at Endersby's knowledge of players. "But it is something I have worn for many a year. Since, at least, I came to London from Birmingham."

"And when was that, sir?"

"Three years ago, Inspector."

Endersby paused to recall the woman in the blue dress who had given testimony at the coroner's inquest. She had witnessed a man with a red beard. Then she claimed she had seen him again with the beard cut off. Surely, thought Endersby, this beard has raised some questions. Perhaps the woman saw two separate men if what Mr. Buckstone swore was true. Endersby resumed his questioning.

"Did Mr. Cake ever threaten you, Mr. Buckstone?"

"How do you mean?"

"Money is the root of much turmoil, as many of your roles in this theatre no doubt have shown. Did he ever press you for his return on his loans?"

The actor shifted. He fiddled with his fencing glove. "Not in so many words, sir. But he did insist. He did like to keep track of his returns."

"Did he lend to others?"

"Perhaps, though I never knew of any. He had me swear to secrecy. He said it was a benefit to us both. He made his interest, and I had my freedom to indulge, if you wish. Why let the world know, he argued."

"Which is why you went to Doughty Street. To keep things discreet."

"I suppose so."

"Do you recognize this signature?" Endersby handed the two other promissory notes of a P. Summers into Mr. Buckstone's hands.

"Not familiar, sir. As I said, Mr. Cake was considerate. I have no idea of the others to whom he lent money."

"What did you have for your supper last evening?"

The actor looked up abruptly. "Ah, beef, I believe."

"Here, in the theatre?"

"At a house down the way."

"An eating house? Where they know you?"

"They should, given what I pay them for their fare."

"And Friday last. What was supper on Friday?"

"I cannot remember. I believe it..."

"And where did you go on Friday, late, after the theatre?"

"I acted until ten, then I went to supper. Yes, and I had prawns. Prawns it was." Buckstone beamed.

"You have rich tastes, sir. On seven pounds a week, you eat like a prince."

Percy Buckstone looked away. "My wife has some means, Inspector."

"Does she, indeed."

The actor now reddened to a degree which shocked Endersby. What was it about the wife? He decided to slow down, let things rest for the moment.

"And then home to bed?" Endersby concluded.

"I beg your pardon?" Buckstone focused his eyes again on the inspector.

"On Friday, Mr. Buckstone. After your late supper, you went to bed?"

Buckstone took a moment to recall. His eyes gazed briefly at the ceiling. "Yes, I believe so, sir. In fact, I dined at home, sir."

"I thank you for your patience and your honesty this morning, Mr. Buckstone."

The actor stood up and shook Endersby's hand. "Good morning, sir," he said politely and left the room.

"Can you speak to his character?" Endersby then asked, addressing the stage manager, who was leaning his elbow against the hearth.

"Even-tempered, sir. Polite to all. Mr. Buckstone loves to gamble, and yet he is prompt in his work here, never coming in drunk, never late. He's a pampered gentleman, sir. Admired by his fellow actors as reliable."

Endersby stared into the meagre hearth and rubbed his

hands, his reason tacking into the waves of facts which swelled his thoughts. It was his method to talk to potential suspects with as much politeness as he could muster. He would proceed gently before launching an attack—if one were called for. He particularly liked to test the memory of those he interviewed; he would ask them about trivial matters, such as their dinner menus, for in them often lay revelations. He refused to indulge in the practice invented by the famed Mr. Mesmer, for Endersby thought it was ineffective. Some fellow members of the London force were now using this method of mind-control by guiding suspects into confession through hypnosis, attempting to capture then tame the wild animal which many in the Detective Police believed inhabited the "Criminal Mentality."

"With your permission, I would like to see Mr. Cake's office," Endersby said, moving away from the fire. "I may need to have keys, if there are any. I may also need to poke into papers."

"You have my permission, sir," said the stage manager. "Anything else?"

After Cake's office had been unlocked and Endersby had entered, the cool damp air of the space reminded him of the cold darkness of the parlour in Doughty Street. The stage manager lit a candle first before lighting a hanging lamp over the room's large table.

"Before you leave, sir, I have one other delicate question for you," said Endersby.

The stage manager braced himself, holding up his chin.

"Did Mr. Cake ever, in front of you, offend any one? Insult, or berate an unfortunate?"

"He never lost his temper, if that's what you mean, sir. He was mostly a quiet-speaking man. He had his ways of persuasion. His ways to make you do things, but mainly he did so by asking you firmly, sometimes demanding. But he was never a shouter, sir. He often took his meals with us all. Like he was one of us...a brother, almost."

"He liked women?"

"Oh, yes, sir. But he never took advantage. Always a gentleman. As far I saw him, sir." The stage manager made a polite smile and left Endersby alone in the room.

Endersby's eyes found an exclusive space—a high ceiling, walls with green paper and cabinets of varnished wood. His gaze wandered from the walls to a long table at its centre, up to a milky-glass lamp, down to a Turkish carpet, along the paintings—portraits of horses, landscapes —round to a desk beside a wide bed with a canopy and finally over to a wardrobe with a patterned curtain as a covering, which his right hand pulled aside to reveal rows of silk shirts and frock coats in black and green.

A pleasing array, Endersby thought, the drawers of the wardrobe subsequently presenting cravats, old–fashioned button boxes and stocking slips. The interior cabinets bulged with rich linens, and below, in a deep single drawer, boots, pull-ons and polish. Endersby tapped at the sides of the wardrobe. He paced and measured its width and length. It seemed the construction guarded no secret *cache*, no place to hide a cash box or mounds of notes. "Just so," whispered Endersby.

He bounced the mattress hard with his right hand. He then lifted the counterpane and rolled up the mattress, to find only a set of bed slats and no other object.

"Cake kept accounts in his head," Endersby recalled out loud.

The table and the desk provided no clues at all to the whereabouts of Mr. Cake's cash ledgers or letters. "Perhaps the thief came here...but no, no." His eyes examined the bed one more time. He noticed the door across from it, the door he had come through, had a brass latch. "To keep out intruders, perhaps? Or to keep in visitors?"

Now the matter of P. Summers occupied his thoughts. Who was this man or this woman? And who would know her or him? It was necessary to question many, for Endersby always found one in a crowd who spoke up. One who inadvertently held onto a tidbit of information forgotten by others. This one would provide him with a new by-way toward the culprit.

Without spending any more time searching, and with

"P. Summers" now firmly in place in his mind, Endersby left and asked the stage manager to show him the way to the costume shop and storage, which was, he discovered, located below the stage itself on the theatre's mezzanine floor. Endersby navigated the narrow stairwell. He ducked his head, holding fast to the banister leading under the stage to a large low room, a sunless underworld full of women in rolled sleeves drawing needle and thread. He watched the heads bent over the cloth, the irons taken from the small hearth and passed across the bangled sleeves of mock velvet. He waited as the grey-faced matron came toward him, her head encased in a black bonnet. The other women raised their heads. For the first time, Endersby noted that each of them was wearing a thin black armband of crepe. This mourning gesture touched him. His memory flashed a picture of the dog-headed walking stick smeared with Samuel Cake's blood.

"Inspector," the matron announced. "Ladies."

The women laid down their handiwork and rose to their feet. Each curtsied. One in particular did not look directly at Endersby, keeping her eyes down. Her face was whiter than the other chalk-like faces. Was she the pale young mistress Caldwell had described at the inquest? The one who had expressed concern over Mr. Cake and his breakfast. "Thank you, ladies," Endersby responded. The matron pulled out a chair. "I have only brief questions, today, and I thank you for your time." Endersby's politeness caused one of the seamstresses to giggle suddenly.

"Mary!" snapped the matron.

Endersby addressed the bold girl. "Mary, I shall ask your opinion first."

"My what?" snorted the girl.

A hush fell over the table. "Mary, I understand Mr. Cake frequently ate his meals here with you all, here in the theatre."

"That don't take my opinion, sir," she retorted, her voice full of mischief. "That is but a simple fact." The others broke into mild laughter.

"Was Mr. Cake a fine-mannered gentleman?"

"Ha," Mary cried. "No, sir. He ate like a sergeant." Loud slapping of hands.

"Ladies!" shouted the matron. "I beg your pardon, Inspector, but this lollying must stop. Mr. Cake dined in his room most often," the matron explained. "But from time-to-time, he took late suppers here in this place with us, the actors and our stage manager. He ate with us on Friday last, in fact. He was familiar to us all, sir." The matron softened as she spoke these last few words.

"He slept here too," interrupted Mary. "Not right at this table, you see. In *his bed.*" Mary's rolling of her eyes brought guffaws.

The pale young mistress looked up just then. In a pained voice she said, "He was always a gentleman, sir. He was much more. His habits were proper. He was a good man."

The others all sighed, and their little moans carried a mocking tone.

"Your name?"

"Esther."

"She was his special one, Mr. Policeman," taunted Mary.

With a sudden leap, the matron made her way to Mary and knuckled her hard on the crown of her head. The girl recoiled. She folded her hands tightly. "I beg pardon, sir."

"Was it you, Esther, who served him his breakfast?"

The pale young mistress admitted. "Yes, 'twas I." Her tears fell now, and the girl next to her pressed Esther to her breast. "She mended his stockings, too," explained the comforting girl. "Once, she mended his cloak, and she liked to brush his hats."

Mary wiggled. "She was in love with him, sir. Lovey-dovey." The other girls all nodded.

Esther patted her eyes. "He asked me," she explained. "He asked me is all," she insisted. The matron clapped her hands.

"Is there anything further you wish to know, Inspector? I am afraid these girls will get out of hand soon enough, what with our long days ahead."

Endersby noticed a sadness enter the matron's face. What loss, what pain had made her so severe, he wondered. "I am obliged, Matron. Did any of you see Mr. Cake on Friday last, before his dinner with you? Did you see him talking to anyone during that day?"

The answer from each of the women was a silent shaking of the head.

"Kindly look at this note, Matron. Do you recognize its signature?"

"P. Summers. I once knew a Summers, a clothier. But no, sir. This hand is not familiar to me."

"And these young ladies?"

The matron tapped the table. The girls were asked to sit down again. The matron held up the promissory note. "Ladies, the inspector has a question." Mary leaned forward. Esther started to thread her needle.

"I am looking for a P. Summers," Endersby explained. "I wish to discover if any of you may know of such a person."

Mary furrowed her brow. "Do we, girls? Do we?"

The seamstresses looked about, whispered, then shook their heads once again. Owen Endersby folded the note back into his pocket and thanked the ladies for their time. He was about to climb upstairs when the matron tugged at his sleeve.

"Mr. Endersby. I predicted this would occur, Mr. Endersby."

"What did you predict?"

"Mr. Cake's death."

"And pray tell."

"Jealousy was the motive. Brutality the means."

"Is there, Matron, a person or persons you can mention?"

"Rosa Grisi, dancer and horse rider at Aston's Palladium."

"A woman?"

"One as fit and strong as a man. She loved Mr. Cake. I saw it often enough. Lovers for certain. Late at night, the two of them. I knew she finished her act at Aston's by eleven o'clock. Out the stage door Mr. Cake would fly to her. An hour later, the love pigeons would be strolling by.

He invited her to supper many a time, to his private quarters upstairs."

"Were there any other witnesses to this affair?"

"My son–in–law, the stage-door keeper. He knew of their business. He was very fond of Mr. Cake and thought ill of Miss Grisi. Foreigners, you know, Inspector. Not trustworthy folk for the most part."

Endersby pondered the matron's words, wondering if they were but petty gossip.

"Miss Grisi had a temper, I suppose?"

"Mr. Cake liked young women, Mr. Endersby. He often walked in with one or another. When Miss Grisi discovered this, she flew into a rage. I swear to you, sir, I saw many a fight from this very stairwell, she shouting at Cake in the wings. Always accusing him."

"Did she ever strike him or…"

"No, she might have done him harm if she had. She is a fine horsewoman and acrobat, Mr. Endersby. Her fists are as hard as any workman's. No, she liked to threaten Mr. Cake in other ways."

"In what other ways?"

"She had two younger brothers. Belligerent young princes. Sailors once, who now work the swings and the canvas dioramas at Aston's. She sent them over a number of times to bully Mr. Cake. My son-in-law had to call a Peeler once to have them barred from entering the theatre."

"Can you describe them?"

"Black hair. Black frock coats. Black caps. A small moustache on the youngest."

"How long did this kind of trouble go on?"

"Most of last autumn."

"What would Miss Grisi gain, do you imagine, from murder?"

"Satisfaction, perhaps. She has a fire within her, Mr. Endersby. A fire in her spirit. Rumours are she once stabbed a man in her native Italy and had to flee to England ,to escape the gallows."

"And her brothers?"

"Foreign brutes."

"Mere violent sport? No money involved here? Perhaps the brothers wanted to steal from Cake."

"It was passion, sir. Plain as sunshine. I think she was driven by revenge, just like the heroine in our drama now playing this season."

Endersby thanked the matron and realized when he was out of the theatre and halfway into the street that he'd forgotten to discuss the promissory note—and this new name—with the stage-door keeper. "Stay alert, old gander," he scolded himself. On his return to the stage door, he waited as an actor collected letters and chatted morosely about murder, then he handed the promissory note to the stage-door keeper, hoping he might be able to illumine the dark matter of this untraceable person.

"Do you recognize this name, sir, this signature?"

"P. Summers. There was an actor once called Arthur Summers. Four, five years ago, at the Lyceum. Was a feisty man, arrested for striking a footman of Lord Carroll's. Married an actress across the river, but I never did know her name. Dead and gone now, I believe. This is a note to whom, Mr. Endersby?"

"It was found in Mr. Cake's house in Doughty Street. I have yet to find anyone who has an inkling of this creature."

"May I suggest old Eleazar on Fleet. Knows most names of the profligate."

"I thank you. And do you have any recollection of a Rosa Grisi and her brothers?"

"A beauty of a kind, I reckon. Very strong acrobat and horsewoman who came by the theatre often enough to see Mr. Cake. She had a temper, I swear. Her two brothers were work, Mr. Endersby. Hanging about and smoking and talking in their foreign tongue. One of them one time struck an argument with Mr. Cake, but nothing came of it. A Peeler was nearby and put the two ruffian brothers off. You think they are guilty, sir? They be the ones who went after Mr. Cake?"

"I cannot draw any conclusion as yet, sir," Endersby said

cautiously. "There are too many directions I must follow first before I point my finger."

"I see your drift. Wise of you, sir. I tell you, I cannot judge others too well myself, seeing I meet most people in passing—coming and going through this door."

"A wise perception of your own. But in time, we can see much if we keep our eyes and ears open. I would ask you to do just that for me. If any suspicious character turns up, or if any memory of yours brings you a new take on things, please send me word at the Fleet Street station."

"With pleasure, Inspector Endersby. I can rely on my sharp-eyed mother-in-law for many a tidbit."

"Indeed, you can. Good day."

*　　*　　*

Into a narrow hall in the New Cut, Inspector Owen Endersby was guided by a young girl. The clock at Waterloo Bridge was striking the hour. The house he'd entered was dingy. Numbers on the doors told him the place was let to boarders, but of a respectable and paying nature, not like the vile lodging houses he had recently seen, not like the fire-ridden hell-hole down in St. Giles. After giving the girl a penny, he was brought into the little parlour of Mrs. Percy Buckstone, the actor's wife. As usual, Endersby needed to verify stories. Was Percy Buckstone a borrower of money? Yes, the promissory notes proved that. Was he one of the frequenters the witness at the coroner's inquest spoke about? Possibly. One of them wore a red beard. Likely it was Buckstone. But was this agile actor capable of violence or murder? *What pushes a man to wield a weapon?* wondered Endersby.

Mrs. Buckstone had arranged herself on a low sofa, oddly placed in the centre of the cluttered room, rather like a large throne amongst the pictures, china dogs, feathers, fans and bowls of boiled sweets. Here, Mrs. Buckstone received. Inspector Endersby introduced himself as a detective. That very word caught the chin of Mrs. Buckstone and raised it to a peculiar angle from which she peered down at his suede gloves and his mud-crusted boots.

Endersby's eyes took in a wide woman with a cluster of loose ringlets popping out from her head in a mass of yellow. She had thick ankles; her lace cap had been removed and was perched ominously on a pillow next to her.

"What?" she snapped.

Endersby repeated the question concerning the where-abouts of Percy Buckstone on last Friday night.

The woman moved her mouth into an irritable frown: "At the theatre, surely, sir. Practising his profession. That is his wont."

"And after, Mrs. Buckstone?"

"After? Why, home to supper."

"With respect, Mrs. Buckstone, at what time was that?"

"Time, sir? Oh, my. By ten or so. The usual."

Mrs. Buckstone rubbed her chubby hands as if she were in a cold draft.

"Not later, by chance?"

"Must I count out the hours, surely? I cannot vouch precisely, sir. No. But near to ten. Percy always comes home near to ten. His habit."

"Does his habit sometimes lead him out late at night?"

"Whatever do you suggest, Inspector?"

"Does your husband spend some evenings with cronies of the theatre? Does he dine out occasionally with them?" Endersby did not want to lead the woman on. He did not want to mention the gaming table or the debts, as yet.

"I am afraid I cannot say, sir. Surely, my husband spends his time as he will. He dines regularly with me, I can assure you."

"Does your husband buy you gifts, Mrs. Buckstone?"

"You are curious, sir. What are you getting at?"

Endersby decided on a quick broadside attack. "Your husband plays the gambling tables, does he not? He has debts? He borrows?"

"He does? I think, sir, you have incorrect information. My husband is respectable in every quarter."

Endersby pulled out the promissory notes with Buckstone's signature. The pink round hand that took them was trembling. The plump face fell on reading them.

"I think this is scandalous, sir. I cannot imagine what my Percy was thinking when he signed these. I give him an allowance. He has his wages. We always dine at home. Is this a jest, sir?"

"They were found in Mr. Cake's house, Mrs. Buckstone."

The pink hands flew up and covered the teary eyes.

"Do you know if Mr. Buckstone had any other kinds of dealings with Cake? Or with other gambling friends?"

"I cannot imagine, sir. I cannot imagine what the man does on his own time."

"On Friday night. What did you have for your late supper together?"

Mrs. Buckstone pulled on her lace cap. "Prawns in sauce, sir. Costly at this time of year, I can attest. A shilling a half-pound."

"You dined together?"

"As usual. And to bed."

"Did Mr. Buckstone rise in the night for any reason?"

"What reason, sir. To escape? To murder Mr. Cake? Is that what you mean?" Mrs. Buckstone was a belligerent bully now. She stood up and her skirt flounced with an angry swish.

"Yes, perhaps. Did he?"

"As far as I know, he remained at home."

"You are certain? Your maid did not see or hear him?"

"My maid? She does not stay in, sir. She is but a daily."

"Anyone else in this hall who may know about your husband?"

"His goings and comings? So I now must play the spy on my dear Percy. Admit that he is a scoundrel?"

"It is a simple question I ask, Mrs. Buckstone. I am not accusing your husband."

"Search them out then. They will vouch for him."

Mrs. Buckstone turned her sights toward the smoky hearth, and from the set of her shoulders Endersby decided it was time he departed. He sensed, even before Mrs. Buckstone showed him the door, that she was telling the truth, as much as she knew it. She held the latch, raised her chin, and looked past him into the hall.

"You might try talking to Elisabetta Mazzini," Mrs. Buckstone confided, her eyes looking right as she spoke. "She is with the opera. Percy told me Mr. Cake was fond of her. She is a clever one, Mr. Endersby. One not easy to catch. My Percy says she is very good at whist and at the gaming table." This last admission brought a hot blush to her cheeks. "Good day, Mr. Endersby," she said, her voice now trembling.

As the door shut, Endersby heard the woman burst into tears. A piece of china smashed against the floor. Retreating to the stairwell, he saw a man below in the doorway.

"Caldwell. How did you find me so fast?"

"The stage-door keeper at the Coburg, sir."

Endersby was with his sergeant a few minutes later walking out of the New Cut and onto Waterloo Road, where they found the eating house mentioned by Percy Buckstone. They entered, checked on Buckstone's story and found he was a regular. Two glasses of claret were ordered. Endersby was restless, kicking the floor with his boot. He peered around the room as Caldwell recounted his morning.

"Seven only, so far, sir. Mostly sellers." Caldwell was holding up the found glove. The blood stains had darkened. "Most shook their heads. Never seen its kind before. Hardy's in the Arcade suggested a maker in the City. He was closing up when I got there—a funeral. He said it was a curious bit. Perhaps a French make. Used for coachmen and horse handlers. He wouldn't swear to it."

Caldwell was wearing his hat, and his face was slightly red from his morning exertion. Endersby encouraged him to keep on talking.

"I will try later today, if you wish, sir. More sellers and makers. They all seemed doubtful. Said mostly the glove was foreign, not English."

"How about glove cleaners, Caldwell? There's a by-way. Cleaners."

"Good point, sir. I shall venture there, too."

"Play the game. Ask for a mate. Get the cleaners to talk about clients. Names."

"Right, sir."

"And the plug, Caldwell? The cheap chomp?"

"Better luck, Inspector. I went straight to Covent Garden to the tobacconists. Two of them told me the name, the weight and the cost of the grain. One said it was a favorite among costers, for its price and flavour. Definitely not a gentlemen's tobacco."

"Perhaps an actor's, however. Let us not overlook that possibility."

"Certainly not, sir," replied Caldwell.

*   *   *

By early afternoon, after a very quick lunch, Endersby knew that a confrontation must take place no matter what the odds. Two names whirled around his mind: Rosa Grisi and Elisabetta Mazzini. Both were in the theatre. Both were foreign. Each knew something of Cake that could reveal yet more names, perhaps even the identity—nay, the identities —of those beasts who beat him to death. Endersby decided to choose one of the women over the other. First comes first, he concluded. He discussed the matter with some urgency with Caldwell, and to his delight found his sergeant not only cooperative but in complete agreement. To show this, Caldwell hid his policeman's baton in his great-coat's inner pocket and hastened to mention that he would gladly go along with any tactic Endersby decided to use.

Thus, the inspector and his sergeant were once again on the streets of London, south of the great Thames river, marching through winding streets of the Surrey side under the shadow of Shot Tower. As the two men rounded the corner of York Road, playbills announced Rosa Grisi's name in large letters. Endersby paused by the arched entrance to Aston's Palladium.

"Over here," he said to Caldwell.

Endersby led his sergeant into an alley beside the

theatre. He withdrew into the shadow of the building and hastily opened his satchel. He lifted from it a pair of thick spectacles. He placed them on his nose.

"Well, Caldwell?"

"They suit, sir."

Endersby then prayed the hairpiece Caldwell slipped on would force the Grisi brothers to trust the two of them as curious spectators, as fans of the horse show. When Endersby returned to the theatre's entrance, he stood before the gaping hall with his eyes quite squinted in trepidation. Caldwell was walking in front of him with a swagger and addressing the stage-door keeper as to the location of the famous Grisi family. "Out in the yard, in the stables," came the man's answer, his palm at the same time receiving a ha'penny.

"Now listen up, Caldwell," Endersby said in a conspiratorial voice. "Rosa Grisi and her two brothers are hot-blooded. The story is she attacked a man in Italy and had to flee here to England. Act slow and listen." Caldwell's wig sat firm as his legs took confident strides into an open yard of sand and a cluster of horse stables. The two Grisi brothers made an appearance, leading a horse from the stalls. The sergeant made the first move, going up boldly to the men, thrusting out his hand. Out of his mouth sprang a broad American accent.

"Fine fine show, gentlemen! I want to congratulate you. Most daring. Impressive."

The brother with the moustache halted. He was a quick-eyed twenty-five-year-old with jet hair and a rough-shaven chin. His eyes were a burnished brown. The older-looking brother, holding the horse, was almost his twin, with the same wiry build and intense gaze. The brothers wore black linen shirts and breeches covered in leather chaps. Their sleeves were rolled up, and Endersby scanned their waists for the telltale belt and dagger.

"*Che succede?*" said the younger.

"What do you want?" said the older, his eyes on the horse, but his attention riveted to the two visitors in great-coats.

"A darn good show," repeated Caldwell. "How do you

boys manage to keep such a tight circle?"

"*Cosa?*"

Endersby lifted up his glasses. A posh palace accent accompanied his words. "A fine specimen. Spanish, is it? Name is Carlton. Lord Edward Carlton. In the market for a good horse, a performer, for my county fair."

"We are not handlers, sir. Nor sellers. I thank you." The older spoke quickly, dismissing them. Caldwell came closer, and the younger Grisi tensed his shoulders. "Yes?" he blurted out in a halted version of the word.

"Mighty pleased," Caldwell said, stressing the "ee" in pleased. He grabbed the young man's hand and shook it vigorously. "You folks from the south? Spain? Italy?"

"We are Londoners," said the older, his voice tired and filling with annoyance.

"Been in the country long, have you?" chimed in Endersby. He circled the horse, inspecting its legs and neck.

"*Calma, calma,*" the older said, patting the horse. The younger came around the back side of the animal and crowded close to Endersby.

"I understand you have a sister. She is the Muse in your spectacle of the Waterloo? Splendid, I understand."

"Sister?" questioned the younger. He cocked his head.

"*Sorella,*" translated the older. The word reached the younger's ears. Without warning, his colour deepened. His mouth pulled into a sneer. Stepping back, Endersby had only an instant to haul in a breath before he saw the glint, the line, the honed point. Triangular in shape, the knife point was abruptly held up and shoved close against the taut skin of Endersby's throat. One extra thrust, and the blade could easily slice the flesh of the inspector's respect-able second chin.

"*Perchè? Chi sei?*" the enraged younger brother spat into Endersby's frozen face.

In a bound, the older rushed to his brother, hand out, mouth open but voiceless. Out came his arm then his fist to yank the knife away from fulfilling its bloody duty. The younger brother pulled back, panting. The knife fell and thumped into the dust of the sandy yard.

"Excuse me, sir," the older brother apologized. "Go, please, my brother and I, we are busy. Lots of work."

"Well, I declare," exclaimed Caldwell, "you are a hot-headed bunch." The sergeant forced a laugh, and Endersby backed off from the younger brother, making a quick mental note: neither brother was wearing gloves, one was the handler of the other. Calming, taking in safe breath, Endersby also noted that the younger had a recent injury to his hand—a cut, as if from a knife like the one he brandished.

"Can I help you, *signori?*"

A tall man in a fur cape was walking into the stable yard. The shadow of the theatre at first darkened the features of his face, but as he moved into the pale afternoon light, Endersby saw he was Italian or Spanish and that he had an air of authority about him.

"*Al lavoro,*" he commanded the two Grisi brothers, who immediately bowed in obedience and led the horse into another part of the yard. The man introduced himself as the agent of the Grisi family.

"Hiram Melville," said Caldwell, shaking the man's hand with vigour.

"Lord Carlton," replied Endersby. He broke into a polite smile, quickly assessing the Italian man's gesture and the look in his eyes.

"People admire my family. Yes, I am a cousin. The brothers and their sister are well-known here in London. It is a privilege to perform before such fine gentlemen as yourselves. Why have you come here this afternoon?"

Caldwell smiled, and before he could come up with a response, Endersby spoke: "We are admirers of good horsemanship, sir. I understand the Grisi family is one of the finest in the capital for performing tricks and stunts. I understand there is a sister, and I would very much like to meet her."

"For what reason?" asked the man. His voice betrayed no suspicion. He was smiling and polite, and his outstretched arm suggested the three of them walk together from the yard into the central ring of the emporium.

"I want to hire her," said Endersby. He hoped his quick response would interest the man and waylay any further doubtful suspicions he seemed to have about the visit.

"How gracious, Lord Carlton," he answered. "But Miss Grisi is not a private performer. Not even for a grand fee. And she has many bookings until the spring, here and in Paris and Vienna." One of Endersby's beliefs was that if a man was lying, there was a hard tone to his voice. The Italian cousin's words took on that tone, its steely nature shaping the pace of the words. For a moment, as the three of them surveyed the rows of seats rising in tiers, the Italian held his stance. Then a flicker came into his face, a hint of fear.

"But of course, we can negotiate a special time for you, Lord Carlton. If you will allow me."

"May I meet with Miss Grisi?" Endersby asked. He half expected the man to refuse on the spot.

But the man responded: "With pleasure. I shall meet with my cousin this afternoon and arrange an *appuntamento*. Please, you can call again tomorrow, so I can give you her answer. She will be most honoured, sir." The tone had returned and with it a touch of malice in the use of the Italian word.

"Good day," the Italian then said, bowing a little before returning toward the stables.

"I thank you, sir," twanged Caldwell. The Italian swivelled around, waved for a second before turning to go outdoors.

"Keep an eye on him, Caldwell," Endersby said in a rush. "Walk around this place. Find out when the Grisi brothers go and come. Stay close by as much as you can, but out of sight, if possible. The question remains as to where in Heaven is Rosa Grisi?"

Asking the same question of the stage-door keeper brought the answer that she was at home, resting, that she wished to remain private, that she met fans, like the gentlemen before him, only after her performances in the evening. Endersby thanked the man with another ha'penny and enquired of her street address.

"Not allowed to tell," said the man, his eyes darting toward the entrance to the stable. "Orders from the cousin."

Endersby was about to ask again but decided to let the situation lie. True, he wanted to coerce the peremptory man, though he concluded the stage-door keeper was most likely telling the truth. It was not Endersby's custom to resort to physical means of persuasion. He was not adverse to taunting or even to hitting a man to get information, but only in dire circumstances. London, after all, was a big, hard city. Endersby knew a policeman had to use force on occasion to get answers. He studied the stubborn stage-door keeper once more. Most likely the man had answered more out of fear than belligerence.

On the street, Endersby eased off his spectacles. "Walk with me, Caldwell."

"You seem vexed, sir."

Rain dotted the pavement. A gust of smoke from a baker's oven momentarily shadowed the street.

"You noted how the young hot-head Grisi reacted to my question about his sister?"

"With the point of his dagger."

"Here, let me see that damned glove."

Caldwell pulled out the soiled glove and handed it to the inspector. Endersby felt the leather, rubbing it between his fingers. He put it to his nose.

"If this belonged to a horse handler, would you not imagine it would carry the odour of horse? With day-to-day use, I cannot believe it *could* not. Here, smell it."

Caldwell took it back and held it to his nose. "There is a faint smell to it, sir. Not of horse, though. Of grease, perhaps. Of oil."

"Yes, indeed."

The men stopped when they reached the steps to Waterloo Bridge. A skiff full of fragrant oranges sailed past, and Endersby was sorely tempted to call to the bargeman and haggle a penny for a handful of the sweet fruit.

"I shall go off and ponder awhile, Caldwell. Give me the glove for the mean time. You get back to Aston's. Rosa Grisi is the one person I sense is most suspicious—so far—in this cruel business."

Caldwell started off into the afternoon. Checking the clock by the river, Endersby hastened over the great bridge, the churning expanse of the Thames forcing him to think of the flow of time. A murderer still remained at liberty. The clocks of London were ticking.

"Blood will out," Endersby consoled himself, though he fervently wished the secret to be revealed to him before night fell. He hurried on. He pondered the wherewithal of the Grisi family and the Italian cousin and their possible roles in the drama of Cake's death. The wind blew colder. With each footstep Endersby's annoyance grew, for he now reminded himself of a most tedious but necessary duty. As was police custom, he must go and present his evidence—the bloodied glove, in particular—to the local magistrate at Gray's Inn. Testimonials required review; forms demanded his signature. The magistrate would want a full account of the murder scene inspection, let alone an appraisal of the surgeon's conclusions. What was most important was Endersby's personal observations as a policeman on the state of the scene and the condition of the body. The items under scrutiny would then be catalogued and handed back to Endersby for his use in pursuing the felons responsible. "A fussy, paper-busy matter," grumbled Endersby. He halted, adjusted his hat to the swipe of the wind and reluctantly raised his arm to attract a hansom.

*   *   *

The magistrate at Gray's Inn fell asleep twice during Endersby's exposition of the crime scene. One hour dragged, with the reading and signing of all the required depositions and affidavits. After much discussion, the session finally ended, and Endersby relieved his mind and his cramped writing hand with a brisk walk. The Strand now shoved, bullied and splattered him. He kicked a piece of broken bottle into the gutter. A man beating a horse found his arm stayed by Endersby's iron grip.

"What good is beating the beast to death, sir? You go nowhere. Feed it instead."

The man, so shocked at the interruption, tipped his hat and laid down his whip.

Endersby marched on. He felt a petulant anger rising. It was difficult, after all, to appreciate a day when there were so few answers to his questions. All he could ponder was the memory of Samuel Cake's bloodied face. He decided not to head in the direction of Fleet Lane, nor to his superintendent, who would no doubt be pursing his lips and wanting an immediate report, nay, a suspect and a conviction by dinner time. *Not possible*, thought Endersby. Taking a rest by a shop window, he stared in at buttons on display. "A puzzle in themselves," he said, noting the patterns and lines. He looked at his own reflection. Doubt added its frown to his tired features.

Logic and perception and persistence: these were Endersby's guiding words. He went over the details, his thoughts first alighting on the redoubtable Miss Rosa Grisi. How, if she were so inclined, did she effect the brutal thrashing of a man she had once loved? Remember the rumour of her stabbing a man in Italy. Perchance Cake had returned late on Friday from the theatre and to his surprise found his former lover waiting for him. They argued; Rosa Grisi lost her temper; the walking stick turned into a murderous bludgeon. Did the smashing then take place after Cake had been killed, a vindictive coda to the sudden act of violence?

So far, logic had brought Endersby to an impasse. He persisted, however. He walked on, and at Brydges Street he stopped to glimpse the crowds lining up to buy theatre tickets at Old Drury. *What do you know, old dowager?* he asked of the building itself. Indeed, what heinous secrets did all the silent fronts of these buildings shelter? If only the inanimate world could speak. But what musing. Endersby entertained the question of how much of this sordid world could civilized beings bear? Back in the fray of Chancery Lane, he stopped mid-street and looked up at the sky. No relief to be had from that ceiling of grey cloud. With new thoughts forming, Endersby realized he must stake out

Caldwell in various places—in disguise—to act the spy. *Deception is often the by-way to truth,* he reminded himself. *That and a little physical exertion. Mind, a roughing up of a villain or two often brings results.* His mind flew back to the spoiled Mr. Buckstone then halted at the vision of the Grisi brother with his threatening stiletto. *In the end, how does the Italian cousin affect all of this? What configuration in the puzzle fits that arrogant liar? And the sister, Rosa Grisi? She is still a mystery, let alone the other woman, the one from the opera, Elisabetta Mazzini. Perhaps she might illumine the pattern of all the interstices and crisscrosses which form the web of the case.*

A nagging breeze of cold air drove Endersby forward until he entered a short street guarded by a large gate and a gatekeeper. Endersby told the keeper his business and was pointed toward the house he had decided to visit before his supper time.

Holborn Row still retained its feeling of grandeur. Like proud galleons, the grand mansions first built in the reign of George the Third held chests of silver and jewels, displayed banners and shields with the crests of ancient families. Greek-styled pillars fronted deep white porches. Endersby pulled the bell at Number 92. When he lifted his gaze toward the shiny door opening before him, there stood a large man in butler's livery. Endersby explained who he was and what he wanted. Soon he was following the butler across a grand foyer domed by a painted ceiling displaying Roman warriors fighting gods. The butler opened a door to a small room. Gold trim emboldened the stiff chairs. In one of these sat Lord Harwood. Like his surroundings, he was gilt-edged: proper, pressed, pointed in tone of voice.

"A detective force? How novel."

There was no disdain, no train of contempt in the aristocrat's words. Merely a haughty curiosity. A moment later, the contract with the broken seal lay in Lord Harwood's silken lap, its journey from ransacked Doughty Street back to the halls of landed wealth presenting an irony, which temporarily amused Inspector Endersby. Harwood's aristocratic signature was on it, as were the names of Old Drury and Samuel Cake, side-by-side in collusion.

"But why Old Drury? And why Mr. Cake? Is the theatre not managed already?" asked Endersby.

"By a Mr. Dupré, sir. Henry Robertson Dupré," answered Lord Harwood. "Practical playwright, among other talents. Thinking of more important matters, I forgot to tell you that Mr. Dupré is also a spendthrift. He indulges in the role of the wastrel at my expense. And despite his recent 'hit', as he vulgarly proclaims it, his rent is grossly in arrears. But then, Old Drury is an eater of coin. What a burden that property has been. Even my father with the great Garrick himself had to call in the bailiff at times."

Endersby noted each step of the narrative, his eyes never leaving the well-fed face of a man whose lineage, he was certain, stretched far back into the fog of time to the era of Elizabeth I herself. Lord Harwood was not only an owner of theatres but also other lease-hold properties in and around London.

"But why Cake, your lordship? I ask you again."

"I beg your pardon. Letting my mind wander to lesser things—a habit of mine. There was the simple matter of a bold offer. Mr. Cake was buoyed by his own arrogance and his investments. Not a scurrilous man, not a dishonest one. Most unfortunate demise, for Cake was a self-made gentleman, as the saying goes. I admired that in him—but I am wandering. I believe it was early December."

Endersby shifted his gouty foot. The afternoon was passing slowly, and the pain was beginning to bother him. "Not to put to fine a point to all of this," droned Lord Harwood. He then proceeded to outline the story of Samuel Cake and his offer to pay the back rent on Old Drury on condition of a new lease to be awarded to him and to him alone, in January next; to take over the management of the great house; to enliven it and enrich its coffers with spectacles not unlike those humble ones he presented in the Coburg—a clever idea, no doubt—money being the only object in sight, for the roof of the old place needed repair, and Cake was the man with the means.

"And Mr. Dupré?"

"Summarily dismissed, sir. Goodbye to the prodigal. A fine talent and a man with a good eye, but a man without discipline for money. Pondering his actions—a daily toil of mine, I confess—I made a decision. Out I sent him with a prompt letter of dismissal. It is our way with such a lease. Each manager is given a year, and delayed payments. But none, it seems, can ever pay. Except for the promise of this poor murdered Cake, I believe no man in London could have done it."

"When was the last time you saw Mr. Cake?"

"A week or so ago, I believe. He came with his offer then."

"You had no other word with him after that date?"

"No, sir. I sent my manservant to deliver the contract. And I had no need to see the man again, nor he me."

Endersby remained silent, thinking over the facts at hand.

"Dupré is a vindictive man, however, sir," Lord Harwood pronounced suddenly. "I have had many a nose-to-nose with him, as the vulgar saying goes. He has the pugilist in him. A touch of Lord Byron—that same arrogant nonsense."

"Is he capable of murder, your lordship?"

"Mr. Cake's calamity has been examined by the coroner, has it, Mr. Endersby?"

"Yes. It was brought to verdict yesterday afternoon." Endersby found himself folding his hands together in a kind of submissive gesture.

"Better early than never, I say," concluded Lord Harwood. "Murder proclaimed then? Beyond doubt?"

"Most surely, your lordship. Do you wish the details?"

"A knife, a bludgeon of some kind?"

"A walking stick."

"How extraordinary. Allowing my imagination free rein—a habit of mine—I can picture the horrible event. The victim struck down. The cries. And as Macduff nobly wept: 'O, horror, horror. Murder and treason'."

"And Mr. Dupré, your lordship?"

Lord Harwood lowered his arms, which a moment before had been raised in thespian despair in front of his widened eyes. He composed himself. "Capable of murder? What a question. Capable of deceit, perhaps. Indolence, certainly, as he has never replied to my letter of dismissal. I would venture to claim he is a man who may give you a clearer vision of Mr. Cake's finale."

"I thank you," said Endersby. The butler led him out through the expansive halls, and when he was outside on the mansion's grand steps, the inspector stopped to repeat facts as was his method. He had honed his mind to draw traces as well, like tracks in sand or like lines in a pencil sketch which in time would form a portrait. In the light of this afternoon, among the houses of the rich, he came up with the idea that Dupré, perhaps, might be the fourth man in the murder case, the man seen by the neighbour scuttling out the back entrance of Doughty Street...*but no, do not jump ahead of yourself,* Endersby cautioned. "Taking a leap too soon," he said to his reflection in a polished urn on the steps of Lord Harwood's house.

He chuckled. "A habit of mine."

*   *   *

Henry Robertson Dupré stood by his desk in his attic office in Old Drury. He read Lord Harwood's words of dismissal for the fifth and final time. "Ridiculous," he said, and tore up the letter, gathering its pieces in his hand and tossing them out the round window. He watched the paper flutter away in the wind and felt a joy in his throat as if he'd just taken a long drink of fine French claret. He patted his hair. He was only too aware that as the manager of Old Drury, he must now concentrate on matters at hand. Serious matters, he thought. And then he smiled. Henry Robertson Dupré reminded himself he was a lucky man. As such, he had to keep up his appearance. For certain he must visit his barber this evening for his once-weekly treatment. Indian henna kept his hair young-looking. "Nothing like it," Henry murmured contentedly, "for brushing out the grey."

He sat down at his desk. This sudden blush of confidence and momentary joy afforded him a moment of imaginative reflection. He raised his quill pen and crossed out the first hesitant lines of his revised script for the pantomime. The simple approach, he thought, is the only way: begin again at the very beginning. The scratch of his quill on the paper inspired his thoughts, but as it did, his inner voice repeated a singular phrase: *finally, finally.* After a few pages of furious writing, the scenes pouring out of his mind as water does from a pump, he sat back, scanned the new lines and nodded with satisfaction. A new promptbook cover lay open, and into it he sorted the freshly written sheets.

And so it is thus.

Henry smiled again. He arched his back. His fine nose and elegant figure seemed even more regal—even more magnificently serene—than ever. He was still a young oak, unbreakable, impeccable.

Henry rose from his chair. His frock coat and pantaloons carried a shine to them, cleaned and pressed earlier this very day by his housekeeper. He patted his hair once more to make sure it was still neatly combed, then left his attic office and locked its door. The short flight of stairs to the stage manager's chamber clattered with his footsteps. Surrounded by the general commotion of the stage, Henry Robertson Dupré felt a driving desire to perform his duties. To say he was vain might be to insult him. At forty, his legs were well formed from years of long morning walks. Ask any one of his fellow theatre managers in London about his talent, and all would agree he was diligent and clever. His hirelings admired him; frequently they likened him in his efficiency to a stiff wind stirring up dust. But to run a theatre like Old Drury at a profit was impossible. No wonder he felt vexed at Harwood's sudden dismissal. It was as if he'd found himself in a duel and been given neither pistol nor dagger to defend himself.

"Never mind," he said aloud, "the letter now is null and void." At five minutes to four o'clock in the afternoon, he entered the stage manager's chamber, a cheery place to

conduct his managerial chores. There was a crackling hearth
and a small window to let in daylight. It was but a few steps to
the table set up for the interviews to secure contracts for the
pantomime with his principal actors. Without further
ceremony, Henry seated himself. He pondered again the
thoughts which had visited him during the night. The prime
threat to his professional life was no longer of concern. He
tried to dampen the glee he felt in his heart. He then
attempted to suppress the deep fear his soul embraced at the
same time. To trump Harwood—that was the easiest of his
tasks. *To trump the world at large was quite another matter.*

The door opened and the stage manager poked in his
head. "Mr. Weston is here, sir."

"Good heavens," Henry said. "You startled the life out of
me." He waved his hand in dismissal. The actor Mr. William
Weston came through the door, his skin its usual milky pallor.
A beaver top hat, thin kid gloves, a frock coat and a French-
style *manteau* with fur collar summed up his outward dress.
He sat down across from Henry. Weston's body contained its
usual nervous rigidity, his back as stiff as a flagpole. When the
actor removed his hat, Henry recoiled at Weston's thinning
hair combed over in a patch of oily strands.

"Good afternoon, Mr. Weston."

"And to you, Mr. Dupré."

"May I enquire after your sister. How is her health?"

"Much the same, Mr. Dupré. I thank you for your concern."

"Nervousness, weakness, the fever?"

"With due medical attention, these shall subside."

"You have a new doctor, then?"

"Shall have, Mr. Dupré. Monday fortnight, my aunt and
I shall have funds from a sale of my sister's necklace to pay
for a new doctor recommended by Miss Root."

"I am glad to hear it, Mr. Weston. Nasty business with
the Cake affair, wouldn't you agree?"

Mr. Weston paused for a second. His face seemed to
whiten even more, turning to a chalky hue. He yanked off
a glove. "Most pitiful, sir. Yet, he was a clever man."

"He was successful enough."

"He could be kind when he wanted to be, Mr. Dupré. I shall award him that." Mr. Weston's voice took on a shade of remorse as he spoke.

"To business, then, Mr. Weston." Henry straightened his shoulders as a signal that money and contracts were uppermost between the two men.

"You wish me to play the prince and the Beast once again." Weston spoke distractedly as if he were in a dream. "The revival, *Beauty and the Beast?*"

"Indeed."

Henry watched the actor's eyes lower. In spite of Mr. Weston's saturnine mood, Henry presented his winning card. "I can readily offer you an increase in wage, Mr. Weston. For your fine service as the prince in *Rachel*. Your scenes of pathos have been the centrepiece of the play and the source of much talk in London. When there is talk, as you well know, there are sales."

"That is most kind of you, Mr. Dupré."

"You are welcome. You deserve it."

"And how much, may I ask?"

"One pound extra a week, with a bonus of six pounds for the panto fortnight performances."

The actor silently pondered the offer.

"Is there anything wrong, sir?" Henry asked.

Mr. Weston did not answer but instead kept staring at the floor before him. *The sum is insufficient, that is what he is thinking,* Henry deduced. He, however, steeled his resolve. "I must, of course, confer with Lord Harwood on all these matters. Our coffers are bulging at the moment, but debts must be paid. And a bonus or two is an extra expense."

The actor before him hesitated. He rose and was about to pull on his glove when Henry pointed to his hand. "An injury, Mr. Weston?"

Weston quickly turned his hand then hid it within the folds of his coat. It was as if he were caught in a sudden flash of footlight glare. "A graze only, Mr. Dupré. From the battle procession."

The deep tone in Weston's voice astonished Henry, who

now feared the actor would turn down the offer. Henry stood up quickly and added: "May I suggest, then, that I ask Lord Harwood for seven pounds."

"Six pounds is quite sufficient, sir," the actor answered in a dry voice, his eyes turned toward the pale light of the window.

"Good then," Henry said, his reaction accompanied by a quick sigh of relief. But he was also confused. Weston was still in an odd state: distracted, fraught with worry. Without any movement, Weston then seemed to awaken from his frozen condition. He blinked, and his staring fell away. He took hold of the contract Henry had placed in his hand, read it and signed it without asking any further questions. Then he put on his glove, his hat, and bowed slightly.

"Forgive me, Mr. Dupré, I was lost in reverie for a moment. I beg your pardon."

The two men shook hands. Weston turned, and as he was walking out the door, a figure in riding clothes rushed in, bumping his shoulder.

"Oh, I beg your pardon, Will," said a flushed Miss Priscilla Root. Miss Root took her place in the chair, having pulled it closer to the fire, her face heavily rouged. "I shall have tea, Dupré," she announced and slipped off her right glove.

Henry was about to call for young Crabb when Miss Root fidgeted. "On second thought, I shall not," she complained.

"Have you thought over my offer, Miss Root? Of the role of Beauty for this year's panto?"

"I am sorry, Henry. I am sorry."

"Can you not see your way to accept?"

Priscilla Root broke into tears, and Henry handed her his handkerchief.

"I am not myself today. I simply am *not*, Henry." Priscilla Root answered him as if she were a prisoner in the dock. "I know you are angry about my late entrance last night, but I am perfectly innocent. I could not hear the stage manager's low whistle. I have never once missed a cue or a performance."

"Miss Root, lateness for any reason is not a virtue in the theatre, need I remind you."

Again, the voice of a protesting victim. "How can you accuse me of negligence? One or two slip-ups. Why, even Mr. Kean was late and very often not word-perfect." These last words were pounded out, the voice slightly raised.

"But at least you have admitted to fault, Priscilla. And now I need your decision on the part. Will you take it? As you well know, I admire your talent, but lately I have had grave doubts about your personal habits, especially your visits to that den in Soho. I can tell you, such indulgence can mar your speaking voice. You must take care."

"Henry, you intrude too much." Miss Root rose in a flurry. "I shall not allow you to bully me. Not at all."

"We are going nowhere, Miss Root. Kindly think on my offer. I need an answer within the hour."

"Henry, I am amazed at you. I have been stalwart and my performances have elicited great applause. You seem deliberately trying to discredit me."

"Hardly, Miss Root. On the contrary. I wish only to assure the continuation of my contract with you."

Miss Priscilla Root walked in a circle before the hearth. Satisfied that he had set her thinking, Henry watched her with careless interest. He sensed she would agree to terms. She would stall, naturally. Hook him with doubt, then release him, gently, with her famous rolling eyes. The silence in the room continued for a few more seconds before Henry abruptly clapped his hands. "Miss Root, I implore you."

Suddenly, without warning, Priscilla Root rushed at him. Her face flushed with erupting fury. She raised up her two fists. Lurching forward, she let out a raspy scream that sounded to Henry like the cry of a desperate child. Henry drew back, but Miss Root swung her fists with such a violent movement that he was forced to raise his right arm in defense. Then, abruptly, the outburst subsided. Miss Root heaved in her chest; she looked up at her raised fists and dropped them to her sides. Henry heard her mutter an agitated, "Oh, dear, oh, dear." Her sped-up breathing gradually returned to normal; her face soon found itself covered in her hands, her mouth proclaiming, "Oh, my

God" in a sorrowful tone. As a final note, a blush of embarrassment scoured her features.

"Sometimes, Henry, one is faced with choices," Miss Root said at last, calmed, collected, her shoulders straight. "Very difficult choices. Often ones which are dark and perilous." Miss Root sat down again. She gathered herself and said, "I cannot as yet ponder your offer. Though I know you need my answer before nightfall. I do not want to give up my position here. I cannot explain why just at this moment. Oh, dear, oh dear..." Her voice sank. She dropped Henry's handkerchief to the floor and dabbed her eyes instead with a square of lace slipped out from her sleeve. Then, slowly and with solemn poise, she rose once again. "Excuse me, please, Henry. I shall be in my parlour."

With no further word, Miss Root departed. To Henry, there was a sense in the air of smoke and chaos. "What has possessed these people?" he said out loud. To clear his mind, he went into the hall. Here, at least, was relative silence and calm. The eerie shadows of the backstage made him think all of a sudden of Samuel Cake. He placed his hands behind his back and paced, refusing all the while to ponder the man's death any longer. He forced his imagination to wander over a multitude of possibilities for the panto's ending. Perhaps, he thought, a fantastic chorus of peacocks, young chorus girls in feathers, dancing as if...but the idea suddenly grew stale. He smacked his palms to clear his thoughts.

On returning to the stage manager's chamber, he sat down at the desk. He folded up the contracts. He sighed. A tense moment held him in suspense. Much to his great distress, he then began to weep without hesitation. He gasped at the flow of feeling. What has come over *me*, he wondered. His fingers turned to ice. He gazed at their trembling. Once again the words *finally, finally* startled his composure like a crack of sudden thunder. Now his hands were shaking.

He clasped them. He heard himself say, "Oh, God."

In horror, he then realized his hands were held as if they were praying for forgiveness.

*   *   *

Reggie Crabb could not stop thinking about his stomach, no matter how hard he tried. One of the ravens—the one holding the cheroot and wearing the gold links in her shirt—had told him to sit on the sofa and be content with the bit of bitter cheese she had handed him from a plate brought in for Miss Root. *Lor' bless me*, he thought, but this skimpy corner of cheese did not fill his ache for the moment.

The clock chimed five. Miss Root was standing by the sofa, as was a woman in a green hat with hemming pins held in her hand.

"There you are, milady," said the woman in green.

"Thank you, Mrs. Edge," said Miss Root, her voice hoarse. "It must be perfect, you understand. For private use, you must know."

Mrs. Edge stepped back, taking up a pin cushion. She surveyed the fall of the blue silk in the dressing mirror, the folds and the fine puffed sleeves.

"It shall do, Miss Root. Splendidly so, if I may add."

Mrs. Edge smiled. She lifted off the cut of the new dress. Priscilla Root pulled in her arms, shut her eyes. Silk slipped up and over her shoulders. It teased her with its thin whispery sound. A yawn then broke over the actress's face.

"Will you come with me, my sweet Crabb?" she cooed to Reggie. Reggie liked it when she asked him, as if he would ever say no.

He stood at attention with cap in hand. "To your place, in Soho?" he asked.

"You are too curious, my boy. But yes. For an hour. I need to calm myself."

The raven puffed out a cloud of smoke and laughed. "I shall be off, then, sister dear."

Shortly thereafter, in raucous Soho Square, Miss Root and Reggie Crabb stepped down from a hackney and walked to the weather-beaten door of Balham and Brothers, Fine Tobaccos. She tapped the brass knocker two hard raps. It seemed that at this hour, the London afternoon was at its noisiest. Soho Square was a village unto itself, market barrels and shops, taverns and stalls and private doors busy with customers and children shouting. In a moment, sooner than he expected, Reggie saw the door of Balham and Brothers slide open. A ghost-like voice from behind enquired as to who was calling at such a cold hour.

"Rachel."

Quick laughter was the response to Miss Root's greeting. The door flung open, as if on its own; Reggie grinned at the short man who greeted them. To Reggie, this little servant resembled a goblin. "Onward," whispered Miss Root. The goblin motioned them in and slammed the door; he turned, and as always, chucked Reggie on the chin. When the three moved along at last, Miss Root took hold of Reggie's hand. Between her and the goblin, Reggie entered a corridor lit by a smutty lantern, its smoke causing the goblin to cough. In turn, the corridor opened onto a large room—like a courtyard—where branching off it were two more halls, one leading into an unventilated antechamber reeking with incense and stale perfume. Reggie could scarcely take in breath. At last, the three came upon a chamber full of cushions and more lanterns, these of a brass kind punctured with patterns, out of which burned a lazy light.

Miss Priscilla Root pulled off her bonnet and pointed to Reggie to sit down. "You remember this venue, my boy?" Miss Root smiled and kicked off her shoes. She lowered herself slowly onto the cushions next to a small glass lamp. "Come, plump my pillow."

Reggie climbed over the folds of the divan. He had never felt such a soft bed before. At the theatre, he slept on a hard pallet by the scene docks. Every day, he was up at five building the fires in the stage manager's chamber and in Miss Root's parlour. Balham and Brothers was a royal palace, carpets over thick floors, windows with lattice.

Reggie punched the pillow, and Miss Root lay back.

"Only one this afternoon. And some hot water, if you please."

The goblin tapped his nose. His bony hand soon found the

inner lining of the actress's coat, which Miss Root had dropped to the floor. In the pocket he retrieved a pound note.

"Then at six o'clock, a chaise to the door, prompt. My boy Crabb shall watch over me."

Like a sigh, the goblin swept from the room. Miss Root began with the clasps on her bodice, then took out the hair pins by her braid. Reggie took each pin and carefully tucked it into his waistcoat pocket. When the door opened again, the goblin entered, carrying a pipe and a small box. A Hindoo woman in a veil walked beside him, holding a basin of steamy water and a basket of sponges. The man opened the box, took out small pieces of fragrant brown chunks and stuffed them into the pipe. With his free hand, he sheltered a taper. Miss Root cradled the pipe in her palm and inhaled deeply. Steam floated into the curl of perfumed smoke.

"Oh, Crabb," she said and tumbled backward onto a cushion. She rolled her famous eyes and laughed. The goblin and the Hindoo disappeared without a footfall. Miss Root took another long draw.

"How cruel I was. I have wept and wept, Crabb." Miss Root laughed for a long time, then quieted herself. "Love is a bitter drink, Crabb. Never forget that bit of wisdom."

Reggie was transported by the perfumy smoke. He gazed on Miss Root until his eyelids drooped. After a dreamy while, he sat up with a start.

A tall gentleman, silent, stiff, clothed in smooth fur and black wool, stood before him.

"Missus, missus," Reggie cried.

Miss Root awoke, rubbing her eyes. Her voice turned to ice. "Go, Crabb, to the chair by the door."

The tall gentleman stepped aside for Reggie to rise. In the lantern light, Reggie now saw the man's high cheeks. His oily hair was long, with side curls, and it glistened like hard wax. Around his neck he wore a twisted yellow cravat. Black gloves encased his thin hands; in them was a packet wrapped in brown paper. "Shoo, pup," he said.

Reggie dashed from the divan and cowered in a musty corner.

His eyes never left Miss Root. She sat up and brushed back her hair. She shuffled to her coat and lifted out a purse, a small wrinkled fold of cloth.

"Crabb, eyes lower," she said, her voice now stinging like a birch rod.

The smell of the lamp hovered sour in the red air. By the bed, Crabb cheated and saw the two figures, one tall and frightening, the other white, delicate, fishing into her purse, handing out a folded note. Yet it was not the tall man's size Crabb worried about; rather it was Miss Root's desperate struggle, full of bewildered sighs. Standing fast so there would be no cause for alarm, Crabb finally shut his eyes. "I cannot see," he whispered.

"Will this do?" asked Miss Root. Her words were spoken without fear.

"Yes, it has your name." The oily gentleman spoke in a flat manner.

"Oh, mercy," Miss Root said.

"I have done what you wanted done," the man then said, his voice lowered to a half whisper. "Done to your wishes. He will not complain any more."

"No doubt," said Miss Root.

"And this boy?"

"Mute. And none of your concern."

"I was not in mind of any threat from him."

"I beg your pardon. What time is it? What o'clock?"

"Near to six."

"I beg you not to come to this room ever again."

"A hansom cab is outside for you. Your factotum told me as much."

Reggie heard footsteps leave the room, a door close, a sigh from Miss Root. When he turned back to see her, alone and shivering on the divan, he watched Miss Root place the wrapped packet into one of her huge pockets. How curious, Reggie thought, as his legs hurried him across the room toward her. The packet held the same shape as a bunch of pound notes. It folded so easily in her hand—but no, this was not his concern. Miss Root was safe, and that was what mattered.

"My hairpins? Where are my hairpins?"

Reggie stepped closer, fully awake, jolted into action.

"Ah, my poor little fish. Dry your eyes. There, there. Now where are my hairpins? Hurry, hurry, goodly boy." Reggie wiped his nose. He pulled out each pin, one by one from his waistcoat pocket, to let Miss Root take every thin point in her pale fingers.

"You must not tell anyone about our visitor, you hear me."

"Yes, missus."

"Especially my sister. Especially her."

Crabb said yes. Yes, most of all. For he knew from that moment on that he, Reggie Crabb, had been granted a secret. He would remain silent to his grave. He would allow his fretful mind to regard the gentleman in the yellow cravat as no more than a dream. Standing, he led Miss Root to the door where the goblin waited, his finger pointed to a distant open door where a hansom cab was waiting.

*   *   *

"Mr. Dupré, sir."

"Am I late, Crabb?"

"Beg pardon, sir. They are waiting."

"Right away, then."

Young Reggie Crabb put his cap back on. As he stepped forward to hold the door for his master, he looked toward the laughing cave mouth where the stage manager stood explaining to Mr. Dupré the need for a new brace. From the scowl on his face, the stage manager was not pleased to have young Crabb's interruption. Dupré held a script in his right hand; he patted his hair and walked briskly toward the door of the scene room. Canvas pillars protruded from the bins. The laughing cave mouth was but paint and wood. Indeed, to Reggie, the scene room resembled a scrap cupboard full of leftover scenes—columns from Shakespeare, trees from the melodramas, all kinds of castle turrets, cottage thatches, archways, vistas of the sea and mountain passes.

Holes from years of use allowed bits of late afternoon light to shine through the canvas backdrops.

"Go. Lead the way," Dupré now commanded.

Young Reggie Crabb dashed down the first two flights from the scene room, down past the realms of the upper stage with its ropes, pulleys, hanging scenery, then further on toward the stage floor and the corridors leading to the offices and rehearsal hall. He thought, *but the master must hurry. The gals and chaps are waiting. Especially the young ones, the little fresh ones all wanting to be stagers.* Reggie had seen their like before, yearning types, all wanting to be like Miss Root or Mr. Weston.

"Onward, lad."

Reggie Crabb skipped toward the large common Green Room. He pulled open the door. Hartley, the stage-door keeper cried, "At last." All the others stood and parted a way for Mr. Dupré, who slowed his pace to an amble and ended up at a large table beside the piano lady. The clock struck six. The piano lady curtsied to Dupré, and as he sat, she banged out a loud chord on the tinny pianoforte. Hartley rose to call out the first names. At first, Crabb thought the try-out crowd was like a ragged army—like the supernumeraries he saw every evening in *Rachel*—the bodies in rows, arms raised, then the voices singing, the feet jumping. Mr. Dupré shouted out orders like a general. Old Hartley scribbled down names, crossed out others. *Lor bless me,* thought Crabb, *but there's the pretty one, a thin one in a nankeen bonnet.* Who was she, pretty girl, with rough hands and blue eyes and a face like a fresh flower? Mr. Dupré clapped his hands. The army lined up, catching its breath, heads forward. Mr. Dupré began his inspection, walking now up and down with Hartley beside him, faces examined, heights measured. Presently, Mr. Dupré stopped in front of the pretty girl in the nankeen bonnet.

"Your name?" he asked.

"Betty Loxton, your grace."

"Have you performed before?" wondered Dupré. The master's eyes were held on Betty's face.

"Nights at the Gaff, sire, near St. Paul's. I do a 'pipe as well as any. I can sing 'Clari', and..."

"Thank you, miss," said Dupré. "Stand aside."

The young gal dropped her head. She stepped out of the line, brushed down her skirt, and as she walked to the far end of the room, Reggie could see how disappointment bent her shoulders. Mr. Dupré meandered through the rest, tapping some on the shoulder, dismissing others to stand aside. Hartley walked behind him, holding the book of names, and Crabb handed the old man the quill pen to dip in the portable ink well and cross out the names of those not wanted. Dupré examined everyone quickly a second time, but Reggie noticed his master kept flashing his eyes toward Betty Loxton. When Hartley had noted all the successful hirelings, he proclaimed the audition finished. Then with gentle glee, the old man related to the piano lady the names of those who would sing and dance. Dupré returned to the table. The stage-door keeper marshalled the beaming faces, handed them song sheets, and the piano lady struck up an arpeggio wherewith the chorus began, a burst of sound filling the cracks of the very ceiling.

Betty Loxton was about to join the unsuccessful ones leaving the Green Room when Mr. Dupré signalled to her to wait. He strolled over to her, straightened the fall of his frock coat and before he spoke, he raised his chin, and with an elegant, quick gesture, patted his henna-brown hair.

"Crabb," he called out. "Come and take Miss Loxton to Mrs. B. in wardrobe."

Young Crabb pulled on his cap. The pretty-faced Betty stood amazed. She held her mouth open at the master's command and did not look him in the eye as Dupré slowly walked around her, his hand on his chin, his eyes hawklike in their peering at her torso, her ivory-coloured skin. His eyes went up and down her figure a second time; his hand brushed back a loose lock on her forehead.

"Take off your bonnet, dear miss," said Dupré. Betty smiled and undid the frayed ribbons. Her hair fell out in a tumble. "Very nice," said Dupré. "You like the theatre, do you?"

Betty curtsied. "I do, your grace. I am not afraid of being on the board. I have a full voice."

"So I heard this afternoon. But for the part I have for you, you must be very brave."

"Why so, sire?"

Betty's tight mouth betrayed her rising fear of Dupré's offer, and so acute were her trembling hands that young Crabb wanted to take hold of them and tenderly stroke them.

"Can you climb stairs, young miss?" asked Dupré.

"But of course, sire. I can indeed," she boasted.

"Do you like being up high?"

"How do you mean?"

"In a tree, say, or high on a roof?"

"I never been to one or t'other, sire, but I show no fear of such, if that's what you're after."

"I am, pretty miss. I shall help you, be assured."

"Thank you, sire."

"Why do you look so sad, pretty flower?" Dupré took hold of Betty's hand. He held it close for a second then let it drop.

"'Tis nothing, your grace."

"I see a tear, do I?"

"No, sire. It is the dust only."

"You are a good lass," Dupré said. "Four shillings for your trouble. And you shall work from Boxing Night until the New Year's Eve. Six days, plus four rehearsals. An extra shilling for a bonus, if you are on time and a good girl."

"I am a good girl, sire. A good strong girl."

"Yes, I can see you are," smiled Dupré.

Crabb took hold of Betty's hand.

"That's it Crabb, to wardrobe. Have her measured. Then bring her up to the fly loft. And get her a harness."

"Yes, sir. Post-haste."

Down the stairs to the costume room, Betty stopped Crabb. "Crabb is your name?"

"Reggie, call-boy. I am but fourteen."

"So you are, sweet boy. I am the same year as you."

"Careful, Betty. These stairs are steep. Don't tumble on your crown."

"I am not a fool, Reggie-boy. Look."

Betty grabbed hold of the thin banister and mounted it. She slid down fast to the wooden floor, landing with a thump. "See," she laughed. She pulled up her skirt, tucked it, did a hand stand, kicking her legs. "I do this at the Gaff. Come along one time. Come and see me fly about."

"I shall, miss. For sure, I shall, Miss Betty."

*   *   *

One half hour later, Betty Loxton was strapped into a thick leather harness waiting in trepidation for the set-up of the flying contraption. A few moments later, Henry Robertson Dupré appeared in the fly loft. "Do not vex yourself," she kept whispering to herself. "This time you shall be brave. You shall impress the sire, show him you are strong." The stage manager blew his whistle. Mr. Dupré raised up his head to watch. Two pulleys attached to a metal track clicked and rattled their way toward Betty. The pulleys held two wires and clips, and its weight was counterbalanced in the offstage by a huge sandbag. Young Crabb stood beside Betty, holding her hand. She shut her eyes. The stage manager approached her and attached the wires to the back of her harness. "Ready then," he shouted to his men below and blew two short blasts.

"Careful," advised Mr. Dupré. "Now slowly let her go down and track across the entire width of the stage and then back up, over on stage right. Give her flight a slight wave action."

The stage manager blew his whistle two more times, and the men below began cranking a drum wheel while pulling on a large rope. Above Betty, another man leaned over a narrow bridge and guided the pulleys. With a slight tug at her body, Betty Loxton rose into the air. The wires jiggled, but she was strong enough and the machine so balanced that she moved as lightly as a bit of fluff. Her feet dangled. She clenched her teeth, and when she began to slowly descend, she suddenly smiled and began to wave her arms. "I'm not afraid, sire. Look, you see," she yelled back to Mr. Dupré.

"Point your toes, Betty miss," Dupré shouted.

Betty's young body floated down into the open space of the stage between the tall flats set for the evening's farce, the wires stalwart in their bearing. From the sidelines, she looked delicate, lighter than down, her body swaying gently as the wires carried her sideways, then up through the dust-motes and the flickering yellow pall from the battens of gaslight. Her flying movement was so breezy, in fact, that Dupré himself broke into applause. "Well done. Smooth as a lark on the wing."

Up she came to the fly loft soon after, her body more relaxed. Young Crabb bolted along the loft bridge to greet her on the far side of the stage.

"My good girl, you have inspired me," cried Dupré dashing up to her. From the way his hands came out to her, it seemed Mr. Dupré wanted to take young Betty in his arms and express his appreciation and his affection for her first attempt. "This waif shall play a fairy in the last two scenes, a muse to Mr. Weston's brooding beast," Dupré announced to the stage manager and his crew, his voice jubilant.

"As you see fit, sir," obeyed the stage manager, his usual huffing and puffing under every syllable. "Crabb!" Dupré shouted. "Tell young Betty to come to me at the run-through."

Dupré pulled down the corners of his waistcoat. He would order a late supper for the two of them. A quick supper. Lovely young Betty would take a bath beforehand, then Mrs. B. could bring her upstairs to the attic office, the one with the desk, the French mirror and the damask-covered *chaise longue*. Henry knew he must write her part by midnight, driven by his inspiration to see her again. He must finish it and send it out to the copyist before dawn.

Leaving the fly loft, he ran down four flights of stairs and practically skipped with joy into the rehearsal hall, where the cast for the pantomime was gathered for the first "walk-through" of all the speaking and the action. As Henry arrived, flushed with excitement, he saw Miss Root in her large skirt and wig looking somewhat fatigued and languid in her stance.

"Are you not feeling better, Miss Root?" he enquired,

not really hearing her mumbled response.

The stage-door keeper came up to him and tapped Henry on the shoulder, prompting him to jump back. "I ask you, Hartley, not to startle me like that."

"I beg your pardon, sir. I have a delay, sir."

"A delay? Whatever do you mean?"

"Mr. Weston has sent word. Illness, sir, has delayed his coming to the rehearsal."

"His own or that of his tiresome sister?"

"He did not say, sir."

"No, I am certain he did not. We have but a half hour to run through before the dinner break. Kindly begin without him then. Posthaste, sir, if you can manage it."

"At once, Mr. Dupré."

The actors took their places where the floor was marked with lines and squares drawn in chalk. Henry and the dancing master read out the moves from the promptbook, and the actors and chorus began reading lines from their folios and moving according to the shouted directions of Henry and his assistant.

"Faster, faster," Henry shouted at the stumbling daughters of the count. Miss Root sang her first song off-key, and Henry delighted in his chance to admonish her. "It was only a D-flat, Henry," she snapped at him, and sang the song again in perfect pitch. The dancing master was in the middle of revising steps for the peasant chorus when Betty Loxton entered the room and took a seat by the door. Following close behind her stumbled Mr. Weston. The great actor's face was white as snow; his hat was off, and his overcoat with the fur collar was unbuttoned. The room came to a halt. Henry stood up from his chair, his hands on his hips.

"Mr. Weston, I must congratulate you. You not only have found us—finally—but you have managed to put on the finest display of a tipsy Irishman west of the Lyceum. Unfortunately, Mr. Weston, you are playing a noble beast this season, not a drunk."

Mr. Weston collided against one of the chairs. "I beg your pardon, sir," he slurred.

The stage-door keeper dashed up to Mr. Weston. He whispered frantically into his ear. Weston shoved him aside. "Nonsense, I can perform my duties quite sufficiently."

"Take your places again, please," commanded Dupré. "Do hurry along, Mr. Weston."

The chorus formed a circle; Miss Root stood with her arms at her sides; Mr. Weston took one step and fell to the floor.

"For God's sake, Weston," Dupré shouted amidst the gasps and astonished glares of the cast.

"Henry, he seems ill," said Miss Root.

"Careless and mad, more likely," retorted Dupré. "How is it possible to run the greatest theatre in London when I must contend with a leading player who comports himself no better than a gin shop fopling?"

A chill came into the air. Mr. Weston attempted to rise, yet even with the arm of Hartley to aid him, he was too dizzy to stand. "I beg...your leave," he said. Hartley crooked his finger, and two younger men from the chorus stepped forward to lead Weston from the room.

Dupré threw his script to the floor. "Damnation," he cried. He panned the amazed faces before him. He wanted to bark at Miss Root for defending Mr. Weston. Instead, he bent down, picked up his script and held it out from his body at an angle suggesting to the tense onlookers that he was holding a smelly cod. "Hartley, I give you leave to continue this wretched task. Run the chorus through. You read and walk Mr. Weston's part. I have work of a finer nature to do, upstairs. Good evening."

On his way out, Dupré sidled over to Betty Loxton and took hold of her cold hand. He stood close to her, "Well done today, miss. You shall be rewarded. See Mrs. B. in wardrobe after your walk-through about a late supper this evening." He touched her lightly on the cheek. The young girl curtsied, and her eyes shone. She was about to speak, but Dupré purposefully turned away, leaving her to anticipate the pleasures of the private dinner he would serve later in the evening.

*   *   *

A theatre manager leaving a rehearsal could consider
himself negligent, but Henry Robertson Dupré did not
care. He had slept little the night before, and his nerves
were jangling. When he returned to his attic office, he was
very much out of sorts, and he banged the door behind
him. A fury erupted in him, and he kicked the chair and
smashed a paperweight against the wall.

He became more agitated at his desk when his revision for
the fairy scene with Betty proved to be feeble on re-reading.
At the instant, he took to his chair and never once stopped
moving his quill until he had scratched out all the lines and
composed new ones. He rubbed his forehead as he re-wrote;
he shut out any noise from the street below, forcing himself to
read aloud the actions and new dialogue until they rang with
his doggerel poetry, until they sounded strong enough to sway
the fickle pit and galleries he had to please every night.

Of all things now, it was the spectre of failure that
frightened him most. "Pull it, send it back." Those terrible
words haunted him. Many times as a young playwright he
had heard them bawled from the balconies, only to
discover the next morning he was without a position in the
theatre. Now he was faced with Mr. Weston and his
unruliness. Whatever could have possessed the man to
sabotage his rehearsal in such a fashion? A piercing fear
bullied its way into Henry Robertson Dupré's conscience.
And what of the matter with Cake?

"Psst," came the voice from the open door. Henry
jumped. The inkwell tipped and spread its black pool over
his newly written words. "God, almighty." Henry grabbed
frantically for the blotter. Alas, his saving gesture arrived
too late—the fairy vision he'd created was already drowned
in India ink. He allowed himself to look back over his
shoulder to the door. He was sure it was stupid Hartley, and
he was ready to beat the man.

"Sire?"

Ah, Henry sighed, as his eyes welcomed the tumbled

hair, the sweet smile, the little waist. "Come in, come," he delighted.

For an answer, Betty Loxton curtsied and dashed up to him. Without provocation, she tossed her arms up to his neck and held him. She pulled back then, her face red. "Oh, your grace, please pardon me. I am so happy. I am so grateful." Her words floated away. In less than an eye blink, she began to weep and knelt to the floor, her hands covering her face.

"Rise, rise, sweet Betty," Henry smiled, his hands stroking hers, his inner self now inflamed.

He held her, took in the heady perfume of her thick hair. Her shoulders were strong and muscular under her cheap clothes. "I cannot help myself, sire," she moaned. "I am so happy." She was like a kitten eager to lap up milk set before its starving mouth. Dupré controlled himself, treating her with some aloofness, for it was not yet time for supper or the pleasures of the *chaise longue*. This temptation must wait awhile before it coaxed one to succumb. Reluctantly, he led quivering Betty Loxton down the many stairs into the deep basement of the theatre. "Rest here," he told her. He instructed the wardrobe mistress to prepare a bath and a cup of tea. Mrs. B. nodded but did not look into the eyes of her employer. She hastened to take hold of Betty's shoulders and steer her toward the hearth. Betty pulled away from Mrs. B.'s embrace and ran back to Dupré, where she whispered "thank you" in his ear, her hunger for his attention forcing her to smile coyly as she returned to the arms of Mrs. B.

"I shall come later to see how you are," Dupré said, his voice slightly higher than a whisper.

He knew he would be gentle with her, at first. He knew without turning back to watch her sit at the hearth he would relish the sound of her footsteps on the attic stairs, her footfall as enticing to him as the taste of the best brandy.

* * *

Time was pressing, even though the smells coming from

the kitchen calmed Owen Endersby enough to allow him to sit down, unfold his napkin and prepare himself for his supper. The aforesaid kitchen was but a narrow cupboard with a small window, a shallow cooking hearth and pantry cupboards. The hearth itself made him proud: in it was the latest iron invention he had purchased for his dear Harriet, a tight square box made of metal, its chimney wedged into the larger flue of the cooking fireplace. On its clanging top, one could place pots to warm, a kettle to boil; its iron belly held coals and embers in a mass of even warmth. Beyond this room, the rest of his humble flat lay in a square of small chambers—the bedroom, the narrow hall, the parlour not much wider than a refectory table, and last, as cozy as a four-poster, his study, crowded by a table and a sofa. Endersby loved his flat, as it was a haven for his mind and body, though this evening it was somewhat stifled by the heat from the cooking hearth and the pressure of a surprise his dear Harriet had prepared for him.

"Here she is," said Harriet, entering the parlour and approaching the dining table, an awkward young woman by her side. Miss Solange appeared to be a quiet woman, never looking Endersby in the eye as she was introduced. Harriet whispered: "She comes highly recommended by Mrs. Paige, whose cousin engaged her in the summer. The cousin left for New Zealand, and poor Solange was without a position. She can cook anything, in the French manner, of course. I thought you and I needed a little change."

Solange subsequently carried the tureen to the table. She was jumpy, her features cramped by her effort. Endersby felt glad knowing she'd been hired to work only in the evenings. The inspector raised his spoon in anticipation. A great slop of white liquid filled with fins and shiny membrane fell from the serving ladle into his bowl.

"Fish soup, *à la française*," chimed Harriet. "Go on, Owen. I tried a bowl in the kitchen. It is delicious."

Endersby proved to be a forbearing man. He ate the soup, then a duck pressed flat into a pancake, then a pot of boiled greens covered with a yellow sauce. He wiped his mouth, shook the new cook's hand, bussed his Harriet and informed her of his appointments for the evening; then, after a short visit to his wardrobe, he descended the stairs to Cursitor Street, wondering whether his food would sit well on the journey to the Coburg Theatre.

The streets across the river were frantic with crowds. Even on a Monday evening, the theatre attracted workers and weary clerks of the city to seek out some entertainment after their long hours of labour. Horses and carts clogged Waterloo Road. A red banner across the front of the Coburg announced the upcoming Christmas extravaganza. Endersby, in soiled cloak, broad hat and spectacles, bravely pushed past young men and women in clothes pungent from the market. He found the stage manager, who let him into the back foyer leading to the gallery stairs. "Beg pardon, sir. I hardly recognized you."

"That is a good thing, then," replied the inspector.

Endersby made the effort to remain as un-policeman-like as possible, given this rambunctious lot of mechanics, costermongers, clerks, lower hall servants and shopkeepers. His mind was preoccupied with the need to find out more about Mr. Cake. Why had Lord Harwood accepted this particular man, when there were other managers—at the Lyceum, the Adelphi, the Olympic, to name only three—who had more established reputations? Surely it was not because Cake was handy with coin? That he knew how to balance a book? A gift, perhaps, for attracting the public—such a thing would appeal to Harwood, even if it were only to amuse him as his coffers filled.

A zigzag staircase led to the gallery, the highest set of seats in the Coburg, a mass of benches crammed under the slope of the theatre's roof. Bodies crowded the narrow confines of the staircase. "Only threepenny a head," shouted the ticket seller. "Hold 'em up, get 'em ready." An echo filled the stairwell as arms reached out to pay a man stuffed into a little wicket by the upper turn leading to the gallery landing. A hat tumbled down over the heads of the mass. Owen could hardly turn to see it caught by a chap with a scruffy beard. "All right there, Charlie, I've got it." As he was shoved further up toward the gallery's entrance, Endersby noted the other motley spectators—lads from eleven to twenty mostly, a few black-faced chimney sweeps and smut-covered dustmen still in their overalls. Endersby guessed, too, at the stranger faces about him. At what he surmised were sellers of pastry, from the flour on their cuffs, the fried-fish hawker sporting his greasy front with blots of scales still hanging from his lapels. But who else, he wondered? The sellers of dogs, the fuzee merchants, the beetle wafer peddlars, the occasional warmly-dressed crossing sweeper? Who else indeed.

He soon found a place on one of the long wooden benches of the gallery. The warmth and smell of the Coburg at first made him woozy—might he bring up his *à la française* dinner in such a fetid atmosphere? Ham-sandwich men vied with sellers of porter, who walked back and forth by the lower railing. The place was nothing more than a heap of moving heads. Below, the proscenium opening had a bright canvas roll. When the drums beat out a tattoo, the gallery and the pit yelled in delight.

The canvas rolled up, and the stage shimmered with blue light. A huge plaster head rose through the centre trap door, and as it began to sing, there descended from the flies a host of young maidens sitting in armchairs—their flight as mechanically wondrous as if the gods themselves were floating to earth. The play was filled with fretting music, sudden scene changes, more flying machines, traps and effects of fire. A real waterfall like a cascade of silver, burst from a rock face concocted of beaten tin. "Lookit, lookit," were the words Endersby heard skimming through the vast sloping faces of the gallery. Applause was thunderous when the ghost of Jack Wilson, played by Mr. Percy Buckstone, floated up and *through* a ship made of luminous gauze. For a finale, the maidens rose in their chairs singing the praises of Jack the Tar, and in a second, canvas trees turned into clouds as paper birds fluttered into a painted sunset.

Owen Endersby let his hands pound out applause. What chaos of joy reigned in the Coburg. So, it was brilliant novelty which Cake proclaimed to his public. When the stage manager stepped before the curtain to ask permission for a repetition, the response was tumultuous. "Bring it on again," shouted the laughing voices. The stage manager raised his hand as if he were the Queen herself and silence fell. "Ladies and gentlemen, I beg your indulgence to remember our sadly departed manager, Mr. Cake." The solemn show of pity moved Endersby. "He was a jolly good man," shouted a lad from the pit.

After the performance, the stage manager led Endersby down a flight of steps and across a courtyard behind the theatre. There was a small workshop, its ceiling hung with levers, hooks and wire forms. A grease-slicked metal table ran the length of the room. Gregorious Barnwell wore a flattened cap. He was short, broad, covered in spots of oil, with thick eyebrows springing from his forehead.

"I cannot now. Please leave me be."

"I am sorry to hear of your loss, Mr. Barnwell," Endersby said.

"You are the police detective, are you? Fine job you've done. My brother Samuel killed right under your eyes."

"I much admired your work tonight, Mr. Barnwell." Endersby pushed on, knowing he must strike quickly in spite of resistance.

"Did you, sir? Did you?"

"Most marvellous visions, worthy of a great theatre."

"Bosh, sir. Worthy of a tinker only." Barnwell lifted a thin piece of metal from the forge. "My brother was an honourable man, sir. Not deserving his fate."

"Tell me, Mr. Barnwell, what scoundrel took such a disliking to him?"

"Some vicious fool." Barnwell took a hammer and banged at the glowing end of the metal.

"From what I have discovered in meeting his acquaintances—his professional colleagues—your Samuel Cake was highly respected."

"Hardly, sir, if one of them beat his bloody brains in." Gregorious Barnwell put down his hammer. He pulled out a handkerchief and wiped his nose. "That's enough, I can say no more."

Endersby walked up to Barnwell and put his arm on his shoulder. It was one of Endersby's ways with people, a way he had of giving comfort that was unexpected from a policeman. Barnwell jumped back. "I blame your kind, sir. Unhand me. These are cruel streets where a man like my Samuel can be beaten to death like a horse."

"Mr. Barnwell, I want to find the brute that killed your brother. I need to find him soon. Vindication is what we are both after, is it not?"

Barnwell replaced his handkerchief. He dragged a chair to the table and sat down.

"I have heard your brother purchased his fine house in Doughty Street not six months ago."

"Yes."

Endersby walked around the metal table. "I much admired it."

"How fortunate for you, sir," replied Barnwell. "I have never seen it."

"Indeed?"

"Never had an invite, you see. Nor the inclination."

"May I ask why?"

"Samuel bought the place to show off his profits. Like a prize pony. A bauble, he called it. He didn't live there but here in the theatre."

"Do you have other kin, sir? Others in your family who might have seen it—or wanted it?"

Barnwell sneered. He took a rag and wiped sweat from his forehead. "No kin, sir. Both of us born on the wrong side of the davenport, if you grasp my meaning. Same mam, different studs." Barnwell smirked, pinched his nose, then he stood up and waved the rag. "Please, it is late. I will not talk about this further."

Endersby hit the table with his fist. This gesture was also one of his tricks: make a noise, distract the man being questioned. "Your Samuel's murderer is enjoying a pint of porter right now, Mr. Barnwell. He may be spending some of your brother's hard-earned coin. Can you picture him in a public house, puffing out his chest?"

Barnwell reddened. "Enough," he shouted. "Leave me be."

"I cannot, sir. I cannot let a guilty man run free when a body is barely cold."

"You are as guilty as the scoundrel himself."

"Mr. Barnwell, I am an honest-speaking man. If we continue to dither, Samuel's killer will never see the doors of Newgate prison. I need to know things that can lead me to this devil."

"Fine words, Mr. Detective. But what I know is of no value."

"Do you know of Rosa Grisi and her brothers?"

"Fools all three. More foolish my Samuel for courting the villainous woman. More a man than a woman, I venture, from her coarse ways. Those brothers are not worth the dung they shovel at that circus."

"Did you ever meet them?"

"No, sir. I thank my Saviour for that. Samuel complained loudly enough so that I needn't see them."

"It is rumoured she stabbed a man once. In her native country."

"I am not surprised. Perhaps it was she, in fact, who killed my brother."

"For what reason, do you imagine?"

"Imagine? For money. For sport."

"And who would put the Grisi family up to such a scheme?"

"You think there is one other?"

"I do not know, Mr. Barnwell. But I have a name for you."

"A name?"

"Henry Robertson Dupré." Endersby had been considering the idea the moment he entered Barnwell's quarters: what if Dupré had hired the Grisi brothers and sister to perform a revenge plot—a house smashing, a head beating. "Is it possible that Dupré was jealous of your brother's good fortune? That he might have paid the Grisis to attack your brother's house as a way of threatening him for usurping his position at Old Drury?"

"I would not put any of this past Mr. Dupré. He was a

rival of Samuel's and despised him." Gregorious Barnwell spat out these last words in a fury of hatred.

"On Friday last, did you see your brother at all during the day?"

"We had a cup of tea together in the morning. Later, in the afternoon, I went with him over Waterloo Bridge and took a late drink with him at a tavern on the way to Old Drury."

"Did your brother mention he was meeting anyone at that particular hour?"

"My brother looked after his own affairs, sir. But yes, since he was now to be manager at Old Drury, courtesy of Lord Harwood, who owns the building. I thought he was meeting the Lord. Instead we both met with an actor, a tall pale man I am not familiar with—a tragic actor at Old Drury—and the two had a set-to in the tavern."

"Your brother and the actor fought?"

"With words only, sir. About a promissory note or two. I was not listening closely. The actor then waxed angry at Samuel. The tavern laughed at his temper, and my brother had the man thrown into the street."

"You do not remember this tall actor's name."

"No inspector, I was staring into my grog. Actors mean little to me."

"Your brother, Samuel, was not married, was he, Mr. Barnwell?"

"No," came the sullen answer.

"He had many young women in his life, did he not?"

"I do not know. I care not."

"He was in love with Miss Grisi, though, was he not?"

"I suppose. And with Miss Priscilla Root."

"The actress?"

"A few years back. Miss Root never forgave him for it."

"Matron tells me he was fond of the young women who worked for him."

"Kind to them, sir, and he never took advantage."

"Young Esther was her name. She was one, wasn't she?"

"Yes. And the little coster girl. A sweet bud. Little Betty."

"A coster girl?"

"She was eager to be in the theatre. Samuel hired her to play in *Jack Wilson*, one of the girls who floats up in the chairs in the prologue. But she fell out of the contraption one day. By accident. He lost his temper with her, and she ran away. Little Betty Loxton. She had a cruel brother, who came calling to take Samuel to task. John was his name. A big man."

Endersby glanced at his pocket watch. It was near eleven o'clock. Sergeant Caldwell was on alert at Aston's and was to follow the Grisi brothers and meet Miss Rosa Grisi. Endersby decided to venture one last question.

"You and Samuel got along well, did you not?"

Barnwell's face darkened. "I loved him, Mr. Detective."

"Did you envy him, too?"

"What do you mean, you scoundrel?"

"He had a fine house. He was handsome. Young women trailed after him. Are you married, by chance, Mr. Barnwell?" Endersby felt a tinge of panic. He was daring to push this man who could, in a trice, smash his head in anger with one of his metal pokers.

"I am not, sir. I was never jealous of Samuel, if that is what you are after."

"But you say you never had the inclination to see his house. Surely, of all people, he would have wanted you to do so."

"No, sir. He did not. He was ashamed of my appearance."

"Why?" Endersby sharpened his attention.

"He wanted the place to be a dream house. Only gentry allowed. He said I would not like it there, it being so big and empty. He said I would laugh at it, and I would look like a servant in it. Do not embarrass yourself, brother, he said. You will think me more the fool."

"Curious," remarked Endersby.

"He gave me this workplace, this forge to let me make my machines. He said that was the only valuable thing he really owned in his life."

Endersby thought about these last words. He thrust his hands into his pockets. The air was growing cold in the room as the fire died down. "Good night, sir," he then said. "Can you tell me where I might find the young coster girl?"

"She is an innocent in this matter."

"In Covent Garden, the New Cut?"

"Near the Garden, sir. By Longacre, I believe."

"I bid you good night."

Endersby thanked the stage manager, who was waiting in the courtyard, and walked out toward the street. By the time he reached Aston's, a light fog had settled.

"Good evening," he said to the stage-door keeper at the entrance.

"No more half-price," came the quick answer. The man was the same one Endersby had questioned earlier in the day. He was sleepy looking and did not recognize him. Endersby walked around the outside of the theatre hoping to find Caldwell, the streets echoing with late walkers and horses being led across cobble stones.

"Caldwell?" he shouted. Endersby rattled the stage door. He leaned his ear to the stable's gate, but there were no sounds of men working. He then moved on, walking to the entrance to Waterloo Bridge, where he spent a few harried moments trying to find a hansom cab. When he finally hailed one, the driver was caustic and rude. Endersby sat back in the swaying coach and ran over the details he had gathered from Gregorious Barnwell. He tried to forego mixing supposition with fact. He harnessed his desire to dramatize the event of the murder. In fact, he forced his thoughts *not* to consider Dupré as the villain of his piece, as a cruel Nemesis, exacting punishment on the innocent Cake. Yet the idea kept rearing up, festooned with those stupendous images from Barnwell's machine play which he had witnessed but an hour before. *Patience,* he cautioned himself. *Do not let this habit mar your judgement.*

* * *

Endersby stepped down at Number 6 Cursitor Street at the precise moment his pocket watch showed both tiny hands at twelve. Harriet was asleep in her bed, and the smell of fish soup lingered. He went to his table by the window and examined the evidence he had amassed thus far. The mud samples, the glove, the promissory note from P. Summers were all he'd gathered. The beadle would deliver Cake's clothes tomorrow. But what else did he have? He needed hard evidence and a confession if he wanted a conviction. Ignorance or careless memory had served him meagre fare for drawing conclusions. Were the Grisi family his only possible suspects? He had yet to meet Dupré, and rumour had a way of warping the truth. And what about the coster girl and her threatening brother? And the relations with Miss Root? Let alone the figure from the opera, the woman named Elisabetta Mazzini. She bore consideration without doubt. Someone in this teeming city had done the heinous act.

He gazed at the clock again. The day was out, and Superintendent Borne had not been given what he wanted.

Owen took a bath. He carried a glass of Spanish port into his room and sat down before the wooden puzzle on the table. Trees and water were the only full pictures he had been able to fit together with certainty. The pieces were well designed to mislead even a practiced hand. He picked up an odd-shaped section, a triangular mass. Was it a gun barrel or a bent ankle? How many human figures were in this landscape-to-be? Owen worked for an hour until he found his eyes squinting, his gouty foot beginning to pang even more dramatically. He tiptoed into Harriet's room, placing his candle on the table next to the bed. The room remained dark except for the pool of light beside the half-drawn bed curtains. Harriet lay in her cap. The pillow cradled her calm face.

Owen crawled close to her, careful not to ruffle the bedcovers, cautious in his tenderness not to wake her. Lying down beside her, he felt much more at ease. He recalled the first time he'd met his beloved Harriet. The set of rooms was on the second floor of a house in Hart Lane. Endersby's youthful self, with his curly brown hair, had seen before him in the party crowd the face of the girl he'd spotted two nights before at Old Drury. "Her father runs a small printing press near the City," said the uncle. Harriet Beaken came toward Endersby. She curtsied and asked him if he'd care to place his name on her dance card. "Rather," he replied, "will you allow me to jump the queue and dance with you now? See, the fiddler has come, and the lines are forming."

It was Harriet's laugh, very quick and warm, then her dropping of the card book into her evening bag that enchanted him. "Such boldness in a man purported to be so shy," she said, taking his hand and following him into the first dance.

Endersby smiled now at the recollection. He felt ready to let her gentle breathing lead him into sleep in spite of his worry that the next morning might bring recriminations, or worse.

*   *   *

Each second, along with every step, Betty Loxton feared for her back. Down Drury Lane to the corner of Longacre, along the pavement past shops, bins, shut doors. Then at home, the doorway to her family's upper flat guarded by the drunken doorkeeper. "Get along, if thou can," spat the foul-breathed creature. A step into the damp hall where John the Pawn was waiting.

"Give it me," he said from the shadows. She handed him her empty basket and her empty purse. "Where have you been?" His voice promised a beating.

Betty lied: "To the City and back, and was robbed." John the Pawn's hand struck hard. She slapped her palm on the splintered floor to break her fall.

"Bring the pennies tomorrow. Steal them, if you must."

John the Pawn shoved her back out, slammed the door and slid the bolt. No matter how hard Betty pounded, no matter how loudly she shouted, no light came on, no sister's footsteps sounded on the inner staircase.

Betty ran alone down Longacre, turned into James Passage, entered the open court of Covent Garden. Dogs roamed the arcade, sniffing for scraps. Betty scurried under a barrow and pulled an oily sheet to cover her head. She lay down on her throbbing shoulder and smelled cabbage and horse dung. She ran her fingertips over her lips; her insides ached from fear. But then she recalled her afternoon in the harness and her soft magical flight across the width of Old Drury's stage. What a good warm supper it was afterwards, and of course Mr. Dupré's sweet words: "I adore you, little Betty." Indeed, she was now a favoured one. Oh, how nice it was to have a hot bath. Oh, how she had trembled on her flight up to Mr. Dupré's private room under the roof of the great theatre. Yes, she was afraid at first of his way with her on the long sofa, his slow approach to her as the evening wore on, his stroking and kissing and finally, oh, yes, finally his violent thrusting and his cry. But all this meant she was forever special to him. Her tears fell hard. He had hurt her, held her too hard, but that was a man's way. She was used to hurt. And she knew too well love can hurt as much as it can soothe. Tears slowly gave way to a secret smile which warmed Betty's cold face.

Presently rain was pelting the pavement, and shivers from the night's damp shook even Betty's toes. A sigh of wind flapped the canvas awnings in the court, and a stench of rotting meat hovered over the oily sheet and wrinkled Betty's nose. Many feelings had run through her mind, most of them joyous, most of them about Mr. Dupré, his long eyelashes, pudgy belly, halting breath. *But you shall be fine,* Betty said to herself. *You have shillings in your pocket, hidden deep down so John the Pawn cannot take them.* Although she knew her family needed her, she was useless to them unless she brought them money. The cold piercing her skin made her life seem momentarily hopeless. But with another smile, she chased away her fear. "I now have what I want," she whispered to the street. "It is not as if I shall starve. *Not I.*"

Chapter Five

TUESDAY, DECEMBER 22, 1840

Owen Endersby rose at six o'clock in the morning to a deep grey light. Fog pressed against the windows. He dressed alone and in silence, choosing a black patterned waistcoat. His head ached, and he feared the gout would punish him even more today. Later, after his ample breakfast, as he rode along in the cab to the station in Fleet Lane, he wondered what surprises would face him in the coming hours, three days before Christmas.

"At last you are here, sir." The admittance sergeant opened a second door into the superintendent's private parlour where a fire was burning high. "He was found near the river, sir, by a couple of scavengers. They took his wallet and coin but were Christian enough to report his whereabouts to a night watchman."

Sergeant Caldwell lay on the sofa. His right eye was shut tight in a bulge of purple skin. A bloody bubble oozed from his lower lip. Scratches under dirt smudges covered his cheeks. The sergeant at hand dabbed his mouth with a cloth dipped in white vinegar. Caldwell lifted up his swollen left hand. He managed to say two pain-filled words: "Grisi brothers."

Endersby scanned the stifling room and began to pace. Everything he had been thinking about the Grisi family was proving right. They were violent, unpredictable, lawless. Such evidence as Caldwell's face convinced him that action must be taken immediately. Beating an officer of the Metropolitan Detective Force was a crime punishable by imprisonment. Witnesses would have to be found. That would be the greatest hurdle. The London public in some quarters remained wary of the police, fearful that many were as corrupt as the old Bow Street Runners. Plain clothes policemen, the Runners had worked on commission as felon-catchers, caring only for the money they were able to obtain. Justice to them had always come second.

Disagreeable as these thoughts were, Endersby admired his sergeant's courage. Would Superintendent Borne deem this attack worthy of investigation? What if no witnesses could testify to the Grisis' actions? Borne despised publicity. He respected his sergeants, but occasionally he would back down from defending their honour and safety if he sniffed a scandal.

The door to the parlour opened, and Superintendent Borne rushed in. This morning his frock coat hung loose on his right shoulder, his trousers had one leg tighter than the other. "Disgraceful," was his opening salvo.

"Yes, sir," replied Endersby, battle nerves readied. Borne pranced toward the hearth. His shiny boots caught Endersby's eye. They were new and too big, and their stiff squeak distracted him.

"We have a calamity, Mr. Borne," Endersby said. "I shall deal with it this morning."

"Deal?" snorted Borne.

"I shall need assistance, at least two men. And a pre-signed warrant."

Borne, not to be outranked, waved his hand in a dismissive action. Endersby anticipated a pompous speech to sally forth. "Quite," was the first word. Then the voice turned decisive. "You shall have all. And without delay."

Borne made an about-face, marched across the room to shake Caldwell's free hand and mumbled a few official words of encouragement. At the door in three paces he called out: "Stott and Birken. Now, on the double."

Sergeant Caldwell managed to tell what he could remember. Endersby gathered his two-man force and assured Caldwell the culprits would regret their actions. Stott was large, burly and square. Birken stood six feet, was similar in build, but wore a beard on his chin. "Gentlemen," said Endersby, "look on your fellow sergeant and remember."

Endersby thrust the warrant into his pocket. He watched Stott and Birken strap their official police batons inside their long-coats. As soon as they hired a cab, it took only six streets and a number of turns before the Thames appeared under them. Crossing Waterloo Bridge, the cab drove south to Aston's Palladium. The sky remained low although the fog was thinning. Inside Aston's foyer, Inspector Endersby heard only the echo of his boots on the paving stones. The pay-box master was hunted down and taken into a small room. Birken nudged him with a bulky elbow to sit. Endersby enquired politely but firmly as to the whereabouts of the Grisi brothers. Shrugs came forth as answers. Endersby haltered his bucking anger, found his way around the pay-box master's chair and from behind, leaned over the trembling man. "I shall not ask you a second time, my fellow. Murder, let alone assault, shall be at your doorstep. Your reputation will not recover quickly if you must spend a grimy holiday in the outer court of Newgate."

"I am at a loss," peeped the shivering man.

"You shall be at a greater one, without doubt." Endersby's hand flew out before he could stop it. His fingers grasped the man's shoulder and with a force surprisingly brisk rattled the pay-box master as if he were a stick puppet. "Now, sir," Endersby started again, "perhaps you could convince me to find the cousin, the chap with the fur cloak. Might he know where the two miscreants have fled?"

"He takes his breakfast at the tavern nearby, The Swan and Reed."

"And Miss Rosa Grisi?"

The pay-box master shuffled his feet. "I beg of you. I truly do not know where she is. Her cousin, the agent you speak of—Signor Fieno—has never divulged to me her lodging place. He says she demands it be kept a secret. And indeed, sir, last night we had great cause to demand where she lives."

"You had cause?"

"You see, the woman did not appear for her performance.

We had to replace her ride at the last minute. I can assure you, our patrons were most displeased."

"And the reason?" Endersby tossed a glance to Stott, who puckered his mouth.

"Signor Fieno announced his star rider was indisposed and begged the patrons to show pity for her. The audience jeered him...so, we were at a great loss." The man retreated into a silent pout. No doubt there was something amiss. But was it an indisposition or a ruse to shelter guilty men? Endersby nodded to his two men-at-arms. Stott and Birken brushed by the pay-box master, with Endersby close behind. Out into the air they marched together, a solid line of three bulky men, words between them scarce, their arms swinging to make up for the solemn silence of their company.

The Swan and Reed was painted blue, and it held a straggling number of mechanics taking porter with their cheese. One of the booths near the back presented an elegant man lifting a knife and fork. Before him were a glass, a wine bottle and a plate of cooked ham. The man wore a fur cloak, and his black hair had been neatly combed. A small pistol gleamed conspicuously in his lap.

"Ah, Signor Fieno."

The man looked up, startled. He reached for the pistol. Endersby shoved his bulk hard against Fieno's arm, and the pistol clattered to the floor. Stott came around the left side of Endersby and lifted the Italian cousin by his shoulders, dragging him quickly out the side door into a narrow lane.

Birken grabbed the pistol then clapped his hands. "Gentlemen," he cautioned the other customers, "enjoy your vittles in peace. Mind your own business, if you know what's best."

Just past the laneway was a small court strung with washing. Stott slammed Fieno up against the brick wall. The beleaguered man's fur cloak slipped off his shoulders to reveal a fine silk frock coat and a large bulge in his upper pocket. Signor Fieno clutched the bulge, but Endersby patiently pried away the man's hand, reached into the inside pocket and extracted a short leather cudgel. Turning it about,

Endersby noted its fine sheath and concluded it was not of English manufacture. He stepped back. He allowed Birken to pat Fieno's waist and legs in a rough examination for other weapons.

"I beg your pardon, Mr. Fieno. My sergeants tend to work somewhat quickly. If they are injurious to your person, do not hesitate to let me know. Your two young cousins, the Grisi chaps—I did not catch their first names—are well acquainted with pummelling."

Signor Fieno did not move.

"Silent, are we, Mr. Fieno? Let me refresh your knowledge of English manners. Beating a public officer of the law is punishable with exile, certainly flogging." Endersby held up the arrest warrant. It contained only the Grisi brothers last names, but he decided to risk a ploy.

"I have here a warrant for your arrest and that of Miss Rosa Grisi."

Still Fieno did not speak.

"The charges, you ask?" Endersby said. He touched Stott on the shoulder, and the young sergeant tightened his grip. Birken was directed to lean closer to Fieno, where he breathed nonchalantly on the man's left cheek.

"The charges are straightforward enough. You, for beating and subduing one Sergeant Caldwell. Miss Rosa Grisi for the suspected murder of Mr. Samuel Cake."

Fieno finally responded with a sly grin. "You are clever, sir. But not so much that you can frighten me with falsehoods."

"Do elaborate," Endersby said.

"Our Italian police are much more subtle in their ways. Yours, it is such a schoolboy trick. You English are a naïve people."

"I thank you for the compliment. Do the Italian police resort to floggings? It is one of our favorite past times for chiding the recalcitrant."

Fieno frowned. "You speak too quickly for me." He then peered at Endersby, and his eyes at first looked full of doubt, soon changing to cold contempt. "Ah, now I see. Now, I know who you are."

Endersby lifted his hat in mock salute.

"What a play-actor you are, Lord Carlton." Fieno broke into a light laugh. "Of course, I suspected you were a police. But I was believing the other man who accompanied you was truly a stupid American."

"The charges stand, Signor Fieno. The Grisi family has been accused of the beating of Sergeant Caldwell. *Habeas corpus*, sir. Bloodied from top to toe."

"He has died?" For the first time, Signor Fieno's cool composure fell away.

"Were you present at the beating, sir?"

"I was only told of it. I am swearing to you the truth. Both my foolish cousins were drunk. They said they saw your sergeant always looking at them, always bothering them, never letting them walk anywhere unless he was with them—close by. I thought, well, he is police, maybe, and they, my cousins, are afraid of the police, and they attacked him."

"Attacked him because you excited the two ruffians to do the deed."

Fieno shrugged and turned down his mouth as if to say he was in no way responsible for the foolish actions of the two Grisi brothers.

"Do you often inspire your cousins to violence, Mr. Fieno? For that matter, do you hire them out for such work, along with the questionable Miss Rosa Grisi?"

"You are speaking nonsense, sir." Fieno's tone had turned arrogant.

"Do you think so? Are you certain you do not find some pleasure in setting the three of these cousins of yours onto rampages—beating others, holding up knives to innocent bystanders like poor Lord Carlton, or smashing houses in fashionable districts where streets like Doughty Street are found?"

"You can say all you wish, Mr. Police. My business is the theatre. My profession is to guide and look after Miss Rosa Grisi, one of the greatest performers you will ever see in this wet, filthy city."

"And why then was the inimitable Miss Grisi absent from the

theatre last night? Surely you cannot afford to lose the money such a performer must garner for you and your paltry cousins."

Insulting a man's family, especially an Italian's, brought out the usual response. Signor Fieno shoved forward. He thrust out his chin. Fury widened his large brown eyes. "You are a dog, Mr. Police."

"Inspector Owen Endersby. May I also present my trusty co-workers, Mr. Birken, Mr. Stott."

Stott once again pinned Fieno to the wall with his broad hand.

"Shall we continue like this for a while, sir, or shall we simply come to the truth?"

Fieno looked away and retreated into silence.

"I see," huffed Endersby. He took Birken aside and whispered in his ear.

Birken, at first, looked shocked. When Endersby elaborated, the man's face softened and a smile of delight appeared. "What an idea, Inspector," Birken said. He then went to his fellow sergeant, whispered succinctly into his ear and said "Do it fast, Stott. It's an Endersby trick." Stott held Fieno hard in his grip as Birken began to unbutton the man's coat, then his waistcoat and the buttons of his trousers.

"Ma, che fai? Che fanno, signore?"

"I find it rather warm here, do you not, Mr. Fieno?" asked Endersby. "I imagine it is our close quarters."

The Italian struggled in vain. The quick-handed sergeants had all his outer garments removed in less than fifty seconds, including his brushed boots. The half-naked man began to shiver in the cold air. Birken folded the clothes neatly over his arm. Stott then let go of Fieno, and the three policemen stepped back.

"Shall we walk, then, sir?" asked Endersby.

"Cane!"

"Still, too warm? I beg your pardon." Endersby came up to the man, and as Stott held him again, Endersby yanked off all the rest of Fieno's clothes. The final piece of linen fell from the man's frame, a sorry length of rag, leaving him stark naked, his chest and legs covered in thin black hair.

"A fine December morning, Mr. Fieno. A good English morning."

To be expected, the poor shivering victim struck out with his right arm, but Endersby jumped back. Then the angered Italian tried to run, holding his hands over his genitals, but Birken grabbed him, shook him hard, held him by his elbows. Endersby, sensing that a final move in this game was necessary, nodded quickly to Stott. His sergeant prepared himself, his mouth turned down in a ferocious frown. Striking a nonchalant pose, Endersby looked up at the sky for a moment as Stott made a fist and directed it rather firmly into Mr. Fieno's cold stomach.

Stott was about to hit Fieno a second time when the coughing, bent man raised his hands in defeat.

"What do you want?" he cried, the sound strangled in his throat. Birken took hold of Fieno and helped him straighten. His eyes had now lost lustre; one arm hung limp by his side, his left hand deftly covering his groin.

"First, I demand a confession from you," said Endersby. "About your two cousins and their deed against Sergeant Caldwell."

"In fact, yes, yes," blurted out Fieno. His lips were turning blue. He was crestfallen, distraught.

"Then, a simple and hasty introduction to Miss Rosa Grisi."

"No, she will not allow it."

"Stott," commanded Endersby. The sergeant jumped at Fieno and pulled his head back by the hair. "I do apologize, sir, for our methods," said the inspector. "We are in a hurry, you see. We could, if you wish, resort to much stronger persuasion. Do we not still have the chair at Fleet Station? You know, the one with the straps?"

"Giulio and Franco beat your sergeant," Fieno shouted. "But I cannot let Miss Grisi be found. I shall take the blame for her."

Endersby was puzzled. He then recalled what the stage-door keeper at the Coburg theatre had told him. "Was Miss Grisi guilty of a crime in Italy? Did she stab a man, as rumour has it?"

"I cannot say."

"Come, come Mr. Fieno. Sooner or later, I will find out where she is. She is far too valuable an income investment for you and your family. You will never allow her to escape, being a ruthless man, after all."

Fieno clutched his shaking body. Endersby suggested to Stott to drape the man's fur cloak over his shoulders. "We do not want a man to die on us from ague."

The Italian slumped against the wall, gathering his cloak about him. He stood still but would not let his eyes make contact with Endersby's. Was this man in love, wondered Endersby? If the story of the fatal stabbing were true, English law had no jurisdiction over Rosa Grisi's fate. So why was Fieno so protective? Jealousy? Passion? The Italian bent over with cold, and Endersby could see in the man's face the terrible contortions of anger, desire and fear. The man was on the verge of either giving in or allowing himself to be beaten and utterly humiliated. Finally, as Stott and Birken waited, Fieno spoke: "Number 20, Roupell Street."

* * *

Rosa Grisi's flat was on the second floor on Roupell Street, a battered-looking alley formed by two rows of buildings of soot-grimed brick. A blacksmith's, a tailor's and a number of shuttered establishments completed the neighbourhood. Owen Endersby had travelled widely in the city; he had been from the flash houses of St. Giles to the newly-erected terraces along Brompton Road. Roupell Street was a narrow passage between the grander streets of the Surrey side, a by-way off the New Cut suitable for those who sought anonymity.

The voice which greeted him sounded exhausted. "Go away."

Signor Fieno pleaded in Italian. Rosa Grisi claimed she *could* not open the door. Endersby stepped up to the polished panels, rather fancy, he thought, given the premises, and said she must open in the name of the Metropolitan Detective Police.

"La polizia?"

Silence, then rustling behind the door. Birken dashed
down the stairs to guard the back entrance to the building,
a door of some weight as Endersby had discovered when he
and the others had first scouted the place. A moment later,
the puffing sergeant returned, recalled by Endersby
himself who now stood triumphantly in the open doorway,
a maid behind him holding the knob and pointing to Rosa
Grisi's three darkened rooms. The far room contained a
large bed, where the woman herself reclined. Beside her
was a gentleman with a black satchel, his hands busy
winding a stiff cloth around her right knee.

Endersby moved forward into the chilly morning air of
the flat. He later described the place to Harriet as a cave
painted in red with leather poufs, mirrors and saddles.
Rosa Grisi's bed was a mound of cloth, a soft hill of satin
bolsters. A strong odour of balsam and raw alcohol
suffused the far room. The gentleman beside Rosa Grisi
claimed to be a surgeon, one well acquainted with the
injuries most often suffered by tumblers.

"Mr. Bennett," the gentleman said to introduce himself.

"And this injury, Mr. Bennett?"

"Most deleterious for the divine Miss Grisi." Bruises
marred her right leg.

"How so, Mr. Bennett?" Endersby summed up the
surgeon as a man in his fifties, an acolyte as well, for his eyes
never left Rosa Grisi's face.

"Miss Grisi shall not be performing for at least two more
nights. This knee is badly sprained."

"Impossible," cut in Signor Fieno. "You say this for three
days now! She rode well enough on Friday and on Saturday
night."

"Recall, sir," said the surgeon, "that you and Miss Grisi's
brothers were forced *to carry* your prize performer into and
out of her carriage before and after each performance, as
she was in too much pain to walk. And remember, sir, how
your wondrous Miss Grisi barely stood erect on the back of
her horse—on both nights—even though she tried her

very best and was able—a superb gesture, Madame Grisi—
to wave the great flag *as she sang* atop her mount."

"*Pigra! Indolente!*" Signor Fieno threw the words at Miss
Grisi.

"*Assassino!* I am not able to ride," Rosa Grisi yelled back
in her defence. "Signor Fieno, he has the idea it is better to
earn money than to have me safe."

"*Bugie!*" shouted Fieno, his cloak held fast against the
cold chill.

"These are not the lies, Luca," Rosa said, her voice
suddenly soft and pleading. "Shall I fall again and crack open
my head? You can show my body to the public and charge a
penny."

Fieno was about to step forward, his fist raised. Stott
grabbed hold of him.

"This is the same *storia* all over again." Rosa Grisi smiled
throughout. Endersby admired the elegant rhythm of her
movements, especially when she lifted her muscular arms. He
felt a rush of heat come into his face, for she was a beauty with
hair short and black, and eyes pale green as Spanish grapes.

"And so, Dr. Bennett, you saw the performance on both
Friday and Saturday last?" continued Endersby.

"I did. Despite her injury on Friday night from falling off
her mount in the backstage, Miss Grisi rode magnificently.
Her one-legged stance on the haunch of her galloping
stallion—she was also balancing the Union Jack on a pole—
well, the crowd went delirious both nights with clapping."

"How was it you accompanied Miss Grisi to her carriage
on these two nights? Were you summoned by her?"

"By her brother, Franco. He was angry." Mr. Bennett's
eyes looked towards the hard gaze of Signor Fieno. "Franco
Grisi and I had met before, as he had a bad cut on his hand
which needed attending."

"Subsequently, you tended Miss Grisi at your establishment?"

"No, Inspector. Here, in this place. On both nights,
Signor Fieno, Franco and the older brother, Giulio, helped
me carry Miss Grisi to this very bed."

"Did she pass a calm night on either?"

"Hardly, Inspector. Have you ever broken a bone? Or sprained muscles? I notice you limp somewhat. From the gout, is it?"

Endersby smiled and explained that on some mornings he had to hobble with his cane.

"I hope it is not for me to do so," said Miss Grisi, suddenly. "I shall not take a stick with me. How can I ride in the arena with a foolish stick?" She tossed her hand into the air as if she were throwing a cane into the sea.

"Miss Grisi paid me to stay late with her on Friday and Saturday. Franco insisted as well. He would not leave her side and watched me like a wild tiger every time I had to bathe her swollen muscles and bind them. He was in tears the whole time, Inspector."

"He is like a child," Miss Grisi said.

Endersby thought: *yes, emotional and violent as well.* "What did you order for your breakfast then on Saturday morning, if I may be so curious to enquire?"

"What a silly English question," Miss Grisi answered. "You English have such terrible food—nothing but mutton and potatoes and tea. *Dio!* I do not remember what we took for breakfast. *Niente.* Mr. Bennett left us just before dawn each day to return to his loving wife and daughter." With this last phrase, Miss Grisi teased the physician, fluttering her eyes as if she were a juvenile lead meeting a lover at the garden gate.

The surgeon blushed. "I felt it necessary to stay with Miss Grisi until she was more comfortable. This is what a surgeon has sworn to do. It is part of our oath."

"Mr. Fieno, I ask you of your whereabouts on late Friday night last."

"I went to what you silly English call a nanny-house."

"He is lying," said Miss Grisi. "He slept in the hall outside my door, where he always sleeps. He keeps me locked inside. It is true. He shuts me in like I am an animal in a cage."

At these words, Fieno raised his chin in an arrogant, dismissive manner, but he remained silent. He had the air of a man capable of doing great harm. A lover then, a man of jealous passion, concluded Endersby. It was so evident. Signor Fieno loved Miss Grisi in a suffocating fashion. Perhaps the rumours of her stabbing a man might bear investigation. Was Fieno himself the victim, scarred in other ways by his love for her?

"Where is Franco?" Endersby then asked. "He helped you for two nights, and then he has run off. Indeed, where is the other brother? Is this the way siblings pay homage to an injured sister?"

"Hiding," said Miss Grisi. "He and Giulio has beaten a police. They will hang for that."

"In Italy, perhaps."

"I cannot let you find him. Or Giulio."

"What shall I do, then, Miss Grisi? A crime has been committed. Shall I arrest you in your brothers' stead?"

"If you must, you must."

"In fact, I am more concerned about your lover."

"Which one?" Miss Grisi leaned back on a pillow.

"Mr. Samuel Cake."

"Ah, I see. Mr. Samuel. So sweet. Did you know Luca—Signor Fieno—wanted to kill Samuel?"

Fieno, who had been sitting down and shivering in his cloak, looked up but did not stir. He shut his eyes.

"He tried it only once. This last summer. Did you not, Luca?" said Rosa Grisi. "With a dagger. And all by himself. It was not so successful, was it, Luca?"

Tears formed in Signor Fieno's eyes. Miss Grisi went on, her words humiliating the man to the point where he seemed to fold under their weight.

"In August, Luca waited for Samuel and struck at him in the night. It was on the New Cut very late. Samuel was a smarter man than he sometimes let you know. Samuel was quick with his walking stick. The dagger dropped from Luca's hand. I cannot remember what Samuel did with it. I think he threw it in the river." A silence attended the final sound of her words. Fieno rose. His skin had taken on the pallor of one who is fatigued from illness and hunger.

Endersby now looked and saw a man once proud, now dazed and defeated by his own passions. Fieno walked up to the inspector. He pulled his coat close and straightened, aware that his stance could be either threatening or entreating. Stott and Birken came close, and Fieno, ignoring them, leaned into Inspector Endersby's face.

"I am innocent, Mr. Police," Fieno said. "My Rosa is not telling the lie. I did want to kill stupid Mr. Cake. But I could not. I wanted to hurt him, to cut his pretty face. I could not. He was not worth it. No, he was nothing to me. My Rosa, she is my trust. My only true possession, so yes, I guard her every night, every single night, to protect her from this ugly stupid country of bully men like you and your peasant soldiers beside me. This is the confession, Mr. Police. I did not know of Mr. Cake's death until the Saturday afternoon. Franco was with me, and we laughed. Yes, we laughed. And yes, with Guilio we saw your other stupid police, Mr. Caldwell. I said we must teach these English how to show the respect."

Signor Fieno had regained all his height, all his vicious arrogance, his majesty. How sad and yet how wondrous was wounded pride, thought Endersby, looking far into Signor Fieno's tired, hard eyes. Fieno turned and brushed by Stott. He stood by Rosa Grisi's side at the bed. "I do not know where Guilio and stupid Franco has gone, but I am swearing to you, they had nothing to do against Mr. Cake. On Friday they both was here with all of us."

Endersby considered these words for a moment. Were they the truth? Or was this an elaborate Italian charade performed by a master of manipulation and disdain? Mr. Bennett was the clue. He could swear under oath that all the men were with Miss Grisi to tend to her need. But then, what about the beating of Caldwell? This was the strangest notch of the puzzle. Why were both brothers so violent to him? And now they were in hiding out of cowardly fear; as Miss Grisi had said, they thought they would hang for beating a member of the Detective Police.

"Can you name anyone who might have seen Giulio in the last two days—particularly yesterday, on Monday?"

Rosa Grisi looked very tired now. She held onto the surgeon's hand as she sat upright and said: "You have no witnesses to their deed, Inspector. They acted on their own, even if Luca made them drunk enough to give chase. I will not tell you where they are, even if you burn me. I have been in the great prison in Rome and seen things you English cannot imagine. You cannot make me betray my brothers."

Endersby resigned himself to Rosa Grisi's words. There was no evidence, no one as yet who had been found to testify. All that was left for him was to send Stott to investigate the scavengers, those rescuers of Caldwell. His seeking for vindication had come against a barrier—the love of a sister for her brothers. How could reason and English law combat such a primal force? To lose her and any lead she might proffer would divert the direction of the investigation.

Endersby sat down on a red pouf and stared around the room. Stott, Birken, the surgeon, Miss Grisi, Fieno—all waited in anticipation. Eventually, Endersby placed his hands in his lap and turned to Miss Grisi.

"I have heard of a man known as Henry Robertson Dupré. He is the manager of Old Drury. Samuel Cake was to replace him in the post of manager."

"I have never met him."

"You, Fieno. Have you had dealings with him?"

"Once. Giulio and Franco, they trained two horses for his opera spectacle."

"And that is all?"

"He paid us on time. His male lead, Mr. Weston, he was obliging enough, though he was not at all a good rider."

"Poor William," said Miss Grisi.

"Why poor?"

"He is an unhappy man. I think of him as a sorrowful man."

"Do you know him?"

Fieno interrupted. "She does, Mr. Police."

"Luca, please."

"No, Miss Grisi, explain."

"I know him because I know of his sister. She is very ill now."

"Mr. Cake knew her as well, did he not?"

"She was delicate and weak. What a foolish man Samuel was at times." Bitter regret seamed every syllable of her speech.

"Cake loved her," Fieno said.

"And you were jealous of his love for Mr. Weston's sister, Miss Grisi?"

"I suppose," she smiled. Her dismissive manner had returned. "That is why I slapped Samuel once. I am sure your spies have told you that story, of how the Italian *puttana* struck the handsome Mr. Cake."

The surgeon, who had been closing up his medicines, came to her side. "Lie down, Miss Grisi. Please."

Miss Grisi composed herself. "Poor Sarah Weston was nothing to me. Cake was a liar. He did not mean to lie. We women, we like lonely men. But he was not true in the end. He came and he went always with promises. For Sarah, it was worse than for me. Samuel did damage to other women. Oh, yes, he left you so confused. He left things behind, like a fox leaves the feathers of ducks he has killed. In truth, his cruelty to Miss Root, it was far worse."

"Miss Priscilla Root?" asked Endersby.

"Yes. Go and ask her yourself. She said she hated him. She told everyone in London she hated him. To make things worse, she goes every week to the cemetery on High Holborn to see the little grave. One she made Samuel Cake pay for."

Endersby stood up and signalled to Stott. "Take Mr. Fieno to the Yard. Have him write down his confession. Afterwards, Sergeant, lead him to Fleet Lane to have Caldwell read it over. I want Mr. Fieno to face the man he has cleverly managed to injure without laying his own cowardly hands on a single part of Caldwell's body."

Signor Fieno did not struggle as he was led from the room. Endersby focussed his attention again on Miss Rosa Grisi.

"How old was this child of Miss Root and Mr. Cake?"

"Go see for yourself, Inspector. The grave is small enough. You can see how Mr. Cake, how he could treat those who loved him."

"I will keep Mr. Birken here to guard your house, Miss Grisi. I shall send constables from the Scotland Yard office to guard all entrances to Aston's Theatre. You know why I must do this. If your brothers have fled into hiding, we must find them. I shall not let you roam free, Miss Grisi. Neither you nor your brothers. We are law abiding people, we English, and our city must be safe for all citizens, children, actors, lovers—all. London is like *my* family, Miss Grisi, and so I, too, must fight to keep it safe."

The maid let Endersby, Birken and Dr. Bennett out the door.

"Birken, stand by the corner and keep an eye on both entrances. I will send you a constable when I can."

"Yes, Inspector."

The surgeon placed his hat on his head. Inspector Endersby took hold of his arm. "Mr. Bennett, I must call upon you very soon to sign an affidavit. You will swear an oath, sir, and tell me all that happened to you and the Grisi family over the past three days. You are aware that you are regarded as complicit if the truth lies in a different state of being than what I heard upstairs."

Dr. Bennett put down his black medical satchel and as if on cue, he began to wring his hands in a gesture which somewhat amused Endersby. The man was obviously stage-struck—fantasy and romance his most intense interest in life. In a flash movement, Endersby grabbed hold of the surgeon's two moving hands and held them in his iron grip. "Be assured, surgeon, I am a man of my word."

Dr. Bennett pulled his hands free. "I do not hesitate in any way, sir, Mr. Endersby. I am well aware of your position. You, sir, are well aware of mine. We are hard-working, honourable men. If you wish, I can swear at this very moment." From his coat pocket he retrieved a small professional card made of yellow paper, on which Endersby read the man's address and, as required by law, his licence number as a surgeon. *"Blood-letting a specialty: Sprains, Wounds, Tendons, Muscles—massage and binding. Particular to the theatrical profession."*

Endersby read the card out loud with some delight. "I

see, sir, you have managed a fine profession, so that indeed you may live your life and practice in the very world of which you want to take part."

Dr. Bennett smiled. "Sir, you are a man of keen perception."

"Expect me to come calling within two days, sir. I am under pressure myself. I must find witnesses and corral them for the purposes of conviction. Your cooperation will be needed, to the utmost."

The two men quickly shook hands; Endersby blew his nose; he searched in his pockets for sweets but found none.

What with the hustle of catching Signor Fieno and the bustle of noting all that Miss Grisi had said, Endersby was in quite an agitated frame of mind. The morning had been full of revelations. He needed corroboration of both Rosa Grisi's and the surgeon's stories, and so headed his way next door. He found the tailor at his table and his wife beside him, as if they were a matching pair of figurines, both stout, both pulling needles to and fro.

"I am afraid not, Inspector," said the tailor. "I remember sleeping soundly that whole night."

"Not I," resounded the tailor's wife. "What noise there was Friday last. Up the stairs, down the stairs, the surgeon first knocking here, then the crowd of 'em taking that damned Italian woman into her chambers. Lights on all the night. That younger brother, the loud one, he was down there in the courtyard pumping water every five minutes. The other two spent the night shouting out their windows at him."

Likewise, Mrs. Bennett, the stage-struck surgeon's wife—not two streets a way by chance—a fussy, yet phlegmatic woman. "No, certainly not, Inspector. Mr. Bennett spent the nights of Friday and then Saturday with those theatre people. He is too fond of them by half. He told me it was necessary to stay by Miss Grisi, for she was in danger of fever. Posh, I say. He is enamoured of her. I dislike her and her two swarthy brothers. Mr. Bennett paid the older rascal for a riding lesson not one month ago. I fear my Mr.

Bennett wants to go upon the stage. Can you picture it? A middle-aged fool in the supernumerary pack of Aston's Palladium?"

But for all that, there was still the missing Franco and Giulio, thought Endersby. Both felons were still at large. *All of detective work*, he reminded himself, *all of it is knots to be untied.* He could not dawdle. Stott and Birken were needed for the rest of the day, and he was now alone. He walked toward the great centre of London, moodily reflecting on the case. Before him opened the winding streets. Hordes of people and carriages and gigs passed him by. His spirits lifted at the merry shop windows; his spirits fell soon after at the sight of the child beggars and the crooked street-sleepers, sad, frightening creatures in ragged clothes scrambling for food.

In Covent Garden market, the central square was filled with hawkers. A family named Barlow—mother, father, two sons—sold lettuce. The tobacco shop facing them displayed pyramids of Dutch cannisters in the window. Endersby entered the place, a bell on the door jingling above his head. There were two attendants, the thinnest a man with a thatch of white hair. The other was a second version of the first, less thin but greying and more nervous in gesture, tapping the counter every second. From time to time, both attendants would look up at Endersby. What *they* saw was a large man with a belly, pockets bulging with odd shapes, a pair of dirty eyeglasses and a turban tightly wound around his head as if he had but lately risen from bed. This same odd creature smacked his lips as he regarded the merchandise.

"I am a distant relative of the mother, you see, gentlemen," said Endersby, pitching his newly-accented voice high. "We lost contact, you see. Most sad, as there is the matter of a purse left to one, a Mr. John Loxton."

John the Pawn, as was his moniker, leased the stall directly across the arcade and sold sundry fruits, explained the two men. In gratitude, Endersby purchased a plug of the cheapest tobacco. "I want to present a gift, you see, to my cousin. He smokes a pipe, I imagine. I want this to be a kind of peace offering." The thinner attendant assured him the brand chosen was often purchased by costermen like Mr. John the Pawn Loxton. And for certain, added the other, John the Pawn was an avid smoker, for he purchased this very brand once a week on Thursdays.

In the flesh, John Loxton himself was taller than Endersby, his hands wide as plates. "Morning," came his perfunctory greeting.

Endersby shuffled and pointed first to a pile of costly Portuguese plums. "For my grandchild," he whispered. John the Pawn wrapped six in a swatch of oiled paper.

On handing him the coin, Endersby noted the man's knuckles and thick wrist. The brown tip of his pipe stuck up from his coat pocket. "A fine day," Endersby said, but John the Pawn did not respond. A young girl appeared behind him. She had ivory-coloured skin and blue eyes. On the right side of her face, a blue bruise spotted her temple. She wore a shawl but no bonnet; black mud darkened her skirt.

"Put 'em here," John the Pawn said to her. The girl curtsied and set the box of pears on the stall. "Git," he said. The thin waif sat down not far from John the Pawn's stool. To his surprise, Endersby discovered her ankle all bloodied. A stretch of thin chain wound about it, choking it; the chain snaked toward a spike to which it was locked, the spike protruding from the wall behind the baskets of green.

"Extraordinary," came the word from Endersby's mouth.

"She's a bolter," explained John the Pawn. "She has a tic, and she bolts," he said. "Thinks her right is to run scaggin'. To the theatres no less," he said, his voice harsh with tobacco cough. "She has a tic," he said again, now turning his attention to a new customer. The girl looked into Endersby's eyes. She did not show fear. Standing up, she curtsied as if she were taking a bow before a curtain. Oh, how charming, how clever she looked—she slid from her boot a short knife and waved it brazenly at the detective as if to dare him to snitch.

"I have not seen, as yet, the great play at Old Drury," he addressed her, meekly. "I hear it is called *Rachel*, and it is remarkable."

The girl's face broke into a smile. "So they say," she answered.

John the Pawn snapped his fingers. "Git, come 'ere."

The girl moved obediently, tucking the knife back into her boot. She held out a piece of oiled paper as John the Pawn filled it with a dozen of the costly plums. Once the transaction had been finished, the girl returned to her post, dragging her clamping chain behind her. She leaned forward to Endersby. "I can dance, you know. At the Gaff near St. Paul's. I also got a piece in the panto. At Old Drury." She placed her finger to her lips to signal to Endersby to tell no one.

"Betty," snapped John the Pawn. "Come, get the cloth and wipe this down."

So, this is little Betty Loxton, Endersby concluded. The girl who fell from Cake's contraption. Endersby ventured one more quick foray. When Betty bent down to wash out the cloth in a bucket, he handed her a penny. "Where can I see this Gaff?"

"Wednesday, ten o'clock, in Earl Street." The girl took the penny, and before John the Pawn could see, she hid it in a fold in her pocket and resumed her washing.

*   *   *

Dried mud like broken pebbles dirtied the stage-door foyer to Old Drury. A woman in black knelt on the floor and scrubbed its stones with a thick brush. Like the other great theatre of London, Covent Garden, Old Drury was a patent house licensed by royal decree to present Shakespeare and classical works as well as opera, melodrama and comedy. Old Drury was a building of grand arches and white walls, and every time Endersby passed by it in daylight, he asked himself if all its phantoms were resting until sundown, when they could come to life under the gaslight. Inside, at the door leading to the great stage, Endersby buttoned his suede gloves. His satchel was once again worn outside his coat, and the spectacles had been hidden away. The turban was folded into a back pocket, and he reminded himself to wear it the next time he met Betty Loxton.

"Come this way, please, Inspector."

The stage-door keeper moved past the flats of the side wings. At the Green Room door, the keeper tapped twice. "He is in conference at the moment, sir. Please take a seat." The old man indicated a wire chair by the railing, and Endersby sat down. The backstage area was as large as the stage itself, reminding him of the great hall in Covent Garden market. There were docks of scenery to one end full of gigantic canvas forms, each varnished with a faint gloss, each with part of a scene: a tree, a pillar, a timbered house. The floor of the stage ran from front to back on a steep tilt. Cut into its oak boards were trap doors, like window shutters, one of them open so that Endersby was able to see below to a platform on which a chair was placed, ready to spring up on cue. He marvelled at the quiet, at the rows of canvas sky-cloths hanging over the deep expanse of the playing area, rather like a host of sails on a clipper ship, he thought. It was Endersby's first glimpse of Old Drury's mechanics of magic, and permeating his delight was the pedestrian smell of oil from the lamps, sawdust and damp rope.

Blood and thunder, he mused, then a memory whisked him back to the age of twenty-five, when he had been taken to this same theatre to see the great Edmund Kean. The actor was performing in one of his "raging" roles, in which Kean struck a pose, hands held up to the sky, calmness suddenly bursting into an agony of remorse, as if all his passion had been forced into his knees and his astonished mouth. It was here as well, in Old Drury's pit, that Endersby had first seen Harriet. She had been with her sisters, both of them spritely, lovely girls, whose faces wept and laughed as easily as the curtain rolled up and down. It was Harriet's whole movement of body which had first attracted him. Endersby touched the edge of the chair. This place would have charmed our little Robert, he thought. He quickly shoved the idea away, got up from the chair and headed toward the door of the Green Room. He knocked and waited and called out the name, surprised at last to see the door open and the man himself in waistcoat and frock coat looking haughty as any aristocrat.

"What may I do for you?" said Henry Robertson Dupré, his right hand suddenly lifting to pat down a stray wisp of henna-coloured hair.

In the room stood a table. There was a young lad in a cap and waistcoat clearing the inkwell and books. He tipped his cap to the inspector and was about to leave.

"I'd like you to stay, if you do not mind, young chap."

"He is but our call-boy, Inspector. I can't quite remember your last name, sir, please pardon my sieve-like memory."

"Endersby, Owen. Metropolitan Detective Police."

The young lad's face registered a gentle amazement. "Pity," he blurted out, "about Mr. Cake, sir."

"Pity indeed, Crabb," rejoined Dupré. "Inspector, need I ask anyone else to come in? I assume you are here to ask questions? I suspect you are very curious about Mr. Cake and his connections to us here, at Old Drury."

"I am, sir. Most curious. I shan't take long. Lad, I shall talk to you as well, in my time." Reggie Crabb sat down on a chair by the door. He placed his cap in his hand and responded quickly to Endersby's request for his name. "Crabb, sir. Reginald Crabb."

"Now then," said Dupré. He held an authoritative stance as he set a chair for the inspector. Dupré's right hand slipped into his waistcoat pocket. His mood was cool, but cooperative; he never stood still long as he spoke, moving continuously around the small room. Whatever seething spite he may have harboured in his heart was not displayed in his calm features. Endersby rather liked the way Dupré proffered information, liked the way he explained before any actual questions were asked.

"It was all a matter of profit and loss," Dupré explained. "Lord Harwood believes in instantaneous returns, a fatal expectation, sir, in a theatre as large as ours. The London public is a hungry maw. Sensation is what they devour. Mr. Cake ran a rollicking success on the Surrey side, and Harwood took a notion that such fare might fill our coffers here. I have no doubt Mr. Cake could have been efficient in his management. Old Drury, however, is a cruel mistress. Even John Philip Kemble himself went bankrupt here twice."

"Were you, Mr. Dupré, in attendance here the night Mr. Cake was beaten to death?"

"I was, sir."

"And later, after the performance of your fine *Rachel*, where were you?"

"I did not imagine that your questioning would veer so suddenly, Inspector. Am I really considered a danger in this matter?"

"All who knew Mr. Cake are in imminent danger, if you wish, of being stamped suspicious."

"'Lor' bless me,'" interjected young Crabb from his chair by the door. "I hope I be not one of them." The young boy's face tightened into a perturbed frown.

"The sun shines in all corners, young master. It can reveal to us many things if we just keep our eyes open," said Endersby.

"Really, Inspector, I do not see the logic of this."

"My needs are simple, Mr. Dupré. A man was murdered on Friday last. I have been speaking with many theatre folk about the matter. You have been named as one who knew Cake. Indeed, I do not often bow to gossip, but it is a profitable by-way in my profession to *listen* to it. And I have found you to be named as a rival. There is an idea that you bore him a grudge."

"I admit it. I had many sour words with Cake. He was an upstart. He stole Old Drury from under my nose. He had a way with his lies and tricks, Mr. Endersby, that I am sure the gossips have also told you. He was wily. Who would not have feelings toward such a man? I did not kill him. I could not. I would not see the purpose."

"Crimes of passion and revenge hide their purpose, at times, behind the fury of their actions. It is only later that reason provides us with motive."

"I commend your analysis, Mr. Endersby. I can attest to witnesses, if you so need them."

"Young lad, were you here on the night of Friday last?"

"Till late, sir."

"And did you closely observe the comings and goings of your superior?"

Reginald Crabb hesitated.

"Go on, Crabb. Quite so. Be forthright," Dupré told him bluntly.

"No, sir. I ate my supper too late, sir."

"With whom?"

"Miss Root, sir."

"Let me proceed in a different direction for the moment."

Endersby pulled the glove from his satchel and asked if either had ever seen it before.

"It is of cheap manufacture," said Dupré, shaking his head. "Many of our actors have gloves similar."

"This one I do not know," answered Crabb.

"You are a good lad, young master."

"I am, sir?"

"Do me the courtesy of waiting outside on the chair by the railing. I will not be long."

Crabb left the room. Endersby rose from his chair and shook out his right leg, which had fallen asleep. Dupré moved behind the table. All the while, the hearth log crackled. Between Dupré and Endersby, smoke floated in a wave and for a split second obscured Dupré's features. Endersby cleared the air with a whip of his hand. "I do not wish to alarm you, Mr.Dupré. I have little evidence at my disposal as to who may have been Mr. Cake's murderer. I must, by needs, talk with Miss Root and others, and I need your full approbation of this."

"You shall have it."

"Here, kindly glance at this promissory note. It was found on Mr. Cake's premises at Doughty Street. Have you, by the way, ever been to Doughty Street?"

"Never, sir. Why would I? The man and I had ice between us, if I may resort to metaphor. He was hardly one to consort with in a private manner."

Dupré read the note. He handed it back to Endersby. He did not hesitate in his response. "It is Priscilla Root's. Plain and simple."

"Your lead player."

"Our leading actress. Please take a seat. I will be brief. And this is fact, not gossip."

Henry Dupré spoke slowly and with a sense that his honesty might redeem anyone guilty of an association with the late Mr. Cake. "Priscilla Root was once married to an Arthur Summers. A brute. He abandoned her. Left the country, it was assumed. She kept his name and signed contracts as Mrs. P. Summers. All legal in the eyes of the courts. Her promissory notes to Cake were personal, but she must have felt they were, in one way, legal tender and so required her official married name, not her stage name. Hence, P. Summers."

"Did you know of these visits to Cake?"

"No. I knew they had once been lovers. And that she claimed she had borne him a child. Not so unusual an event in our profession. I ask that you remain discreet in these matters."

"Discretion is only one part of our valour as detective police, Mr. Dupré."

"An apt turn of phrase, Mr. Endersby. I congratulate you."

"Here is another. 'Lord, lord, how this world is given to lying.' Henry the Fourth, sir. An admirable play."

"I do not see your thrust."

"What witnesses, Mr. Dupré? Whom may I speak with that can vouch for you without fear of reprisal?"

"You have taken a turn, sir. A blaming tack."

"Rumour is a pipe blown by surmises, Mr. Dupré. A quote from the same play, and indeed, it well expresses the sentiment I hold to. I surmise there is more to your involvement with Cake. Will your witnesses claim as much, do you think?"

"This is preposterous baiting, Mr. Endersby. I am clear of such a crime. I have nothing to hide."

"You are the only man in London who would have been most severely compromised by Mr. Cake. You more than anyone had the most to lose. Your reputation, your income. Your very self as a man of means."

"I am not given to beating my rivals to death with sticks, Mr. Endersby. Such was the way the crime rags described Mr. Cake's demise."

"You had strong motive to do so, nevertheless."

"I am not a bear in a pit, Mr. Endersby. You may prod me, but I shall not fight."

"Lord Harwood does not think you a capable man."

"Lord Harwood is indolent and naïve."

The two men sat looking at each other. The hearth kept fuming with smoke. Dupré rose, went to the door and called for a boy to come and tend the fire. Without hesitation, he extended his hand to Endersby, and with an even tone asked him to return again at his leisure. For a moment, Endersby begrudged the peremptory dismissal, but his instinct prompted him to accept it temporarily. He walked to the door and even shook the man's hand.

"Good morning, I thank you at least for your patience. I shall enquire of your stage-door keeper as to witnesses."

"Most certainly."

The door to the Green Room closed behind him. Endersby thought for a moment before seeking out young Reggie Crabb. The inspector then led the boy downstairs into the lane next to the theatre and suggested he take him for a muffin at the corner. Crabb dashed to tell the stage-door keeper of his temporary absence then rushed back to Endersby, who was already on his way to the steaming wagon and its brass coffee urn. The muffin was round and full of raisins, and young Crabb bit into it with much relish. Endersby sampled the coffee, thick and full of sugar. The two of them then sat flank-to-flank on the kerb, like father and son, and chatted.

"You like the Old Drury, young master?"

"I do, sir. A good employ, even if my stage manager is gruff, sir."

"An honest man, he?"

"Most, sir. Punctual, too."

"You eat in the theatre most nights. You take supper there?"

"And tea and dinner."

"And Mr. Dupré? He is also fair and good?"

"Most times. 'Cept when he's angry."

"Does he frequently lose his temper?"

"Daily, sir. On little things. Him and Mr. Cake had it out. Bad words between them."

"When did you last see Mr. Cake?"

"Friday last. In the backstage."

"Did he speak with you?"

"Not me. To her, the strange lady, and Dupré. And he took a moment to visit with Miss Root."

"Tell me of this strange lady."

"She came to see Mr. Dupré. In his box. A beauty, and foreign. Very dark hair. Cake and her, they talked, then she left, then Dupré came and he was very angry, then him and Mr. Cake, they had very, very angry words."

"Can you recall any of them?"

"Dupré said he would damn Cake. He did blaspheme him."

"Did they resort to fists, young master?"

Crabb now broke into a quick laugh. "They kicked chairs, sir."

"You keep a keen eye out, don't you?"

"I have to. As call-boy, I daren't be tardy. I daren't miss where my actors stand."

"You are a good lad, young Crabb. Let me ask you this, then. What is your Mr. Weston like?"

"Fair and honest, sir."

"He played in *Rachel* on Friday and Saturday last, did he not?"

"The Prince, sir. Fine playing, too. On Friday night he took late supper with Miss Root. I was there, with him. He was jolly for a time."

"I hear Miss Root has a sister. Does she frequent her rooms backstage?"

"Daily, sir. And her friend, too."

"Here is a penny for you, young master. Hold it against a favour I am about to ask."

"Yes, sir."

"You are quick and bright. I want you to be my eyes for me in Old Drury."

"Your eyes, sir?"

"Keep your eyes upon Mr. Dupré as much as you can. Stay in the shadows. Do not let him know where you hide."

"If you say so, sir."

"Here is a shilling. To be yours in two days. Payment for your Christmas duty of helping out the Metropolitan Detective Police."

"What shall I do if I see anything?"

"See that tavern over there, across Vinegar Yard? I shall be there tonight and for two days hence for my supper. Keep an eye out. Let me know who comes and goes each day. If by chance you see something you want *me* to see immediately, come and fetch me posthaste."

"I will not fail, sir."

"I know that, young master. Now be off."

* * *

Young Reggie raced back into the theatre, proud to be a lad who now could help the detective police of the great city of London. "Cor," he whispered. Reggie had a sharp memory; he had to have one to do calls; he was trusted by Mr. Dupré and the stage manager to know who was to be ready, where they were to go, and at what time. Without Reggie Crabb, Old Drury would not run well. Actors could miss their cues.

"Remember," he said to himself. And certainly Reggie remembered all he ever heard, all he said in return. "It's my gift," he said and wanted to boast.

Clattering into the wings, he remembered the very words and gestures he witnessed between Mr. Cake and Mr. Dupré last Friday evening. Angry words they were.

Reggie remembered watching Mr. Dupré enter his private box. Through the crack left open, Reggie saw how Dupré's eyes took in the orchestra and the bright furniture of the farce, all lemony in the gaslight. As for the silhouette before him…perhaps the light was playing tricks? Where was the slender waist, the dark hair with its coronet of white roses? Instead of the strange woman, Mr. Dupré found a lithe young man in a cloak and beaver. A smell of onion sauce fleshed out this male apparition, which broke into a mocking laugh.

"She's left, Dupré."

"Cake."

"She's left you. Gone to the Strand, to supper."

"On your purse, no doubt."

Samuel Cake raised his young chin, and his mouth curled slightly.

"Doing your rounds, are you?" Dupré asked.

"Fresh meat for the pit, Dupré. Requires me to go out hunting each night."

"Commendable," replied Mr. Dupré. "You actually pay that little orchestra of yours? You support a roster of actors, do you?"

"None in this city is so extravagant as you, our Prince of Cleverness. But my dear Dupré, I hear Harwood remains displeased. He does not like failures. Small houses. No rent. Even with your *Rachel*, you are still in danger. So say the gossips."

"Envy has a crooked tongue," smiled Mr. Dupré.

"Your *Rachel* has been called for by audiences each night. London demands more performances. Fifteen repetitions so far and no booing."

"Twenty-four repetitions, in fact. And a mention in *The Times*. A veritable hit."

"A fine title. *Rachel; or, the Hebrew Maid*. I like it."

"She's a little heady for your gallery of costermongers."

"Heady? No. Your *Rachel*—I beg your pardon—is too slow. Old hat. Too many speeches."

Reggie watched how Mr. Dupré shoved his quivering left hand into his pocket. "So, Cake, the diva Elisabetta has left me. Gone to supper, you say?"

"Fickle is as fickle charms," Cake answered.

"And pray, what brought you into my private box?"

"Yours, my good Dupré? But for how long?"

Mr. Dupré puffed out his chest. "Has Harwood told you?"

"I, too, received a letter," grinned Cake. "You have dined too long on Harwood's mercy."

"Then it *is* you, Cake. You, of all people, you upstart. No doubt London will howl when it hears a mud lark has been offered the lease to Old Drury."

Samuel Cake tipped his beaver hat in mock salute.

"The truth is"—Mr. Dupré hesitated to make sure Samuel Cake paid attention—"that you yearn for reputation and to eschew that cockpit you run across the river."

"Oh, mercy," Cake cried. He crossed his arms, shoving his cloak brusquely aside. "Not cockpit, dear old Dupré. You must see it. A money pit, a shilling sack. I sup on champagne paid for by my hungry dogs."

Mr. Dupré bowed his head, though Reggie saw how his teeth were held tightly. Samuel Cake strolled past him and stood at the door.

"Dupré, do these hens always treat you so poorly? Perhaps your Italian beauty was too ripe for you?"

Dupré flicked the lapel of his frock coat. "They are dust, Cake. A penny-a-throw."

"That frock coat becomes you. Come January, will it keep you warm, I wonder?"

"*Damn you,* Cake." Here it comes, thought Reggie—Mr. Dupré cannot hold back his fury. Samuel Cake placed his hands in the air as if to beg for mercy, but then broke into a taunting grin. He kicked over one of the gilt chairs in the box. "I shall have to rid myself of these. Old Drury will have a different kind of crowd come New Year's."

"*Get out!*" Dupré shouted. He bolted forward.

"Beware, Dupré," Cake said, retreating. "Her Majesty may admire you for the moment, but you are no longer the doyen of our grubbing fraternity of players. You, too, shall fall."

"I'll damn you first, Cake."

Henry Robertson Dupré waited as his rival headed toward the stage-door foyer.

Reggie shivered, remembering how he had tentatively approached his master, how his own eyes had burned from what he had just witnessed. "Sir?"

"What is it?" growled Mr. Dupré.

"Permission to leave and do calls?"

"Indeed, Crabb."

Reggie had stood at attention with a worried look, his cap held in his hand.

"Do not fret, Crabb. We are not undone as yet. Not undone at all."

As Mr. Dupré spoke, Reggie wondered how his master would recover from his anger. "Not undone, *perhaps,*" Dupré swore, as he waved to Reggie to go and set the gilded chair in its rightful place.

Cor, Reggie thought now. *I must say these words again. Save them for the Inspector. For I am now his eyes. And his ears, too.*

*   *   *

Although the morning was waning, Endersby was still sufficiently curious to wander back to Old Drury and continue his questioning. What to think of Dupré, he wondered? If young Reggie Crabb could be trusted, Dupré's fight with Samuel Cake sounded suspicious. Damning the man, kicking chairs? And now there were new leads to question and new doubts to mull over. Crossing Vinegar Yard, Endersby pondered the life of a detective, its ins and its outs, its daily round of probing. To this philosophical turn, Endersby submitted his mind with the same ease that he would slip his bulky body into a hot bath. He enjoyed the calming effect of his pondering; he let argument and rebuttal wash through his imagination. As he approached the arched entrance of the theatre, his thoughts emerged from an idea about guilt, an idea which drained away into the depths of his inquisitive mind the moment he raised his eyes.

There at the door stood Dupré. With sudden eagerness, he presented his right hand to Endersby. "I have had second thoughts," he said, shaking hands. This sudden turn intrigued the inspector—his instinct again affording him patience, for Dupré bore watching. What had come over the man? Beside Dupré, under the open arch, stood the doddering Mr. Hartley, the stage-door keeper.

"There, sir," announced Dupré. A folded note thrust at him from Dupré's left hand mentioned a man's name and an address not far from Old Drury.

"My gentleman's club, sir. On Friday last, the night of Mr. Cake's demise, I went there at five minutes past midnight, took a cold supper, and remained until two or later. My club man can verify my comings and goings. Hartley, can you recall that same late hour when I bid you good night? I was on my way to my club."

"I think so, sir. Yes, if you wish."

"Come, Hartley. This is Detective Endersby. He shall want 'the whole truth and nothing but' from you."

"If you wish, sir."

Mr. Hartley invited Endersby to step into his small, unheated room by the theatre entrance. Alone together, the older man provided some brief narratives of the people who had come and gone on Friday night. "I am clear on most matters," Hartley said; clear on the dark foreign lady, Miss Elisabetta Mazzini, who had arrived at seven o'clock on Friday to visit with Mr. Dupré. "Elisabetta Mazzini." Hartley held up her calling card. "A singer at the Italian opera. No formal address given." He also recalled Mr. Cake coming in unannounced. Hartley complained of his brusque manners.

"How long did Mr. Cake stay at the theatre?" Endersby asked.

Hartley pondered the question. "Not long, perhaps a half hour. He paid a visit to Miss Root, so I heard. And had words with Mr. Dupré. He left alone, I remember. But before he left, the dark foreign woman—Miss Mazzini— left wrapped in her cloak. She was dressed for the evening with flowers in her hair. I believe she wears them always, sir. It is her signature from her great role as Norma at the Italian Opera."

Endersby smiled at the sharpness of the man's diction. But how reliable was his memory? Endersby tested the man with his usual questions about food and luncheons, and the poor old man got muddled.

Hartley then brightened. "On Friday, yes, it was Friday, Mr. Dupré *did* leave. He ran out of the theatre before his *Rachel* had ended. Odd, too, he did not wish me his usual good night. Moreover, he wore a long old cloak, one he hasn't put on for a number of winters now."

Endersby thanked the old man and walked back into the dark hold of the stage. The breeze that so often set the canvas scenery to shudder reminded Endersby that this great theatre was indeed like a ship at sea. And what a tempest-tossed ship it was as well, he thought. This cold December morning had been full of revelations. And it was time, as was his way, to recall the witnesses' testimonies at the coroner's enquiry on Cake's murder. The three men in caps. The lone figure in a cloak at the back entrance to Number 46 Doughty Street. The frequenters—a veiled woman and two men. Who were they? Perhaps the threesome had been Rosa Grisi and her two brothers. But they had alibis for Friday night, as did Mr. Buckstone, the actor. There was Miss Root, who must be questioned, and the elusive, mysterious Elisabetta Mazzini. There was also the matter of Cake and the little grave in Holborn cemetery. Above all there was the suspicious Mr. Dupré— arrogant and secretive, perhaps protesting too much to prove his innocence. In the corridor leading to the Green Room, Endersby found Miss Priscilla Root by chance walking down a branch corridor which led to a row of dressing rooms. She was alone, dressed in a cloak and a bonnet covered in feathers. Her hands were covered in fine leather gloves.

"A detective?" she said.

She then burst into tears and ran to one of the doors. She took out a key, and when Endersby tried to be of some assistance, she shoved him away.

"Miss Root, please, let me help you."

"No one can help me, sir. How dare you come here this very day, so soon after..."

The door was finally opened, and she rushed into the darkened room beyond. Endersby remained at the threshold. From the dark came the sound of a glass breaking. Miss Root cried out: "Leave me, please. I cannot see you now." A moment later she appeared, with a tear-stained face. She slammed the door in Endersby's face.

"Ah, me," he whispered and waited. Weeping filled the inner room. "Best not," he grumbled and rightfully concluded to his own satisfaction that it might be prudent to let her calm down. Even so, he remained alert to the inkling that both Mr. Dupré and Miss Root were reluctant to speak. Hesitant and angered at being approached. Moats and walls, thought Endersby, to defend a besieged castle. But what are both of them hiding beyond those barriers? He nodded sagely to himself and wandered a little, talking to stage hands and to the gruff stage manager, who claimed he had no time to watch for the comings and goings of visitors, let alone his master, Mr. Dupré.

"Thank you in any case," said Endersby. He left Old Drury still dissatisfied, with many questions unanswered. "Time and patience will out," he quietly reminded himself.

The heart of London had become green with holly around windows, wreaths of mistletoe and boxwood on door knockers. Endersby's foot had not been paining him as severely this morning, and he was glad of that. He took a quick luncheon on the Strand, standing in a public house with a rum and hot water in his hand. A light rain was falling by the time he passed through Pickett Place. His hat was dripping by Shoe Lane, his boots soaked through when he finally reached the entrance to Fleet. He had been on foot for over seven hours, and during that time had humiliated a man, bribed a child and been rejected by a star player in the capital's finest theatre. He shook his coat in the vestibule on his way to the second parlour of the Fleet Lane station. Caldwell was still sleeping on the sofa. The admittance sergeant asked Endersby to follow him to Superintendent Borne's chambers. Now, as he heard his own footsteps tread upon the floor, Endersby smelled the soot-thick rain of London on his skin, felt the grime of his livelihood on his clothes.

A faint glow of light brightened the office of Super-intendent Borne. When Endersby had first met the man, he had not liked him. Fussy and preposterous were two of his favourite words for him, but others were frequently less complimentary.

"Please, do *not* sit down, Endersby." Borne's voice seemed hollowed out by the rain. He circled the table and faced his inspector. "I need your advice."

With no mention of anything but the filthy weather, Borne led Endersby out to the slippery courtyard of Fleet Prison, which stood but a few paces along an arched passageway. The scene before them was oddly calm and innocent at first glance. Barrows were covered with thick cloths. Borne instructed a sergeant to pull them off. Endersby gazed at the blackened faces, the mounds of cindered clothing. Seventeen bodies from St. Giles: the reek of fire and the rot of flesh drifted through the sheet of rain.

"What to make of this?" Borne said. "Look on these, Endersby. I had them brought here to Fleet so our surgeons could be sure of the initial coroner's decision. Witnesses have claimed they saw two men with torches run into the place after one o'clock in the morning. The two appeared ragged, street-sleepers no doubt, too mad and penny-pinched to afford a pallet in the foul place. The *Chronicle* has written up that we have been slow and negligent. Not interested in the poor but rather in nabbing thieves for the rewards. But *this* is murder on a grand scale."

Borne remained still, his eyes panning over the soaking, bodies. "Well?" he said finally. "This is a calamity, Inspector. On top of this we have the wretched murder of Mr. Cake to solve. What have you found?"

If Borne were thinking of closing down the Cake investigation, a great deal of effort would have been wasted. Endersby decided to answer carefully. "Two men, dangerous sorts, are still at large. I fear they may attack innocent people. The two Grisi brothers are foreigners. One pulled a knife on me while in the midst of a simple conversation about his sister."

"Are they capable of murder?"

"We are not certain, sir."

"Conjecture, then. And what of this Cake and his associates? Who had motive to take a stick to him in the first place?"

"It turns out he was often mistrusted, sir. He was ambitious, ruthless."

"So are many men in London, Endersby. I cannot tie up Stott and Birken for much longer."

"I understand, sir."

"In fact, Endersby, the whole business seems watery to me. The coroner decided it was assault. Well, find a ruffian and arrest him. Get one of these foreign men into Fleet and question him."

"If we can find him, sir. He has gone into hiding."

"How did that happen? I thought this was under your control."

"Men run in fear, sir. Their sister has sworn to protect her brothers at all costs and will not divulge their whereabouts."

"Wretched. Let Caldwell take this one over. He'll be on his feet in a day or two."

"A delay will cause us to lose the conviction, sir. Lose our grasp on possible suspects."

"You move too slowly for me, Endersby. I am sorry to say it, but this seems a straightforward matter of revenge. You have articulate witnesses. Let your sergeant run after them. We have seventeen bodies before us here and two madmen ready to burn down half of St. Giles."

"Is this your opinion, sir, or that of the *Chronicle?*"

"You are impertinent, Endersby. I consider your callousness reprehensible."

"I cannot allow you to dismiss the case of Samuel Cake, sir. The efforts we have put forth are leading us toward finding his killer. It would be folly to stop now."

"I did not counsel you to stop, Endersby. But to pass the

damned matter to Caldwell. Please do so at your earliest convenience. And tomorrow, I want you and Stott to begin the hunt for the torch-bearers."

Borne headed back to the office and paused out of the rain under the arch. "I want a report on this lodging house catastrophe as soon as next Friday. Just a sketch of the matter, the coroner's findings and a plan of attack. You can also write up a short description of the Cake business, so we have a record to hand to Caldwell."

"He has been assisting all the while, sir."

"All the better, then, that he take over."

Endersby wanted to cut out his own hasty tongue. Borne had manoeuvered him into the very corner he wanted to avoid. The puzzle of Cake was to fall apart before his eyes.

The rain began to fall more heavily, as if it were in an accusatory mode, an extended arm of Endersby's impatient superior. He moved under the arch. Sergeant Stott appeared before him in the courtyard as if that same crashing rain had conjured up his burly form. "I got your message, sir. Signor Fieno is in custody, and he wrote out his confession."

"Now, Stott. We have precious little time left us. Ride, fly, swim if you must, but get up to Gray's Inn station and find the beadle. Get Cake's clothes from him, even if you have to berate him. Then go about the houses near Number 46 Doughty Street and rap on doors and tell them who you are. Go after the neighbour next to Number 46 and talk to his servant. I need a refreshing glance at this case before I lose it."

"Lose it, sir?"

"Never mind, Stott. Ask at Gray's Inn of Mr. Rance, their superintendent. Tell him you want stories of similar crimes in the area, if any. Take sharp note of what he says. I want to know whether schools of thieves and bully gangs are common up there—though I doubt it. Then spend the rest of your afternoon at Eleazar the Jew Lender on the Strand. He is well-known in the theatre circles. Find out what he knows of Miss Priscilla Root. Tell him this matter concerns murder, that it concerns justice, and it also concerns his neck if he does not provide us with a lead or two. I have a vague notion he knows something. Once you have succeeded in all of this, meet me at the tavern across from Vinegar Yard at the hour of the farce."

Stott blinked at his superior. There was no time for him to ask for clarification, as Endersby had turned and with an uncharacteristic speed walked off in the direction of the Thames.

*   *   *

At the age of eight, Owen Endersby had been taken by his father to see a public hanging. This was done in the father's belief that all events contained in themselves a kind of justice. And it was up to man and woman alike to seek that justice out, to see the world as a rational place. Endersby never forgot that outing with his father. He ardently believed it had helped to shape his way of thinking and prepare him for his vocation as a policeman. Owen desired reason and balance above all things, searching out miscreants sometimes to the point of exhaustion.

The case of Samuel Cake was resting on conjecture. Worse, it was to be taken from him, and all its horrific mystery left in limbo while the murderer still breathed the cold holiday atmosphere of London. Endersby pushed his way through wet, grumpy fellow city-dwellers, their "pardon me's" lost on his ears. London was full of brutes, he thought. All of them wearing top hats and fine coats. All unaware that *his* mind was set on finding one responsible for a young impresario's death.

Twenty minutes of walking found him at the river's bank. Endersby had shuffled the Cake murder puzzle around, and like any man in a hurry, he had occasionally miscalculated one piece fitting in for another. But he sensed he would soon find a clearer picture. There was, after all, Cake's clothing still to examine. The cloak, for instance, had blood spatters. It also had deep pockets, but

Endersby had not taken enough time to look at them all thoroughly. "Must be done, old gander," he scolded. Fifteen minutes later, after walking through more busy streets, the rainy sky now clearing above him, promising sunshine, he stood at the stage door of the Italian Opera in the Haymarket. He asked for the singer, Miss Elisabetta Mazzini, and was delighted by the warm reception he subsequently received from a fine-looking woman. "Most kind of you, Madame Mazzini."

The woman was in her late thirties, round, blithe in gesture, her voice deep and smooth, and when she began to speak, she astonished the inspector, who stood for a moment with his mouth open. "Yes, from Manchester. Last name of Stork. Not a proper name for an opera singer. So, I trained in Naples and dyed my hair and married a Mr. Mazzini, who has passed on and left me comfortable. Clara is my real English name, but London knows me by Elisabetta."

"A fine ruse indeed," Endersby finally said. "You are truly an actress."

"Well, there are many of us who must play at disguises in order to earn our suppers, Mr. Endersby. Come into my private rooms. I am sure you will be wide-eyed on hearing about Mr. Samuel Cake. A man of mask and mystery much more than I."

How fortunate Endersby felt to find Elisabetta Mazzini so accommodating; how delightful to see her in her chamber at this late afternoon hour, meeting her pianist, listening to her voice trill and play in the realms of Mozart and Bellini. Elisabetta Mazzini poured him hot coffee and allowed him to listen to her for a few moments as she was learning a new part. Afterwards, she led him into a small room and sat down across from him.

Endersby asked her first about Friday last and why she had dressed and gone to visit Henry Robertson Dupré at Old Drury. "Vanity, Inspector," she answered frankly. "I am getting older. My singing voice is fading. The great Malabran knew of this aging, although she died too young to suffer its consequences. I dressed and agreed to take supper with Dupré—a difficult but sly man—on the hopes he might consider hiring me to act at Old Drury." Endersby pondered her story. "But then, I met up with Samuel Cake. By accident. He told me he was to be the new manager and superintendent of the theatre. Mr. Dupré was no longer in a position to hire. Indeed, Samuel Cake was kindly and offered to meet me for supper later on and discuss a possible post for me under his new management."

"I am certain Mr. Dupré was not pleased with the outcome."

Elisabetta Mazzini smiled then moved on to talk about Mr. Samuel Cake. "These facts are known by only a few— Samuel Cake swore me to secrecy. But now that the dear man has been buried, it is time I told you all." For the next twenty minutes, Elisabetta Mazzini astounded Endersby even more than when she had first opened her mouth and revealed she was an Englishwoman born and bred. She freely told him things which from now on would make the murder puzzle a tighter fit.

"Dear Samuel was a gentleman of sorts, sir," she explained. "I dare say he had a problem, however. He was charming, seductive and yet, after a time, one realized that all he wished for was companionship. If you catch my meaning."

Endersby found himself somewhat bewildered. "Was he diseased? Forlorn?"

"Perhaps the first...we never moved in any intimate manner to consummate our relations with physical pleasure—if you catch my theme."

"Was he then incapable of indulging in manly pursuits?" asked Endersby.

The vivacious woman broke into a sharp laugh. "Such pride you men carry about when it concerns your perform-ance—what we women consider to be but the brief crowing of the cock—a strutting about, a shove or two followed by a loud sigh, then a tumble into sleep."

"I see," said Endersby, his professional smile betraying a sudden hesitation at the woman's frankness. Elisabetta Mazzini's eyes sparked with merriment, and there was no hint of cruelty in her voice. "I cannot say if it were by choice or hindrance or even the 'French itch'—which may have been the reason. But dear Samuel was not excitable in that way. I have heard he was never intimate with any of the women he met nor even with the boys and gads of lower Great Windmill Street. Many of our older tenors here at the opera often indulge in that particular taste of meat—if you see my picture—but dear Samuel, oh, no, I think not."

The woman's face then changed; a cool, shadowy expression of seriousness removed the merriment Endersby had seen earlier on. "But there is more," she whispered. She leaned closer to him. Endersby listened and nodded and joined fact to fact, hearsay to gossip, forming a new picture of the motives and events surrounding the Cake murder. A feeling of relief—much like one has in recovering from a bad cold—began to suffuse his mind. Elisabetta Mazzini had given him new direction.

"Your discretion, Madame Mazzini, has been most appreciated."

The woman stood and put out her right hand, prompting the inspector to take it, bow and lightly kiss the ring on her middle finger. "A pleasant gesture from the Continent, do you not agree, Inspector?" Endersby agreed, and with his mind chock full of ideas and names he bid the diva *adieu.*

Soon after, Endersby indulged in a brisk walk through Covent Garden, then a ramble northward along High Holborn. Steeples and rooftops wavered in the damp air. At an open ground, the gate he pushed screeched from lack of oil. Before him he found headstones, carved dates and names. He studied the stones for a while and came to a conclusion. On leaving the graveyard, he decided to ponder his findings in a small tavern outside the gates. After a hot gin, the hobbling Endersby hired a hansom then presented himself to the stage-door keeper of Old Drury and made a polite, but firm demand. Hartley sent off a messenger; the young lad returned and led the inspector down halls and toward doors. Within moments, Endersby was met at the parlour entrance of Miss Priscilla Root's dressing chambers. A tall woman dressed in a man's black frock coat and trousers peered at him. Her hair stood spiked in short strands, its coif having been disturbed by the recent removal of a beaver hat.

"She is drunk and asleep."

"Wake her, then," Endersby commanded. "And be quick about it."

The tall woman did not move. "I can tell you all you want to know. I am her sister."

Behind her sat another woman dressed in the same manly outfit. Her boots were removed, and her feet rested on the arm of a sofa. A spaniel circled the room, panting.

"Take cold water and splash her," Endersby ordered.

"You are an old bulldog," the woman snapped. She flicked her cheroot, and ash floated to the carpet.

"I have run out of polite requests," Endersby said. "I have no time left to brook tantrums."

The woman gave in; she stepped aside and extended her arm as if she were a hostess welcoming Endersby into a dining room. The door shut quietly behind him, prompting the other manly woman to rise from the sofa. She jerked her head and led the impatient Endersby into an inner room, its colour and furniture grey and wan in the late afternoon's gloom. "Here, Inspector," the woman whispered. "But she is in a sorry, sorry state."

"I do not know what to tell you, Inspector," the sister then said, stepping gingerly into the room bedside her look-alike companion. "I don't know what is proper."

Endersby stared at the prone figure before him on the rumpled bed. He pulled from his satchel his ear trumpet and placed it on Miss Priscilla Root's chest. "She is breathing, at least." He could make nothing more of her state, given the dimness of the chamber. "Light a candle," he said. Both the sister and the other woman scuttled and scurried and returned with a massive light in a brass holder.

"Close, close by," Endersby ordered.

Twice the flame flickered on a face lined and crumpled by fitful sleep and worry; the cheeks looked desperate with rouge and smudged rice powder, as if messed by a violent hand. Endersby had feared a suicide, but the smell of rum on Miss Root's moving lips convinced him otherwise. Miss Root's hair matted her forehead, and with a tenderness even he found surprising, Endersby lifted the mass of wet curls away. With his arm under the actress's neck, he placed Miss Root into a sitting position against a stack of cushions. The manly sister handed him a wet sponge. Endersby dabbed lips, forehead and lower neck, and soon with only silence and curious eyes about her, Miss Root surfaced from her stupor.

"Good afternoon, Mrs. Arthur Summers," said Owen Endersby.

On hearing Endersby's voice, Miss Root tried to raise her arm to push him away. Her heavy shawl prohibited her from reaching the point where she could strike. Miss Root gazed at her attendants with weary eyes. "You again, sir?"

"Inspector Endersby, Mrs. Summers."

"You have come to take me to Newgate Prison?"

"Are you indeed worthy of a visit there, I wonder?"

"You do not lack charm, sir."

"I thank you, Mrs. Summers. You, in your turn, tend *too much* to dissembling."

"That is my *métier*, dear man."

The inebriated woman tried to lift her hand again, but it fell back with a plop on the cushion. "Let me be, please. Let me have a moment to myself."

"I have precious little time, Mrs. Summers." Endersby's foot was aching. He was wet and very tired; he knew he must not falter. It was an awkward situation, yet he must drive her into soberness. Endersby took the nearby basin and splashed water onto Miss Root's face. She turned from side to side. "Oh, please," she wailed. He took the sponge and dipped it lightly, then squeezed drops onto her wrists. Endersby placed the basin on the floor, dragged his chair closer, and with his face next to London's great *tragédienne*, he began the first of many thrusts and parries in the process of finding the truth.

As he spoke, his voice was calm, as if he were conversing with a stranger on a coach ride. "What do you see here?" He held up the promissory note with the signature, P. Summers.

"Paper and ink."

"And what else?"

"Naught else, dear man."

"You can see a bribe, of sorts, can you not, Mrs. P. Summers?"

"Can I? How you twist things, sir."

"Yes, this is a promissory note signed by you for money lent. It was money easily got by you, got with a low interest, much lower than Cake demanded from others. And we *know why.*"

Endersby let his face break into an encouraging smile. Always with Miss Root, he figured, there was a need to cajole. Some game to amuse her, then trap her.

"All I know is I needed money," she answered in a languid manner. "Dear Samuel lent it to me. I tried to repay him, but he was selfish and cruel and kept after me, after me, oh, you do not know, sir, how pressing and unreasonable that man could be."

"The cruel and selfish one was you, Mrs. Summers. You were a liar as well. You told all of theatrical London you carried the baby of a man you knew could *never* have given it to you."

The sister leaned down to Endersby's ear. "Not worth your trouble, Inspector. Believe me, it won't hold water with her."

"Blood, perhaps," he retorted, and demanded again of Miss Root what he believed was a truth held close in the hardest hearts of that darkened room.

"Take my word, dear man," Miss Root said. "You can claim no truth in that."

"Admit it. Cake was no more than a capon. A man who could not fulfill his manly duties, no matter how he was tempted, even by you."

No response. Then a sigh. Then a hand raised to strike, and that same hand dropped. "Falsehoods, all of them."

"And Mrs. Summers, the truth of your lost baby. You

wanted Cake to love you. You held him in thrall, threatening to tell London he was not a true man, and so you lied to keep him by your side. You also borrowed his money and forced him to give you special, lower rates of interest. All for the sake of revenge and foolish pride. Your own bitterness at being rejected by the poor man."

The actress turned her face away, as if Endersby's words were flames burning away her protective skin. A sob convulsed her chest. "The son you bore and lost was not Cake's. It was from none other than Mr. Arthur Summers, your erstwhile husband and your occasional bedmate, even though he had officially abandoned you. Oh, yes, to spite him *too*, you preened and cooed as if Cake were his bed rival, until the business came crashing down. Until the poor babe was stillborn, and you were left in shame by the husband who despised you."

"There was no baby," Miss Priscilla Root insisted, her voice quavering.

"I am deeply sorry for your loss," said Endersby, his voice genuinely sympathetic. Strengthening his resolve, however, he set aside his emotion and continued. "In High Holborn cemetery, Miss Root, there lies a headstone, a tiny grave. On it, the name of Master Lewis Summers."

"There is none such."

The sister again implored. Endersby reluctantly pulled back, staring hard at the actress, whose eyes now shone wide and whose flushed cheeks were glowing as if she had been dancing in drunken revelry.

At last the voice cracked; tears welled up. "I will not say it," the actress whispered. "You are full of lies."

"Tell me why you wanted so much to hurt young Cake. You loved him. You wanted him. When the baby died, you blamed him for making you so tired. You made him pay for a grave that belonged rightfully to the father—Mr. Arthur Summers."

"I will not look on this," Miss Root cried.

"The grave still stands, Miss Root," Endersby said. "You played on this cruelty, mocked Samuel Cake, paid your debts at your leisure and took delight in his anxiety."

The beleaguered woman lay on the rumpled bed and began again to weep. Suddenly, she laughed, wiped her tears, and smiled.

"You see, Inspector, I can fool you, even up close. Some wretch has filled your ear with poison. Has doused the light of your reason. Cake was my lover, true enough. He then found another, we made amends, and I borrowed his money because he was kind and generous."

"Generous to a point, Miss Root. But what I said to you was not lies. Not fancies. Many other women in London who loved Samuel Cake knew his charm and money were his only compensations for acts he was unable to perform."

"And why, then, if this was true," Miss Root argued, rallying a little, "would any of us have wanted such a monster?"

"Why indeed?" asked Endersby. "Whenever you went to visit Mr. Cake in Doughty Street, you wore a veil and were accompanied by your sister and her friend. You took them along as a general might take his colonels to ensure your safety."

"We went only twice to that lovely house in Doughty Street, did we not, sisters? Cake let us into his fine parlour with his piano and his painted walls and all his statues, and we took tea, and then we departed. A simple call, Inspector. Common in London's fashionable circles."

"Except that for you, Miss Root, it was but the lower kitchen you were let into. That was all. Mr. Cake did not allow his sordid business to take place above stairs. Indeed, if he had, you would have seen barren rooms. No statues, no painted walls. I have seen the place myself. And on Friday last, late into the night, did you three go again to Cake's house? Go, perhaps, to taunt him. To play at sport with him?"

"How novel you are, Inspector. We were here dining. Ask of Mr. Weston, he can tell you."

"Mr. Cake did not leave his private club in Swan Yard until two o'clock in the morning. There is a reliable witness to that fact—Miss Elisabetta Mazzini—who was there dining with him. He left the club and walked toward his house in Doughty Street."

"But we were in our beds by two, sir," blurted out the sister.

"Who can attest to that?"

"Why, all of us, sir."

"Each for each?" Endersby waited for a reply. Could a maid, a footman ever be trusted to tell the truth on a master or mistress? Could a sister, who might also be an accomplice? How could such an alibi be accepted in spoken testimony? Here was the crux, Endersby reminded himself. To be sure, on Friday last, Miss Root had motive, she had opportunity, she knew two women, manly and thin, who in darkness could be mistaken for men. This moment made Endersby feel he had lost the match. It took all of his sense of reason for him to restore his stance. But now he had to guess. He had to turn the puzzle upside down and see it from another angle. By doing so, perhaps he could discover a fact; he might be awarded a confession.

"You, Miss Root," he said, confident his new approach would be sound. "You have saved your own neck from the gallows yard at Newgate." Endersby confronted the three women, now in a row by the bed, the actress sitting up, the two manly companions at attention by her side.

"But how?" breathed the sister.

"Mr. Cake visited you on Friday last, did he not?"

"Yes, he came to this very parlour," said the sister quickly.

"He came to collect his money, did he not?"

"Who told you this?" asked Miss Root, her voice growing heavy with fear and anger.

"Two reliable men who work here—one your stage-door keeper, the other—not really a man as yet—but a young call-boy who sees with innocent eyes and speaks the truth."

"Yes," said the wearied voice of Miss Root. "Yes, and no. He came to get a sum of money owed to him."

"Precisely. A *partial* sum, which he had to beg to receive. For there was no reason for him to bring this very promissory note—the one found in Doughty Street— knowing it would remain only half paid. He left it, therefore, at home. He left it until he figured he could tear it up. You paid him some money Friday last, but then something else occurred in this room. Words or threats from him that if you had been in a sporting frame of mind, Miss Root, you could have gone in anger to his house after midnight to smash his things, to punish him more by stealing this last bit of evidence you had between you. *If* you had thought this way! But the promissory was left lying on the floor in a house you rarely visited and, as your silly lie about its decoration amply proved, was unfamiliar to you and your sisters."

The three women stared in mute amazement at Endersby's barrage of words. At his quicksilver deductions.

"Did you and Cake have bitter words Friday last?" Endersby asked directly.

Miss Root stood up, her cheeks flushed. Her sister was about to open her mouth when the actress teetered over to her dressing table. "Sisters, leave me, I beg of you. *Leave.*" The two other women walked out in silence. Miss Priscilla Root closed the set of French doors that separated her sleeping chamber from her parlour. Standing tall now, her back arched, she turned, faced the inspector and pointed to her dressing table.

"He stood by me there once he had received his money. I had no intention of ever paying off the full amount of the note, and he knew that. But on Friday last, he wore a different face. No longer pleading, no longer like a frightened servant. He stood here, and he threatened me with dismissal if I did not stop taking rum and hashish. 'Into the street, Miss Root, where starvation awaits you,' he said. It was that simple. He was to take over Old Drury as its manager, and he warned me if my debts remained unpaid, and if I did not present as professional a behaviour as I could, I would find myself taken into Bow Street. I tried to persuade him. He said he had my promissory note as proof—a legal document with my legal name and signature—which could be used against me in court. I wanted to kill him right there. But I could not move. And I had no idea where he kept his money, where he hid his records. He would gladly put me in my coffin, no less. I spat in his face. I tell you that with little pride, for I did love him."

The voice cracked, tears and heaving of the shoulders replaced the flat words. In a second, her arm flew out, smashing a bottle to the floor. "That night my sisters and I and Mr. Weston took dinner here and drank ourselves into sleep and oblivion—at least I did."

"How can I be sure of this?" Endersby then asked, his voice held low, his attention showing respect to Miss Root and her painful confession.

"Go and speak to little Reggie. He is all I have, really. He is a good boy and honest, as you say. He can tell you where I was and what state I was in late Friday. Disgraceful a state, as it was. There, it is all said. Grave deeds and a confession. Need I give you more?"

Endersby, weary and wet, desired to lie down, but he knew the evening ahead required more of his patience. "Not for now, Miss Root."

Endersby left the dressing room, reflecting on his minor triumph. He set about immediately searching for young Crabb and located him in the downstairs costume room. He asked the boy questions of a different sort this time, mainly to test Miss Root's veracity. Crabb was honest, and for what he knew and was able to tell, he was valuable to Endersby.

"You are sure, young master?"

"It was me, it was Mr. Weston, Miss Root and her two sisters. Mrs. B. brought us vittles from the house up Hart Street, boiled bones and oysters. 'Cept I had none of them oysters."

"What time did your supper take place?"

"Right after the comedy, come midnight perhaps ten minutes thereafter."

"Can you remember what Miss Root said to you?"

"About what, sir?"

"Any matter, young master. I am hear to listen."

"They talked about the play and the oysters. And Mr. Weston, he always talks about his sister, how poorly she is."

"Did Miss Root speak of going home, of going out to a party?"

"No, sir. She never goes out in the night. She sleeps in her parlour because it is warmer there, she says. I see her in the mornings when I come to tend the fire."

"Can you remember if she was asleep Friday last and remained in her rooms all night until Saturday morning last?"

Reggie Crabb hesitated then said, "Miss Root could not *but* stay there, sir. She was too drunk to walk. Her sisters were asleep on the floor. Cor, they stunk of too much wine. Miss Root became ill all over her dress. Lord, she was mewling like a baby. I helped her lie down in her bed. I stayed with her for a long time and fell to sleep myself. Yet, she woke me very early just near sun-up, because the window showed pink. Her little Kean had soiled the carpet, and I had to clean her up. Miss Root threw up again, the stink was terrible, sir. Cor, I had to clean that up, too." Young Crabb blushed on those last words. "I said no secrets. Miss Root will not like it."

"You have done well, Reggie. In fact, it was Miss Root who bade me speak to you about Friday last. She trusts you as I do."

"Thank you, sir."

"Here's a penny extra, lad. Remember, I am across Vinegar Yard tonight. Keep your eye out and sharp."

"I shall, sir." The boy ran off to do duties.

On his way out, Endersby decided to test another hunch, one that could still implicate Miss Root but more likely would exonerate her in favour of a guilty verdict for none other than Henry Robertson Dupré. It took Endersby a short walk northward, his mind reviewing facts. The club man at Litchfield Street was wearing a black topcoat, and his waistcoat reminded Endersby of a Persian carpet.

"You are here to ask about Mr. Dupré?" said the club man. "We are always obliged to serve the constabulary in any way we can." Dupré's private gentleman's club was furnished with private rooms and nooks for supper. It had an inner courtyard with an elm, a mournful cousin to the great trees leading out from London toward the southern counties.

Endersby immediately did not like the club man's manner. He acted glib, and he cut too quickly into Endersby's questions with what seemed liked rehearsed answers. Yes, Mr. Dupré was here from half eleven until past two in the morning, early

Saturday last. Yes, he was escorted afterwards to his house in
Woburn Place, a fashionable address, most respectable.

The club man called out, and the club's link boy was led
in. He was sixteen; he removed his cap, his hands dirty
from the black pitch of the torch he carried nightly to
make his living. He recited the walk he had lighted for
Mr.Dupré, from the club northward to Woburn Place, the
greeting of Dupré's housekeeper, and the quality of the
weather. All in a halting, practised manner.

"Your receipts, then, sir." Endersby knew establishments
of this kind gave credit and ran up tabulations for special
clients.

"Confidential, I am sorry, sir." The club man smiled stiffly.

"A fee is required, is it?" The club man cocked his head.
Endersby did not balk. He undid the clasp on his old
satchel. His purse lay in the flap and from it he produced a
sovereign. The link boy gasped, as if such money were a
discovery to him.

"Most preposterous, Inspector," the club man protested.
"Confidentiality is a principle of a gentlemen's club. I cannot
and will not allow such Bow Street vulgarities in this place."

Endersby replaced the coin, closed the satchel and walked
toward the door. "Murder is rewarded, sir, by hanging. As you
well know. Those associated with the obstruction of justice
and truth fare little better. When a conviction is successful,
those people who were deemed willfully associated with the
felon are also in peril of punishment."

The receipt book showed three signatures, all written by
the club man, all pertinent to port wine and beef and French
tobacco, credited to Mr. Henry Robertson Dupré. "How
curious," mused Endersby. "These entries were penned in at
one o'clock in the morning on early Saturday—you are
thorough. Which means, if I gather from typical practice,
you had closed the club and its kitchen by one and wisely
tallied all your receipts for the day. Which means that Mr.
Dupré left your premises perhaps a little earlier than you
had previously mentioned."

The club man insisted; the club man argued; the link

boy was berated by the club man for lying. The link boy broke down, slapped his cheeks in fear, told the inspector that it was not so late now that he thought about it, maybe half twelve. "I had to run on the double with Mr. Dupré, for the gentleman seemed in such a hurry to get to Woburn Place." The link boy was dismissed.

Endersby snapped shut the receipt book. He walked into one of the empty supper nooks, where he accosted a waiter setting a fresh table. The waiter knew of Mr. Dupré and told Endersby his regular patron had dined on beef and taken French tobacco on early Saturday last. "Very well," said Endersby. "And was Mr. Dupré in good humour, in your opinion?"

The waiter did not hesitate. "Mr. Dupré is often in good humour. But he was not his merry self Saturday. " Endersby asked why. "No, reason, sir. Only a surmise. He left long before his usual hour, about half midnight, I'd say."

Back in the entrance foyer, Endersby again confronted the club man, who remained adamant, hard-edged, stubborn but nervous, for his hands could not stay still. "I have an old watch, sir," Endersby began. "To my perpetual delight, it keeps perfect time." Endersby slid out the watch and fob from his waistcoat pocket, and as he spoke he gazed at it fondly, smiling with pride. "Now, I spoke with Mr. Dupré this afternoon. He told me he left the theatre for this club at five minutes past midnight. His stage-door keeper, however, remembered him leaving earlier, before the curtain dropped on Dupré's hit play. You claim he arrived here at the club at half eleven. I am bewildered, sir." Endersby stared hard into the club man's darting eyes. "Indeed," Endersby continued, still turning the watch in his hand, "both your link boy and waiter agree it was half twelve when Dupré left—not at two—which would jibe with your own receipt entries at one o'clock. Do you wish me to go on?" The club man remained silent. Endersby raised his eyebrows, put away his watch, and listened to the other man sigh. Endersby did not wish to prolong the agony of the situation. "How much did he pay you to lie, sir?"

The club man hesitated and looked over his shoulders to be sure he and the detective were alone.

"Two sovereigns," he whispered. "I knew not of any matter, sir. I still do not. It is none of my business to know. We often prevaricate for our members to avoid curious wives, creditors, nosy relatives. A club, Inspector, is a man's last bastion of retreat."

"So it seems," answered Endersby. "Certainly that is true for scoundrels."

*   *   *

The hackney cab almost ran into a wagon on its way to the house of Henry Robertson Dupré.

Woburn Place was an elegant street with newly planted trees set between the paving stones. Along both sides stood rows of houses painted in white stucco. The kitchen entrance to Number 12 was shaded by the front steps. Endersby was curious to see Dupré's abode, having met with him twice already this day. The housekeeper introduced herself. She was in a nervous mood, and Endersby, examining her face, worried she might become his adversary. He raised his hat and stepped across the threshold.

"Is Mr. Dupré in, by chance, Mrs. Croft?"

"Hasn't been all day. Not since he left for the theatre this morning."

"I am Inspector Owen Endersby of the Metropolitan Detective Police."

"I am honoured, sir." Mrs. Croft's face betrayed one feeling—worry—but her voice was welcoming. "This is about the terrible death of Mr. Cake? We read about it in the paper not a day past."

A clatter from the kitchen interrupted Mrs. Croft. She turned her face from Endersby to shout for quiet, but the noise did not cease. "I beg your leave, sir. But do come in. I can offer a cup of tea at this hour, although we are preparing for six gentlemen at half past eight, as Mr. Dupré is entertaining cousins from Shropshire."

Endersby watched Mrs. Croft's quick movements. Her irritated face softened a little. He had the impression her ire could be easily raised, but then her kindly side could just as easily reappear. He followed her into the broad, bustling kitchen. What a space it was, worthy of a theatre manager of Old Drury: two servant girls, a cook, a footman, all at the long wooden table, the footman with his silver polish, the servant girls at their chopping blocks, and cook, robust, merry, her large arm stirring a pot. One of the servants with a bright complexion was talking merrily.

Mrs. Croft introduced the inspector. The servant girls bowed, the girl with the bright complexion turning a brighter red. "He will want honest answers," she explained. Endersby thanked Mrs. Croft and outlined briefly the story of Mr. Cake's murder and the subsequent search for the culprit guilty of the crime. "Terrible, terrible," muttered the cook.

The questions were simple: "Tell me, please," said Endersby, "of the events that took place in this house on the night of Friday last. Who was here? What time was supper served? What were your duties? At what time did Mr. Dupré return home?"

Mrs. Croft answered the last question. "It was early for him, sir. At between half twelve and one o'clock. I was up then, doing accounts, and I noticed a link boy coming up the street with his torch ablaze. Mr. Dupré was behind him, and in a great rush from the way he was walking. The night was very dark, and I was surprised to see him at that hour."

"Yes, sir," the footman added. "Mr. Dupré is a hard worker. Home from the theatre most nights by two at the latest, into his bath and then to his bed. He is an early riser. Up at dawn for his *Examiner* and his breakfast. We were not amazed, in truth, but it was unusual."

"I heard not a sound," the cook said. "I sleep like a dead woman."

One of the servant girls meekly explained: "He greeted me and said he'd been to his club. He said he needed brandy and bath water and then sent me to fetch Jane, here. Didn't he, Jane?"

Mrs. Croft shot a worried glance at Jane, the talky girl with the flushed complexion. The footman lowered his gaze. The cook began stirring the pot with a renewed vigour. Endersby marvelled at the abrupt coldness which had befallen the company. He was even more amazed at Jane. She had gradually looked down as if she were searching for a fork on the floor. Indeed, in her attempts to answer his questions, Jane's lively voice began to squeak. What only moments before had been a jolly girl now became a stumbling child.

"I-I-I don't recall. B-But of course. I-I fetched his nightclothes from the dr-drying rack."

"And then?"

"T-T'was all, I r-recall."

"Then to her bed, Inspector," aided Mrs, Croft. "Our Jane is nervous, when she is met by strangers. It is nothing."

Endersby stood before the crew a moment more with his face quite openly curious and contracted with concern. "Did any of you hear Mr. Dupré moving about once he'd taken his bath?" Silence as the motley bunch reflected.

"I believe so, sir," the footman said. "I removed the tub and water to the courtyard, and I assumed Mr. Dupré took to his chores, then to his bed. One does and does not hear such common sounds, if you catch my drift."

Endersby tried a different question. "Was the front door locked when Mr. Dupré arrived home?"

"Yes, and I locked it after he came in," said Mrs. Croft.

"Did Mr. Dupré go out after he'd finished his bath?"

"But why would he do such a thing?" asked the footman.

Why, in fact? But then Endersby considered that the household had been performing its rituals for the night, and most likely they would not have imagined, nor had the temerity to admit, that Mr. Dupré was indulging in any untoward behaviour. Mr. Dupré was a man of some influence, both in the theatre and in his own home. Certainly, however, Endersby could not leave the situation entirely as closed.

"May I ask when you expect Mr. Dupré for this evening?"

"At half past seven, sir," said Mrs. Croft.

"For his relatives?"

"Yes," replied the footman.

"And would you kindly inform him that I would very much wish to visit him later this evening, simply to confirm what you have kindly told me."

Mrs. Croft was cordial. "At ten o'clock sir, if that is convenient."

"I shall send word."

Endersby thanked the assembled company for their time. He discovered on leaving Woburn Place that the winter's evening was closing in. Gaslights began to sputter. He felt grimy from his exertions today and wished only for a bath and the company of Harriet. "Move on, old gander," he said gruffly. It was a long walk to Cromer Street and one Endersby did not find pleasure in, as the rain was once more whisking around him in a flurry. But at last—out of professional necessity—he stood before a house that in grander times had been a mansion. It was divided into smaller chambers now, some of its larger passages and foyers converted into apartments, one that contained four rooms leased by Old Drury's leading player, Mr. William Weston.

Mr. Weston's apartment was sad-looking, melancholy in light and space, not unlike its prime occupant, the princely lead actor with the tall body, the pale face and the thinning hair.

The inspector was met at the front door by a dour older woman with a pursed mouth. "I am Mr.0 Weston's aunt," she said in her curt introduction. "Come this way, but please be quiet, as we have an invalid." The sour woman, her meagre body clothed in black cotton, pointed to a closed door and explained to Endersby that it sheltered the sickbed of Sarah, Mr. Weston's bedridden sister.

The reticent, cold-voiced aunt then told Endersby about Mr. Weston's whereabouts and activities on Friday night last. Her answers had a dry, fatigued quality to them.

"Mr. Weston arrived home at his usual hour of one."

"Were you waiting up for him?"

"I think not, Inspector. It is my custom to retire early, after tending Miss Sarah."

"Had you been tending her long?"

"Oh, my, yes. I was half asleep after two hours. You see, sir, she has the fits sometimes, and is in one of her periods where she cries and is very restless. She needs to be calmed. I often draw a hot bath for her to control her ranting. Though with our new physician and his sleeping powder, my work is made easier."

"Miss Sarah then slept, did she?"

"She did."

"Were you by a clock when Mr. Weston returned for the night?"

"How do you mean?"

"You said he came in at one in the morning. You were very precise as to the hour. I imagined you were waiting or perhaps preparing something for him and glanced at your clock."

"No, Inspector. I was in my bed. I do not prepare for my nephew unless he requests it. On Saturday last, he came in at one in the morning, as I heard his latchkey. And I always hear his latchkey at the same hour."

"But you did not *see* him come in?"

"No, Inspector."

Mr. William Weston at last appeared from a chamber next to the parlour, where the aunt and Endersby were seated. The actor's face was care-lined, but he had majesty in his straight posture and height. Seeing the actor in domestic circumstances, rather than on the stage, Endersby felt sudden awe. Mr. Weston explained through an apology that he had been preparing himself for the evening. "I beg your leave, Inspector," he said with much deliberation. "I hope my aunt has been helpful."

"Indeed, Mr. Weston."

Endersby was further delighted when Weston suggested they walk and talk together. "Would you care, sir, to come my way to the precincts of Old Drury, where I take supper?" the actor asked. The inspector agreed. Weston pulled on his overcoat with the fur collar. To Endersby's eyes, he then seemed even more stately. Weston's beaver hat extended his height: it was as though he carried his own light to show off his high cheekbones. Mr.Weston bid good night to his aunt.

"Shall you need supper on your late return?" she asked, her mouth thin and tight.

"I think not, Aunt," he said. He bid her good night again and led the inspector from the apartment into Cromer Street.

In spite of the hour, and the fatigue he had been feeling, Endersby found his energy and interest revived by the presence of the pale-faced man who now walked beside him. Mr. William Weston did not hesitate to share the domestic details of his life as the two of them crossed the street and turned their way south toward Drury Lane. He explained that each weekday evening before seven o'clock, he would walk to the chop house on Hart Street, take a hot meal, then prepare his face for the performance at eight.

"You have made a great effort," said Weston. "I mean, you have come to my home to examine me, because you wish to know if I have an alibi for Friday night last."

"Indeed, Mr. Weston. I must examine every by-way, and I must talk to anyone who was involved even in a marginal fashion with the terrible event. I have come to you as you seem reasonable, and to check on the alibis of others."

"Do you consider me a suspect?"

"I cannot say as yet."

Weston pondered the response for a moment. "Conjecture is the first step in solving a crime?"

"Always, Mr. Weston. You, as well as anyone I speak with, are in the shadow of suspicion. It is the nature of my profession to cast you there."

The two men moved slowly on, Weston controlling his wide steps out of deference to the limping older man beside him.

"I can tell you but a simple tale." The actor then continued, his voice low. In it, Endersby heard a refinement of feeling. "I performed the role of the Prince until ten o'clock on both Friday and Saturday last."

"A fine role, indeed, sir, as I was in the box on Saturday night. Most impressive show of remorse in the final act." Endersby could not help himself. He felt honoured, in one way, to be seen along the streets with such a well-known figure. He could not quell his praise of Mr. Weston's look of despair in Act Two.

"I thank you, sir, humbly."

Endersby pulled back and re-directed his passion. "And then?"

"On Friday, I played in the last piece, a comedy, until midnight and took a late supper with Miss Root and her sisters, oysters of a fine quality. I like to walk slowly home afterwards, to reflect, and so I reached Cromer Street at half-past one and went to bed, my sister having been given a sleeping draught, as is usual."

"Did you and Miss Root speak of anything in particular at your supper?"

"She told me that the singer, Elisabetta Mazzini, had been in Mr. Dupré's box and that Cake had stolen her away for the evening."

"Did Miss Root say why Mr. Cake had done such a thing?"

"Cake saved her from the clutches of Mr. Henry Robertson Dupré."

"Is he a dangerous man?"

"He seduces women, sir, and cruelly so."

"And Mr. Cake? Was he not also a seducer?"

"You refer to my Sarah. It is hard for me to judge, since I have seen so much of the aftermath of her infatuation with him. He was most kind to her, and he was most kind to me as well."

"How?"

"He lent me money."

"Was he discreet about it?"

"He was generous and practical. He was a man whose interests lay in building profit."

"How often did you visit Doughty Street?"

"Two or three times. No servants to the place. And I was always kept down in the kitchen to wait."

"You were required to sign promissory notes, then?"

"I was, and I did, and once my debt was paid, I usually tore them up."

"So, Mr. Cake returned them to you."

"He was fair-minded in that respect."

"Were you in debt to Mr. Cake? Recently."

"It hardly matters now. But yes, I was. Sixty pounds owing."

"Did you see Mr. Dupré at any time on Friday last?"

"Late in the evening, you mean?"

"Yes, any time after your supper."

"No. I would not have had opportunity, as my dressing room is in the back corridor."

"Did Mr. Cake have any enemies that you were aware of?"

"Other than his rival, Mr. Dupré? No. He was not the type to engender such."

"No jealous or vindictive lovers?"

"I do not think so."

When Mr. Weston looked at the glove taken from Endersby's satchel, he immediately tried it on and expressed both delight and trepidation. "It is a perfect fit."

"So it is," said Endersby quietly.

"A badly made glove, sir. One not worth wearing. It seems to have been made by an amateur at best. The crime rags mentioned a bloodied glove found in the backyard of Doughty Street."

"It was, sir. You were aware there was a laneway?"

"I once walked about that empty set of rooms and saw the stairs and the gate. I was always amazed that Mr. Cake did not have locks or latches."

"Is this glove yours, in fact?"

"If I say yes, what would that mean?"

"A difficult question. It is a piece of evidence found on the site. Evidence which could be incriminating."

"It is not mine. I must have fine gloves for fencing, sir. Such a glove as this would not be useful to me."

"You have sustained an injury?" Endersby noted a long, fresh scab on Mr. Weston's hand as he gave back the glove.

"A graze from a blade two days ago. A swordsman in the play, by accident. Common enough."

Endersby replaced the glove. He had recorded the smile, the occasional pause in Mr. Weston's dialogue with him, actions innocent enough in themselves.

"Mr. Weston, do you have any vices such as Miss Root's?"

"Do you mean that I take to drink?"

"Yes, I mean that."

"I cannot afford to. I cannot be drunk if I must sword-play. I may take a life, and my purpose is to feign violence, not to perform it. Yet, I shall admit I sometimes drink a tankard of ale. Maybe two, to give me strength."

"And what of Soho and its dens?"

"Never, sir."

"Even if the desire be there?"

"You mean the despair. I must be sober enough to care for Sarah."

All in all, the words were spoken in rounded tones and with an even pace, and although Endersby's nature was inclined to wariness, he decided for the time being to let what he had learned about Mr. Weston sit comfortably. The two men stood on the rushing street before the theatre where they had finally come to rest. They spoke further of trivial matters. Of the death of Madame Malibran and the great success of the Italian composer, Donizetti. And of the fires in St. Giles and the state of poor lodging houses, where so many of the less fortunate actors of the capital lived.

"I bid you good evening, Inspector."

"If you have any other memories, any revelations you feel the need to express, I am at the tavern across from Vinegar Yard."

"Thank you."

"One last request. Is your sister in any state to be questioned?"

"Whatever for?"

"I am a man searching for the truth, Mr. Weston. It may be necessary for me to ask anyone connected, as I said before. To clear up sudden doubt."

"I understand. If you can grant me the courtesy, I shall certainly arrange a time for you to meet her, when she is feeling stronger. She is, however, frequently sedated these days, as our physician has recommended a sleeping cure. To calm her ravings."

"What a pitiful situation for you, Mr. Weston. However, even in illness, truth can be spoken. But I appreciate your generosity. I bid you good evening."

*   *   *

"There you are, at last."

"I cannot stay long."

"Embrace me, dear Owen. At least an embrace."

Harriet was flushed. She had been setting the table. A fresh cap topped her curls. Perfume wafted about her, which Endersby loved—a faint touch of lavender, sweet and womanly. He held her, felt her softness, and as if a balm of oil had been applied to him, his own cranky, paining self dissolved. Evaporated into the air, he mused, kissing his Harriet and taking her warm hand in his.

"You seem most distracted, Owen. It is that time, as always, is it not?"

She was referring to the long familiar stand-off between them, the turn in the path of an investigation when he withdrew more and more into his own thoughts, leaving her outside of himself, as if she were locked behind a solid window of glass and could not reach out to touch him.

"I beg your pardon."

"Pardon granted. Habit is a great forgiver of sins."

"Harriet?"

"Never mind. Solange has made you a fine soup. But, oh, I see resistance. What? You cannot stay? Is that what this look is all about?"

Endersby was about to tell her he must rush back to Vinegar Yard. It was a few minutes past seven o'clock, and Stott was to meet him. Vital information was forthcoming. There was Samuel Cake's cloak to be examined, among other facts and findings. Endersby wanted nothing more than to take a bath and lie beside Harriet on the divan before the hearth. And then he felt the need to confess his anger.

"I have been removed from the Cake investigation, as of this afternoon."

"How do you mean?" Harriet led him quietly toward the dining table. She slipped off his rank coat and pulled at his suede gloves.

"Borne has commanded me to lead troops into battle. To secure a victory over some vicious creatures guilty of setting the lodging house fire in St. Giles."

"He has great need of you, then, Owen. A great need to vindicate the deaths of those children and women." Harriet held out the chair and gently pressed her hand on her husband's shoulder, all the while looking toward the hesitant Solange who, with tureen in hand, and with sweat upon her forehead, dared to take one step toward the dining table.

"Indeed, yes. I cannot fault him in the end. It is a noble gesture."

The ladle poured a beef-smelling, onion-rich stream into the bowl. Endersby breathed in the aroma of what his mind immediately labelled as ambrosia.

"Indeed, noble. You are worthy of the task."

"I am, certainly." The spoon rose to his lips; the spoon dipped again and again, and Endersby realized he was at last dry and comfortable and that Time, a wanton and oft-demanding master, could stand and wait until the second full ladle had been downed.

"Caldwell is to take on the matter of Cake's murder."

Harriet shook out her table napkin, secured it over her bodice, and dipped her spoon. Solange retreated toward the kitchen door.

"Will he be worthy of such a responsibility?"

"I cannot say. Well done, miss," Endersby spoke to the lurking girl. His mouth was full of a toasted square of bread so heavy with garlic, he needed to dab his eye. He then wiped his chin and rose."I cannot say, but I venture, I shall have to direct him."

"He seems a willing enough man for that."

"Indeed. I must run to Vinegar Yard."

"So, you said, my dear. There is jellied eel for later, when you return."

Endersby could hardly contain himself: eel was his favorite dish. Arms outstretched, he bussed his Harriet, and even had the quick wisdom to address the hard-working Solange. *"Merci* to you, young woman," he said, and pulled on his coat before struggling to put on his suede gloves with Harriet's gentle help.

The tavern across Vinegar Yard was not crowded. Plates and jugs were carried to and fro, and the smoke from pipes floated up to the massive rings of candles over the tables. Endersby took a moment to unwrap his coat, shake his hat and peel off his gloves, looking all the while at Sergeant Stott standing at attention in front of him with a tired look on his face. Beside the sergeant was a handsome younger man. He had oily hair and wore a yellow cravat.

"Gentlemen, please," said Endersby. He ordered a round of brandy and hot water.

"This is Josef, nephew of Eleazar the Lender, on the Strand."

"My pleasure," Josef said. He placed on the table a raft of folded papers. Each bore the signature of "P. Summers", and each recorded a sum lent on promise of repayment with interest. "Mrs. Summers, alias Miss Priscilla Root, frequently comes to us, to my uncle. We know she owes other lenders as well. Of course, she can pay, and she does pay. But it takes time."

"Have you seen her recently?"

"Oh yes, yes, in Soho, at the club at Balham's, which she frequents with her sisters. I went to inform her that my Uncle Eleazar would no longer be angry with her if she would agree to pay him more regularly with extra small sums. Miss Root was generous, oh, yes and grateful."

"Had she been tardy?"

"Yes. I had come to the theatre Sunday last to collect. She sent out to me her little call boy, oh, certainly a good boy, and the money was right. I am back-and-forth between our clients and my Uncle Eleazar. It is our business, you see."

"Was she then agreeable?"

"She was most agreeable after my Uncle Eleazar had agreed to arrange these weekly payments, and they include the one sovereign she already pays once a week." Young Josef was imposing, clear-headed and straightforward. He had a quiet, mysterious air about him, however, that to an innocent eye might seem frightening.

Josef rose to leave and gathered his papers.

"Did you, Josef, ever meet Mr. Samuel Cake?"

"I knew of him. I had taken my cousin to his theatre. But I never made his acquaintance."

"And your uncle?"

"My Uncle Eleazar knows all of London. You best ask him. He did not lend money, however, to those with a full purse."

"Did you or your uncle ever lend money to a man called Giulio Grisi?"

"Only to his younger brother, Franco. Giulio is too proud for money lenders."

"Do you happen to know where he is at this moment?"

"In London."

"In hiding?"

"Is he? I have not heard."

"If you do, if you meet Franco within the next day or night, do not hesitate to send word to me."

"He has committed a crime?"

"He has beaten a policeman."

"What a foolish thing to do," said Josef. He shook the inspector's hand and left, not having taken a drop of his brandy.

Sergeant Stott then spoke up; he described his journeys into Gray's Inn and his particular discoveries. "Super-intendent Rance beckoned me into his office. I did not know how to acquit myself, except to come right out with my request. I asked about thieving schools and about gangs. As Mr. Rance was half amused by my queries, he continued to listen, and then told me blankly that he knew of none. That the Cake matter was singular, in his opinion. That theft was not rife in the area, despite its respectability, no doubt due to the efficiency of his policemen. I then enquired as to the procedures on Friday last, the night of Mr. Cake's murder. Rance complained that the station was awakened at a very late hour. The admittance sergeant showed me the records. Mr. Merron, the servant sent by Cake's neighbour, arrived at the station at fifteen minutes before three and had to summon a constable who was sleeping in the back chamber. According to the record, the constable in question reported that he first viewed the body of Mr. Cake at the premises of 46 Doughty Street one half hour later.

"I then ventured to Doughty Street. Slipping from door to door, I gathered scant information and only one offer of a cup of tea to chase away the dampness. Until I came to Mr. Cake's neighbour. His old servant, the one who had fetched the constables on that fatal Friday, was most forthcoming, chattering like an old monkey. I was reminded of such by his broad sideburns as he went on. As it was raining hard, and the kitchen door was unprotected, he waved me in. I sat through his entire description of the events, from his being wakened by his master, from his hearing the noises in Cake's house at such a late hour—loud enough for a man partially deaf—it being past two o'clock, to his putting on of boots to run to the station. He made a point I had him repeat. On his way back with the constables he took a shorter route, down an alley, and he saw through a break in the houses the dark outline of a costerman's cart. Most odd, he claimed, most unlike costers to lurk on the streets at that hour. Few of them come this far from Covent Garden. A figure sat holding the reins. The figure was smoking, wore a cloth on the head, wore what seemed to be a skirt, seemed most woman-like. And that was all."

"Enough, and well said, sergeant."

Stott then asked if they could find a private room upstairs. Endersby called over the barkeep and made his query. He and Stott were summarily led past the bar itself, through a curiously wide hall, and into a small room with a cold hearth.

"I shall send the boy to make a fire," said the barkeep.

"Do not bother, my good man," replied Endersby. "We shall return to the main room presently for our pie."

From a hefty sack, Stott drew out a long black woollen cloak. "At last," said Endersby. The cloak collar was of silk. Its hem and side pockets were still spotted with Cake's blood. Stott spread the cloak over a set of chairs Endersby had clustered. Both men rubbed their hands and blew on them from the cold. The light was dim. Stott searched for a candle and was forced to run to the barkeep to find one. In the meantime, Endersby walked around the cloak, lifting its weight and peering into its underside. An eerie feeling it was to touch the material, as if Cake were still a part of it, as if his body might suddenly materialize from it, popping out at Endersby like a demon in a stage melodrama.

When Stott returned with the shuddering light, the cloak took on vibrant new life. Its lining was of scarlet, and it shone as if polished with chamois. Endersby brushed his fingertips over its surface. He began to pat it. He lifted it to his face and pressed its corners. Running it through his hands, he found along one side a row of very small buttons, every one square and sewn over with a sheath of the scarlet cloth. He unbuttoned all of them patiently, with Stott holding the cloak apart. The entire cloak then widened to twice its width. It was as if Endersby had uttered "Open Sesame", and the cave of the Forty Thieves appeared before his amazed eyes.

"Curious, Stott. It is a bank."

In small folds, there were hundreds of pound notes. The folds were clasped by eyes and cloth hooks. It took Endersby and Stott ten minutes to pull from the folds over two thousand pound sterling.

"Mr. Cake's balances," marvelled Endersby. "He walked with his own money box around his shoulders. Pray, what if by chance he'd left it in a cab?"

"Not likely, Inspector. Do you think?"

Endersby hands flew into other interior pockets. Here was a notebook hand-sewn of flattened sheets. Names appeared in columns. There was Mr. Buckstone still owing. There, too, Miss Root as "P. Summers". And Mr. Weston with his sixty pounds. "It hardly matters now," quoted Endersby.

"I beg your pardon, Inspector."

"Those words were uttered by Mr. Weston about Cake's business of loans and notes."

The buttons were re-buttoned and the cloak folded shut.

"Ah," cried Endersby. "How clever."

"What, sir?" Stott had taken to stamping his feet to chase the damp air away.

"Hence the shy seamstress. Esther by name. The 'lovey-dovey' girl. Another quote, I am afraid, sergeant. A worker for Mr. Cake, a seamstress. I surmise this is her excellent handiwork."

A pocket inside one of the outside pockets was yet another discovery. "What a trove," exclaimed Endersby. "Ah, look at this."

The paper was soiled but readable. One signature was large: William Weston. The sum, however, puzzled Endersby. "Look, Stott. Read out the number to me. What is the amount of this promissory note?"

"Thirty pounds, sir. In number, and written out in full. And Cake, the lender. Weston is debtor. Both have signatures."

"Hand it to me."

Endersby took the note. "But the actor told me he owed sixty pounds, as the ledger recorded."

Was this a separate loan? A loan in two parts? Or was this note a balance of some kind or other?

"Read the date out to me, Stott, if there be one. On the note."

"Fourteenth October, of this year."

"Over two months."

"Yes, Inspector."

Endersby mumbled thirty pounds again and placed the note in his satchel.

"Stott, take the cloak back to Scotland Yard. Take the money in your sack and go as quickly as you can and lock it up. We have not been spied on here, so you will be safe.

Once you have done that duty, return here, take your pie and stout and sit with me, for we have more things to do this night, and some of them may not be very pleasant."

.   *   *   *

Henry Robertson Dupré awoke at his desk in the attic of Old Drury, the candle gone out. His bizarre, narrow office felt colder than an iceberg, at least as Henry imagined an iceberg being cold. He read his watch. Nearly half past nine o'clock. He smiled to himself and sat up. He gathered the pages he had written and placed them in a corner of the desk. He trimmed and lit the candle before shoving back his chair. With all this movement, he was silent and cautious, the night outside full of shouts. He took from the drawer a short iron staff and pried up two of the broad floorboards, which helped make up the narrow terrain of his office. Had his architect not built him a new floor, Henry's secret cache would have been hidden in a cupboard or behind a cloth. But it was the floor, and how well it yielded the folded cloak. This evening, Henry decided the cloak was enough. Perhaps he would risk a broad rimmed hat. He pulled on his blue waistcoat and frock coat. The candle sputtered, and its flickering jarred his concentration.

"And so, *guv'ner,*" exclaimed Henry to himself, as if he had just split in two and become Master and Familiar. "So, off we trot." A not unpleasant swirling overtook him, as if he were mounted on a racing steed and had lost hold of the reins. Ignore the clay bottle, counselled his Familiar self, leave its oil and sheaths. No time, no desire tonight for reaming and ramming. "Ah, no," he whispered. He smiled again as he looked for a second time at his watch. Then he resumed his dressing. He tied on the great cloak. He tugged down the broad rim of the hat.

On the shy side of half past nine o'clock, Henry Robertson Dupré descended the back stairs of Old Drury. He hurried out, passing though Vinegar Yard into the bustle and shadows of the street. There was a dour expression on his face, as if he had just eaten a cut of lemon, but perhaps this was more a forced look, more to do with his disguise than his temperament. His marching feet led him down Bow Street. Clouds blotted out the stars, and the rain was light. Gaslight softened brick and cobble, giving to Henry's mind the appearance of a painted canvas streetscape. There was a wild beating in his heart now. Ahead, in the meandering lanes, waited the brothels and nanny-houses of London. The thought made him thirsty, and he made a quick turn, walked briskly up a shallow court and entered a cosy gin shop.

"A moment only," he chided himself and signalled to the barkeep to bring him a glass.

* * *

"I know it's you," said young Crabb to himself, escaping from the shadow of the building, his eyes wide and aching with wonder. "What else can I do but go?"

Dupré was therefore left to his drink in the tavern and Reggie Crabb, spy and professional aid to the Detective Police, ran along the street. A rabbit could go no faster, since the inspector had said be sharp, be my eyes, so now Crabb must be his legs, too. He ran and stumbled and careened around corners. It would be true to say Crabb was frightened. *Lordy*, he thought, *if Mr. Dupré was to find me out. Then it's the mines, it's the streets for sure, a crossing sweeper's broom.* Now he saw the tavern door moving toward him, his own legs in a big ache from the pounding of the cobbles. The door grew, then it opened, and the smoke took hold of him. *Cor*, where was the old fat man? Crabb's first thought was the inspector had left him to be caught. He pushed from table to table, and in a panic tripped and fell. He brushed himself off, grabbed his cap and ran to the barkeep. By the time he shoved his way forward, his eye caught a figure at a table. It was Mr. Endersby, lifting his glass of rum and hot water. He was already talking, cheeks flushed with hearth-warmth. *I hope he will listen.* A rougher, burly man sat across from him, shovelling pie and pastry into his wet mouth.

"Sir," shouted Crabb, his breath shooting forth.

"Lad, come here. Calm down."

"He's run out, sir. Run to a gin house on Broad Lane."

"Who do you mean, lad? Take a breath."

"Mr. Dupré, sir. I was your eye. Sharp, sir. And he ran out."

"Here, sit here. Now look at me. Once again. Start at the beginning."

"Where, sir? All I know—he took a supper in the Green Room, went upstairs to his attic at half past of seven and shut the door."

"Dupré did not go home? He took supper in Old Drury."

"Yes, sir. Lordy, that is but the start."

"At half of seven, he shut his door," repeated the inspector.

"I hid—like you said—I hid at the stair-top, under the fly drum. I waited and I waited, and he came out after so long a time. After more time, he went back in and fell to sleep."

"How did you see that?"

"His door, sir, he left it ajar. I sat and hid—like you said—and when he woke, he lit his candle and then he bent over the boards in the floor and took them up with an iron staff. He pulled up the cloak, sir. The black cloak then a hat, and he put them on."

Crabb held his hand to his aching throat.

"Stott, hand me your porter. Here, lad, take a slow slip. Easy, now."

Crabb gulped the rich liquid and coughed. He drew his hand over his mouth.

"Tell me more about the floor, lad."

"But sir, he is out. He is in Broad Lane. I was alert—like you said—and he will go on."

"Right you are, lad. Stott, come with me now. You, lad, you go back to your stairwell and wait. Hold up there and do not move. Mr. Dupré may return, and if he does, you somehow come back here. If you cannot find us, tell the barkeep you came in and ask him to tell you the time. Then, go back to your bed. You have done well, my young eyes."

Crabb pushed the chair back. He listened to the inspector with only half an ear, for he was more interested in going along. "May I not come, sir?" his little voice asked. But the noise of the other men and the scraping of chairs drowned out his request. The inspector and the burly man threw coins on the table and made for the door in such haste the old man's limping leg seemed to fly by itself. *Lordy,* thought Crabb, *what is up now? What is the mischief?* Crabb's brain was sick with watching. He wanted to drink a draught, and he wanted to run with the inspector. He sauntered out of the tavern, ambled into Vinegar Yard and stopped to take in the rain-filled air of the city.

At the stage door, he tipped his hat. The theatre was full again tonight. The crowd burst into applause as a trumpet sounded. Crabb climbed the stairs, once his cues were done, and sat once again, alone, under the fly drum.

"Lordy," he grumbled. Such a strange life. He still had a few moments before his next rounds. "I wonder," said he to the drum, half hoping it might answer him back. "I wonder if I will ever see that lovely Betty again."

*   *   *

Dupré entered a narrow passage. Stale cold rimed its walls. Nary a sound he made, as if his presence would jar those who appeared before him. Figures in black and grey, feathers and fringe on all of them. And all of them lining the curved staircase which rose into a heady gloom. Their movements spoke of pleasure, secrecy, coin. Of physical delight, thought Henry, of a kind known to Jezebel and the acolytes of Sodom and Gomorrah. Beyond the cramped curve of stair came the noise of laughter and drum roll. For here, and this fact brought a quick grin to Henry's face, here was his rival house. Here was the great Covent Garden, but not its grand foyer and its saloons. Rather, this was its infamous back stairway full of women of the town. Henry climbed further into the curve, and a legion of black, bobbing bonnets came into view. Regimental formation, he surmised, a woman to a step, shawl pulled tight, bonnet loosened, mouth busy, knees bent. And the clientele—not the pay-box kind, indeed, but the shilling-a-throw gentleman, top hat on, legs astride, buttons undone before the bobbing head, posture as straight as best a man can do after pints of ale, dignity only slightly compromised by a pair of teetering boots on the step slant. There, to Henry's right, a frail eight-year-old girl peddled paper violets.

"Ha'penny a gather, your worship."

Henry tossed the waif a penny, snatched the bunch and mounted more steps. "Trot on," he said under his breath. Where was one pretty enough in this smelly light? "Ah," he cried, moments later.

Near the top of the staircase, he handed his gather to a young bonnet, her black hair pulled tight into the frame of her rim. "What, hello," Henry said. The girl's lips smiled bright red from grease paint and spittle.

"'Allo, squire," she said, eyes aglance, hands already twisting open Henry's trouser buttons. She began, slowly, sliding and sliding, the rim of her bonnet brushing against Henry's groin. On and on, slow, up and down, and it was as if in this moment of lust, Henry was transformed from a man into a frigate, his topsails all trimmed, his body into the wind ploughing through swells. His yardarm was straight; his mast at full height. "Easy," he cautioned his bonnet. "Easy, there." He pinched his thumb and forefinger on the girl's shoulder and slowed her down. "Steady, careful."

The bonnet did his bidding. Henry raised up his head and breathed. He readjusted his stance. "Go on," he bade her. The bonnet began again with some vigour. Henry stared at a stain on the wall beyond her head, a hand mark, greasy and small. This was but one distraction which bothered him among many. What joy he had entertained by his disguise, now faded.

"Damn," Henry said again and pulled back. His bonnet took hold of his thigh.

"Come along, squire," she said, her voice low and hoarse. "We ain't done as yet."

Henry had already started to button his trousers. He proffered her a shilling, tossing it at her face.

"Aaooh. Christmas come early. I thanks you, squire."

Down the stairs Henry pushed. He shoved his hat from his sweaty brow and finished buttoning himself, keeping his head low as he strove through eager men making their way up the crowded stairs.

The brutal air of Bow Street awakened him.

"Ah, Mr. Dupré. A fine supper you've taken."

"What in damnation are you saying, sir? I beg your pardon."

Before him in soiled hat and shabby suede gloves stood the bulky, broad-smiling Inspector Owen Endersby.

"Relatives from Shropshire, I understand," queried the inspector. "Six of them. All lined up in a row."

"I do not see your jest, Inspector."

"Meet my sergeant, Mr. Stott. He will aid me in escorting you home to Woburn Place."

The burly man's hold was already pinching Henry's arm. "This is outrageous and preposterous, sir. Leave me be."

"Mr. Dupré. I need only a few moments of your time. Over the matter, sir, of a pack of lies."

"Let me go."

But it was no use. The door to a hansom cab was already held open, and with a hard, cruel shove and a clamp on his wrist, Henry found himself beside the gruff but still smiling inspector, whose firm hand held him all the way to Number 12.

* * *

"Now then, ladies and gentleman."

The kitchen at Number 12 Woburn Place was lit by two candles placed on the long table. Mrs. Croft stood by the dying hearth in her night dress and cap. The cook, the two servant girls and the footman held close their flannel night robes. Henry Robertson Dupré removed his cloak, and on instruction from Inspector Endersby, handed it to Sergeant Stott. For the past five minutes, as the company was hastily assembled, Dupré had said not a single word.

"We are here in this kitchen to come to terms," said Endersby. He was tired. His leg panged so much, he stopped for a moment to rub his knee. Mrs. Croft stepped forward and told the footman to fetch the inspector a chair.

"'Tis better if I stand, madam. I thank you."

Jane, the stuttering servant, girl began to sniffle. Mrs. Croft was about to go to her side when Dupré's voice resurfaced. "Leave her, Croft," he said, his tone so vicious, the housekeeper backed off to the hearth. "I want all of you to know…"

"I beg your pardon, Mr. Dupré," Inspector Endersby interrupted, his voice raised. "You shall be called upon presently to speak, once I have had my say."

"This is not a court of law," the theatre manager spoke back.

"No, indeed. But you shall see one of those soon enough. Do not try my patience. I shall be forced to have Mr. Stott come forth."

"Beware, Inspector," countered the irate Dupré. "You are acting like the secret police. Something the heinous French might invent. I remind you we are in England. And I am a free man."

"You *are a liar*, bar none," retorted Endersby, turning to the arrogant man. Endersby's hand lifted ready to strike. The inspector checked himself, however, on hearing a faint gasp from the sniffling servant girl. Stott came up behind Dupré. The sergeant placed his hands on the manager's shoulders and persuaded him to sit down.

"Now, ladies and gentlemen, I shall not take much more of your time," Endersby said, his voice calming. "No doubt you are exhausted from having made a grand dinner this evening. It was for six men, I believe, six cousins from Shropshire. A pleasant number for a table. Pray, cook, what was your fish dish?"

The cook stood silent, bewildered. "Madam?" insisted the inspector. The cook glanced first at Dupré, who ignored her. Mrs. Croft was implored next, but no response.

"There wasn't any, Inspector," came the answer at last from the cook.

"What a pity. I myself am fond of fish as a first."

The footman made a gesture to speak.

"Yes, sir. Memory jogs, does it?" said Endersby, his voice taking on a pleasant if still edgy tone.

"Only mutton stew, tonight, Inspector. And that's the truth of it."

"Well, not quite, my man. A footman is a respectable profession. I admire your patience. But it is not in my experience a posting which requires a man to obstruct the course of justice."

"I do not follow, sir," said the footman, now demonstrably nervous, as his left eye-lid had suddenly taken to fluttering.

"Oh, do not go on," whined Dupré. "What a hopeless ninny you are."

"Mr. Dupré, I shall not warn you again," said Inspector Endersby.

"Sir?" enquired the footman.

"We were speaking of the truth. It is my impression, from my earlier visit this evening, that the truth has somehow been warped. The cook made no fish, you speak of stew, and yet I understood there was to be a dinner. Well, what happened to it? Were the relatives delayed? Did they float into the ether?"

"They came and went. Nothing more," said Dupré.

"And fed on dust, did they, Dupré?"

"My servants do not lie, Inspector."

"Unless paid to do so. The club man I spoke with told me a fine story. Until I checked his receipt book. There was the matter of time being conveniently manipulated."

The present company made no sound.

"What did you gain, Dupré, from these arrangements? Your servants stand in fear before you. I can see that. The club man made a fool of himself and you."

"This is preposterous. On Friday, I went for supper, I came home, I went to bed."

"Granted, you did those things. So, you are innocent?"

"Most certainly. You are here to berate me into a false confession."

"I am here as a public official to find out the truth about a man's death, Dupré. You have set up a wall of lies to stop me. Or, at least, to make me jump and fall about. Yet, you say you are not guilty. Here sits, ladies and gentlemen, London's greatest theatre manager. A man who pays off his club man to secure his innocence. But why? Is this innocence the dream of a madman?"

"Sir," spoke Mrs. Croft. She reached behind her to the hearth and took down a jug.

"Croft, leave that be," ordered Dupré. "You shall find yourself without employment, I assure you."

The woman stopped.

"What are you afraid of, Dupré?" asked Endersby.

"I cannot oblige you, Henry," said Mrs. Croft. She took the jug, walked to the table and turned the jug out. A jingle of sovereigns rolled onto the surface. "Take your money back, Henry. I, for one, will not stand by and support a lie for little reason."

"You stupid beast."

"Dupré, control yourself."

"I ask you to leave, Inspector." Henry Robertson Dupré stood up. Endersby signalled to Stott. The sergeant's strong arms took hold of Dupré and forced him back down into his chair. The inspector then walked over to the seething man, sat on the edge of the table and faced him.

"If I cannot persuade you here, Dupré, it is my duty to escort you to Scotland Yard."

"On what charge? You have no right to touch me."

"On suspicion of unlawful acts. You are man of logic, Dupré. Imagine my perspective. I see a situation wherein a powerful man is usurped by another; I see a man whose anger is immediate; I hear from others that this same man—who professes to be a gentleman—takes advantage of women. Indeed, he seduces them. Nay, he threatens to rape them at his pleasure. And not just penny-a-throw whores. No, leading singers of the Italian opera. I hear from reliable sources that Mr. Cake came to warn a certain Miss Elisabetta Mazzini to beware of you, since you are considered a dangerous man. This careful Samuel Cake, on the same night, was found beaten to death in his house. A man in a cloak was seen leaving Mr. Cake's house in Doughty Street under suspicious circumstances. You own a cloak, Dupré, you hide it in the floor of your office, and you use it as a disguise for visiting whores. I discover, *in fine*, that you have bribed a man to say one thing against another. And that your household itself is a bastion of tongue-tied individuals who received a clutch of sovereigns to keep their mouths shut. All this, Mr. Dupré, leads me to believe you are hiding something. You are indeed hampering an investigation into a murder. This is serious on all counts."

"Miss Mazzini is a liar."

"To what purpose? She is a woman of reputation. She gained to her advantage from what Mr. Cake told her. She became safe from you."

"Cake was a coward. And a thief."

"Worthy of a beating?"

"I wanted to make sure the club man would not lie about me."

"Was it worth so much of your time and effort? To secure a sycophant's tongue?"

"Inspector, men such as he are always ready to deride. He is a snake in the garden. I wanted to be sure his memory could not falter."

"But if you are innocent, why did you need to pay out coin? Especially since you are a man who is on the brink of financial difficulty."

"This greasy world runs on money, Inspector. Reputations rise and fall because of it."

"But we are still missing the mark, Dupré. You claim you are innocent. Yet, you sully the water you bathe in. I am not certain I can see the run of the plot."

"He is protecting himself," the stuttering servant girl cried out.

For the second time this day, Inspector Endersby was astonished by this girl named Jane. A moment before, she was sniffling. Earlier in the evening, she had been stammering with shyness. Now she stood by the footman, her head up, her tongue steady in her head.

"Protecting himself from what?" asked Endersby.

"His own shame," Jane said, coming forward.

"Quiet, Jane. She is innocent in all of this, Inspector," said Mrs. Croft. She stepped into the circle of light at the table.

"I am not, mum," cried the girl.

"Let me speak, Jane," said Mrs. Croft. "Inspector, I am a good Christian woman. I work hard in this fine house. I work beside good people. Mr. Dupré, he is an artist of sorts. Men like him need their pleasures and their private ways."

"No, mum, no," argued Jane.

Dupré put his head in his hands.

"Mr. Dupré cannot help himself, sir," the servant Jane then confessed.

"I am not sure, Jane, what you mean," said Endersby.

"He is afraid, sir. Afraid for himself, for his soul, for us here. Look, yourself, you said it, he is London's finest. Yes, he is. But he cannot let little men bring him to his knees."

"Jane, you are talking gibberish," said Mrs. Croft.

"No, mum. I ain't the fool. I can see what I can see." The girl's outburst of passion astounded the others. Jane was breathing hard, as if she had been chased by a wild dog. Her face was red. Endersby wondered if she might spontaneously combust and burn down the kitchen in the process.

"Tell me, Jane, what you know then," said Endersby. "I want to hear from your memory what happened in this house on Friday last. Shame or no, I want you to tell me about your master. To be sure his reputation—and his innocence—is worthy of your praise."

"It is. It is," the stalwart Jane now said. "My master came home with the link boy just after half twelve, as he said." Jane hesitated; she considered a moment and went on. "On Friday last, after he came in from his club, I took him his bedclothes as I always do."

"Jane, it is not your place," said Mrs. Croft. "Inspector, I cannot let this child speak of such things. It is not right."

"Let her be, Mrs, Croft," said Henry Robertson Dupré, his voice quieter now.

"He loves me, is all, sir. He always comes to me at night. He says he must. So, he does. So, he has shame of it, too."

"Is this the truth, Mrs. Croft?" asked Endersby.

"Yes, sir."

"How old are you, young Jane," Endersby said.

"Fifteen, sir."

"And so, Jane," Endersby continued, "go on. What happened?"

"He came to me, sir. He took his bath, and he came into my bed as he always does."

Mrs. Croft sat down at the table. In her sad, tired eyes Endersby noted a sense of defeat.

"Did he stay there for long, Jane?" Endersby asked. The servants stood in the outer ring of light from the candle, their faces glum.

"Of course, sir. He always does. That's his need and his shame, sir. He always falls to sleep, too, in my arms, and he did on Friday last, he was so worn and tired."

"The rest of you," said Endersby to the watching, silent figures in the room. "What do you have to say to this?"

Mrs. Croft raised her worn face. "I can speak for them, Inspector. Jane tells the truth. Mr. Dupré did not leave on Friday night after he arrived home. He is a man of custom, in his own way." The voice of the woman was so sorrowful and full of pity that Endersby had to pause. He looked toward Stott, whose eyes were held hard on Dupré.

"Mr. Dupré, you are a great fool," Endersby said, breaking the momentary silence.

Dupré looked up with a pained expression.

"You are a man protected and secured by this company," Endersby went on, "and yet you deigned to abuse them with your own mistrust. What did you fear losing?"

"When Samuel Cake was found dead on Saturday morning last," Dupré faltered, "I had a terrible fear. I feared that someone like you might come knocking at my door, a finger pointed. Lord Harwood was ready enough to throw me into the gutter. Who else was ready to do so? 'Down, down I come like glistering Phaeton.' Am I not like that very king, sir? Subject to the jealousy and spite of others?"

"Mr. Dupré, you are a man who trades in fantasy. Perhaps you have let that blind you to human kind."

"Human kind, Inspector, as you no doubt have seen more than I, is no better than dung in the road."

"But not in this room, sir. Surely you can see that."

Inspector Endersby pulled out the bloodied glove from his satchel. He unfolded it and handed it to Jane.

"Have you ever seen this item before, Jane?"

"No, sir."

"And you, Mrs, Croft?"

"No."

"I found it at Doughty Street. Those marks you see in this light are spots of Mr. Cake's blood."

Jane pulled back.

"Blood from his skull, which was beaten so badly his face was not recognizable. May I ask you to put it on, Mr. Dupré."

Henry Robertson Dupré leaned forward, and in the hushed room surrounded by candle-shadow, he pulled the glove over his hand. He held it up. The glove was loose, slipping. He pulled it off.

"But what does this prove, Inspector?"

"Unfortunately, nothing. It is the only piece of evidence left by one of the intruders, perhaps even the killer. It seems it is not yours, if I can believe your servants' testimony."

"Inspector, my servants have told you the truth."

"You admit this now, Dupré?"

"I came from my club by half twelve or a few minutes past. I took by bath. Miss Elisabetta Mazzini was to have supped with me, but she had left. I had only Jane, here, to keep me company. I admit to that."

Endersby moved from the table and walked slowly to the kitchen door then back. Sergeant Stott came up to him. "What do we do now, sir?"

Endersby rubbed his knee. He was still wearing his hat, gloves and wet coat, and he was feeling so tired he wanted

to lie on the stones of the floor. "Fetch paper, ink and pen."
The footman opened a drawer and drew out the items.
Endersby took hold of the quill and handed it first to
Dupré. "You shall write out what you did, detail by detail, on
Friday night last. Just as you have spoken it. Afterwards, add
your signature to the page. A signature is binding, Dupré.
Please remember that. Mrs, Croft, can your servant girls
read and write?"

"Jane can, sir."

"And cook?"

"I believe so."

"Take each one alone into your pantry. Those who
cannot write, have them tell you what they saw and did on
Friday night last and then sign the paper. Do not collude in
any way."

"Yes, sir."

"Mrs. Croft, a quick pot of tea for us all, please."

"Yes, Inspector."

The rain began again to beat the windows. When Dupré
had finished writing, he handed the paper to Stott with a
brusque flick of his hand and stood from his chair. He
came up to Endersby.

"Are you satisfied?" His voice in Endersby's ear. "Are you
at last satisfied?"

"Justice, Mr. Dupré." Endersby put down his cup and saucer.

"I shall report you to your superintendent. I shall tell my
man at the *Chronicle* this sordid story."

"To what purpose?"

"To my satisfaction, Inspector. That is enough. You Bow
Street donkeys believe you can run our streets, bully gentlemen in their own homes. Unconscionable."

"Justice is a harsh mistress, Dupré. Luckily, she is blind."

"Get out of my house this instant!"

"I cannot, Dupré, until I have performed my duties.
There are papers still to collect."

Dupré clapped his hands. "Get on, all of you." He glared
at Stott, then he left the room. A door slammed upstairs.

Mrs. Croft gathered up the tea things then came over to Endersby with the signed sheets. "I beg your pardon, sir," she said. Endersby took the sheets, checked them and put them into his satchel. In the doorway, Mrs. Croft took hold of Endersby's arm and stopped him. "Pardon me again, Inspector."

"Yes, Mrs. Croft."

"I cannot in good conscience let you leave without telling you this."

"What is it?"

"It was us, sir, the footman and me that made up the story about the dinner. Mr. Dupré came home in a hurry this afternoon and asked us to protect him. He gave us the coins to be sure we would speak 'straight' to you about his comings and goings. He was so frightened, sir, he could not speak clearly. He broke down, in fact, in a most sad fashion. You see, Inspector, his life *is* the theatre, and in the last two days, Lord Harwood decided to take that life away from him. I am fond of Henry. I raised him, in a manner of speaking, after his mother died. I cannot say Henry is a practicing Christian, sir, but he is a clever man. He brought in little Jane from a workhouse and gave her a living. Like man and wife they are in some respects, sir. He is not a murderer, as you shall see in our written stories. Please, forgive us."

For answer Endersby gave but a quick nod. The woman before him was no adversary. What her face told him was a matter of anguish and fear. Stott signalled to Endersby, and the two of them heard Mrs. Croft sigh as she closed the door. Endersby slowly climbed the area stairs to street level. His mind sifted and sorted facts as fast as he could gather them together. Stott stood behind him for a second and allowed him to catch his breath. The two men then entered the street with heads held against the rain. "You go on, Stott. I shall walk apace."

The route home to Cursitor Street was fraught with barriers. There were private gates at Southhampton Row. A fallen horse and its overturned cart blocked Eagle Street. Holborn presented rain, mud and chaos—and no hansom cabs. Hell itself has become a sea, thought Endersby. The night deepened as he walked into Chancery Lane, his body wracked with pain, his neck sopping. Facts and suppositions clamoured for his attention as if they were a cluster of rollicking schoolboys. But Endersby knew at this point in his fatigue that he *must* let his mind relax. The rain let up for a moment, and it was as if all motion and fury had come to rest. Endersby opened his coat to shake off the wet. He removed his hat, brushed off the residue from the street.

He was shivering. "You are the wretch, you old boar," he chided himself. When his feet stumbled forward, Endersby needed to touch the walls to steady his gait. "Murder and mayhem indeed," he said to the cobbles. After a time, the familiar steps and the welcoming lights of Number 6 Cursitor Street appeared before him. Endersby found his latch key and stumbled into the downstairs hall. "Harriet!"

Endersby pressed his bulk against the railing leading up to the flat. He called again: "Harriet."

The hall and stairwell filled with candlelight. Two figures came toward him. A frightened face came first, holding up a candle. Behind it came the familiar cap and rosy cheeks of the one woman he knew could give him comfort.

"Embrace me, Mrs. Endersby, I beg of you."

"Dear Owen, what a state of disarray." Harriet folded her arms about Endersby's neck and held him. Releasing him, she turned to the wide-eyed Solange. "Put on the kettle, cut some bread and stoke the hearth in the parlour." The girl hurried up the stairs, the circle of candlelight rising with her, leaving Harriet and Owen in clammy darkness.

"Now, dear one," Harriet said. She lifted Endersby's hat and placed it on the newel post. She relieved him of his satchel and placed it on her own shoulder. "Lean on me," she said. He held the railing and pulled up. At each step his gouty foot dragged in agony. Harriet slipped on the edge of one stair but kept her balance. "Come, we'll find our way."

Once inside the cosy apartment, Endersby fell against Harriet's breast. "I am weary, my dear one," he admitted, his breath short from the climb.

"You are also very dirty and greasy from the street," she

answered. She led him to the parlour sofa, where he fell into its softness.

"I am nothing more than a fool, Harriet." Endersby wiped his cheek.

"Well, you are most certainly a hungry fool at best," soothed Harriet.

She pulled off his gloves and his filthy boots. Solange appeared with a flannel and soon, with wiping and rubbing and general patting, Endersby felt drier and better. With much delight, he was soon at a table set with knife and fork, a plate of jellied eel and a warmed glass of Spanish sherry. "Fine, indeed," he said to the two tending women. Solange had taken on a glow from her running about, and for the first time Endersby saw in her a gentle beauty, her hair a soft brown, her curious eyes not without compassion.

"You shall make a fine wife, young Solange," he said, downing a second glass.

The girl blushed.

"I am to take on a new case, Harriet," he said later from his steaming bath. Harriet sat beside him by the fire, her hand pulling a thread through her needlework screen.

"Yes, I know. Burned bodies. You are worthy of the task."

"I told you already?"

"Over soup."

In the study, Endersby hobbled to his table. His hand flew out. In disgust he shoved the French puzzle he'd been working on to the floor. Wooden pieces lay in a heap on the carpet. His mind was full of misgiving. No puzzle, no game is this business, he thought.

Harriet came in. "What have you done?"

Shame reddened Endersby's cheek. He stood and looked at her, not knowing what to say.

"Surely, dear Owen, only you can pick them up. How can we know what pieces fit where?"

"How right you are," he said. Harriet stood off and did not move to help him. She held the candle as he bent to the floor, picked up each piece and laid it back on the table. The light glistened on the pieces, and with their glow, Endersby felt suddenly better, as if there was to his tumultuous world the capacity for order. There was no doubt he had the ability to allow reason to gather the terrible bits and shards of the truth he now held in his mind.

"Good night," Harriet said. She left without another word but with a gentle movement that gave Endersby a sense of calm. At his other table by the window, he laid out the glove; he stared at the dried mud samples he had collected Saturday last. He pondered the sound of the rain, and he prayed that what he knew and what he feared might somehow come together into a truth he could present to the world. It had been a long day, many secrets unveiled. *Caldwell would mend,* he thought. *Rosa Grisi had revealed her loyalty to her brothers as well as her innocence with a credible alibi; the sad Betty Loxton and her cruel brother, John the Pawn—where do they fit, and what could they reveal?* This and the extra promissory note found in Cake's marvellous cloak were byways yet to explore. And what of Miss Priscilla Root? Was her confession merely a lie, or did Reggie Crabb relieve her of guilt with his innocent recollection of a drunken party? Mr. Henry Robertson Dupré—well, here was a case of a man bent on falsehood, on disguise—and yet a man not necessarily given to physical violence.

Owen Endersby breathed out.

Such is the toil, the meandering manner of the detective mind, he thought, congratulating himself on his accomplishments, relegating his doubts to a far corner as he turned to find solace in his bed.

*   *   *

Betty Loxton raised the skylight pane as far as she could, and when it moved no farther, she refused to be defeated and shoved her head and shoulders through the narrow space, her feet lifting off from the wiggling chair. She found herself lying face down on slimy steep tiles two storeys up from the alley. Holding fast to the window brace, she checked behind her to be sure no light had been lit.

The snoring and snuffling from the other room went on unabated. Betty slid toward the gutters; she let go of the brace, and her feet swung down in an arc. Pain racked her back, her elbows, her shoulders. She crawled slowly along. Her feet caught the gutter edge. She kept looking up until she found the small jut-out with the broken sash. Inside the dormer, the smells of refuse and the scurrying of rats greeted her. On the floor, she paused and her chest began to heave with great gasps of air. The coins sat safe and sound in her deep pocket. The bonnet was her sister's, but Betty did not care. Her skirt was the good one she kept for Sundays, though she regretted not taking her dirty one with her. But you can purchase same, she thought. *You are free.*

She found the door and yanked it open. The stairs screeched under her boots, like they were souls being torn from their graves. Each step was tested; one, then two were missing. Betty held onto the railing and shimmied down two more flights in the inky dark. *You are free,* she thought again. This, the pain and dark, this is what you must suffer.

Out on the street, she ran so fast, she bit her tongue. She ran toward the great portico of Old Drury. She ran behind the building to the horse stalls, found the metal-covered coal chute and climbed in. Down she slid, holding her nose. The costume room was black. Betty crawled carefully under the hanging garments. She smelled the stove and Mrs. B.'s metal pressing irons. The hearth gave off faint ember-light, and the little girl who tended it was asleep on her pallet. Betty pulled off her bonnet. Lastly, she folded her skirt up and touched her ruined ankle. The chain had rubbed it raw. The vinegar her sister had applied still burned the skin. She tapped the scabs and knew they were not as yet puss-filled. She went to the hearth, found the bucket of water and dabbed the wound. A strip of clean cloth was on the table, so she bound her ankle, her eyes squinty in the dim light.

Behind the wicker baskets, the ones full of soiled shirts and stockings, Betty settled herself. She found a velvet waistcoat and balled it into a pillow. She knew she must never leave the building. Not for a long while. She would plead with Mr. Dupré. Of course, he loved her and would guard her. What if he was angry? Angry because she did not show for the rehearsal this past afternoon? *But I couldn't come, sire,* she argued as if Dupré stood before her. *No, I was clamped and held back. Oh, sire, I am grateful to you.*

Betty found her eyes closing. She was so hungry, she could eat a piece of wood. Tomorrow Mrs. B. would give her vittles. Betty reminded herself the dearest Jack in London town was Mr. Henry Robertson Dupré. She would risk death for him, as soon fall from a roof as lose his loving attention.

Chapter Six

WEDNESDAY, DECEMBER 23, 1840

It was at the hour when old Hartley, the stage-door keeper, unlocked the stage door, at ten o'clock in the morning to be precise, that Betty Loxton opened her sleepy eyes to see Henry Robertson Dupré standing over her. Betty had been curled up, shivering, the velvet costume she had used as a pillow crumpled by the baskets. Dupré was wearing a green frock coat and a frown. *He is not pleased with your mischief,* she whispered to herself as she stood up to face him.

"Good morning, Miss Loxton."

Betty curtsied. Reggie Crabb appeared beside Mrs. B., who came up to Betty and took her hand.

"Leave her for a moment," said Dupré.

"She is cold, sir. And hungry."

"Leave her."

Betty rubbed her dirty wrists. Her skin itched, and her mouth was dry and bitter.

"What are you doing in here?" asked Dupré.

"Hiding, sire."

"I can see you have been rummaging in the coal chute."

"I came down it, sire. Last night."

"From whom are you hiding?"

"My brother, John, sire. I have run away from him."

Betty lifted her soiled skirt and showed Dupré and Mrs. B. her scabby ankle. "He clamped me down, so's I could not run. Said I could not come here again. Said I was no stager and must stay put."

"Poor rose," said Mrs. B. "Fetch me water, Crabb, and a flannel."

"You cannot live here, Miss Loxton," Dupré said. "Nor can you rush in here every night when you are at odds with your family. May I remind you the street is your home."

"Yes, sire, I know it *was* my home. But now, as you know, I wish my life to be here."

"We have a busy day. Feed the lass, then send her off."

"No, sire, I beg of you. I shall be a good girl. You know it. You know I can be."

Betty thrust her arms out to embrace Henry Robertson Dupré. A stiff, cold hand prevented her. A haughty voice addressed her. "Miss Loxton," said Dupré, "I am not in the habit of feeding and scrubbing coster girls. I am a man of the theatre. I must find someone who can do your duty and not shirk rehearsal, leaving me high and dry."

Young Crabb put the steaming basin on the table. Mrs. B. knelt, and holding the skirt up, began to dab the ankle wound with water. Betty moaned as it stung. Dupré smoothed the front of his frock coat.

"Crabb," said Dupré.

"Yes, sir."

"Call the company, posthaste. We are on the stage this morning."

"One word, sire, if you please."

Dupré turned his back to Betty, and pretending not to hear her voice, walked away, passing between the cutting tables toward the staircase. Mrs. B. held Betty's skirt and dabbed again. "Don't move, little rose. Now, that's better. Come and have some tea and a bit of bread."

"Oh, no. I must go on up."

"I shall call you," said Crabb.

"But he is so vexed with me, Carrot," cried Betty. "He won't find no one else, will he?"

"Little rose, take my advice. Rest here, drink your tea. By and by, you shall go on up," said the gentle Mrs. B.

Crabb patted Betty's shoulder and dashed from the room. Whistles came from above as the stage hands began to set the wings and the cloths overhead. Betty gulped her tea. She was so cold, she ran to the hearth and thrust her head and hands nearly into the flames.

"Careful, foolish child," admonished Mrs. B., who pulled her away from the heat and circled her with her arms. "You can stay awhile down here. On the floor. I shall get Crabb to make you a pallet. See, our little Judy, our hearth gal. She finds it comfortable, as shall you."

Betty wiped her eyes. "Sire is so vexed, he is. I must not let him be so." She bit into the bread, and she licked hot lard from her lips. Today was Wednesday, she knew. Her mam would be frantic. Her brother John would be in a swatting mood. Today was a big selling day for fruit, tomorrow would be as well, then the great day of Christmas. Plums, apples, Spanish oranges newly come from the ships with their boxes stamped with red ink, the little oranges all together in straw, shivering like me, thought Betty, and so far from home.

As was her way, Betty managed to pull her strength together. She washed her face. She plaited her grimy hair. Although her leg pained her, and despite the doubt that poked her like a hunger pang, she did not entertain the worry that her sire would stay angry with her. She loved him. He would not beat nor swat her. She knew this as she climbed the stairs to the stage. She knew one other thing as well: she would do what he asked of her. Fly, climb, lie at his feet—for she was his now. As Betty walked through the rushing scene, as she saw amongst the scene shifters the straight posture of Mr. Dupré, she felt hope grow in her breast. The stage opened before her, an immense plane of wood, cracking with the feet upon its surface. Above her spread the high shadowy sky of cloths, ropes and fly drums. Gas jets flickered on the standing side poles. Mr. Dupré was pointing to the back of the stage as Miss Root pulled on her feathered helmet. There, beside the first entrance, stood the majestic figure of Mr. Weston.

"Places all, please, ladies and gentlemen."

Betty Loxton walked into the crowd. Miss Root stood in

front of the mass of bodies. A wooden tree rose through a trap door. Mr. Weston cupped his hand to his mouth and shouted from the wings: "Gooday, Lady Bright, the sun has risen to greet thee." Like a single wave, the chorus moved, bowing before gathering together to surround Miss Root. When Betty stepped forward with the other actors, she sensed Mr. Dupré's eyes ready to cut her. Her sire was a particular man. Betty realized she was in danger of being lashed by his temper. She remained stalwart, however; her only desire was that Mr. Dupré might show his kind side to her. If so, she might beg him once more to be his flying maiden in the pantomime. He walked up to her, and his first words were spoken in a quiet manner.

"Miss Loxton, you are to leave the stage, please. And quickly."

Betty curtsied but did not move. As the cluster of other bodies widened around her, she felt even more alone.

"It is not your place here, Miss Loxton. You are no longer needed."

He waited for her. Still, Betty did not move. No longer was she the collared dog of her brother. No longer the kicking post for her own mam.

"I can do it, sire. You know it. I shall not leave you."

Betty Loxton had become bewitched by this stage world, with its oil and dust, its blue fire and canvas vistas. "I shall not ask you again," said Dupré.

"I cannot leave you, sire. Let me show you."

With a burst of life in her legs, Betty ran toward the back of the stage. She mounted the stairs, two by two. She came to the corner, hung on to the railing, swung herself onto the skywalk, the massive stage below her. The moment she saw the other girl, a red-haired girl from the chorus hooked into the harness, Betty took herself to the edge of the fly walk where she placed her toes over its frightening edge. She raised up her arms. She sang out a song, a Gaff ditty about a Queen and a Tom, and she sang and sang and held her balance. The red-haired girl screamed. The fly-loft assistant leapt forward. The stage manager's whistle pierced

the dusty air. Though Betty teetered, she held herself steady.
She drove her eyes skyward. No way, she thought, no way but
to hold on. She refused to let fear push her. Each word she
sang brought footsteps nearer until a strong, hard arm
grabbed her waist and pulled her back.

"We've got her, Mr. Dupré."

"Put the baggage out."

But Betty was already loose. In a flash, she fell upon the
back of the red-haired girl. She unlatched the harness,
shoved the crying creature onto the flywalk. Her voice kept
on singing, the Queen and the Tom. A fever of desire
quickened her arms; she fitted herself into the harness.
The cloth bands, the eyes, the hooks, all obeyed her
fingers. Betty Loxton was no longer anyone's servant. No,
now she was a bird. An angel. "Here, there," shouted the
stage manager, now coursing along the skywalk. The
grump's face was redder than an apple.

Then the air flowed under Betty's feet, though she
would not look down. Pray the wire is strong, she
whispered. Betty Loxton spread her wings. A slight jerk
told her the counter balance and the control ropes had
taken hold; the lifters guided her down, running the
pulleys. Now she looked down; the stage rose toward her as
she floated, arms lifted, a fragile sparrow. Miss Root and
the chorus broke into clapping. Shouts swelled from the
stage hands. The stage manager greeted Betty as her toes
touched the stage boards. She stood alone for a second, the
harness embracing her skinny chest. As Mr. Dupré walked
toward her, the crowd hushed.

"Let her be," came the harried voice of her sire. Betty
curtsied to Mr. Dupré. "Let the foolish bird fly," he then
said, his mouth breaking into a thin but tight smile. "Keep
her on, or she will dash her brains out on all of us before
we can shout Happy Christmas."

*   *   *

Endersby placed the last wooden piece into the centre.

Now it was clear. The French puzzle presented a scene in a jungle with an elephant, a rider and palm trees. "Well done, old gander." His night's sleep had abandoned him at two o'clock in the morning; in desperation to win it back, Endersby had taken tea, soaked in a bath. Then, by four o'clock, he had given up and retreated to his puzzle table. Every muscle was now aching in the morning light, and his damned gouty toe pinged with sharp jabs. Nevertheless, he nibbled at another piece of cheese. He dressed—suede gloves, sombre blue waistcoat, hat. In the kitchen, he procured an apple, wrapped bread and more cheese in a cloth and rummaged until he found Harriet's cache of candied almonds. Hobbling downstairs to the door, he opened it and was greeted by the clamour of London's daily business. He hired a cab; it rattled over broken streets, knocking him about from heel to forehead. Half-awake, he descended at Fleet Lane.

"Good morning, Inspector."

The admittance sergeant led him up to the second parlour. "Much better, are we?" were Endersby's first words on seeing a revived, shaved and somewhat rosier Sergeant Caldwell.

"Yes, sir, and I thank you." The lip was still puffy, and the bruises were yellowing, but Caldwell stood firm and ready.

"You know of the development, do you?"

Caldwell nodded and said: "Superintendent Borne has asked us both to come in."

Endersby threw off his coat and gloves and followed Sergeant Caldwell into Superintendent Borne's office. The man was scribbling on a sheet of paper. His frock coat was wrinkled, and Endersby noted a small stain—butter, perhaps?—on the left lapel. "I shall be brief, gentlemen." Borne did not stand. He folded his hands before explaining in a flat tone that Caldwell was to assume the responsibility for the Cake murder case. "Endersby shall brief you on its matters this morning." Stott, who had just entered the room, discovered that he and the inspector were to investigate the lodging house fire and its subsequent calamities.

"No further ado, sirs. I bid you good morning."

In the hall outside of the superintendent's office,
Endersby gathered Stott and Caldwell and led them into an
antechamber which faced the inner court. "As we know
gentlemen, time is running down. London is filling up with
corpses, and we have serious duties to perform." Stott stood
at attention, his face full of concern as Endersby began to
explain. "No word yet from Birken as to the hiding places of
the Grisi brothers, but we shall, my good men, bring those
ruffians to justice for their attack on you, Caldwell."

"Thank you, sir."

"Our puzzle is coming together," continued Endersby.
"We have new clues as to the horrible implications
surrounding Mr. Cake's death. I have been asking myself,
these past sleepless nights, many new questions. And I have a
new tack to offer. May I suggest we work together and
quickly." The two sergeants agreed. "Would either of you care
for a candied almond?" asked Endersby. Both sergeants
politely declined. "At times like these when sleep denies me
comfort, I take to sweets and cheese. But onward."

Endersby opened the door to the antechamber to check
if the hall outside were empty.

"No use taking risks to thwart us," he explained. "Now,
men. You, Caldwell, will go this morning and take this
wretched glove with you once again. This time complete
your rounds, but go instead to glove makers in and around
the theatres. Start near the Surrey side, near the Coburg
and work your way toward Old Drury. Ask, too, if the
costumers and haberdashers at the theatre have been
asked to sew such a glove. Make your presence known as a
policeman and force confession if need be. At the same
time, call on the cleaners of gloves near all the same
establishments and ask if clients have ever appeared with
this piece of merchandise."

Caldwell did not question Endersby. He took the glove
and left the room. Stott stepped forward.

"You, sir. I shall trust you to Covent Garden. Find the
stall of John the Pawn Loxton and watch him today. Watch
him until the evening. Make sure, if he has a waif with him,

you watch her, too.'Keep an eye out for his cart and a dame with it. I might also send you to Cake's gentleman's club to review the comings and goings of Samuel Cake Friday last. Be prepared to do both. I shall be in Vinegar Yard for supper, as usual." Stott put on his hat.

"I shall fool Borne, mind," Endersby said. "I shall go to the lodging house presently. If Superintendent Borne asks of your duties, tell him I have instructed you thus. Tell him it concerns the fire. But Cake's killer must be *found.*"

* * *

Lying stiff and granite-like in its coffin, the body of Samuel Cake faced upward, its sightless eyes seeming to peer through pine board and piled earth toward the distant sky. In the misty morning, the graveyard itself held a suspended deathly breath of its own. A crow in a crooked tree took flight; its path followed the inner-city streets, over parks and turrets, to Number 46 Doughty. Rising high over the mournful house, the bird did not see the man standing on the front steps. The figure paused for a moment to watch the bird's erratic flight. Mr. William Weston then hurried down the area stairs, broke the police lock on Cake's kitchen door and entered the basement floor.

He held his hand close to his heart. He called out and listened for possible voices. He walked up to the parlour, where he knew Cake's body had once lain. The furniture had been stacked against the wall, broken, random. Mr. Weston stared at the blood specks left behind; he stared at the broken shutters. Upstairs, he sat on the smooth bed. Then he began to search. He pulled up the mattress and replaced it. He stuck his head into the hearth. The desk gave out a squeak when he yanked open its drawer. On the third floor, he tapped the floorboards. "Nothing."

Coming down into the basement kitchen, he was startled by a figure standing in the open door of the area entrance. A short, stocky man wearing a grease-spotted coat. An unfamiliar profile, but he knew from the man's stance, he was harmless. There was a look of awe and bewilderment on the sorrowful man's face. "I beg your pardon," said Mr. Weston. The short man jumped and grasped the handle of the door.

"Who are you, sir?' the awe-struck man asked, his question that of a proprietor rather than an uninvited guest.

"I am Mr. William Weston, sir. I apologize for startling you. I am at your service."

"I am most sorry, sir. Gregorious Barnwell. And your business here, sir?" queried Barnwell, who seemed as unsure of his presence in his brother's house as the great actor's.

"I beg your leave, sir," replied Mr. Weston. "I was out walking, as I do often to take exercise after morning rehearsal. I came by the place and discovered the door with a broken lock."

"You knew my brother, sir?"

"Well, and respected him. I came on a whim to pay respects of a kind. I wanted to see the place one last time. I shall leave you and bid you good day."

Barnwell waited as Mr. Weston slowly made his way to the street and climbed the area stairwell. Weston turned to see the door shut behind him. He knew of Barnwell casually, from secondhand gossip in the theatre, knew him as Cake's half-brother and as the greatest stage machinist in London. Mr. Weston moved on to prolong his morning walk, though he felt tired. He felt sorry for the short man. His face appeared to Weston's inner eye, twisting, accusing, untwisting and twisting yet again. "Enough, enough, demon," Mr. Weston said to the shadows in the street, thereupon deciding to clear his mind of the matter and vouching never to visit Number 46 Doughty again.

*   *   *

Upon entering the private club with Inspector Endersby, Elisabetta Mazzini called at once for its director, a homely, easy-going man with chestnut hair. He suggested tea. "I can also offer a light luncheon, sir, or a meat pie at this hour. Would they suffice?"

"Indeed. Most kind of you," answered the delighted Endersby. Madame Mazzini had arranged the interview at Samuel Cake's gentleman's club in Swan Yard to accommodate Endersby's request to check her alibi. There also appeared to be a curious story about a tall man that required detail. Once the food was brought in, Endersby began in earnest, keeping in mind that time was flying. A tin clock tick-tocked in the corner and rang out twelve chimes.

"Most simple, sir," replied the club director to the inspector's first question. "He was a tall man in a costly cloak, and he refused to give his name. He enquired after Mr. Cake and was told he was taking a late supper and could not be disturbed."

"You had never seen this man before?"

"No, Inspector. I am occupied with much work here. I rarely venture forth beyond Somerset House."

"Cake and I dined in room three," said Elisabetta Mazzini.

"Beef and oyster pie, if memory serves," said Endersby with a smile.

"To your odd notions and your capacity for recollection, Inspector," said Madame Mazzini, her face rosy and smiling as she toasted Endersby with her tea cup.

"Yes. And then Cake left at two o'clock to walk home to his house in Doughty Street."

"On Friday last, this tall gentleman came at what hour to enquire after Mr. Cake?" asked Endersby.

"Around half one o'clock in the morning. He was most insistent, and he had been drinking some draughts of rum, I believe."

"What did he do when he was refused by your keeper to be let in?"

"He demanded we hire him a cab, sir. Which we did and with some relief."

"Why so?"

"Why, he became suddenly belligerent. A most haughty man. Well groomed, I might say, but showing an arrogant streak in 'im. We run a calm establishment here. Gentlemen are expected to act properly."

"Even those with rum on their breath?"

"Even so, Inspector."

"And, by chance, would you have noted the cabbie's coach number?"

"Of course, sir. He is one of our regulars. He stalls his horse here in our very yard. Night shifts only, of course, to service our clients."

"Most convenient and fortunate. Please welcome a Sergeant Stott later this afternoon. He will come by to ask some more questions. I am especially interested in what your cabby can tell us. Before I leave, would you kindly afford me a fuller description of this arrogant man in the cloak. A sketch, if you will, and please be certain of his hair colour, size of cloak and, if possible, his gait and tone of voice."

"I'd be honoured to oblige, Inspector."

* * *

Young Reggie Crabb held the basin. Mrs. B. washed Betty's wound again and bound it with a clean strip of flannel. "What a way to treat your own blood and flesh," Mrs. B. said. Afterwards, Betty and Crabb drank a cup of broth by the hearth.

"He's let me back, Carrot," Betty said, her face beaming.

Crabb looked into her sad, cold face. He read in her eyes not joy, but loss. What did Betty—the sparrow—want after all, he wondered? A tap on the bannister leading to the stage above called him, and he set down his cup.

"I shall return, wait here," he said.

Betty grabbed his sleeve. Her face was now streaming with tears. "He don't love me, do he, Carrot?"

"What you mean?"

"Is all for naught. He said he did, but he don't. Not now."

"Come, come," Crabb tried to comfort, using words he'd heard Mrs. B. use.

"No, it is no use. What am I to do?"

"Who is crying here?" said Mrs. B., walking into the

hearth light. "None of this, young rose. I want you up on your feet. Come, come. Off you go Crabb. To your duties. You, rose, come here, and I shall set you a task."

Crabb reluctantly left Betty Loxton and climbed upstairs. At Mr. Weston's dressing room door, he knocked twice then entered. A rum bottle sat on the actor's table. Crabb placed the letters from the stage-door keeper on Mr. Weston's desk. "I am his eyes, and his feet," Crabb whispered. "Hallo, sir?" he called out and waited.

But the room remained quiet. Crabb took in a breath. He remembered that evening, knocking on Mr. Weston's door, hearing Mr. Weston shouting and angry, and Crabb thinking there was someone with the great actor. No one was here now. "Lor' bless me," Crabb said and looked over the top of the dressing table. He looked under the chair, behind the screen. Footsteps approaching made him scurry, and he was able to get out of the dressing room before the steps turned and came down the hall. At Miss Root's dressing room door, there hung the sickly smell of sweet smoke. He tapped twice, and when the door slid open, it was Miss Root herself, still wearing her feathered helmet from the rehearsal earlier that morning.

"Ah, my goodly boy. Letters?"

"None, Miss Root. None this afternoon. I come only to see if you need anything."

"What a lad. Do I need anything? I wonder, I wonder."

Miss Root stood still and in a daze. She held up a little brass pipe from which the smoke curled.

"No, I think not," she said, and with a nonchalant brush of her arm, she closed the door.

Crabb ran down the hall and up the long sets of stairs, passed the fly drums and the sky cloths and came to Henry Dupré's attic office.

"Go away," was the curt answer to his tapping.

"Crabb, sir. Letters."

"Damn you, Crabb." There was scuffling, then a muffled cry. The door flew open, and Crabb glanced the dashing bare legs of a young girl. He could not see her face. She hid behind the door, and Dupré, waistcoat open, trousers buttoned crookedly, snatched the letters and held up his right hand as if to box Crabb's ear.

Taking control, his breath even, Dupré said, "Thank you, Crabb. Quite. Send up for coffee. I shall go to the Green Room presently." Like a stiff breeze, Crabb hurried back down the flights of stairs, across to old Hartley, told Hartley of the coffee request, was handed a slip of paper on which Hartley had scrawled the word "Coffee", took the paper and descended into the warm, busy air of the under stage and Mrs. B.'s domain.

"Coffee order, Mrs. B. From Mr. Dupré."

Betty Loxton was passing a hot iron over a set of linen fairy wings. She rubbed her nose.

"Careful, rose. Do not stain 'em. I've enough running to do without an extra wash."

"Hallo, Carrot," Betty whispered.

"I can go to the muffin man, if you wish," said Crabb.

"Tomorrow, you shall see a new sight, Carrot."

"How do you mean?"

"I shall be a new gal. One you will see once and not again."

Crabb wrinkled his forehead. "Betty, what mean you?"

"You shall see. Come tomorrow. But come now and sit here."

"I have errands. I can stay but a minute, no more."

"Sit and let me tell you a tale."

"Will it be long?"

"Long enough. But someone must know it. You can keep a secret, can you?" Reggie nodded and sat closer to Betty so she could whisper. "So, Carrot, only you shall hear of it. I regret to tell it, but I must." Tears filled her eyes. As Betty began her tale, Crabb listened, held his breath, widened his eyes and knew he had to remember every word she spoke.

*   *   *

"She came down with the chills and a hot forehead just after breakfast. After you left."

Endersby held his wife's hand and looked upon the sallow face of the cook, the young Solange. Her hair was damp. Little tremors shook her body and made her lips quiver.

"Had she taken anything?"

"Not that I know," Harriet said. "She could not say. Suddenly, she fell to the floor. Your luncheon soup, I am afraid, fell with her and scalded her ankle."

A red patch of skin was shown.

"And the physician?"

"My brother has run to fetch him."

"There is no fear of cholera, Harriet, if that is what you were thinking."

"Was I, my dear? Cholera was not on my mind. But fatigue and love-sickness were."

"Love-sickness?"

"A note was delivered last night. By hand, by a relative who spoke no English."

"A note for Solange?"

"Yes, dear Owen. You need your luncheon, even though you have eaten us out of home with your sleeplessness and appetite. I have pork pudding and a cold potato with vinegar for you."

At the dining room table, the note was proffered for Endersby's inspection. Even though he had taken food with Miss Mazzini, he indulged his appetite which, in these days of work, lack of sleep, and general toil, had grown more demanding.

"It is in French."

"Yes, dear one. And my capable brother has translated it. It seems the marriage for little Solange has been temporarily postponed."

"For what reason?"

The potato was bitter and salty, and the pudding too small. Endersby nibbled at the cheese set for dessert between bites of the pie.

"The army, dear," Harriet explained. "The man has been called into the French army. For a six-month sojourn in the south of that fine country."

"Then, all the better for us. We can afford to pay the woman. She can console herself with making fine dishes. All is settled."

"If you say so, but thwarted love, may I warn you Owen, has a way of finding its own level. Tantrums, pouts, and the like."

Endersby put down his spoon. His mind had been so full of hatching schemes that he was glad of the respite, of the domestic tragedy before him taking precedence.

"I beg your pardon, Mrs. Endersby. I have been precipitate. And thoughtless," he admitted. "You are right, and I shall endeavour to show Solange much gratitude and to offer her comfort."

"As you shall, Owen. Now on to your dessert and to your duty."

"Aye, to that. Much planning and much deception, my dear. But I cannot avoid any longer the problems of the fire. St. Giles calls, and with a hard voice."

In his gouty misery and with his stomach still rumbling after his second luncheon, Endersby turned to the window of the cab and the mist of the afternoon. Smoke from bakers' chimneys, flying slush and mud, the odours of horse and wet wool coats on shoving pedestrians clouded his view of the goodness in the world. The streets closed in, as if their age made the buildings huddle closer in wintry despair; their façades looked sooty enough in their dilapidation. There was a light breeze, enough to wet his face and assault his nostrils with the additional stench of London sewage. In Saint Giles, the horse clattered over wet stones at a slowed pace. Inspector Endersby thoughtfully brought his sharp eyes to bear on each and every thin, haggard, torn-capped, pale-skinned creature that eked out life in this sordid corner of the metropolis. Wooden houses, wracked and cracked with ill repair, sagged, sank and generally seemed to moan under their yoke of poverty. Endersby descended from the cab, the horse giving off puffs of sweaty steam.

He entered the confines of the burnt lodging house at St. Giles. He took time to survey the space before him, observing as thoroughly and precisely as he could, leaving no detail unnoticed. Owen Endersby was convinced this case, chaotic as it was, might prove less troublesome than the Cake murder. After all, two madmen had been seen brandishing flames. Reliable witnesses had made testimony. Cabbies, sweepers, lodgers—those still alive—all could be questioned, the two villains' identities determined by a thorough search through other lodging houses. But what if the culprits had decided to end it all? To jump into the Thames, knowing their deed had damned them to the fires of Hell?

It was most difficult to think further on the matter when the odours of scorched wood and burnt human bodies surrounded one, when the presence of a short, soot-covered man interrupted one's musing. Endersby's mind was now sharp and vivid with supposition. In this way, he followed the sooty man through crumbling ash and broken beam into a large blackened room, partially collapsed, some of the beds of the lodgers still intact, their pallets whole, the singed blankets still upon them.

"You need speak with anyone?" came the question from the man.

"Perhaps, later on. Allow me a moment to ponder."

"Not a sight for gentle eyes."

"This is murder, in fact," mumbled Endersby.

He spent minutes walking, looking, asking the sooty man about habitual lodgers, wondering if there were records he could consult. Where were the survivors?

At one of the burnt beds, the sooty man pointed. "Here rested one of the victims," he said. "They sleep through drink and smoke. Like they was babes."

"Sleep of the dead, sir."

"Doubtless, Inspector. It's the smoke that smothers them. Here look."

The sooty man raised up a flaking mattress. Under it was shoved a hat, a pair of boots, a paper, a glove and a quill.

"This one, he was a scrivener by trade. Could pen a fine

complaint. He died, but his stuff, see it here, all safe from the flames and smoke."

"Flames did not consume this pallet nor its hoardings."

"They all take to hiding stuff under the mattress. Even in here, no one dares to steal from under them."

"Curious."

The bed and the mattress took Endersby's attention for a few minutes more. His stomach demanded an almond. He obliged it and went on pondering but also scheming: how might this sad place help him unravel the knots still left in the Cake case?

He found attendants and interviewed them. Their teary eyes told of the noise, the crying out, the terrible smoke and rush of flames over the shabby roof. He collected confessions and descriptions from those who could write. He paid a penny to lads in the street, the usual loiterers who will sell truth or lies or their own bodies sometimes for a tiny profit. One lad, thin and coughing, told of the two madmen and from where they had come: "Down the alley yonder, big chaps, seen 'em before," the lad said, "at the Crown and Spit, bad-mouthers, one a rat-catcher by trade. Bites all over 'im."

"And perhaps mad from the rats, you think?"

The lad shrugged. Endersby returned to the entrance of the lodging house.

"A hard afternoon, sir?" said the sooty man on meeting the inspector again. Endersby took note of the alleys leading away from the heap of charred timbers.

"No, indeed," he answered gruffly. "An afternoon, so far, of revelation. I thank you, sir."

Endersby bid the man goodbye and returned to the pavement. He moved ahead with purpose, keeping his eyes wide and alert. He would search out the Crown and Spit later on, but for now he had more urgent business. He doubled his pace and watched for frantic rats running ahead of him in the gutter.

*   *   *

Henry Robertson Dupré stepped briskly along Piccadilly. The sun appeared briefly and noted his polished boots, the nap of his overcoat, the brilliant metal of his gold watch chain. Indeed, passersby would remark on his hair, visible and groomed under his high hat. Recently cut, Henry's pride glowed with a fresh application of Indian henna. Entering the Burlington Arcade, the manager of Old Drury visited his tobacconist and purchased a packet of cheroots. He was on his way to the Italian Opera to persuade Miss Elisabetta Mazzini to dine with him when he ran into a man stumbling along the cobbles, his mouth reeking of rum.

"For the love of God. William Weston."

The actor raised his head. Weston drew his ill-met companion into the darkened turn of the passage.

"Ah, my good Dupré. What is your matter?"

"My matter, sir? Why, look at you at this hour of the day. What has brought this on, my lost man?"

William Weston's face was more pale than usual. His chin was unshaven, and his entire mien was that of a man run ragged. It was as if he were shouldering a great burden on his back, and his entire body was ready to fall into the deepest sleep of oblivion. As a consequence of this sight, there arose in Dupré a curious sensation. Not the expected disdain, but instead a tug of sympathy. In fact, his hands reached out to hold up the teetering Mr. Weston. "Come in here for the moment, Will," said Dupré. The door to a small chop house stood nearby, so the two men went in and sat together in a booth. A serving man came toward them, and Dupré ordered a pot of hot coffee with milk. He asked the server to make up a plate of toast.

"You are in need of some food above all, Will," said Dupré.

This sudden kindness on Dupré's part resulted from his having seen a familiar look on William Weston's face. The look expressed feelings Dupré had often confronted—both as a young man on the rise and as a successful man of the London theatre. The eyes emptied of light and the cheeks whitened from a terror in the mind—the death of hope.

"Henry," said Weston, "I am not much company, I fear.

I have done a thoughtless deed. Taken the rum bottle as a friend, and as you can discern, I have been heartily betrayed by my liquid friend's false promises."

"Take some of the coffee, Will."

Weston drank slowly. He went on to tell Dupré of his fatigue and his sleepless nights over the past few days. He also admitted to Henry something he had feared to tell him in the past. "Henry, you have known me for three years. I have always been one who can learn a part word-perfect. I can play what you or any manager can ask of me. But this past year, with my sister's illness growing worse, I find myself more and more distracted. I cannot concentrate as I once was able to do. I cannot remember passages well. I am most concerned. Most beleaguered by doubt, I can assure you."

"I have not doubted your talent, Will. You have infuriated me with your taking to rum. But other than that, you have been sterling."

"You are kind to say it, Henry."

"I am a gentleman, sir. We are fellow artists and must defend each other, even to the point of recognizing our misdemeanours."

William Weston put down his coffee cup. He stared for a long time into Henry Robertson Dupré's face. He then rose very quickly. He downed the last drops of his coffee. It appeared to Dupré as if a demon had suddenly leapt into the muscles of William Weston to drive him out of the chop house. Indeed, Weston did not stay a moment longer. He did not bid *adieu*. His transformation was complete: he had returned to his former, distracted, stumbling self, and pushed his way into the street, his cloak unfastened, his gloves held carelessly in his hands.

It took Dupré a moment to gather his composure. He asked for the bill and paid it. He left his seat, his mind quietly recounting the abrupt event which had just taken place. In the crowded street, Dupré tried to orient himself. Mr. Weston's action had troubled him. The caring sentiments he had expressed toward the actor were not foreign to his nature, but such compassion seldom found occasion for expression in his life and therefore was infrequently indulged. He felt he should shake his head, as if he had just awakened from a dream. "Damnation," he muttered. His proud, elegant manner returned. He patted his hair and glanced at a shop window to check the fall of his waistcoat and the angle of his hat. He decided not to think further on the matter and moved on to his destination. At the entrance to the great Italian theatre, he presented his calling card and was led into a small hall by the stage-door keeper's foyer. The sound of a piano filled the hall as a door opened.

"This way," said a young woman in a black dress.

With some trepidation, Dupré followed the woman into the room. Was he foolish in coming to her? Might Elisabetta Mazzini mock his attempt at expiation? The room was large and airy, full of sofas and bookshelves. Dupré wanted to exact justice—of a kind—and to present his credentials to her, for Cake had robbed him of his chance at seduction Saturday last. At the piano by the far window stood Elisabetta Mazzini. She acknowledged his entrance with a slight turn of her head. He breathed in at the sight of her black ringlets framing a face still holding a version of its younger self; he wanted to touch her cheeks, the colour of rich cream. As everyone knew, Elisabetta Mazzini's shoulders were famous in London, and once, years ago, had been compared in their shape and smoothness to the ice cream *bombes* served at the Café de Paris on the Strand. A moment elapsed; Dupré found himself briefly at a loss.

Miss Mazzini's silken skirt hissed as she approached. Dupré marshalled his words. *I invited you to supper, my dear,* he recalled; *you betrayed me Friday last by going off with Samuel Cake; yes, I shall forgive you but only on condition you dine with me tonight.* Henry Robertson Dupré took one step forward. He opened his mouth to repeat those practiced words aloud, his smile automatically preceding the rise of his voice. Before a sound could be uttered, however, he balked. What appeared up close to him was a woman with a raised hand. Elisabetta Mazzini's own smile had hardened into a look of contempt. The raised hand moved so suddenly, the force of its slap against Henry's left cheek sent him back into the edge of the open door.

"Samuel Cake warned me about you," she said, breathing calmly.

"I beg your pardon," croaked Dupré.

"Samuel was a good man, Henry," Elisabetta Mazzini said, speaking with a frank tone. Leaning into Dupré's face, she said, "He could not help what he was."

Dupré wiped his mouth. The hand struck him again. This time his upper lip caught the edge of his teeth, and he tasted sudden blood.

"*You alone* are the villain," Elisabetta Mazzini said, her voice now sharp with venom.

"Now, now, Elisabetta, calm yourself," said Dupré, calling up his soothing voice, the one he always used to placate angry females.

"Do not cajole me, Henry," she said, full of warning. "But go. Do not ever come near me again."

"Now, listen here…" But Dupré had no chance to finish his sentence. Two strong female arms shoved him out the door, which subsequently closed in his face with a loud slam.

"Damnation," Dupré mumbled. "Whatever has possessed that foolish old vulture?"

*   *   *

Betty Loxton carried the linen wings in her arms as if they were a newborn and hid them in a cluttered corner of the basement costume room. From a storage trunk, she pulled an old gauze gown. It fit her slim frame adequately enough and soon found a place beside the hidden wings. When Betty came afterwards for her soup and bread, Mrs. B. patted her head.

"You can work hard, young rose. You can stay down here for the season and help me, if that is your wish."

"I thank you. You are a kind woman, Mrs. B."

"I am obliged is all."

After soup, Betty left the basement and climbed up to the

highest fly loft over the stage. Leaning out from the wooden guard railing, she counted the heads of the scene shifters and carpenters far below. Tops and toes meandered over the dusty, boot-marked boards. The height played a game with Betty: she imagined the gaslit depth of the stage as a pool of restful water. Here—up in the loft—was the perfect place for her deed. It would be Christmas Eve; she would be like an angel. *I shall, I shall,* she smiled to herself. Having decided on her plan, she flew like a breeze down two flights, ignoring the cruel attic door of Mr. Dupré's office; down further she raced through the side stage and again into the basement by the hearth, where Mrs. B. was sitting and pulling a thread through a pair of britches.

"Take up your needle, child," the kindly woman said.

Presently, young Reggie Crabb appeared.

"In a pickle, Carrot?" said Betty.

"I needs to speak with you," he whispered in her ear. Mrs. B. smiled. "What has got into the two of you?" she said. "Young Crabb, go and fetch a chair and sit with us."

"I must—and I beg your pardon, Mrs. B.—but I must speak with Miss Betty alone."

"Why then, go to it, lad," she said.

Crabb took hold of Betty's wrist and led her behind the racks of shields and helmets in a far corner of the room. "I been pondering," he said.

"My tale, you mean?"

"Yes, your tale."

"You must keep it secret. You swore."

"I know. I shall. But you must tell it again."

Betty was coaxed into the darkest part of the basement room, where above her head hung carnival masks with leering faces. There, Reggie Crabb explained himself a little more, filling in details, giving Betty names. She listened patiently; she held in her tears when Reggie mentioned the name of Samuel Cake.

"I am his eyes and ears, Miss Betty," Reggie said. "I have to honour him. And his case."

"Carrot? You are shaking all over."

"You must do this, you must," Crabb pleaded. "I beg of you to come with me."

Betty worked her arm free, pushed past dusty trunks and broke into open space by the cutting tables. Reggie pursued her, desperate to grab her elbow. Betty scolded him, her ire rising. "I will not budge."

"Now, it is your turn to promise," pleaded Reggie, not unaware of Betty's scowl and her planted feet.

"What?"

"Promise to follow me and tell your tale one more time."

"You are making me the fool, Carrot." Betty slapped young Reggie playfully on his shoulder.

"I beg of you. Just this once."

Betty hesitated. She glanced over her shoulder at the round figure of Mrs. B. by the fire's light. "Will I do you harm, if I do not promise?" Betty asked.

"Yes, yes. Please!"

"Then I promise."

Triumphant, Reggie clutched Betty's cold hand. He waited for a second, checking her gaze to be sure her eyes were not full of fear, then he yanked her up the stairs. "Wait!" she cried. But to no avail: Reggie drove her through the stage-keeper's foyer and into the din of Vinegar Yard, across which they ran until they entered a tavern full of pipe smoke. Betty was coaxed like a reluctant pony up to an empty table, where Reggie begged her to sit down.

"Now, Miss Betty," Reggie said, breathless, still shaking, his voice taking on a sour tone. "Now remember where this table sits in this room. Will you?"

Betty nodded, but her eyes kept peering around at the other tables, the scattered men and women drinking and eating cheese and bread. "When the time comes, you will stand with me at this table…"

"Whatever for, Carrot?" Betty interrupted, rising to return to the theatre across the way.

Reggie took hold of her right elbow. "What for?" he said. "Why to tell your story to Inspector Endersby."

*   *   *

"This way, sir. It is close by."

The young constable from the City proceeded down the alley, followed by Sergeant Birken and Inspector Endersby. Under an archway, the young City constable, his face made jolly by a large, curly beard, stopped and pointed to a second-storey window, its outer shutters closed tight.

"There, sir. Both of them," the constable said.

"Cautiously, gentlemen," replied Inspector Endersby.

Slowly up ten inside stairs, then down a corridor on soft feet. The three—the constable, Birken, Endersby—approached the door of a small room in a crumbling house fifty paces from St. Paul's. Sergeant Birken afforded the door a swift, brutal kick. Feet dashed about behind it. Once again, the burly sergeant's body performed. This time his left shoulder smashed wood and groove to greater effect, and the door fell from its hinges to reveal a bare room inhabited by two men, one with a moustache, both with black hair, and in shirts and trousers hastily pulled on. Each man brandished a dagger. The single window now gaped open. The shutters thrust aside let in creeping mist.

"Guilio and Franco Grisi, I arrest you in the name of the Law," shouted Inspector Endersby. "Stand and be taken into custody."

Endersby began to cross the crooked floor. His face remained ruddy from climbing the stairs. His right arm with its closed fist resembled a battering ram. Behind him, in forced unison, Sergeant Birken and the City constable. A phalanx of the Law, Endersby thought in a flash of pride. "Do not move, brothers Grisi," he commanded. But the two felons—betrayed, discovered, cornered—were not in a mind to obey. They both dodged to the left of the phalanx in the direction of the open window. The mustached Grisi hopped up and down as if to frighten the advancing cohort. The other Grisi, dagger held forth, shouted in Italian what Endersby surmised were vile curses.

"Onward, men," said Endersby.

Sergeant Birken leapt forward in a display of muscle and speed and grabbed the mustache by his neck, consequently to wrestle the hopping villain to the floor. Seeing this, his eyes widened in sudden terror, the dagger-slashing Grisi took a stance against Endersby, blade to the inspector's throat. A black expression froze the ruffian's face. "*Muori,*" he spat at Endersby.

The inspector stamped his foot. His allied City constable raised his fists, ready to pummel the glaring miscreant. "Dodge 'im," whispered Endersby. Quickly, the inspector winked. Mustering his energy, he raised his threatened throat from the vicinity of the pointed blade. *Brave of you,* his thoughts flashed. Now rise—his sudden tip-toes distracted the frantic dagger holder. The constable—on cue—dashed this confused Grisi from behind. He shoved hard. The blow found its mark. Rammed on the back and forced forward, this Grisi brother's chin collided favourably (in the Law's eyes) with Endersby's suede fist. The dagger clanged to the floor.

"Hold him," shouted Endersby. From his satchel he yanked out two pieces of stout cord. He threw one to the constable. In a turn, he moved to Sergeant Birken, who now after much tumbling, rolling and slapping, had secured the other Grisi by pinning his arms down. Endersby wrapped the cord around the writhing man's wrists. A hard knot held tight two crossed hands. In a trice, the two felons were upright, their energies and curses falling low and silent.

"To Scotland Yard, gentlemen. Have them give out a confession and write it down. Take no resistance and force them if need be."

Sergeant Birken and the constable led the Grisi brothers down to the street. Endersby meanwhile wiped his hands on a cloth and sat for a moment. He recovered his breath and planned his next move.

"Come, old gander. No time for resting. Move on, quick."

*   *   *

Without delay, Endersby found a cab and was soon on his

way toward Old Drury and its busy neighbourhood. He always pictured the theatre as a great moored galleon—flags lowered, its portico like a prow—permanently in dry dock. Still, despite its age and faded façade, the grand place had the capacity for adventure, the promise of golden lands of the imagination within its fabled reach. By its side, Owen stepped from the cab and gazed at the theatre's steeped roof before paying the driver and walking with purpose through the coaches and pedestrians, first to call for Reggie Crabb, then to cross Vinegar Yard. The tavern welcomed him with its smoky air and the cheery smile of the barkeep. Endersby quickly found his appointed table, and within minutes he had assembled a young company of two companions.

"You are Betty Loxton," said Endersby in a tone of voice which carried curiosity and gentleness. "I am Inspector Owen Endersby of the Metropolitan Detective Force."

"You, sir, are a policeman?" Betty wondered, her face pinched.

"He is that and more," said young Reggie Crabb. "And you must call him that. Inspector." The noise from the tavern intruded their enclave—laughter, coughing, the clink of glasses. A hearth was blazing.

Betty Loxton put her hand into a pocket of her skirt and lifted a dried flower into the dim light of the late afternoon. "'Tis all I have for my memory of dear Samuel," she said.

The character in her face touched Endersby, though it was pity he felt uppermost for the pretty street girl. She seemed a proud, hopeful child, no more than fourteen. In this tavern smoke, her face looked much healthier all in all than the last time he'd seen it, when its youthful mistress stood tethered to a wall like a nanny goat.

"Go on, Betty. Tell him," prompted Reggie.

Betty raised her eyes to Endersby and curtsied. In his turn, the inspector sat forward and removed his coat. Betty seemed incapable of knowing where to place her hands, tucking them under her shawl, fiddling with a strand of hair. Her voice started husky and low.

"My mam, known in these parts as Pineapple Pol, she has

a brother, Thomas, from Surrey. He come up last Friday, and he and…" Betty stopped. Endersby believed he saw an expression of horror mixed with sadness on the poor girl's face. Thus, he felt justified in reaching out to her and asking her to sit down.

In gratitude, Betty sat on the edge of a chair pulled up for her by Reggie.

"It were done for me, they said. Even Stephen. Eye for an eye."

"Go on," said Endersby.

"Mr. Cake, he comes to me one afternoon on the street. Not a fortnight ago it was. He says to me, 'You wish to make a penny or two, pretty gal?'

"'Yes, sir. How sir?'

"'Come to the Coburg, Surrey side, Waterloo Road. This afternoon at two.'

"The street was so busy I daren't leave, what with apples to shout and all. But I wanted so to go. My mam, she is hard with her hand and said to me never to think of the stage. Though I go to the Gaff on Wednesdays to dance and do jiggling. So, I hawked my ware, I threw the rottens to the gutter, and I went to Waterloo Road.

"'Ah, there you are, young Betty,' says Samuel Cake. 'This way.'

"'Now it is only a contraption,' he says in his sweet voice, and I sees this odd man beside him, all greasy and wearing grease on his face and hands. 'No harm to you at all. It goes up and then down.'

"'And who are you, sir?' says I, bold as brass, to the greasy man to show I takes no mischief.

"'I am Barnwell, Gregorious Barnwell, brother to Mr. Cake.'

"'There, good girl. Now stand still and let Mr. Barnwell fit the harness.'

"'She is ready, Samuel.'

"'Hold on, little Betty,' says my sweet Samuel. 'There is naught to fear.'

"And so I did, I held on and up into the air the contraption flew. A flying chair it was, and it was so slippery and so wobbly,

I moved and kicked. Down I come so fast I hit the floor. Lucky I was not so far in the heavens to crack myself.

"'Oh, girl, are you all right?' says the greasy man. 'Get up, that's it. Now Samuel, we need to put the brace on her and attach her to the chair. It'll hurt a little, Miss Betty. There, now let me tighten it. There, all is safer.'

"'Hold on, Betty,' says Samuel. 'That's it. Four pennies, and you shall fly every night.'

"But no, the chair tips, and the wire works loose, and I comes down a second time and with a crack on them boards, and poor Mr. Cake, he was sad, and his arms came out to me. They did, they really did, and he held me. Oh, but the greasy man said 'No, she cannot, she's too fidgety, she's a pretty one but she is no stager.' Then my Samuel, he lets me go, out to the street once again. Pays me but a penny. My mam, she shouts at me when I comes home afterwards. 'What nonsense now, girl...and you black and blue. Who done this to you?'

"'Mam, t'is nothing," I said to her. "But my mam takes no guff. Never takes never for an answer.

"'You foolish git, look what you've done. How can you carry a basket with your back all hurt and bent.'

"'Don't, mam, don't.'

"'I told you, no scamping about. I'll none o' that nonsense.'

"'What is up, mam?' says my brother John the Pawn, he coming in just then to settle the ruckus.

"'Lookee, John, a scoundrel has hurt our Betty. Look on this. This ain't right. Not right, and now we are to be without her neck to carry apples. Stupid girl.'

"'Who done it to you?' he asks me, his hand ready to hit me. 'Speak up, Betty.'

All this story was uttered in a passionate way. Endersby watched astonished as Betty acted it out, her voice changing as the characters in the story came and went. Her face screwed into a frown to show Pineapple Pol; her eyes fluttered every time she said the name of Samuel Cake.

"And then what happened?" Endersby had little time to surmise the answer, for Betty was quick, almost furious in her response.

"All I knows is they planned to scare him. Thomas with his club. And my brother John the Pawn and Peter the Stick, he went, too. Mam drove them in the cart, and we was told—me and Clare, my sister—to hush and tell nobody. They went and came back late, and they was laughing, and they was telling how they broke up the house. John the Pawn, he was hoping to meet Mr. Cake. He been to talk to him once after the contraption hurt me…just to warn him…but Mr. Cake, he was not frightened of John. And I knows John, he likes to scare people."

Sergeants Caldwell and Stott entered the tavern and walked over to Endersby's table. They took off their hats in silence and stood by their chairs as Betty Loxton finished her story.

"Can you write and read, Betty?" asked Endersby.

"No, Inspector. Only my numbers."

"Can you tell your story again if need be?"

"But where, sir? You mean to you once again?"

"Or in the courts. Or to the magistrate."

Young Reggie Crabb took to his feet like a soldier bracing for battle. "You cannot, sir, cannot let her go in there. They will *damn her* for sure."

Endersby took Reggie by the shoulder. He held him face-to-face. "No, young lad. It is not of my doing. It is the Law which requires it."

Young Reggie withdrew, his head held down. "She done nothing, sir. I seen her do nothing but good," he said.

"I believe you, young lad. But it is she who must stand by her tale. It is as true as you can tell it, young miss?"

Betty now shoved both hands under her shawl and carefully regarded the assembly before her. She passed her eyes around the room, first to Endersby, then the two waiting sergeants. Such a sigh of remorse escaped her lips that Endersby himself was surprised by it. "Tell my sergeants the tale once again," Endersby said softly. "Let them hear the part about the club and what happened on Friday night last. This is very important, young Betty. For you, and for Mr. Cake. We do not want the courts to send the wrong folk to the gallows, do we?"

"The gallows, sir?"

It was obvious to Endersby—certainly, it was clear even to the staring eyes of Reggie Crabb—that Betty had not considered this consequence. Her own mother and brother and uncle—all were culpable, all were candidates for Newgate prison. Worse, any one of them might swing from a rope if her own words were to make it so. Endersby was moved by Betty's wild eyes, now full of tears.

"I tell the truth, even if I lose my old mam. But I can only say what I know."

Against what seemed her better judgment, Betty told the tale again, making sure she spoke slowly, with eyes held on the inspector's face. Sergeants Caldwell and Stott stood as witnesses. No change to the details was proffered: the costers had gone to Cake's house, smashed it, and come home. Betty then asked if she could be allowed to return to the comfort of Old Drury. Endersby suggested young Reggie Crabb accompany her.

On the boy's way out, Endersby cautioned him once more. "Here, lad, is your shilling as promised. Keep an eye out for tonight and tomorrow. Keep your ears open for any word that might help. We are busy tonight, but on the morrow, I shall call for you, if need be."

The boy tipped his cap and led a pale Betty Loxton out of the room.

Soon after the two waifs had shut the door, Endersby called over his sergeants and asked them to share pints of porter and to begin their own peculiar tales.

*   *   *

Endersby first drew Stott into his confidence, where he hoped the trials and journeys of his sergeant's afternoon might bring forth facts which could serve to enlighten the three men, all of whom were on the brink of discovery, even if they still hovered in a limbo of swirling suppositions.

"And so, Sergeant Stott," he began, "what revelations do you bring us?"

Stott's face did not light up with enthusiasm as Endersby had hoped; nevertheless, his story was recounted with vigour.

"They work hard, John the Pawn and Pineapple Pol. She is a tough hen, sir. All afternoon, I lurked in the Garden, watching them sell. I followed the hen to a flat, where she led out another young gal and sent her forth with a basket of lemons. I took coffee beside them, heard them talk in their coster language—it is hard to follow at times. But I found out that Wednesdays, tonight for certain, they go to the Gaff. It is a kind of entertainment, a make-shift theatre near St. Paul's. A place of lewd ballads and what the costers call 'jiggling'."

"Young Betty Loxton claimed she dances and sings at this odd place."

"Yes, Inspector. It is a place where the young coster lads take their gals to dance. The tobacconists—across the way from the Loxton stall—they claim much more goes on there."

"More of what?"

"Thieving, jostling, rogering, sir."

"A stew, then. A nanny-house?"

"On occasion, so they said. It's a place for bucks to mount does in the back corners behind the rows of men and women watching the shows."

"A penny an entrance, no doubt."

"A ha'penny, sir."

"So, tonight John the Pawn and Pineapple Pol shall go."

"For certain, sir."

"We must risk going too, Stott. Indeed, we must conjure up a game for them. A ruse to trap 'em."

"I would not frame such a thing on my own, sir. They are a hard lot. They carry clubs and knives."

"Stott, I mean that we—Caldwell and I—shall go, and with a constable to aid us. A constable to catch any bolters who try to run outside of the place."

"It is not for me, then, to come along?"

"Ah, believe in me, Sergeant Stott. With all that I know to this point, I shall need you in reserve. But tarry a moment."

Endersby looked at his two sergeants with a hard gaze. His impatience and ever-nagging hunger were driving him to act on impulse. He had reviewed all the facts, fitted the puzzle, tried to see a series of scenes as in a play, his memory traces affording him perspective. This thinking did nothing, however, to calm his doubts. In fact, they drove him to know the end of the rigmarole. Endersby leaned into Caldwell and examined his face.

"As you can see, sir," responded his sergeant, "my wounds have healed somewhat."

"But you still look the tough fighter," said Stott.

"One who has lost the latest scuffle," quipped Endersby. "But such yellowings and scabs shall provide us with our ruse."

"How so, sir? And what shall we effect by it?'

"My good man," retorted Endersby gruffly, "let me explain when I come up with the ruse itself; you are too impatient, and I am in need of some supper."

Uttering a cry to the waiters, the irritable inspector stamped his healthy foot. Presently, a server appeared and was commanded to bring a hot eel soup, a potato pie and a plate of cold tongue. Endersby also asked for a quill, a scrap of paper, an inkwell—all brought to him within a wink—and a runner-boy who could be trusted. "Do not figure this to be a note for our superintendent, gentlemen," Endersby spoke as he wrote on the scrap of paper. "It is, rather, an apology to my wife whom I must abandon this evening at the supper hour." A rush of colour entered Endersby's cheeks as he wrote. The two sergeants meanwhile pulled chairs from the table behind him, sat down nearer the hearth and began warming their hands. From the mantel Caldwell took two clay pipes out of a cup and filled them with caches of his own tobacco. Both men lit up and relaxed in their chairs, their feet pushed out before them.

"You see, gentlemen, my wife is my life's accomplice." Endersby's voice took on a tender, musing tone. "I must keep her informed, more for my own peace of mind than hers."

The running-boy was summoned. Endersby gave him a penny, with the promise of another, and drew out for him the direction of Number 6 Cursitor Street. "I knows it, Guv'. Sure as the back of me hand. Past the hospital, in the shadow of the prison."

"Run then, and quick."

The server now entered. Plates of food clattered on the table. Endersby moved like a man starving on a desert island. To be precise, he lurched at the food, and with fork and spoon ate his supper without a word to his more leisurely companions. Wiping his mouth at the end, Endersby sat up. "We have precious time tonight, Caldwell. We must use rag and string to make up our disguise."

"But sir," replied his faithful sergeant, "you have yet to be astonished at what I have for you in this small envelope."

"But what is it, my good man?"

Sergeant Caldwell handed the soiled, folded paper to his superior.

"Do you know its contents, Caldwell?"

"I do, sir. And I have been patient enough with its withholding."

"You have held something back?" Endersby cried in amazement.

"No, indeed, sir. Not held back at all. I was waiting to save for you the finest tidbit."

"I do believe it," grumbled Endersby, somewhat humbled by Caldwell's assertion. But his heart was leaping with anticipation. "You have locked me out, sir. Let me in, I beg of you."

"It is a most singular story," Caldwell began. "I spent the first hours at the glove sellers near all the great theatres, at Old Drury and Covent Garden, then to the Surrey side and the Coburg, the Victoria, then back over Waterloo to the King's, the Italian opera. The answers came in a chorus: never seen the glove before. The leather and canvas palm were poorly sewn, said one; the canvas and leather are cleverly combined, said another. At the theatres themselves, the outfitters for leather could not place the item.

"Well, Inspector, I took the glove away, and I looked at it smartly, and it was my opinion it had been cleaned at least once. Given the blood on it, no doubt the glove was smutty, but there was to the leather a look which sulphur and rosin give, that cleaned 'feel' which a glove tends to have more often than not. So, I take myself to my haberdasher, then to his brother, a glove cleaner, near Lamb's Conduit Street.

'What do you say, Richard? This glove been cleaned, do you think?'

'Most definite. Cleaned not too long ago. Can tell by the feel of the leather. The rosin still lingers on it.'

"He lifted it to his nose and smelled. 'Could be taken for oil, he said, but that is definitely a smell of rosin mixed with sulphur. The blood spots need attention. Someone cut who was wearing these?'

"'Aye, Richard. Whoever has done the cutting, he must beware soon enough.'

'I'll tell you what. There are no more than seven or so reg'lar glove cleaners in London. I think I can spare you their addresses. I knows for certain that two of 'em, next to Bow Street itself, use a fine kind of rosin, smelling like this yellow leather. A respectable cleaner, of course, keeps a client list, so you may discover your man—or, indeed, your woman—who is the owner.'

"I went off, and according to his directions, I went here and there.

"'No, sir, said one.' 'No record,' said another. 'Thank you, sir, never seen its like before.'

"I sat down after three hours. I was exhausted as a man can be, with no respite and the cold air taking its toll on my weakened state. I simply couldn't find neither man, woman, nor child that had cleaned this lost mate. As I made my way south to the river, I wondered if all my efforts had been in vain. It was into the sixth hour of my search, and I decided— since the Lyceum was close by—I would visit its backstage and enquire once more. At the stage-door stood a young man, a quiet, modest gentleman who was conducting business with the keeper. When he stepped aside, I made my plea to the keeper himself, and in the midst of my request, the young modest man stepped forward.

"'I could not help but overhearing, sir,' he claimed. 'I beg your pardon.'

"'You, sir, are most obliging. But I am at a loss.'

"Forthwith I lifted the glove and showed it to the modest

young man, who with no hesitation broke into a smile.

"'You must excuse me,' he said. 'But I must walk on and cannot stop here very long. But if you will accompany me a short distance, toward the City, I may be of help to you. I must begin my work within the hour, for I am forced to be in good time, and early, for the night.'

"'You work, sir, at night? But you do not impress me as a baker.'

"The modest young man said: 'No, I am not a baker. Nor an actor.' He began laughing, and we walked on a step or two before he spoke again. 'You may be astonished, sir, at what I do at night, considering your questions to the stage- door keeper.'

"'How so?' I asked, full of curiosity as well as doubt. Was I, perhaps, being taken advantage of?

"'I am a glove cleaner.'

"The words out of his mouth struck me as the most singular coincidence. 'I cannot believe this, sir. You are leading me astray,' I argued. 'I must bid you a good afternoon.'

"'Yes,' he laughed. 'I told you so. And this piece you carry. Well, it is another odd chance, and one which may shock you as well.' I was not in the frame of mind to contradict the pleasant-seeming man. He dressed as a gentleman of modest means. He did not appear to be a strangler or a pickpocket. I was strong enough, despite my injured face, to hold him down if need be. He took hold of the glove and turned it once more in his hands. He stroked its leather backing.

"'I've spent half my day,' I said, 'searching out cleaners and sellers of gloves.'

"'On account of these blood spots?'

"'Precisely.'

"'And you are, no doubt, a sergeant with the Metro- politan Police.'

"'I am, sir. A sergeant with the Detective Police, in fact.'

"The man smiled and handed back the glove and raised his hand to point toward a broad house not forty paces away. 'Bless you, sir, I know this glove and its mate well enough. It belongs to a particular party whose name I cannot recall for the moment.' I feared as much. Here was the rub, the pull-off. But before my own disbelief could hamper my better judgment, the congenial chap said: 'If you shall trust me, I can lead you to the man who cleaned this item and to the owner's name.'

"'Then you know for certain who did the cleaning?'

"'Rather so,' he beamed. 'My father himself.'

"We went round to the broad building, up a set of clean stairs. There we found in a set of cleaner rooms an old man in a green apron, with a daughter on either side, rubbing and dabbing away at a lot of gloves. 'Good evening, sir,' said the old man. The daughters rose to curtsey, then resumed their work. The pleasant, modest young man told the story of the glove, and the old man gazed at it, turned it over in his hands, passed it to one daughter and then to the next, the latter rising from her chair and taking the liberty to walk with the glove into a second room. She returned with a box of slips and papers. She ran through the slips with her fingers, as fast as she could. She checked the slip, read with her lips moving in silence, a name, the description of the glove. Then she retreated into the second room, re-appeared with pen and paper and envelope.

"'Are you certain?' I asked of her.

"'Certain of what?' came her curt reply.

"'I must demand you are certain,' I said. 'For this is a matter of grave concern, and a matter also of life and death'.

"The old man stood. He took the glove and checked it again while reading the name and address of its owner which his daughter had freshly written. 'No doubt of it. The man is a regular patron. And he pays on time.'

"I thanked the family and offered to buy them a supper in gratitude, but they would have none of it. With this envelope in hand, I made my way back here, to Vinegar Yard. I think its contents, sir, will be of paramount interest."

Without hesitation, Endersby tore open the envelope and read the name and address to himself. He handed the information to Stott, who had come forward. Stott read the contents, handed the envelope back, and the three men stood in silence.

"Click, click," whispered Endersby.

"I beg your pardon, sir," said Caldwell.

"Stott, we have no time now. We have only our legs and our hearts to guide us. I want you to forgo sleep if need be. Get to Swan Yard, to Cake's gentleman's club, and ask for the cabby who serviced the man who called for Mr. Cake, on Friday last. The proprietor is reasonable, and he knows you are coming. Find out from the cabby where his fare went at one o'clock or thereabouts on Friday night last. Ask, too, if the cabby can remember the clothing of his passenger and any outline of his features. Once you have this information, meet us if you are able, at the Gaff in St.Paul's. If you cannot find us, then go on to Number 6 Cursitor Street, and bring a warm coat. Do not take to your bed, Stott, for I have a mission for you which will require of you much daring."

Stott remained still, taking in all that Endersby had said.

"You, Caldwell, must perfect a limp to accompany your bruised face. And we are now off, with turban and string to catch us a costerman and his ruffian friends." Endersby spoke with a direct, cold, earnest voice. "Remember, we are in the business of exacting the Law and must not fail to believe that our means, often suspect, bring about a just end."

* * *

In the distance loomed the dome of St. Paul's Cathedral. Owen Endersby could never have pictured himself dancing in a lewd working-man's theatre. Yet the moment he and Caldwell alighted from the hackney-coach and made their way down the streets of the City, no subsequent hesitation rose in his mind. Only a few words were spoken between them as they walked. Endersby had already drawn out his ruse, carefully plotting what kinds of responses he anticipated from the costers and what he must do in the event a knife was drawn and pointed at his throat. Their disguises were simple. Endersby wore his old canvas coat inside out, and Caldwell had pulled up his collar, put on a flat hat borrowed from the bar-keep in the tavern of Vinegar Yard.

"Tie it up tight, if you please, Caldwell."

Endersby waited as his sergeant wrapped the turban around his head, his theory being that John the Pawn might recall him as the fussy fruit buyer of a few days ago. The broad end of Ludgate Street glistened with light snow. Caldwell practiced his limp and told Endersby he would attempt a posh accent tonight.

"Add a touch of the fop, Caldwell. It'll give the brutes a sense of advantage."

The jingling sound of a piano rose and fell in the misty air. As Endersby and Caldwell came closer, turning south into narrower quarters, the stretch of Earl Street before them took on a new shape. One of its shops on the ground floor had been torn open: its front entirely removed—door, wall and windows—and its gaping entrance strung with crudely painted canvas squares.

"Them the performers, you figure?" said Caldwell.

"I thought you'd decided on posh words, Sergeant."

"I beg your pardon, sir. What has come over me? Be they the vulgar dancers, in those canvas portraits?"

Endersby smiled at Caldwell's quick turn. "You could have been a stager, I swear," he said. Walking in single file— Caldwell as "The Lord" and Endersby as "his valet"—the two of them strolled into the garish light seeping out the Gaff entrance. The colour of the light shone orange-red—its source a candle hanging inside a giant paper lantern suspended just inside the cavernous entrance. Across from the Gaff itself, this same lantern light gleamed like sunset in shop windows. The red-orange faces caught in the reflection of the window glass were those of the rough crowd of twenty-year-old men in cloth caps and kerchiefs. The thin girls on their arms looked no older than thirteen or fourteen, dressed up in soiled bonnets and tattered shawls. Outside, Endersby spotted the back-up constable he'd asked Fleet Station to bring in, and he nodded to him as a signal that all was set. The constable tapped his baton on the pavement to the two men and watched as they joined the crushing figures. The mob pushed toward the money-takers, and greasy, soiled hands stretched out to tender their ha'pennies. Another police officer—from the local station— stood by the entrance to preserve order, and he occasionally shoved the boys off the pavement amidst swearing and shows of fists.

Inside the Gaff, the air was fetid with tobacco smoke. The stage, a large platform of boards, dipped and warped, pulling against the nails hammered into its surface onto three wooden sawhorses. Streaks of red paint smeared the walls. Endersby looked up to note that the ceiling plaster of the room had been removed, though the white-washed beams still stretched from wall to wall. Above them was another storey, now open and gaping over the milling bodies below. The second-storey room displayed remnants of its former state as a parlour, its soiled wall paper daubed with large black letters announcing the performers. Like coarse playbills, thought Endersby, who marvelled at the space, festive despite its ruin. Around him, such shoving and pushing; such puffing of pipes; such a dense damp stink of market dung, unwashed skin, sweat-soaked canvas and wool. The piano in the far corner—a low, battered instrument with keys as yellow as a tobacco chewer's front teeth—pounded out a chord. A man wearing a long dress and a crown ambled onto the makeshift stage.

Whistles, stamping feet and hollers greeted him. He curtsied, his tongue lolling from the side of his mouth. A young, broad boy in a leather apron came out behind him. A drum roll, the piano again and the two men began a lewd, pelvis-to-pelvis dance, each grinning at the audience and winking to the delight of the spectators.

"Keep an eye out," said Endersby to Caldwell, his voice lost in the tumult.

Ragtag couples began to dance. After a while, porter cans passed around. A young woman, no older than Betty Loxton, rushed onto the stage after the bows of the two dancing men.

"Alloo, Lucy Light," cried a bunch of rough boys, their pipes smoking in their mouths.

"There he is," said Endersby. Caldwell followed the line

of Endersby's pointing finger. John the Pawn leaned against the wall directly across from the entrance curtain. Beside him was a haggard, pock-marked woman in a red bonnet.

"Pineapple Pol, we assume?" asked the sergeant.

"Perhaps, Caldwell. Let us perambulate."

"Hi, Lucy Light, freckled girl," yelled out more of the boisterous young men. The girl appeared no older than fourteen, slim, her face all smiling. She started to sing and dance with her arms thrown up over her head.

"Flash us, flash us, Lucy Light."

The girl broke into laughter and raised up her hem. John the Pawn lit his pipe and drew in smoke as Endersby meandered his way through the sweaty bodies. Pulling close his turban, Endersby tapped John the Pawn on the left shoulder.

"Good evening, sir."

John the Pawn looked at Endersby then turned away. The inspector tried again.

"What want you, man, with your tap tapping?"

"But a word."

"I am busy, scab."

"A word, sir. Money is in it for you."

"What you say?"

"Coin, sir."

"Get away, rum lot."

The dancing Lucy Light sauntered over and lit a cheroot on one of the thin gas jets. She puffed, then began a song which brought howls and much clapping.

"Duck-legged Dick had a donkey, And his lush loved much for to swill..."

Endersby tapped again then stood back, anticipating that his persistence might bring the elbow of John the Pawn squarely on his jaw. The other man did not budge.

"You are John Loxton, sir? John the Pawn. The man who does jobs?" asked Endersby, his voice pitched up to bolster his disguise.

"Cool! Look there. Two Bow Street scars," warned the haggard Pineapple Pol. She wiped her mouth with a dirty hand and drew on her pipe. Across from her and John the

Pawn, two local policemen had entered the space, both of them wearing white leather gloves and brandishing their batons. A low whistle arose in the Gaff on their entrance.

"Gentlemen, hope you ain't doing arrests, since there is no cross chaps here," cried Lucy Light from the stage. The costers and their gals laughed at the joke, and the boys in their kerchiefs tipped their caps to the policemen in mock salute.

"Give it me," said John the Pawn to Pineapple Pol. She was holding up a plug of tobacco. He tore off a bit.

"You think, Pol, we ever find the git?" John the Pawn asked.

"She'll turn up here, sooner or later, the stupid gal," she replied.

"No, mam, I think not. Our Betty's bolted."

"Scamming child. I shall beat her senseless when I sees her. She's scamping. I told her no to scamping."

"Kind sir?" said Endersby once again.

"Leave me be, plaguey man. Or you shall have the Bow Street scars over there upon you for your broken head."

"I beg a moment only. Look upon my master there, the pal over by the door with the bruised face."

"I know him not," replied John the Pawn.

"Who are you?" cried Pineapple Pol. "What scam are you playing?"

"None, missus," Endersby replied. "I come but as a gentleman's man to ask John Loxton a favour."

"And who is that fool to send you?" Pineapple Pol asked, squinting her eyes. "What foolin' are you up to?"

"I beg only a favour. A cousin, you see, of mine...we is both in service...he knows of a chappy, a coster by the nickname of Peter the Stick."

"A rotten herring for sure," laughed Pineapple Pol.

"Get on with you, or I'll crack your skull for you," muttered John the Pawn.

"My master, there, by the door. Him with the collar up and the flat hat. Beaten and hurt by a terrible footman, in employ to none other than Lord Harwood...a rascal. Mind, this same cousin of mine tells me that Peter the Stick and you, sir, was in a fleece, or at least a lark and a game, last Friday night. You and the Stick against some chappy in Doughty Street, what a ruckus was caused, so he tells me, and..."

John the Pawn grabbed hold of Endersby's cravat and pulled his face up to his stenchy mouth. With the odour of onions and rotten molars in his face, Endersby heard John the Pawn say, "Lies and foolery. I sell but apples and plums. Get away."

"Kind sir, I but promised my master at least a word with you. He is sore oppressed. What with my cousin giving him some promise of revenge—hoping it'd be you and the Stick to do it on this ponce of Lord Harwood's. I come only to buy a favour and pay for a kindness."

"Flash it, then."

"Pardon, sir?"

"Flash it, fool. The coin."

From his inside pocket, Endersby slid out a sovereign. He held it to John the Pawn's nose. Leaning in close, Pineapple Pol grinned and snatched the coin from his hands. "'Tis stinking fake," she said, holding the sovereign out before her in a clutch of black-nailed fingers.

"Nay, missus, genuine as the Queen's arse, I swear," said Endersby.

Pineapple Pol broke into a cackle, coughed and turned the coin twice around.

"Bless her, and her German prick," she laughed again, her throat catching a harsh cough, forcing her to spit on the floor. In an instant, John the Pawn grabbed the sovereign out of his mother's fingers. "Get out of my hands, Johnny boy," she yelled, pawing at the air as he now held up the sovereign. "That is my privilege," she bellowed.

"No, mam, it ain't. But 'tis mine," John the Pawn growled, the words between them fierce. Slipping the coin into his upper pocket, John the Pawn followed this gesture with a reminder to his mother: he elbowed Pineapple Pol in the neck so hard, she tumbled against the wall. Her pipe clacked to the floor.

"Scamp boy," she yelled, but she rose up quickly, forcing a laugh, her eyes narrow with anger.

Endersby was not surprised to see her raise her fist to

retaliate but then to reconsider. In one clear way, she had common sense: her son's violence cowed her, and it gave to Endersby a clear configuration of the kind of deed the man was capable of doing, to either a young girl like Betty or a grown man the size of Samuel Cake. With Betty's confessional words in his mind, and his own desire to make the ruse work, Endersby sallied forth again.

"There is another of those—and a guinea, too—if you shall but hear out my master," Endersby said, winking at Pineapple Pol. "He is most insistent, sir. Most brutal in remark if he do not get his way."

Endersby was aware of John the Pawn's change of heart, for now the costerman was fingering the sovereign, having slipped it from his pocket to pass it across his blackened teeth. Knocking the tobacco from his pipe, John the Pawn grabbed hard the upper arm of Endersby, and with a wry smile said to him to lead on and no farting on the way.

Midway through the crowd, John the Pawn stopped still and looked furtively around the room. He hesitated, looking back at Pineapple Pol, who was re-lighting her pipe. He took a moment to wipe his mouth. He yanked Endersby's arm. "That your master, yonder?"

Caldwell turned and sneered at Endersby on his approach. "Stinking dog, what has taken you so long?"

"Here is one, sir. The one does jobs. John Loxton."

John the Pawn glanced up and down at Caldwell's clothes. "He is no master, plaguey man. Look at his shabby dress and stinker hat."

"Look at my face," said Caldwell. "Shall I come to such a place as this in lawn and silk?"

Caldwell managed to lisp his words, the sound making John the Pawn grin.

"And who beat you, sire?" The costerman's voice was full of mockery.

"That was a wretched arrogant footman," said Caldwell, dismissive in his manner, his arm fluttering, as if he were batting a fly from his cheek. "In Lord Harwood's employ. A gad of a man."

This was the second time this evening that Endersby realized that Caldwell was a man of some playfulness. In the aura of his sergeant's most convincing performance, Endersby was struck by the power of Caldwell's play-acting, let alone the look of hardy belief on the face of John the Pawn.

The coster is waiting this out, Endersby thought. Waiting and weighing the risk.

"The poxy shit would not lower the steps for me to my carriage," Caldwell went on. "Claimed he was only footman Number One, doors only, and that Second Footman was off ill. Stuff and shit I said to 'im and struck his curling mouth. Whereupon the rascal knocked me down."

John the Pawn slapped his knee. "Serves you right. Serves you so, pricky Jack."

"How dare you, sir. I come to you for a favour."

"How dare I? This is how." John the Pawn shoved Caldwell to the wall. He pressed his bulk against him and looked hard into the sergeant's eyes. "Aye, you been properly thumped. Rumbled to a bruise."

Having crossed the room unbeknownst to her son, Pineapple Pol sidled up to Caldwell. "This is the plum, Johnny lad?"

"Get you hence, mam. Get on."

"You leave me be, lad," she said. "What you roughing this poor pal up so? He is kindly enough."

"Indeed, missus," cowered Endersby. "It is but a small favour we come for."

"What is your cousin's name, sir? The one that knows Peter the Stick," asked John the Pawn, still holding Caldwell to the wall.

"Gaffy is what he's called. He is a cutter, sir, in Holborn."

"How does he know a coster, then, fool?"

"His sister, sir. She knows well of Peter."

John the Pawn let Caldwell go. He stepped back and gazed about the room now filled with dancers and a tumbler on the stage tossing balls into the air. If the ruse were to hold, Endersby could not afford further delay. He did not want John the Pawn to doubt any longer. He pulled another coin from his pocket—a mere shilling—but he hid it in his fingers so that in the light it could not be easily read.

"What of this matter, then," barked Caldwell. He flashed an uncertain glance at Endersby, who held his arm fast.

"We are undone, master," said Endersby, making his voice quiver in mock subservience. "Here is a man of no consequence. Peter the Stick has lied."

Such an utterance caused Pineapple Pol to grab John the Pawn and swing him around. "Move on 'em, lad," she urged. There was a glare of anger in John Loxton's face tagged by a flicker of disappointment as Endersby started to walk away, slipping the coin back into his pocket. Acting true to his disguise as a pandering servant, Endersby allowed Caldwell ahead of him and diverted him toward the Gaff's entrance to the street.

"You, plaguey man," John the Pawn shouted at them. "Come back. I see your coin. What is it you wish of me?"

Pineapple Pol laughed at her son. "You lost 'em now, Johnny lad." In answer, Caldwell turned to see John the Pawn shove Pineapple Pol into the crowd, the scrawny woman laughing and pointing at him like a witch in the Pantomime.

"How do we know *we* can trust *you?*" hissed Caldwell. By now he was halfway toward the curtained archway leading out to the street.

The coster hesitated for a second; he then leapt forward, trotting after Endersby and Caldwell and almost crashing against them in the entrance. "Come into the street, gits" he said, pushing past the two men to hold open the curtain for them. Outside, the sky was now full of cloud. Endersby's back-up constable was waiting by the doorway ready to witness. The bitter chill caused breath to smoke in the air. John the Pawn stood in front of the two men, gulls he figured, from the way he was grinning. It was clear to Endersby the costerman must honour his pride, or lose the coin. And so the ploy was set in motion.

"You can trust me," John the Pawn said.

"I think not, if your playing with us is such," whimpered Caldwell.

"I hears, sir, you thumped a man good, Friday last," ventured Endersby. "Some ponce from the theatre."

"Aye, you heard rightly, wormy man. Tell your master we did a good one on 'im, too."

"Sir, stories do not interest me," said Caldwell in a haughty manner. "I bid you good night. We must find another, for it is heartily worth my while."

"Stay, sir. I can attest," said John the Pawn. "I can show you if you wish. 'Tis but a cab ride north to Doughty Street. The house stands empty."

"And you, sir, in your coster's wisdom, have a key to the place?" sneered Caldwell, leading the man on. "And can you also beat away the poor man's servants?"

"The man had none, I swear to you."

Caldwell affected a pealing laugh. "Such a jest," he cried. With a surreptitious toe, Caldwell knicked Endersby in the shin, who responded with a slight grimace but also a nod. Endersby was also noting the details of John the Pawn's admission. To the two seasoned policemen, it was obvious the costerman was well acquainted with the place, but the facts on its lack of servants had been reported in the gutter press. Could John the Pawn read? Would he have cared to find out the consequences of his rumbling? Rumours amongst the costers would have flown—a few facts of the case were public knowledge. What Endersby needed was a confession of a singular fact. One known only by John the Pawn himself. The press had not described the crime scene but only reported the coroner's proceedings. Endersby remembered that all the confessions at the inquest concerned the body, the possible manner of murder, witnesses' recall of visitors and such. What was needed from John the Pawn was an admission of an action only *he* could have performed or commanded during those dark lawless hours.

"Don't believe it," said Endersby. "The man was rich. So said the press. And do you read at all, sir?"

"Well enough, serving man," John the Pawn answered with some hesitation. "But I tell you, come and witness. The house had little furniture, bare as a bone it was. Me, my mam's brother Thomas and Peter the Stick, we does our best up and down the place, smashing. Scared the rheumy man off, we did. He daren't come in while we was there."

"But I need you to *beat* the rascal footman, not frighten him away." Caldwell had now affected a piercing whine.

"Fair enough," said John the Pawn. "We thought he'd be at home. We thought it, and we brought a club, my cousin Thomas from south of Surrey."

"All supposition, my man, but not evidence of deed," said Caldwell.

John the Pawn rubbed his forehead. He was angry now. "Damn you, sir. I have had enough. I swear we went to beat a man that hurt my own flesh and blood. We wants to thrash him. We even nailed the shutters tight so no one could see us. And we smashed up the glass in his door."

There, at last. Two single facts Endersby was waiting for.

"Nailed shut?" cried Caldwell, to emphasize the point.

"Yes, man. Hard shut with Jew seconder nails. Cheaper by the handful, I warrant. We thought the noise might amuse the chappy." John the Pawn pounded one fist against the other as if to illustrate his hammering method.

"And the back window, sir?" Endersby asked, carefully.

"Smashed. So's to show 'im we'd been round the place. Since he warn't at home—and he never came—we left soon enough. What with our ruckus, the scabs from Gray's Inn be upon us in no time."

"After you nicked his silver and coin?" Endersby said, to goad.

"Ha, the rub. There was none of either. A bare bone, I tell you. And the man staying out all hours. We could do what we done, in fact."

"Enough, John the Pawn," said Caldwell.

Endersby then gave the sign. They had arranged en route to the Gaff that when the jig was up, Endersby would pull at his left ear.

John the Pawn spotted this, lofting a suspicious glance at Caldwell and the inspector through mist and red light. "You 'ave an itchy ear, wormy man?" The costerman bent forward as if to blow his nose. He completed the gesture by suddenly reaching for a knife hidden in his left boot. "You plaguey gits, this be a scam," he yelled. He waved the knife high, jerked his torso into an attack posture, and, aiming the knife's snout end at Endersby's chest, he took short, frantic jumps forward. The back-up constable watching by the Gaff's door rushed into the scene, for now it was certain this was a game of life and death. The constable dashed in front of John the Pawn. His baton came down swiftly cracking the costerman's wrist.

"Halt, scoundrel!" the constable shouted. The knife bounced on the cobbles. John the Pawn made a tentative start to recover, a start inspired by seeing Caldwell pull out a police baton from under his disguise. It was the bear pit, indeed, with the dogs on the winning side, but it took fully half a second before John the Pawn got his legs (and his wits) and began truly asserting himself. Poking hard with his elbows, he first knocked the wind out of the constable who had been bold and brave enough to initiate the sally. He then tried to run, but Caldwell came round his right side and slammed his full weight into John the Pawn's back, grabbing hold and twisting up his fisted right arm.

"Let me be, scummy rat," the struggling costerman cried. Endersby pulled from his satchel—closely hidden under his coat—a pair of cuffs with a latch and chain.

"No, no you don't," cried the John the Pawn, his eyes wide with terror. Clamping them on, Endersby watched John the Pawn howl, his voice breaking into panic laughter. Caldwell then completed the routine: he lifted his coat and produced a link chain attached to his waist. To it, he clamped a second set of smaller links and fed them through the slots of John the Pawn's cuffs—in the end a kind of steel umbilical cord securing criminal to constable.

"I done nothing, gentlemen. You got no proof of me. I was telling you tales, you gulls."

"There were two witnesses to you leaving Doughty Street, John Loxton. They can attest." Endersby knew he'd just taken a risk in bending the truth. His and Caldwell's remarkable ruse had developed nicely into a capture. The inspector's offense was simply justified by the costerman's actions, and so Endersby would not really have to face any tough opposition to his methods. Besides, he also surmised the costerman could never challenge him.

"You're fools. Scum." John the Pawn said, his attempt at disdain failing to gain attention. The beleaguered felon broke out of his fury with an attempt at ineffective authority: hands clasped in irons trying to hide themselves under his coat, he demanded the inspector take his pipe from his upper pocket, fill it with plug and light him up. "A gesture of police courtesy, you understand, guv," the costerman said. "As is my rights as a British subject."

"You can wait on that pleasure, my man," said Endersby dismissively.

"Who in Hell's dominion are you in the end, sir?" John the Pawn demanded.

"Inspector Owen Endersby, Mr. Loxton. My worthy sergeant, Caldwell. And a respectable constable from Scotland Yard. At her majesty's service."

John the Pawn turned down his mouth. He began to breathe hard. He shook his tethered hands. He fought back tears. He took his manacled wrists and swept them over his eyes. He laughed again, swaying his head from side to side. He tried, without success, to spit at the inspector's shoes, but soon relented, his resignation drooping his once proud brutish shoulders. "You ever seen a man so knocked over with surprise?" said John the Pawn, his voice lying low in his throat. "I mean me, inspector. You grubs took me. You nabbed me. But, I wager, you ain't done it much. I was the dupe."

"Come along, Mr. Loxton," said Endersby. "Most like you come peaceably, decorum being the greater part of a thief's manner."

"Well, I ain't no shit-bucket thief. I'm an honest, back-broken worker. Never a scam in my life."

"Until this Friday last."

A scream behind the party rent the air. Pineapple Pol was rushing into the street. The young constable turned in time to catch her arm. Much of her subsequent movements took the form of slugs, kicks, choppings of the jaw. The constable held her still.

"What, Johnny lad, what is this? They nabbed you," she screeched.

"And you, mam. You were in the cart, after all. 'Twas you that drove us north."

"Ungrateful pig," she yelled, a gob of her spit flying into her son's face courtesy of her quick forward head thrust. The constable held her wrists behind her as Caldwell found another set of cuffs in his pocket.

"I hope you'll let me have my coat, sir," John the Pawn said, his voice suddenly polite, if guarded.

"You attacked Mr. Cake's house out of spite then, sir," asked Endersby, unwinding his costume turban.

"Eye for an eye. Simple justice."

"Not English law, however," Endersby reminded him.

"Off to the 'factory' then," John the Pawn said. And with that, Pineapple Pol was duly secured while Caldwell held fast to her glum son. Endersby spoke briefly to the other constable about keeping an eye on the place. Without further delay, a hackney coach was summoned. The young constable climbed aboard, hauling behind him a swearing, coughing Pineapple Pol. Around the street, a few peering young people circled. This was, however, a common sight. Arrests for thieves, window breakers, drunks, slag women for hire—the daily bread and lard of this rough, mean quarter of the city. While Endersby commanded the cabby the route first to Fleet Street and then Newgate Prison, Caldwell draped John the Pawn's coat over the costerman's shoulders and shoved him into the cab, next to his squalling mam.

Sticking his head out the cab window, the costerman grinned and said to Endersby, "I ne'er been to Newgate, myself. Do you think me mam will like it?"

"For one thing, Mr. Loxton, the wintry wind blows hard through its stone walls."

John the Pawn saw it was no use carrying on further. Sitting back in the cab, he closed his eyes as Caldwell tapped

the roof, and the hackney coach proceeded to drive on to
Fleet Street. Alone, now, cold and hungry, Endersby walked
back into the noisy confines of the Gaff. He hoped he might
see the sad little waif, the sweet Betty Loxton and her dancing
feet. The smoke was pungent and blue. The stage was full of
antic jugglers. Endersby remembered that Stott might
appear, and so he scanned the room, the two doorways, the
back shadows for any sign of him. Alas, all he could find were
runts and brutes, drunken girls with faces smeared by beer.

"Nowhere," Endersby said under his breath. The freckled
girl called Lucy Light returned to the stage, dancing with a
man in a bear's head mask. "What a folly," Endersby said out
loud to no one in particular. Betty should be here, he
thought, but he sensed she had decided never to return to
the place, its smoke and laughter no longer enticing her to
sing. Leaving the noise, Endersby walked for a long while
westward out of the City. He drew in his mind the by-ways and
highways of the case, a map of its motives and opportunities.

"Propensity," he whispered.

He was convinced he knew who the murderer was. But he
needed more—crucial items and a confession—to close up
the case. To this target he planted the word "conviction".
Now to get one, he mused. Here was the final challenge—the
rub. Indeed, it was the key piece of the Cake puzzle.

*   *   *

Sergeant Stott was waiting on the steps of Number 6
Cursitor Street. His face was brisk from the cold. Even his
large, beefy hands looked blue. "Did you not call up to my
wife, sergeant?"

"No, sir. I thought it too late."

"She is a woman used to the strange hours of policemen. Come inside, then, and warm your hands. I need
them soon enough to be dexterous and quick."

The front door closed behind the two men. The street
lay quiet and misty, a breeze rising from the river. Smoke
from chimneys floated like fog over the eaves of the houses.

A light appeared in the far left second floor window of Number 6 Cursitor Street. Behind it, Endersby listened to what Stott had to say about the cabby and his fare on Friday night last. Endersby did not flinch at the descriptions, nor did he leap to a conclusion right away. Stott, who was precise in his way of speaking, told his tale methodically. Endersby then instructed him on his next set of duties to be performed in the subsequent hours of the night.

"I am too clumsy with my gouty foot to accompany you, Stott. You are a brave man and capable."

"Thank you, Inspector."

Endersby took a large muslin bag out of a drawer near his puzzle table. Its top was gathered with a string.

"Here it is, Stott. You know where to go. Be on guard, and if worse comes to worst, our respected superintendent will stand by you—I shall make sure of that."

Stott opened the bag then drew it closed to be sure it was sturdy. Endersby led him down the inner staircase to the street. "You shall have to walk, sergeant, but be quick." From his satchel, Endersby drew out a final item for his sergeant. "Take this," he said. He handed Stott a fork made of the finest German steel. It was broad, its handle made of wood. Stott turned it over in his hand and gave his superior a brief, but confused look.

"I wondered if you might enquire," chuckled Endersby. "No, this is not a jest. It is a trick of mine. I use the steel as a lever. See, its handle is well made and strongly attached to the spine. It is the best implement I have found for sliding under sashes and lifting windows."

Stott grinned at the novelty of the object in its new-found function. "I shall endeavour to perform to the utmost, sir, fork and all."

Endersby shook his sergeant's hand. "I am depending on you, Stott. Very much, indeed."

The sergeant set off into the smoky light of the street. On his way back upstairs, Endersby had a hunch that this trick would work. He was certain his instinct in this instance would not prove him a fool.

"At least, I hope not, old gander."

After his bath, he found to his surprise, a thin band of flickering light coming from under Harriet's bedroom door.

"I can hear you, dear one," she said. Without knocking, Endersby entered and beheld Harriet standing by her bed, dressed in a long blue gown.

"I bought it for tomorrow evening," she beamed.

Her hair was done up in her nightcap, and the incongruity of the two items of her dress made Owen Endersby smile with delight.

"A fetching *ensemble* I might say, Harriet."

"Owen, I see that Solange has had an influence. You are now speaking to me in French."

"One word at a time, madam. Slow and steady am I."

Harriet reached out and held Endersby in her arms. "I have procured a box for the opening night, tomorrow, at Old Drury."

"Splendid."

"A Christmas extravaganza. *The Beauty and the Beast.*"

"Indeed."

"And rumour has it…"

"From whom, may I ask?"

"Why, Mrs. DeForest next door."

"Rumour has it…?"

"That Her Majesty will be in attendance. With the Prince."

"Splendid again."

"You shall accompany me, of course."

"Most certainly. On two counts."

"How do you mean, dear Owen?"

"Pleasure *and* business."

Chapter Seven

THURSDAY, DECEMBER 24, 1840

Snow had been light for the past hour. Owen Endersby let himself out again and stood in the back courtyard of Number 6 Cursitor Street, staring at the leaden sky. A breeze, chilly and wet, swept the cobbles. Endersby heard footsteps. He stepped under the porch, and while waiting, listened to the cry of a baby in rooms above him.

"Hurry up, man."

Endersby peeked out from the porch and squinted. Had the man gone home and slept? Had he been caught?

"What are you doing, Owen dear?"

Endersby turned and addressed his wife, whose head had popped out of the second storey window directly above him.

"Taking the air, Harriet."

"Indeed you are. And, I presume, the snow and wind. What about your breakfast?"

"I shall come up in due time."

"Please invite Mr. Stott to join us, will you?"

"I shall, I shall."

The window clicked shut, and Endersby marched briskly through the slush of the courtyard to the street entrance. He left footprints in the mud by the doorway. His slippers felt clammy with water. He regretted dressing so quickly this morning. He wore only a frock coat and trousers and his coat over his shoulders. He reminded himself that he must choose a waistcoat for today, one suitable to the evening he would spend later on at Old Drury. The street was empty and cold. Behind him, a rushing of feet. Endersby swivelled and beyond the passage on the far side of the courtyard, through the other entrance, Sergeant Stott came pacing like a soldier into battle. "At last, here he is, old gander," Endersby whispered.

"Sir," cried Stott and held up the muslin bag. It bulged at the bottom. For answer, Endersby clapped his hands. "Is it a hit, Sergeant? Have we our quarry?"

"We do, sir."

Endersby inspected the bag. Snow fluttered onto its crumpled contents. Drawing the string tight, Endersby shook the hand of his sergeant and invited him for morning tea and toast.

"If it is all the same to you, sir, I shall go home to my bed for a few hours."

"You were not caught then, nor discovered?"

"No sir. Quiet as a flea."

"And it was where we guessed it was?"

"Exactly as you had surmised, sir. An apt deduction, I might add."

"Thank you, sergeant. Off you go then."

"At what place shall we meet next?"

"'In thunder, lightning or in rain?'" quipped Endersby.

Stott looked bewildered for a second, his large face showing the effects of a sleepless, harrowing night of house-breaking and thievery.

"Never mind, Sergeant. It was a joke of mine. A quote from Mr. Shakespeare."

"I see, sir, thank you."

"Gather Caldwell and Birken—I think we can fool Borne for the moment—and claim I have duties for them all if asked by our noble superintendent. I shall have to make an effort today, in fact, to delve into the lodging house business. Even on Christmas Eve day, I know. Nevertheless, we shall then meet at Vinegar Yard for our strategy."

"What, sir, shall we do in the meanwhile? We shall no doubt be discovered for last night's foray?"

"No doubt. But our culprit will wonder who could have done it. And what to do about it? In my ken, the guilty always choose to seem innocent and oddly enough remain so even in light of their imminent capture. We shall wait and see. There is far too much at stake today for our felon to flee. And indeed, sir, given what you have just seen these past few hours, we may safely wonder if any discovery will be made at all."

"Most likely, sir."

"Now to your sunny bed. Tonight, just past supper, at Vinegar Yard. No. Better meet me with Caldwell in the backstage hall of the theatre. Send Birken to guard, as we discussed. Before you sleep, please attend to the safe-guarding of this bag, as we have also discussed. Let us meet just at curtain-time, at eight o'clock. I am attending the grand Christmas extravaganza and shall be on guard within the pit itself."

*   *   *

"Damnation."

Henry Robertson Dupré once again undid his unruly cravat and started over. Fold to the left, fold under, once to the right, and balance.

"Jane!" The room was cold. His hearth fire lay in ashes, greyer than the snow-swept street outside. "Mrs. Croft, damn you!"

Dupré stepped to his dressing table, picked up a bell and rang it. No more than five minutes later, he drew on his Turkish robe, tied its silken ropes around his waist, and went into the hall. "Is anyone stirring in this confounded house?"

Down the stairs into the hall, he called out again. The faint morning sun ushered him toward the staircase to the kitchen. Shafts of light were the only illumination afforded him as the tapers in the hall and foyer were unlit. The stairs creaked as always, but this morning they resounded with a cry which alarmed him. He half expected to find his rooms ransacked, his furniture broken into pieces, his servants bashed and bloodied and lying face down on the floor. The large windows in the kitchen remained dark, as their muslin curtains had yet to be pulled open.

"Jane? Mrs. bloody Croft? Where in Hades are the two of you?"

No kettle boiled, no pan sat on the fire. Where was cook? The table lay empty. Five wooden chairs pushed close against it, their tight formation impressing Dupré as sulky resistance to his domestic authority. Dupré scraped one of the chairs out from the table and sat down. What he wanted was his tea. What he needed was medicine for his tumbling stomach. He also feared something worse, though he refused to say it to himself. An old complaint had returned—an itching, a burning sensation, a discharge. And to think he had been careful, cleaning himself afterwards, always pissing right away, always checking his sheaths to be sure the oil kept them pliable. Wretches, all of them, he thought. Sows and bitches.

He banged his fist on the table. A door opened, and he saw a figure in a bonnet carrying a portmanteau. The figure ran past him and through the area door into the street. "Jane? Where in God's world are you going?" Jane mounted the outdoor steps and ran off. Dupré smacked his lips, rubbed his eyes and wanted to go back to bed. He marched into the pantry. Here he was accosted by a familiar figure in a shawl and bonnet and gloves. "Mrs. Croft. At last! What in the devil are you doing dressed in street clothes at this hour? May I enquire as to what you and the rest of your paltry company are doing?"

Mrs. Croft swept passed him. Dupré could see she had been weeping. He trailed her into the kitchen. "Where are you going, Croft?" he asked, his voice plaintive as a lost boy's.

"Henry, I shall not stand for this arrangement any longer. This time you have done harm and gone too far."

"You are impertinent, Croft. Come to your senses."

"Do not speak to me in your master's tone, little Henry. You are a prodigal son, if ever there was one."

"What have I done then?" Dupré whined, impatient and hungry.

"Are you blind as well as senseless? You never were a cruel child. You were once so…"

"Stop this, Croft. I wake to find my house cold, my servants fled, and you are babbling about my childhood."

"Your poor mother would have been ashamed of you."

"My poor mother would have exulted in me. She was a greedy, stupid woman, as you well know. A whore of the first order. She would have loved this house and my money. Please, Croft, you are carrying on."

"Miss Jane is ill, Henry. She is ill because of you and your carelessness. She is bleeding. She has been to a physician, and she has lost a mass of blood."

"And so?"

"Henry, how can you be so thoughtless? Jane was carrying a baby. *Yours.*"

"Claptrap. Even so, dashing into the wintry street at year's end is no way to protect one's self. Has the ninny gone completely mad?"

"She is ill in another way, Henry. The way your mother was."

"Nonsense," Dupré bellowed. "I've not harmed that child."

Mrs. Croft sighed. "Do not lie, Henry. Face your evildoing."

At these words, Henry Robertson Dupré halted his breath, as if he'd fallen into a deep crevice of glacial ice. *Finally, finally.* His mind jumped back and forth in time. His hands fidgeted, became slippery with a cold sweat. *No,* he thought, *I will not admit it. I will not reveal to the old badger my own present physical discomfort.* Would he have to restrain Mrs. Croft somehow? What a temptation there was to strike her down. To punish her for her searing tongue.

"I have decided to leave, Henry," Mrs. Croft said in a quiet voice. "As a caring, responsible Christian, I must look after poor Jane. Your house is no longer a welcoming place to work. I do not need references, so do not try and bully me into staying."

"Preposterous," huffed Dupré. "What a smarmy Evangelical idiot you have become." His voice shouted now with pain and betrayal. "You are far worse than my poxy mother."

"I am sorry, Henry. Jane is distraught. But I think it best for her to be away from you."

"How can you punish me like this?" Dupré's voice fell into a sob.

"Goodbye, Henry."

Mrs. Croft reached out to touch him on the head. In response, he slapped her away. She moved closer to him in spite of this, grabbed his wrist and when he tried to strike his fist against her, she pulled it to her heart and held it tight against her bosom. "I forgive you, Henry," she said. "I turn my other cheek toward you. You are a man who must find his righteous way alone."

"Get out, you mewling sod. I shan't suffer your righteous Christian dung any further."

Dupré struggled free, and with neither a feeling of regret nor a backward glance, he ran away from Mrs. Croft, crossing the kitchen and bounding up the back stairs. He waited, panting, to hear the area door to the kitchen click shut. Henry continued up the stairs from the kitchen until he reached the front hall and its adjacent parlour rooms. Out on the street, the figure of Mrs. Croft passed by the front windows, her head bowed into the new slanting snow. Henry scowled.

As the moment wore on, an impatience grew in his heart. A surge of anger, like a gust of winter wind, thrust him into a frenzy. First he threw a Chinese vase onto the floor. Not satisfied with its shattering sound, he kicked a precious wooden chair, its clacking on the parquet so irritating, he instantly found himself in the parlour, fists clenched, his eyes roving the room. The urge to destroy felt as full of intent as his sexual appetite. He tore down a curtain; he hurled a table—chess pieces and all—at the cold hearth. Shoving over the sofa, then the writing table, then the hearth screen brought red to his cheeks and water into his eyes. When he had finished, he looked down at his right hand. A large, bloody gash cut across it like a gaping mouth. Blood dripped onto his Turkish robe.

What he wanted now, more than anything, was the figure of Mrs. Croft to stand before him so that he could beat her, take a horsewhip, perhaps an umbrella, and whack her across her head and torso. He wondered if his very veins might burst. He ran upstairs. He splashed water onto his hand. Calming down, strolling into his cold bedroom, he fell across his bed. "Oh, oh," he wept into his pillow.

He lay still until the chime on his mantel rang out in silvery tones. Then he rose, wiped his mouth and wrapped a cloth from his washstand around his hand. He straightened his cravat and smoothed his hair. For a quick second, he stared at his posture in the looking glass then raised his chin.

"Damnation."

*   *   *

Sun broke through the clouds, falling snow veils melted, and the breath of the city—chimney smoke—rose in regimented columns to combat the sudden brightness of the air. As Endersby and his two sergeants, Stott and Birken, approached the bank of the Thames, a sorry sight appeared before them. Gangs of mud larks, young, thin, sickly children, were scouring the banks' muck for broken glass, tin, old leather—all of it rubbish for a penny to salvage. Beyond them in a small wooden boat, an oarsman pulled toward shore, his net bulky with a slimy object.

"Bring it in," shouted Endersby. Stott wiped his nose with his handkerchief.

The boat ran up on the bank. The net was hauled in, and a body turned out onto a lone patch of stones. The mud larks ran over, and without a question or a sound began to rifle the soggy pockets. "Get away," said Endersby. The wild-eyed children did not listen. They grabbed and pushed, and when nothing was found, they ran off down the bank like a pack of dogs. A lad, familiar to the inspector from the St. Giles district, stood by Endersby and pointed to the wrists of the corpse.

"Must be him, sir. Look'ee at 'em. Sliced, like Mr. Peacock said."

"The body's not been in the water long," said Endersby. He instructed Stott and Birken to note the face and scratched hands. "Turn him over," Endersby said to the oarsman. The man did as he was told, his face half-covered with a kerchief. His young daughter sat watching from the stern of the boat while she attached the net once again to its clamp.

The corpse had one eye.

"'Tis him," said the lad. "He and t'other set the fires."

"Stott, have this river-washed man brought to Scotland Yard. And call a surgeon. Superintendent Borne will be happy. We have been fortunate with witnesses to this man's demise and testimony as to his deed." Stott wished them a profitable day and went about the business of having the oarsman row him and the body across the river toward the docks, where a police waggon would be secured.

Meanwhile, the lad led Endersby and Birken to the waiting cab, and together they bounced through the slippery holiday streets of the capital. Shop windows were festooned with wreaths and garlands of holly; butchers' windows displayed squadrons of hanging capons and geese. Tonight, London would shine with frost and gaslight, and the grand theatres would unveil their pantomime extravaganzas to crowds eager for spectacle. The cab drove between tumbledown buildings, under a covered alley into St. Giles. At the burnt lodging house, Endersby and Birken went in and found the sooty man perched on a broken-down settee.

"Inspector, I see my trusty lad has found you. And the body?"

"Wrapped and delivered to Scotland Yard, Mr. Peacock," said Endersby, laconically.

"I imagine the reward, sir?" said Peacock, lowering his voice.

"I beg your pardon?"

"You Bow Street men, you always get a bonus, nay? For getting the body, the conviction?"

"May I remind you Mr. Peacock, with due respect, we are now the Metropolitan Detective Police. Bow Street runners and their ways are a thing of the past."

"But still, sir. Remuneration of one kind or another is surely part of police procedure?"

"If you are looking for payment for doing your duty as a London citizen, may I suggest you approach my super-intendent, a man most generous in his capacities to re-ward and punish."

Mr. Peacock fell silent. Endersby asked to be taken to the tavern, the Crown and Spit. On their way, he pondered the Cake murder, hoping that the new-found evidence was safe for the time being. Concluding a murder case was always a difficult business, as Endersby's years with the City of London had taught him. Capture was important; charges to be made had to be accurate; the courts were often ruled by biased judges—these things, however, could not concern him. He had proof and motive, and all he needed now was a confession from the felon. All would then fall into its necessary order.

"Here we are, Inspector." Mr. Peacock opened the door to the tavern.

A man was waiting for him at a table. He stood, showing due respect by removing his cap. Endersby called for a round of gin and hot water, hoping his gesture might loosen the man's tongue but also encourage the truth. In fact, as his questions proceeded, Endersby was impressed by the clear, detailed accounts of how the drowned man had been one of the madmen with the torch. "Lead 'im to the other fire-setter," said Mr. Peacock, prompting the man with his elbow. The man picked up a small stick and led the inspector and his sergeant out a back door of the tavern. Down two streets they went, through a broken archway into a dark courtyard full of hens and dung; finally, they came into an open field thick with mud. In the distance, a wooden shack buttressed a long wall of tin slatting. Endersby could hear the river beyond the wall. A muddied, scab-covered lot of several men and women huddled by the door of the wooden shack. Each was holding a stick. Endersby approached, and one of the women of the lot ran over to him. "You the guv, then? You the Runner?"

"Detective Endersby. And this is Sergeant Birken."

A thumping came suddenly from behind the closed door of the shack.

"The villain is in there," explained the woman in a hoarse whisper, pointing to the thumping door. "The burner. The torch-man from St. Giles."

A moan not unlike the screech of a colicky baby shot out of the shack. Cries and more thumps were issued as Endersby walked into the huddled crowd of watchers, the stench of their clothing making him cough. The woman whispered to the group that Endersby was a policeman.

"Get away, sir," said one of the grubby figures, a man with a palsied face. "He is ours. He run from the tavern like a horse on fire—like them poor beasts he killed himself. We got him in here. We can corner him."

Endersby leaned into the door of the shack. "Who's there?" he shouted. The justice-seekers raised their weapons. A volley of harsh curses and kicks began on the other side of the shack's door. The inspector pressed his ear against a crack. "He's working at something," he said to Birken. The ragged vigilantes all planted their ears to the side of the shack.

The door of the shack burst open, catching the crowd off guard. A figure in rags flew out, scrambled past the astonished justice-seekers, broke through one of the tin slats, and ran toward the river.

"Let's grab him," screamed the men.

"Wait!" shouted Endersby. But the disorderly gang had scurried. The woman in the lead bashed down another tin slat, and the crowd crawled through the opening.

"After them, Birken. We want the poor madman alive, if we can catch him first."

Endersby and Birken gave chase, clambering through wet mud and sharp-edged tin before stepping onto a long parapet of wooden piles tilted into the bank of the Thames. Ahead of them, the stumbling, ragged felon. The mob after him yelled and hollered, arms waving, their make-shift weapons poking up as if to tear the sky. Birken blew his whistle. Along the precarious ledge, he and Endersby placed their feet with care. The fleeing man sailed into the air, jumping down from the ledge onto the river's bank. The human hounds wanting his blood halted, pulled back, lowered their arms. An inhuman cry arose from where the harried arsonist now held his ground. Birken pushed ahead. He blew his whistle again. Finally, Endersby arrived, his chest heaving. The huddling mass fell silent. Before him, Endersby beheld a sight full of desperation: the bedraggled madman stood with a razor held above his head.

"God curse you all," he shouted, the spit spraying from his mouth. In an action fast and horrific, he sliced open his wrists, his howls mixed with a choking laughter. The unfortunate villain fell shaking to the muddy earth, fresh blood spurting from his cuts. "Come, Birken," commanded Endersby. They climbed down to the mud below. Taking hold of the shuddering man, they struggled to lift him up. Birken pulled out his handkerchief and tried to staunch the wounds, pressing his weight down on each of the wrists in turn to retard the blood flow. To the mass of ugly humanity above, Endersby shouted out for help.

Just then a woman with a haggard face broke through the callous onlookers and tumbled her way down to the flat below. "He is a brother in Christ," she screamed. When she reached the three men, and in particular the failing culprit, her eyes widened. The slowly failing arsonist was turning white from pain and exhaustion.

"Hurry, woman, give us a hand," shouted Endersby in a gruff command. But the woman could not budge. The gawkers above froze in amazement as the murderer's body shook with spasms, his voice whimpering.

"Oh, mercy," the haggard woman cried. She stretched out her hand and touched the creature's cold forehead, a sheepish look in her eyes. "He has come to this," she said, "so far from his mother's womb." Endersby loosened his grip on the man, grabbed the woman and shook her. "Take this," he growled, forcing his handkerchief into her grimy hands. The woman immediately did Endersby's bidding: she wrapped the cloth tightly around the man's right wrist. By this time, Birken had done likewise to the left, and now ran off up the bank blowing his whistle to summon a Peeler. At that same moment the mob scattered, turning away from the scene as if it were nothing more than a wave lapping the shore. Endersby held the man's head up; the haggard woman wept, her face covered by her stringy long hair.

"Thus, is justice," said Endersby, with resignation. In the distance, gulls cried out over the water.

"God help us all," murmured the woman, raising her head. Birken and a constable were presently loping along the bank, coming toward Endersby and the bleeding man. Standing up, the woman shouted at them and began waving her arms until the two men arrived and knelt down to help.

*   *   *

Back in Scotland Yard, Endersby prepared to meet with Superintendent Borne. He waited in the second parlour and tapped his gouty foot to distract his mind. When Borne broke into the room, he stumbled on the door jamb and clacked into the door itself, banging it against the wall. He regained his composure, though his cheeks burned with embarrassment.

"Fine work, Inspector Endersby."

Endersby got to his feet. He lifted off his hat. "We have confessions in writing, sir. I had a clerk at the tavern take them down."

Endersby pulled two folded sheets from his satchel. Borne glanced at them in a cursory fashion, and for a moment was not sure where to place them. He decided to shove them into his coat pocket for the moment.

"Caldwell? Has he done much more on the Cake business?"

"We have proof positive."

"Good heavens, Endersby, such confidence. You have been busy night and day, it seems." Owen Endersby noted a touch of jealousy in his superintendent's tone of voice.

"Only doing our duty, sir, following your exact demands."

"Indeed," said Borne. He waited. He turned down his mouth. Endersby watched Borne's eyes cast about the room, searching perhaps for some object to comment upon. At last, with a brief sigh, he engaged his inspector once again.

"You shall, of course, arrest the felon?"

"Certainly, sir."

"But why waste time and money. Get to it." Borne had taken on a stiff, commanding manner.

"Right away, sir," said Endersby, putting on his hat, knowing he could now leave and get on with his work.

"Shall I accompany you in your arrest, Inspector?" the superintendent suddenly asked. "It has been a while since I have done such a duty. I might find pleasure in it once more, and to be sure, I think it proper I come as a gesture of police dedication. A good show from a public official."

Endersby reacted without thinking, hoping his response, despite its lack of truth, would stop Borne in his tracks. "The felon has been taken into custody already, and is at this moment to be formally arrested—that is, the paper work and the record keeping are to be completed. He is being held in the station near Doughty Street."

"Why there, for the sake of Jove? Surely we are not granting that constituency credit for this arrest?"

"Convenience, sir. And the crime was committed in a house nearby, so I felt it was appropriate if further questioning and clarification were needed."

"You felt, did you?"

Endersby hesitated, his tongue beginning to regret the lie. If Borne persisted, the strategy for the day would collapse, the conviction based on the confession might be severely hampered. Physical evidence was but one element in the edifice of crime solving, but as all detectives in the city knew, the confession, the heartfelt, soul-revealing glimpse at the dark motive of murder, was the cornerstone.

"I see, I see," Borne then said, distracted. He had lost interest. He turned and walked toward his office. He carefully opened the door, looking down first before stepping forward.

"Carry on, then, Inspector. And have a jolly Christmas Eve supper."

Endersby found his way to Vinegar Yard. He took another hot gin and water to ward off the chill of the streets. Sergeant Stott had secured a small room on the second floor and had, with the generosity of the bar-keep, found a safe hiding place for the muslin bag. Endersby knew it was essential that the proof be guarded, but also close at hand for the upcoming evening's work. He climbed the stairs, paused to catch his breath, entered the room, and with a key provided by the trustworthy bar-keep, unlocked a cupboard.

On its bottom shelf, under a pile of washing-up cloths, lay the muslin bag. Endersby pulled it out and opened it. At a nearby table, he spread out its contents, examining each of the pieces and making sure he could connect them with the testimonies he had heard at the coroner's inquest not four days earlier. He wondered how he would question his suspect, and if, indeed, with hidden witnesses— Caldwell and Stott—how he might exact a true confession. This could prove to be the stalling point.

"Indeed, old gander. So plan your way well," he cautioned himself.

Placing the bag back in the cupboard, Endersby felt a quick surge of disappointment. The case was coming to an end. If he succeeded, the intense connections he had made would dissipate. He regretted that he had to move on; he would no longer have the privilege of haunting the backstage world of the theatre. He had enjoyed questioning the artists and the workers of that ephemeral kingdom of make-believe. No, he must move on, his reason forcing him to re-enter the sordid streets of London.

"Such is the way," he then said, and turned the key.

*   *   *

Betty Loxton stood up from her bath. Mrs. B. had left her a cloth. She dried herself while she pondered her fate. Tonight she would fly. Tomorrow...well, Christmas was the Lord's birthday. *Our Saviour loves and forgives us,* Betty thought. She could not remember much of his story. He said that children were to come unto him. He made a blind man see. He could, if need be, bless a wretched coster girl and forgive her her sins. *He must,* Betty thought.

She dressed and could no longer sense herself as a complete being, any more than she could imagine herself as a dog or a toad. She had never seen a toad and wondered how she knew of such a thing. Yet she figured that at this time of day, such a matter was hardly important. A man had been murdered. She had been acquainted with him—slightly—but her heart, her fourteen-year-old soul, had been miraculously touched by this brief encounter. She knew now that his death had brought forth strange feelings in her. It must be a *kind* of love, she thought. Her own kin had been part of his ill fortune; she had been aware, too...but, no, do not let that terrible day shadow your life; do not be clamped and beaten down by its presence. She lifted up her shawl, but then she put it away again. She searched in the costume room, going first through a trunk full of skirts and gloves. Then through another she found pieces of red cloth once used for brigands' sashes, she'd been told, for Mr. Planché's play. She pulled one of the sashes and wound it around her head, shawl-like. This will do. Slipping on her shoes, she found her way to the back door and climbed the steps into the bracing, bumping street.

When she reached the arcades of Covent Garden, she was shaking with such fear; she wondered if she might faint. She did not look for her brother's old stall. The tobacco shop was open. Plums, oranges and all kinds of holiday greenery filled the inner court. Even as the fear of a beating, so hard she would cough blood, made her hesitate, Betty Loxton walked forward into a small shop, its windows full of dolls and whistles. She found a penny whistle painted yellow. A parrot adorned the mouth piece. It was wrapped in plain paper for her. She curtsied and left the place with the door tinkling behind her. Across the courtyard, she caught a glimpse of Clare, her little sister.

"Clare," she blurted out, but the girl kept going.

Betty ran under the arcade, down a side lane and onto Long Acre, where she saw her sister in her bonnet carrying a large basket of lemons. Clare's body was tilted to the right as she hauled the heavy object down the street. She stopped ahead. Now Betty saw her sister try to lift the basket onto her head, like Pineapple Pol had taught both of them to do. The basket toppled, the lemons spilling into the sludge of the gutter. Betty waited in the distance. She dared not run up to help her poor little lamb. "Ah, Clare," she sighed. Now her sister, pale, thin, dirty, knelt in the street, and Betty saw in her face all the despair of the world. How she wished she could help her. How she wanted to take her away from this grimy pit. But all she could do was watch little Clare bend, retrieve, spit on each lemon, place one after the other into the basket. Finally, her face showing anger and fatigue, Clare tried again, and with greater skill, placed the basket on her bonnet and marched off, her left arm steadying her teetering load.

Betty wanted to cry. The tears refused to come. She ran back to the door of Old Drury. On her entrance she heard the voice of Henry Robertson Dupré. He was holding a newspaper, and his cravat was tied loosely. His face was wrenched into a frown, and as he began to ascend the stairs to his attic office, he stopped and gazed about the backstage.

"Good morning," he shouted.

The gruff stage manager dropped the whistle from his mouth. "Good morning, Mr. Dupré." Betty heard the two men test each other: Dupré asked if all was ready; the stage manager responded by complaining there was so much to prepare for tonight's great performance that he was tired, at a loss, fearful the whole matter might not come to pass.

"Buck up, my good fellow," came Dupré's answer. "You are the master stage manager of London. You shall do it."

Dupré climbed higher. Betty tiptoed up behind him, and at his door she spoke to him in a soft voice.

"Good heavens, Loxton. Do not startle me so."

Betty unwound her shawl, and from her pocket produced the whistle in its paper. She handed it to Dupré.

"What is it now?" he grumbled. He stepped into his office. He threw off the plain paper and stared at the whistle. "I have no time today for jests, Miss Loxton. Get yourself downstairs and to your tasks."

He handed back the gift, his arm out behind him as he walked toward his desk. Betty had to scamper to take the whistle before Dupré let it drop to the floor. Without a second's hesitation, she understood that she was right. That she was in no harm, in the end, but wise in what she had prayed for, had prepared for. She took the whistle. She picked up the discarded paper from the floor and left the room. It was then, as she descended the stairs, she realized to whom she must give this trinket.

First, she went down the hall to Mr. Weston's door. Then she listened at Miss Root's. After checking the foyer, the backstage, the hallways to the upper and lower saloons, she clambered down to the mezzanine below the stage and she found him, watching a carpenter rig one of the mechanical trees onto a trap. She ran up to him and kissed him lightly on the cheek.

"Here you are, Carrot."

Young Reggie Crabb blushed as he unwrapped the plain paper. He held the whistle up. The carpenter and he pointed to the painted parrot.

"For Christmas, Carrot. For Old Drury's prince of princes," Betty said, her r's rolling, her o's rounded.

"I thank you, Miss Betty." Reggie Crabb blushed. "But I have naught for you."

"Oh, but you have." Betty's face ran with tears. She threw her arms around Reggie's neck. The carpenter let out a sly whistle. Crabb pulled away. He was red and grinning.

"Come on, then," said Betty. "Hurry up here. We'll do your rounds together."

"Right you are," cried young Crabb. He picked up the whistle and blew it hard.

Betty wiped her face. "May I?" she asked the carpenter. She pointed to the tree, its leaves and branches of painted canvas. The two dimensional object was braced to the trap door surface by a wooden T and two bolts. The carpenter smiled, and Betty climbed onto the trap itself. She grasped one of the branches of the tree. The wooden support wiggled.

"It is sturdy, miss," said the carpenter.

"Shall we try it?" Betty reached out to Reggie Crabb. He took her hand and climbed onto the trap. The two of them held hands and leaned into the canvas trunk.

"Trap six," shouted the carpenter.

A creak, a jiggle, the trap mechanism clanged into place, and the ropes on either side began to roll. With breaths held, Reggie and Betty began to rise. "Hold on," Betty said. Up and up, the trap itself steady, the tree pointing into the opening straight above, a little square of stage sky.

"Hold on," Betty said. "We're on our way to heaven."

*   *   *

He needed his suede gloves and his large coat. He placed them into the satchel. He smelled the soup, and with a sense that his plan would work, Endersby left his room and found himself happily within five minutes of his early supper. Harriet arrived at the dining table wearing her new brooch and her new blue frock. Owen stood up and pulled out her chair. He gave her a quick kiss on her cheek. She smiled at him and patted his elbow as he passed her to sit down again. His mind was jumping and turning, and he needed to eat something very soon. The door to the kitchen opened, and Solange entered with the tureen. Her face was noticeably more cheerful at this hour. Had she received another letter, wondered Endersby? Or had she instead recovered, pulled her senses together, forgotten the chap and gone on to cook a meal for which she would be duly commended?

"Soup, *madame*," she said. Her voice was chilled, flat. Endersby decided the woman had returned to her duties, but not to her normal self.

The salty broth wanted stirring. This was not a good sign. Endersby shrugged and began lifting and lowering his spoon. Harriet remained quiet. Harriet's younger brother, Caleb, rushed into the room a moment later, a flustered man, his hands with plasters on them from being cut by the paper he was selling below in his shop. He apologized, sat down and started into his soup. Wine was desired next, and Caleb waited patiently as Solange went out to fetch the carafe. All three of them finished the soup, their eyes down at their soup plates. No word was shared among them.

"Fish, *madame.*"

This course displayed a runny sauce. Through all of this, Endersby remained complacent. In no way would he allow this incident to thwart his expectations of a fine night in the theatre. Like a bird intent on its solitary flight, he thought intensely of how he might address, let alone cajole the person he knew he must face later on in the evening. He examined his own motives, he reviewed his need to pursue, he formed words and steadied his resolve. There would be re-criminations; there would be denials. Then again, he thought, there may be resignation, then confession.

"Fowl."

The pigeons were delicious. Succulent, plump, the sauce full of sage and butter.

"Well done, indeed," said Harriet. Solange managed a smile.

Caleb raised his glass, proposed a toast and offered a glass to Solange. "It is Christmas Eve, my friends, and I wish for all of us a happy Christmastime."

Solange downed her glass. She dashed into the kitchen and returned with a mound of sugared cakes, all piled like little snowballs into a pyramid.

"*Joyeux Noël,* " she said.

Endersby smacked his lips. He chased murder, blood and fear from his mind.

"Now," said Harriet. The pyramid had disappeared by this time, and she was on the verge of rising. "I have a great surprise for you."

"Yes?" said Endersby. His wife paused before her attentive company.

"Mrs. DeWinter has informed me that the *Chronicle* this morning confirmed a most wondrous fact."

"Yes," said Caleb, now impatient.

"Her Majesty will attend Old Drury this evening with the Prince."

"Wonderful indeed," said Endersby.

"Most wonderful, husband. So we cannot be late."

Harriet ushered her men into the hall. On with their coats and down the stairs where Solange stood holding an umbrella over the doorsteps. The cab arrived in good time, and the doors were clacked shut. The whip cracked, and the bouncing ride took longer than expected, given the huge crowds along the streets. Even as he witnessed the joyful chaos around him, Endersby sensed a feeling of desperation. Christmas was a time of much sorrow for many. The faces in the streets told him people were anxious, excited, expectant, fraught. There was one person who by now must be full of trepidation. But Endersby decided he would not imagine what would soon come to pass.

"Good evening, sir," said the ticket-taker.

As Harriet and Caleb charted their way through the thick mass of chattering spectators, Endersby found the hall to the backstage. He met the stage manager, who bowed to him, recognizing him and pointing to Sergeant Stott and Caldwell waiting in a corner. Endersby approached them.

"Birken in place?"

"Yes, Inspector," said Stott.

"Fine. And now the boy?"

"Coming presently, sir," said Caldwell. His face was healing. His cheeks rosier.

"Happy Christmas to you both," said Endersby.

"Thank you, sir," said both sergeants in unison.

"Remember to be stalwart and quick."

"Without fail, sir."

"I have brought a whistle, too. If I need it."

"Stott will stand by the pit door, sir. Two blows was it, sir?"

"Correct, Caldwell."

"We are ready then. Good luck."

*   *   *

"You look so lovely, truly you do," said young Reggie Crabb, out of breath from running all the way downstairs to the costume room. He gazed at Betty Loxton in her glittery costume for the pantomime.

"Do I, Carrot?"

"You will see her majesty from up in the flies. You will see her better than anyone when she comes in."

"She will look at me, too, Carrot. I have a surprise. But tell no one."

Plates of mutton stew were handed to him and Betty by Mrs. B. The two sat together at the long table in front of the hearth. Mrs. B. put the lid back on the great stew pot and came to sit across from the two of them, their spoons poised to dip into the steamy food.

"Well, my rose, you shall charm the queen herself, I hear."

Betty Loxton smiled and started to gobble down her dinner.

"You can stay by me—stay here in Old Drury, I mean—if you want," said Reggie in a whisper, chewing and swallowing as if he had never eaten hot food before in his life.

"What are you two ragamuffins doing?" asked Mrs. B. She reached over and patted Reggie on his head. "Now don't hurt yourself eating like a madman. Take your time. And do not go making any plans, Mr. Busybody. You have no say as to where or how Miss Loxton shall live. She can come and go as she pleases."

"But what shall I do, Mrs. B.?" asked Betty with a concerned expression. "I have no home any more. My brother John will kill me for certain for bolting from him."

"Let me speak with the stage manager. He is a testy but a kind man. I am certain we can find you some work here. We don't take in many orphans, mind. But we do make exceptions."

Betty smiled and wiped her greasy mouth.

"Who knows," said Mrs. B. "Mr. Dupré himself might want to keep you on as a supernumerary. Stranger things have taken place in this old theatre, I can assure you."

"What do you think, Carrot?" asked Betty.

Reggie put down his spoon. "As I said, you can stay by me, on a pallet in the scene room. It's warm there. Lots of room. And most mornings there is sunlight in the window."

"Let me think on that," said Betty. But she was grinning as she spoke. When she and Reggie had cleaned their plates, they rose and went to warm their legs by the hearth. "You keep an eye on me tonight, Carrot. I want to surprise you as well. I have put some extra things on my costume. Sssh, do not tell a soul. Watch me when I fly for her majesty."

Betty saw Reggie's face fill with curiosity, then she tapped him on the shoulder, her own features full of smiles and mischief, and ran off upstairs to the noise-filled stage.

Reggie Crabb watched her go; he pulled out the tin whistle she had given him. He blew it once then shoved it into his pocket. He thanked Mrs. B. for his dinner and scampered up the same stairs to the stage. He was panting and hot. *So much to do this evening,* he said to himself, but not aloud, not so the others around him, the chorus, the shifters, the actors waiting in the wings could hear him. He ran into the hallway, out to the stage-door foyer, where the old stage-door keeper was arranging letters and warding off a long line of women in holiday bonnets.

"No passes this evening, none at all," Hartley, the stage-door keeper, kept crying. There were moans and arguments. Carriages splashed by the entrance, and shouts of complaint filled the air as disgruntled ticket-holders brushed slush from their clothes.

"Yes, boy, what is it?"

"Mr. Hartley, sir, you sent for me?"

"Not at all, boy. Get on with your calls."

"But Mrs. B. insisted, sir. Told me before my dinner. Said an urgent matter. A packet."

"Packet? Packet? No indeed. Now do not pester me ...oh, a moment, boy. Yes, of course."

Old Hartley led the boy to a nearby door. He opened it and pointed to a man with a bruised face, a black hat and long coat. "Caldwell, the name is, lad. A trusty man. Mr. Endersby the detective has sent him, and you, boy, are to be given a task."

"But I cannot, sir, with all respect. I have calls to do. And it is Christmas Eve."

"No carping now, boy. Get on with it. You shall have plenty of time for your calls."

Young Reggie Crabb walked through the door and headed toward the man with the bruised face. The man saw him coming and took off his hat. Reggie stopped for a second. A shadow fell between him and the man in the distance, the flickering gas jet making the man's face look like a mask. Reggie took one step forward. The man motioned him to hurry along. Passing through the shadow, Reggie brushed his coat front and removed his cap.

"Young Crabb, I presume?"

"Yes, sir."

"Sergeant Caldwell, at your service."

"Yes, sir."

"You have calls to do, I know."

"Yes, sir. I do."

"I will take none of your time, lad. Here is a small packet."

Caldwell pulled a long, soft object out from his coat. It was wrapped in brown paper.

"Most urgent that Mr. William Weston receive and open this before the performance."

"Mr. Weston, sir."

"Do not hesitate, lad. Off you go."

Young Reggie Crabb ran past the sergeant, up the stairs and onward to Mr. Weston's dressing room door. He tapped.

"Enter, Mr. Sprite."

"Five minutes, Mr. Weston. And a happy Christmas."

"Thank'ee, Mr. Sprite. You have brought me a gift?"

"A packet, sir. And I was instructed to have you open it before the performance."

"Who told you to do so, lad?"

Reggie had not anticipated this. He had not been warned to lie. But to save time, as time was running out, he said. "Mr. Dupré, sir. A gift, he claimed."

"How kind," said Weston. He was covered in a white powder, even his arms. On his head sat a great mass of wool curls and the snout of a lion. "I shall open it as soon as I have finished dressing. A happy Christmas to you, young boy."

"Thank you, sir."

Crabb, breathing hard, closed the door and went to Miss Root. She did not answer right away, but after a third tapping, the door flew open, the spaniel began to bark and the two sisters in black top hats stood at attention.

"Miss Root?"

Young Reggie Crabb's voice fell into silence. Before him framed in the far door stood a tall, magnificent creature. It was blue and green in hue; its feet were clad in white leather boots which sparkled with rubies; its face, rounded by curls, and painted a shimmering gold, was surmounted by a helmet piled with feathers, beads and a tiara of diamonds. A shield with a dancing unicorn was held in its right hand.

"Well, my dear Crabb. What do you think of Miss Beauty?"

"Time, Miss Root. Lor' bless me, but lovely you are."

"Ah, Crabb. Lead me on then."

With majesty in his steps, Crabb walked ahead of the splendiferous Miss Root, down the corridor, through the crowded and hushed side stage and up to the second set of wings, where a wooden pony on a rail was latched to a chariot of peacock feathers. The stage manager blew his whistle in one sharp blast. Miss Root climbed into the chariot. "A pause, ladies and gents," said the stage manager in a loud whisper. "Her Majesty is about to enter. Once the trumpets are off, we go."

The shifters and actors, all with glistening eyes in the half-dark, bowed their heads.

"Run, boy," whispered Miss Root. "Finish up." She took Reggie's hand and gave it a squeeze, then let him go. Blushing hot, Reggie Crabb ran toward the wooden stairs to the fly loft. Was she ready? Was she in place? He climbed and scampered, past the huge fly drums, over the ropes laid out for the pullers. The lines of gas jets blazed by the wavering sheets of canvas. The sconces below had been turned up by the light men, and the blue and yellow gauzes set in place. He looked for her. He asked the carpenter on the loft. He said he had yet to see her come up. Where was she? Her wand and spear were laid out by the harness. She would come alone, then, he said, and ran across the bridge to the other side of the stage. There, the chorus of birds, young girls in masks, waited, and they curtsied to Crabb as he checked and counted all six of them. Down the far stairs, across the back stage he marched, and as he did so his heart leapt, and he heard from the orchestra beyond the curtain the sound of a regal fanfare.

*   *   *

"Oh, my, she is beautiful."

Harriet Endersby had tears in her eyes. The trumpets and drums played in full force a tune by Mr. Handel. The audience, all in holiday finery, stood in rapt attention. Into the centre box of the Grand Circle, a short, slim woman with black hair moved with a delicate grace. On her head sat a diadem which caught the light in such intense flashes that Owen Endersby had to blink. The woman had a small chin and skin the colour of a white rose. Behind her came a cluster of larger women, ruffles, sashes, evening caps, brooches of rubies and emeralds and hands held crossed in front of them. A tall man with chestnut sideburns and a small beard stood next to the Queen. He wore a blue tunic and a sash with a diamond studded star pin on it. The older gentleman to his side raised his hand, and the orchestra finished its fanfare. A silence of tense expectation filled the auditorium. Not even a baby in the upper galleries dared to cry. The Queen took her seat. The Prince, with his stern face and his sideburns, sat beside her. The older gentleman then lowered his hand, and the others in the royal box sat down.

Within a second, before a breath could be taken, whistles, laughter and huge clapping stormed the auditorium. Huzzahs and shouts of "Your Majesty" blasted the air. Harriet took out a second handkerchief to wipe her eyes. Endersby counted hats off, hands up, babies held aloft, children bent over railings to get a glimpse, clerks, servants, merchants, soldiers, matrons, all with cheering mouths welcoming the diminutive figure in her flouncing gown and bare shoulders. The Queen smiled. The cheering increased. The curtain parted, and the entire cast of the huge extravaganza came forward, helmets and spears, all before a grand forest of trees on banks, on platforms, all the figures of the play taking a short bow to their sovereign. The players stepped back. The huge chandelier full of light flickered with the sitting down of three thousand spectators. Owen Endersby reminded himself to memorize this sight. This was a great occasion.

The orchestra now drummed out a long tirade. The curtain rose a second time, and a chorus of maidens began to sing. Miss Root entered in her chariot, and once again the theatre filled with claps and shouts. She stepped down and came to the front of the stage, the footlights making her boots shine like mirrors.

"Oh, Beauty bright, oh Queen of Light, this night of nights shall be."

She had to pause as the audience again huzzahed the Queen. Harriet handed a sugared orange to Endersby and whispered in his ear. "Are we not so fortunate, dear Owen?"

Endersby chewed on the sweet rind. He mumbled a response and turned his gaze toward the small door opening near the proscenium arch, where Sergeant Stott was quickly stepping in.

*   *   *

Betty Loxton snapped on the harness.

"There you are, miss," said the carpenter. "What are those you've put on?"

"Wings, sir," she said boldly.

"But those aren't part of the costume Mr. Dupré wanted."

"He has changed his mind."

Betty readied herself. The music swelled. The carpenter gave the signal, and Betty was lifted into the air. She pointed her toes and began her descent. As she approached the batten of tiny gas jets that lit the canvas scene, she tipped her right shoulder forward to get a quick glimpse of the Queen in her royal box. Betty then closed her eyes. She folded her hands and thought of herself as an angel.

*   *   *

Endersby looked up. The cry from the auditorium tore through the air like the howl of a banshee.

The young girl's wings were afire.

"*Stott!*" Endersby yelled.

The sergeant leaped to the stage over the steps beside the orchestra pit. The wire kept descending. Flames ran down and sheathed the girl's slender body like a silken coat of blue and orange. Betty's face grimaced; her hair blew into a whirl of sparks and white smoke. The wings attached to her back glared a sudden red. Members of the orchestra clambered to their feet. Shouts, yells and hollers cracked the walls of Old Drury. The burning angel kept floating down from the flies, then the fly wires snapped. Harriet buried her face in Endersby's shoulder. A woman fainted in the next box. The body, jumping with dying flames, rolled onto the stage floor, where Miss Root stood paralyzed in her place, her mouth a frightened O. Mr. William Weston dashed forward and raised his arms to calm the multitude. At the same time a man with a whistle ran in from the side of the stage carrying a bucket of water, and the green curtain closed on the scene.

A moment later, Endersby had made his way through the astonished audience into the backstage area. Panicked shouting and weeping filled the air. Shifters in their paper caps scurried about. Fairies and beasts held to each other in convulsions of tears. Young Reggie Crabb—his face contorted in terror—rushed past him carrying a pail of slopping water. Endersby found his sergeants amid the chaos: both Caldwell and Stott had taken their places.

"A great horror and pity, gentlemen," Endersby said in a hurried voice. "But let them look after that catastrophe," he added quickly, holding the two men with an intense look in his eyes. Endersby felt his heart pounding. "We have our own chase upon us now. Come and be quick!"

The three men ran down the corridor by the dressing rooms and took their places. After waiting a few moments, they signed to each other, and Endersby stepped into a dark corner by the stage entrance. He waited, hearing the cries, the tumult, the sudden blast of trumpets which quieted the theatre. As he watched his quarry leave by a side door, he let his two sergeants begin the chase. He hurried back to the auditorium. He looked at his watch and figured ten to fifteen minutes would be all he needed before he must make his final move.

In the grand house of Old Drury, the smell of acrid smoke floated over the hushed audience. Queen Victoria was standing now in her box like one of her new public statues. She took on a solemn gaze. The audience rose with her in silence and in awe. The Queen bowed her head and raised her right hand, pointing it toward the stage curtain. All eyes followed her. Endersby sensed it was as if her royal presence had a magnetic power, as if her outstretched hand could, over space and through smoke, bless the charred form of little Betty Loxton who lay dead on the stage under the guard of a weeping boy of fourteen.

Endersby signalled to Harriet. She held her head high, her handkerchief in her hand. She nodded twice back to him. The Queen then turned from the sorry sight, and with no fanfare left her royal chair behind, taking with her the Prince and her entourage. The audience remained standing, and Endersby without further delay went from the auditorium and pushed his way through the backstage halls and foyers into Brydges Street, hired a hansom and rode onward to the house of a murderer.

*　　*　　*

"We're ready, sir," said Caldwell in a low voice. Endersby took the muslin bag from him. In the distance, Birken stood in the shadows by the back door of the building.

"Stott's gone inside already, Inspector."

"Wait here, then Caldwell. For five minutes only. Then come upstairs and stand by the door, which I shall leave ajar."

Endersby did not attempt to explain his presence to the agitated dour aunt when she confronted him in the hall.

"Are they together?" he asked her.

"Yes, but what...?"

Endersby reached for the doorknob and left the confused woman covering her face with her hands.

The bed was in the centre of the room, facing a crackling fire. The figure of Sarah lay propped up on pillows in the four poster with a canopy and side curtains. Her eyes were closed, her face so death-like and pallid in hue that Endersby feared she had taken a turn for the worse. The thin mattress under her no longer had a skirt around it. The cloth had been removed and now lay spread, like a banner, over one of the chairs near the window. Under the canopy sat a man with white greasepaint on his face, his eyes outlined in black, his tall bony frame still clothed in woolly fur and green spangled boots. He was holding Sarah's thin hand.

"Mr. Weston."

"Please come in, Inspector. I beg your pardon for the disarray."

Endersby left the door ajar, placing his satchel by it to keep it still. He walked forward, his shadow running beside him on the wall across from the brilliant hearth. The shadow lifted up the muslin bag and placed it on the bed. Endersby's silhouette then faced that of Mr. Weston's.

"Please sit down, sir, if you so wish," said the actor.

Endersby took a chair and pulled it toward Mr. Weston. He noticed immediately that the mattress sat unevenly upon the bed frame.

Weston looked down, his face coming into the glare of a candle on the side table, his eye sockets lighting up as if he were out of doors in sunlight. "I thought it the best place to hide things, Inspector. I kept my money, my cancelled promissory notes and other possessions under her. Who would have considered disturbing a sickly girl?"

"Who indeed?" replied Endersby.

Weston reached for the packet young Crabb had brought him earlier in the evening. He took it from the side table and opened it. Out came a clean glove, the match to the one found at the murder scene, a coster's cap, and a slip of paper. Mr. Weston read the number on the paper in a whispery voice. "He is a fine cabby, this chap," the actor said, handing the paper to Endersby. "I assume you shall want that returned to you, sir?"

Endersby placed the paper in his coat pocket.

"Now look in the muslin bag beside you, Mr. Weston."

Weston let go of Sarah's hand. He placed it tenderly on the counterpane and reached for the muslin bag. Endersby spotted Caldwell's face in the shadow of the hall.

"I imagine we are not alone, Inspector?" queried Weston. His face fell once again under the shadow of the bed's canopy. He opened the bag and lifted out the soiled glove found at Doughty Street. He laid it on top of the other, the two a perfect match. Next he noticed the collar of a mackintosh coat peeking out of the bag. "Ah, you have that as well, sir," said Weston, his voice feigning delight and surprise.

"One of our witnesses at the coroner's inquest mentioned she had seen, on and off, a tall man in a coster's cap and mackintosh coat. She imagined he was a frequenter of Mr. Cake's residence, as you certainly were."

"Often. The man was generous in his loans. Demanding, of course, when it came to repayment. But always fair. I admired him. I found him eccentric, especially his empty house with his unlocked doors. He seemed content without servants."

"You knew better than most that his house was empty, easy to break into."

"Child's play, sir. But I had intended only to retrieve this last item. This promissory note you have folded in the bag. I knew there was one left—for thirty pounds—but I could not find it that evening, Friday last. It was all I wanted other than ready cash."

"Mr. Cake was diligent in his bookkeeping. He kept all of it in his head and on his person."

"How so?" inquired the actor. His sister opened her eyes for a moment, then closed them again, unaware of Inspector Endersby sitting close by.

"Sewn into his cloak."

"How clever." Weston stared at the muslin bag in a frozen reverie. He then mumbled a single word.

"I beg your pardon, Mr. Weston?"

"Evil," replied the actor. "It shows itself in odd ways, sir. It was a simple thought only."

"I wondered when I saw the beds in a burnt lodging house if perhaps you thought as those men did," said Endersby. "Secrets hidden in obvious places."

"Perhaps, Inspector. I thought of my dear Sarah as a kind of guard. Her illness allowed me to take advantage of a place of which even my aunt was unawares." Weston began stroking his sister's hand, the shadow over the bed casting a line just below his eyes, so that the lower part of his face was in light, the upper in dark, his whites barely visible. He picked up the promissory note. "I meant to tear this up if and when I found it."

Endersby leaned forward quickly. Here was a piece of valuable evidence he could not allow to be destroyed. Caldwell had made a slight move, and his foot was inside the door. But then Mr. Weston folded the note and put it back in the muslin bag. "Why bother," he then said. "The gallant man is dead."

Weston stood and stretched. He turned and noticed Caldwell by the banister in the hall. He smiled and sat down again. "Provocation, Inspector."

"Yes?" said Endersby, attentive and waiting.

"What provokes a man?" asked the actor. "Fear? Anger? Love?"

"All three from time to time," said Endersby, his eyes held hard on Weston's face.

The actor pulled on the pair of gloves. He examined them, turning them in front of his eyes.

"Sarah made these. She could hardly pull thread, let alone cut and make a glove. But she insisted. She wanted me to have them for rehearsals. She said they were one of a kind, and that for me, they would always remind her of how grateful she was."

"Grateful, sir?" asked Endersby.

"She does not wish to be in this cruel world of ours, sir," the actor said. Tears came quickly to his eyes. "I have tried to warn her. I have bought antidotes, prayed with her, paid doctors to dissuade her. But she insists. She must be tethered from time-to-time. She has fits of joy followed by fits of inertia and terrible melancholy."

Endersby moved his eyes toward Sarah, her frame but a gentle stretch of skin and bone under the covers.

"Why did you kill him, Mr. Weston?"

"Provocation, sir. One can never predict what one is capable of doing under duress."

"You are an actor, sir. You are used to reining in emotions, shaping them, controlling them."

"Ah, sir, you sound like a mesmerist. Do you detectives use mesmerism to trick your felons into confession?"

"On occasion. But I sense that shall not be necessary with you, sir."

"You have invaded my house, ransacked my hiding place, thrown my old aunt into tears. There is provocation, sir. But as you see, I am calm and collected."

"Why did you kill Samuel Cake?"

"Ah, Inspector, the tale is simpler than our own panto-mime."

Again, Weston stared off in reverie. He asked permission to take some refreshment. Caldwell entered and stood by the closed door as the actor went to a sideboard, opened a jug and poured out a glass of dark rum. He offered some to Endersby, who refused. Weston drank half the glass and went to stand by the hearth. Given what he knew, given what he feared could happen, Endersby sat forward in his chair. Mr. Weston was a strong man. He was London's finest fencing actor. He could, if inspired, begin to fight. He might even consider an escape through the glass of the bedroom window. To his relief, Endersby noticed that Stott had been thorough in his break-in: he had removed the poker and shovel from the fireside. The only weapon the actor might use, other than the jug or a glass, would be his large fists.

"We have time, sir," said Endersby, "if you wish to regale my sergeant and me with the tale. We are all ears. I am most curious to know why and how you killed Mr. Cake."

*   *   *

Owen Endersby learned this much: it was on Friday night last, late after the performance. William Weston washed his face in his dressing room basin before making his way to Miss Root's parlour at the end of the hall. He looked in upon her, her two female cronies and the young sprite, Master Crabb. Indeed, they were all waiting for him. He did not guess the oysters had been served already. He jested to the gathered company: "I am a beggar invited to a banquet, yet not like a beggar, but a prince-come-lately."

The company dined and spoke of the play. And of Mr. Cake and his feat of stealing away Elisabetta Mazzini from the dragon claws of Henry Robertson Dupré. "As if," Miss Root said, "Samuel Cake was a knight in armour. Off to Swan Yard to his club he has taken her."

The night grew late. Weston still harboured anger at what Cake had done to *him* earlier that evening. In a tavern, behind the great theatre, he and Cake had agreed on a rendezvous of sorts, Weston preparing himself to beg a loan for medicine for Sarah. Cake, dressed in his showy clothes, started to dispute over a few pounds owing. He dared to call Mr. Weston a careless debtor, "ready for Marshalsay Prison". Weston held defence against the insult; he had no choice; blaming words meant nothing; could he persuade Samuel Cake to soften—to grant but an extra small loan to a loyal borrower? Was Cake capable, at least, of simple compassion?

No one could predict Samuel Cake. He refused his friend. He mocked him again, exciting Weston to shout, whereupon Cake had the tavern-keeper shove the actor out the door. Later, when the performances were finished and Weston had dined, he left the company in Miss Root's parlour and decided he would assail Cake once again. After all, he was desperate. Sarah lay on her bed in Cromer Street needing sedatives, leeches for clearing her blood. Unless she received these, she might fall into a death-like sleep. Possibly, she could become like the heroines in Italian operas and slip into madness, tearing her clothes, harming her body with pins, broken glass.

"I, therefore, put on my cloak and hat, determined to walk to Cake's club in Swan Yard. I felt lightheaded from the

French wine." Not fifteen minutes later, when he confronted the club's proprietor, an arrogant Jimmy-Know-All, Weston stank of rum he had purchased on his way, for this sweet-bitter drink gave him courage.

"Mr. Cake asked not to be disturbed, sir," the man sneered. "You've cheap drink on your breath, my man. Off with you." The proprietor crooked his finger to a ruddy Irishman behind him, holding a thick cane to beat off intruders. The two approached Weston with threatening glances.

"Call me a hansom, you insolent donkey," Weston demanded. The Irishman stopped grinning. He stepped forward, spat on the floor, then after a mock bow, mouthed a whistle and a cab instantly appeared.

That was the start. "I was in no state of sound reason," Weston said. "The rum cut apart my logical senses." The cab drove north towards the Foundling Hospital; the wobbly wheels shook the cab so hard, Weston feared he'd lose his fine supper, and so asked the driver to pull over. Descending from the hansom, Weston decided to walk through Mecklenburgh Square to clear his head, to balance his thoughts. "I stopped to gaze at a new lot being dug for a house. The earth was blood red, thick, and like a curious boy I decided to walk through it to see the back end of another house with a large open court. It felt a fine, brisk evening, and since I had no intention of giving up my quest for a loan, I came to my senses. Leaving that square, I decided to stroll to Cake's house, to Number 46 Doughty Street, with which I was familiar, and wait for him to return from Swan's Yard. How could he refuse me yet again, I argued. The man was, at bottom, not a monster."

Fifteen minutes past one o'clock in the morning, the lone parish bell gave out one tinny clang. Though Weston had been walking for a short while, he was not restless nor did he doubt that Cake would lend him money. Anger, it seemed at that moment, had retreated from Weston's sensibility. The street was dark and empty. "Why not enter Cake's house and wait inside, in the kitchen. I'd done it often enough before," explained Weston, his tale-telling voice devoid of emotion. Quietly opening the unlocked door to the Cake's Doughty Street kitchen, Weston crept in, out of sight of any passerby. He lit a candle in the hall and shielding it, climbed to the first floor then to the second, the cold empty rooms resounding with his footsteps.

Whereupon he set his mind on searching the bedroom desk, remembering the note for thirty pounds he had signed. "Why let him throw that in my face?" Weston said, pondering his actions. The desk drawers were full of documents, other notes but nowhere did he discover his thirty-pound promissory note. "I could simply tear it up, I thought," said Weston. "Cake would not remember such a trivial item." He searched on, but became disappointed. The room was ghostly; Weston looked back at the track of red mud he'd made. He thought: *But how will the foolish man with no servants clean it all up?* Weston was about to leave when he heard glass breaking. He paused. He heard rough voices. It sounded as if the basement door was being kicked open. More voices, footsteps, raucous laughs.

Weston stood stone still. The noise flew up the stairwells. How had this happened, he wondered? On the night he plays the thief, there are others like him mad enough to rob the rich young man from Surrey side. "Come, let's come out Mr. Arrogance," shouted a countryman's voice. It carried a violent threat to it. It could crush a skull, thought Weston. "Come ye out, Mr. Contraption," yelled another, and this was followed by stamping boots and slamming doors. More laughter erupted, but soon the curses and questions began to get closer. Men were climbing up from the kitchen.

Hurry, you must hide. Hurry.

"Hoi, hollah," shouted the voices. Feet tramped, shouts threw out more insults; the intruders then began the ascent to the second floor. Weston looked to the bedroom window. He hid behind the drape. He moved so quickly, he knocked over a chamber pot, with its stale piss, clack and spill, all in a second. He held his breath. He covered his mouth and held his body close to the window as he heard one man enter the door opposite him and pause.

"No sleeping body here," the man shouted. "Where are you, Mr. Cake?" a deep hoarse voice cried. "You aren't safe, Cake. Nor be your fine house...we have truncheons, we have clubs, Mr. Cake. Come out, wag, Mr. Contraption Man." The bedroom was left untouched, unexplored.

Weston stepped from behind the curtain. Now a new noise commenced, one as frightening as the bawls of these violent bullies. Smashing, crashing had begun. Glass shattered; heavy chairs cracked. All the while there was a constant hammering so sharp Weston felt the banging through the boards on the second floor.

But what kind of house thieves are these, he wondered? No, rogues like these are not after cash. Thieves want silver not broken furniture. These folk are murderers, indeed. They are savages. Best to stay hidden in the shadows. *Will not the neighbours complain?* Weston wondered. "In such a locked-up street, I wished the constables good speed. But then, how could a young baton-wheeling constable overpower this congregation of hammers and clubs?" The noise remained for a time on the first floor, down the stairs into the basement. Then voices and feet disappeared; the house fell quiet as a grave. Weston said aloud, "They have gone, oh mercy. Come and gone. And what have they done?" Cake ought to have been home by now. But then Cake, he'd heard, slept at his theatre, dined with his seamstresses. He ought not to have this shell of a house. To what purpose? To show his fat purse to the world? Weston began to curse him. Not only for his money. But for something much stronger. Cheap rum had brought on a sharp headache and a melancholy. A rising memory of sorrow accompanied them. All rested on the face of dear lost Sarah. Once, Cake had cherished her. "Like a lover," whispered Weston. "Like a true love." Cake had thrown Sarah aside. Such abandonment was too brutal for Sarah. Such infected her mind so that she hid away inside her feelings of loss. Closeted her reason until it shrivelled away like a plucked flower. "Guilty you are, Cake," Weston mumbled aloud. *Certainly you broke her heart and brought sadness into the Weston household. How could you do this?* "Dog, charlatan, vulture!" Weston stopped on the stairs wanting rum, railing against Samuel Cake with mounting obscenity.

In the moonlight from the window, Weston became a dark wrathful figure descending a darkened staircase, his mind full of bitter words. The vexed actor touched his forehead; he drew his hand hard across his skin. Like a binding cloth, the cold house closed in on him. Moving again, he went into the parlour on the first floor. He passed through the room, stepping over cracked chairs to an upright desk. Its drawer proved empty like the other one upstairs. He stood and looked about in silence, and turned. A night breeze seemed to brush his cheek. He could feel it touch him as he had never felt air before. The room stretched before him, and there was silence, but then other movement.

"Well, Will," said a voice. Slurred, calm, a silhouette in hat and walking stick.

Weston stumbled face-to-face with Samuel Cake.

"But why, Will? Did you think I hid my money here?" The tone was gentle, steel-edged.

"You have been angry, I see. Look at this place. I must consider you for my next extravaganza. 'Jack the Giant Killer'. What arms you have!"

Cake's voice entangled him like a hangman's rope. Cake tipped the brim of his hat, at the same time swirling his cloak. His cane tapped the edge of the sofa. Weston was standing very near, breathing hard. His mouth dried up, his tongue grew heavy. Cake struck the sofa then danced on the crunching floor.

"Why, Will?" he mocked.

Weston shivered, ignoring a pain cutting into him. Words were lost; only a shake of his aching head responded to Cake's needling voice. His hand suddenly showed a cut. Blood like a red line drawn through chalk. He looked up. Cake was grinning, his walking stick held high and ready to strike and cut once more.

"You are a stupid man, Will. Sick and stupid. Get out of here. Go on."

The stick fell whizzing again at Weston's shoulder. He

ducked, luckily thrust his body backward. Blood shimmered on his skin. From his pocket, he pulled out his gloves, the ones his Sarah made him wear. He slipped them on, one looser than the other. He plunged toward the hall. He wanted only to run, to breathe in street air. "Get out," screamed the drunken Cake. But the voice Weston heard through his headache and his terror was not an angry male voice. It was, instead, the voice of a woman. A dour, petty woman. *The familiar screech of a cold-hearted, mean-spirited hag.* How often had he run from his aunt's rasping tongue? How frequently had he wished to strike her down after she had beat him, to trample her pious humiliating presence under his boot.

Weston's glove hurt his cut hand as tears flushed his eyes. *"Run!"* he commanded himself, heading confusedly for the open front door. Cake's sharp-headed walking stick hit him again from behind.

"Stop this, for God's sake!" Weston shouted. He turned. "I will not be humiliated!" he cried. Cake sidled up to him until the two men stood chest-to-chest. Lifting his cane, Cake pressed its carved ivory head into Weston's right cheek. The man's breath stank of wine; the man's odour sharpened Weston's headache.

"What did you say, Weston, you rummy fool?" Cake scratched the tip of the cane against Weston's face. "And how is the little Sarah?"

"You harmed her, Cake. Made her ill with your cruelty."

"I did?" Cake sneered, raising his chin to step back. "Oh, for some sweet punch, what do you say, poor Weston?"

"For God's sake, Cake," the actor moaned.

"What a stupid, hopeless girl she was. And not so pretty after all."

"Do not insult my sister, sir."

"Well, hardly, Weston. How does one insult a sparrow? For is she nothing better now than a puking animal?"

"Stop, you demon," cried Weston.

Cake pushed his cane against Weston's shoulder. "Get out and go to your sister," Cake laughed. He began to whistle nonchalantly.

"A blackness fell over my eyes. I swear it. I could reason no more," confessed Weston. "I sensed only muscle and force. *Stop, stop, you demon.*" Moments later, when the blackness lifted, Weston found himself grasping the walking stick in his right hand. Samuel Cake, meanwhile, was reeling backwards. "Good God, Weston," Cake shouted. Tumbling into the sofa. Cake laughed while raising his hand in defense. His beaver hat rolled to the floor. Laughter such as Cake's inspired a sudden piercing wail in Weston's ears. Blackness returned. Weston—surprised, daunted, yet still mobile and strong—dreamed he saw a tall man like himself hitting another, a helpless drunken man in fine clothes, his tongue mocking the air, horrific as a hyena's howl. The ivory dog bit Cake's ear, cracked his temple, tore hard at his eyes and cheeks, hard, *harder.* A warm spray of liquid rose in the darkness as Cake fell onto the floor. His huge cloak settled over him as he floated on a spreading pool of blood.

The night air blew cold and damp.

"What in God's mercy have you done," Weston rasped as his mind cleared and he saw the walking stick clutched in his right hand. A few feet away, Samuel Cake lay sprawled face down on the bare floor. Weston heaved the stick at the wall. His glove scraped his cut, so he pulled off the itchy leather. Struggling downstairs toward the back door, it was as if the Devil's minion were driving him. Weston stumbled on the outside steps; his hands grasped the brick wall to steady his balance. Then he ran down the alley. Stars blinked high above him before hiding themselves behind icy cloud. Weston ran and felt for his glove and found it gone. But he was so tired, so needing to be at home in his own bed, he did not go back for it. Racing, he felt oddly free, as if he were a wild beast set loose from a trap. He ran and ran until he barged into the midst of the city's chaos, ran until he finally reached his house, where the dour aunt greeted him in her nightgown, her face tired, her mouth angrily spouting words about the late hour, the sick sister.

"Yes, Auntie," Weston cried. "Please forgive me, I beg of you."

The taciturn aunt nodded to him. Leaving her, Weston rushed to his bedroom to pass the rest of the night in torturous, dream-racked sleep.

*   *   *

The confession finished, a silence entered the room seconds before Inspector Owen Endersby witnessed William Weston fall to his sister's bedroom floor, totally spent. The glass he was holding broke against the hearth rail. Stott and Caldwell moved quickly into the room. The dour aunt, who had heard all, wept quiet tears. She was holding a flannel cloth and went to the canopied bed. She began to pat the sweating head of Sarah Weston. Neither she nor Sarah seemed to notice the group of men behind them, two of them lifting William Weston to his feet, one pulling from a satchel a pair of wrist irons, a third coming into the room, dripping from being outside, and all of them as a herd, trotting quickly out of the chamber, their eyes and mouths held in serious manner, the bulky inspector himself blank-faced, staring ahead with much concentration furrowing his brow.

A hansom cab was secured. William Weston was accompanied to the Fleet Lane station of Scotland Yard. Up the stairs to the admittance sergeant, then into a small room, where the actor was given a cup of tea, then courtesy of the inspector, a second cup filled with rum and hot water. Inspector Endersby called in Stott and Birken, and the three of them, while sitting across from Weston, took quill, ink and paper and wrote down all the details of the murder story, word for word, strike by strike, as Weston had told them. The actor wept. He rubbed his wound. He was then requested, in very polite terms, to take quill and ink and paper and write down the same story. He was so tired he could barely lift and dip the quill, but the inspector said, "Come along, Will. You are a good man, a caring brother. You did all for your Sarah. Ne'er forget that."

"In vain," came the whispered words from the princely figure.

After much coaxing, the confession was written. William Weston was then led to a smaller room behind the open courtyard and placed under custody until the magistrate and Mr. Borne could speak with him. Endersby ordered all his three sergeants to follow him to a club he knew nearby—a public house with a private kitchen—and there, with plates of steaming sole in butter and roast beef—they read to each other their own versions of the Weston confession. "Remarkable, gentlemen," said Endersby. "All of a piece."

Caldwell then recited the words written by William Weston. To the group's astonishment, the actor's were almost word for word the same as his spoken version. And on hearing them, Endersby could imagine the tones, the tragic emphasis of the man's voice, as if in his most brutal hour of life Mr. William Weston had turned all into the finest expression of his art.

"Until tomorrow, gentlemen."

The sergeants were dismissed. Endersby walked to the courtyard. He glanced into the high window of the cell where Weston lay. The leading star of Old Drury sat upright, his eyes moist and dull in the candlelight. He was speaking under his breath, arms moving as if he were on the stage. Endersby could not decipher the mouthed words, but he imagined from their shape they were from the recesses of his troubled soul. As he left Fleet Lane to walk home, Endersby recited favorite words of his own, taken from William Shakespeare: "I have lost my reputation. I have lost the immortal part of myself..."

*　　*　　*

Snow piled onto the sill. Harriet Endersby rose from her dining table, having left part of her late supper untouched. "How can you gobble so?" she reprimanded her husband. The night was very dark. Solange stood by the door leading to the kitchen. Endersby finished his plate of oyster pie and wiped his mouth. "I have learned, dear Harriet, one cruel fact in my profession. It is hard to bear, I admit."

Harriet raised her chin. She waited, and as she admired the freshly scrubbed but tired face of her husband, she let out a small smile, knowing that justice had been performed.

Endersby went on, taking a last sip of his French wine. "Never bring the corpse home with you to dinner."

Solange gasped.

"Never," reiterated Endersby. "Or you shall find it next in your bath, then in your bed, crowding you from under the covers. And you will end up raving, alone, without prospect, and bloody cold."

"A happy thought, dear Owen," said Harriet, her tone lightly sarcastic. "But a wise one, indeed."

Endersby rose from the table. He put his arms around his wife. He thanked Solange for her meal, and after she had gone into the kitchen, he led Harriet into the small parlour, where she had decorated a little pine tree. He took a taper and lit the seven candles on the meagre branches. "It still has a forest perfume," said Harriet. She strung her arm into her husband's and pulled him closer.

"It is time, I believe," said Endersby. He found a sudden surge of energy, and he scampered as best he dared to his study, where from a trunk he pulled out packages and bottles. Quickly, he found his way back to the cheery parlour. At that same moment, Solange entered from the kitchen with a plate of fruity tarts. After the three of them had toasted the season with French wine, they said a prayer before Solange went off to her bedroom. The inspector and his Harriet opened their few lovingly wrapped presents. "It will be the great day soon enough," Harriet said, pulling at a string.

"Indeed. A day of joy for us all."

Chapter Eight

FRIDAY, DECEMBER 25, 1840

P oets say all great cities are alike. They have their mighty towers and their hovels, their heroes and villains. In all men's hearts, regardless of station or purse, one thing remains immutable: the desire for merriment. Inspector Owen Endersby felt that very emotion as he dressed for his breakfast, pulling on a bright red waistcoat for the special day. He had arranged to meet the staff of Old Drury. On his way there in the hansom, as streets pulsed with voices and laughing children, he reflected on the grand theatre. It was but a glance at the place he wished to take on this sleety Christmas morning. Old Drury, he believed, was not so different from a great lady in the aristocratic circles of the capital. Both had long lineage; both admitted to admirers and critics; both remained glorious despite the ravages of age, the vicissitudes of Fortune, the ever-pressing need for gold and diversion.

He thought of his favorite old stager, the comedian Mr. Beazley, who wore his britches up and a frayed powdered wig to cover his bald pate. He thought of his neighbour on Cursitor Street, Mrs. DeWinter, who habitually left her dining table early to attend the play, having taken an early supper with Mr. DeWinter, a draper. A commodious man, thought Endersby, a clever one to have secured his success with Scottish woollens. His wife hated the farce, was never fond of Beazley or indeed of Mr. Jerrold's light wit, yet she was mad for the melodrama. So was Mr. Potter, a copy clerk who lived under the DeWinters, a man overly fond of the installments of Mr. Dickens and who, having never married, dined alone on a single cutlet in a chop house near the theatre. He did so in order to arrive early and take in the heady odours of the pit, of onion, lamb and beer, as well as the delicate aroma of the gas lamps.

Indeed, the place was a world unto itself, and as Endersby alighted at its stage-door entrance, he allowed his powers of recollection to subside for the instant as he was met by a serious-faced group. Endersby spoke to them quietly. He had arranged to meet with a number of the staff, and he gathered them together in the stage-door entrance. He told them the coroner's surgeon had declared the death of Betty Loxton an accident, and so the little coster girl would be allowed a Christian burial. The coffin makers near Chancery Lane had wrapped the blackened body in a white sheet and lifted the pathetic mass into its final wooden cradle. Sharp new coffin nails secured the top. Endersby gave young Crabb two pennies and told the mournful boy to buy a flower bunch, as the hearse was on its way.

With Endersby now was Hartley, the old stage-door keeper, Mrs. B. and the haughty Henry Roberston Dupré, all at attention in Vinegar Yard. The theatre people witnessed the scattered procession of coster lads and Betty's weeping sister come around the corner and move past the stage door. Heads bowed behind the slow-moving hearse. It was a simple flat cart pulled by a blinkered dray. The small coffin lay in the embrace of two worn leather straps that kept it from sliding onto the pavement. Endersby knew it must have been Dupré who'd paid for the funeral. Mrs. B. stepped forward. The hearse stopped as she laid Betty's soiled bonnet on the coffin's lid. Catching his breath, young Reggie Crabb returned in time and held up his bunch of flowers in a salutation to his lost friend.

At the final moment, before the driver cracked his whip to drive southward to the pauper's cemetery, an elegant carriage drew up. On its door glistened a royal insignia. A thin man in velvet stepped down into the street. His sense of majesty, his air of power, prompted Endersby and the others to take off their hats. The man was indeed from the palace. He spoke deliberately in an official tone. His words included pity, goodness, a reference to the baby Jesus. And then he took from a footman's hand a small cluster of white roses. The thin man handed the bouquet to Endersby. "Sir, Her Majesty asks that these be put on the coffin of Miss Betty Loxton. In respect for the poor child." Endersby obeyed and gently placed the blooms on the top of the pine box, while two of the gathered company quietly wept. The hearse then rolled forward; the royal carriage went on its way; Endersby shook hands with Dupré, Mrs. B. and Hartley.

"Sir?" said a small voice.

Young Reggie Crabb stood with cap in hand at Endersby's elbow.

"May I be dismissed, sir?" the boy asked.

"I beg your pardon, lad?" asked the inspector.

"From my duties." Reggie Crabb lowered his voice. "Your eyes and ears, sir."

"Ah, indeed, brave boy. And here, take this bonus shilling for your pains."

Young Reggie thanked the inspector, stuffed the shilling into his waistcoat, and in a dash, ran off down the street, his cap back on, his right hand holding up his bunch of violets. Eventually, after a turn or two, he caught up to the hearse and soon was seen marching in time beside the dray, the costers and Betty's sister, holding up their heads with pride as they went along.

Brydges Street on a cold Christmas Day. Here is the end of our story. The hearse trundled around muddied corners leading towards the murky Thames, its box of fresh-smelling cut pine, its rough surface decorated with a snow-speckled bonnet and a white bouquet. Only those who knew her story remembered the thin waif inside the coffin, her hands folded like an angel's across her breast. It was a frosty morning; here and there people hurried along the cobbles bearing brightly wrapped packages. Owen Endersby walked slowly home toward Number 6 Cursitor Street, his mind pondering the life of his city, noting how the death of a mere child made but a faint mark on this huge metropolis of souls, this London, returning yet again to its noise, bustle, smoke and labours.

And when the fall of midnight comes and trumpets sound no more, the great house of Old Drury shall empty of spectators. The thin women with twig brooms will begin their own peculiar dance, sweeping the pit for lost buttons and spots of tobacco and hat pins and pennies. The great tiers above once crowded with fine silken gowns inevitably become like ancient mausoleums, abandoned places of pillars and grandiose arches. And the galleries, trampled, pounded, porter-stained, pissed-upon, once hot and swarming, resign to fetid darkness. The street portals close for the sleep of a few hours, the lamps grow dark. With all her phantoms fled, Old Drury stands for a blink in time as nothing more than a bulk of stone.

Acknowledgements

This is a novel created out of research, imagination and inspired commentary from a number of people. I wish to thank those people for their kind help: Cheryl Freedman of the Crime Writers of Canada, Catherine Gildiner, Eric Hanley, Allan Hepburn, Pat Kennedy, Toni Laidlaw, Susan Lewthwaite, David O'Rourke, Victor Pianosi, Andrew Podnieks, Cathy, Joan and Gladys Redfern, Margaret Van Dijk.

Special thanks to the creative team at Rendezvous Crime, and to Sylvia McConnell for encouragement and editing advice. I also owe much to the staff of the Map Room at the John Robarts Library in Toronto.

A number of references were also consulted. I took liberties on occasion by changing names slightly, and dates, but for the most part all the street and theatre names are accurate to London in 1840. The fictional characters are entirely my own invention; however, there are touches here-and-there—minor details—based on historical figures: *Madame Vestris and the London Stage* by William W. Appleton; *The Revels History of Drama in English*, volume VI, edited by M. Booth et al; *Jack Maggs* by Peter Carey; *Bleak House* by Charles Dickens; 'Household Words', Volume 1, 1850, edited by Charles Dickens; *The World of Charles Dickens* by Martin Fido; *The Development of the English Playhouse* by Richard Leacroft; *The Diaries of William Charles Macready* by William Charles Macready; *Recollections and Reflections* by James Robinson Planché; *Madame Vestris* by Clifford John Williams; *Mayhew's London*, edited by Peter Quennell.

Finally, gratitude forever to Betty Munsie who said: "Go do it!"

author photo by John Parkes

Jon Redfern was born and raised in Alberta. He has been a free-lance journalist for both the *Toronto Star* and the *Globe and Mail,* a story editor for the CBC and a children's playwright. His short stories have appeared in numerous literary journals.

Jon's first novel, *The Boy Must Die,* won the Arthur Ellis Award for Best First Crime Novel in 2002. Since that time, Jon has been researching, writing, teaching English as a professor at Centennial College in Toronto and serving for two years as the Vice President of the Toronto Chapter of the Crime Writers of Canada.

He lives in Toronto and in Waterton Lakes, Alberta.

Printed in the USA
CPSIA information can be obtained
at www.ICGtesting.com
JSHW022209140824
68134JS00018B/946